INVISIBLE ENEMY

She thought she heard the softest scrape of a footstep near where the door would be. Her feeling of dread increased. With a sudden move, she rolled from the gelbed to the floor.

The motion saved her.

Blinding violet light cut a swath over the bed, leaving shimmering afterimages and a smell of scorched plastic and acrid steam. Jemi shouted and flung herself to where she thought her attacker might be, knowing that he must be able to see in this darkness, knowing that in another moment he'd find her . . .

Other Avon Books by
Stephen Leigh

THE BONES OF GOD

THE CRYSTAL MEMORY

STEPHEN LEIGH

AVON
PUBLISHERS OF BARD, CAMELOT, DISCUS AND FLARE BOOKS

THE CRYSTAL MEMORY is an original publication of Avon Books. This work has never before appeared in book form. This work is a novel. Any similarity to actual persons or events is purely coincidental.

AVON BOOKS
A division of
The Hearst Corporation
105 Madison Avenue
New York, New York 10016

Published by arrangement with the author
Library of Congress Catalog Card Number: 87-91162
ISBN: 0-380-89960-4

First Avon Printing: September 1987

Printed in the U.S.A.

K-R 10 9 8 7 6 5 4 3 2 1

This one's for Hania, a better friend than I probably deserve and one of my favorite critics.

And it's also for Jerry, Michaele, Charlie, Ric, Diane, and Lisa—along with (why not?) Art, Louise, Tony, and Chuck. You know why. For those of you still with me, I wish you few but wondrous deaths.

Homo sapiens is the blame-casting animal. When disaster slams into us it's never our fault. A bad situation is always due to someone else's evil intentions. If no one is close by to take the guilt, we accuse the weather, the time of year, or an old football injury. Hitler is reputed to have said to Goebbels after the failure of the Russian invasion in 1941–42: "It was the snow. I never want to see snow again. It is physically repulsive to me."

Given this, it's not surprising that when we found the resources of our own solar system too few and easily used up; when the T'Raijek came and demonstrated by their very presence just how poor and backward we were; when we realized that to ultimately survive we had to escape the trap of our own sun, most of us shrugged our shoulders and said it was simply Fate.

We gave up.

It's a damned good thing that mankind, while admiring the concept of democracy, is also not an animal that follows the lead of the majority. Homo sapiens is also the rebellious animal. In that, at least, we found that we are the equal of any other race.

It's probably the snow.

—from *The Cage of Sol: Mankind Trapped* by David Morris; Avon Publications, NY, Earth; published May, 2175.

We're dogs fighting among the ruins of a past civilization. We fight among ourselves for the scraps left by our forefathers. We see only what we might scavenge from the remnants left us, blind to the possibility that we ourselves might do better.

Humanity once looked outward. Now we look only in the mirror and scowl at what we see.

—from a pamphlet distributed by the
Saliian Peace Committee.

CHAPTER ONE

Jemi pushed the welding equipment into the navigational compartment. Even in free-fall, the inertia of the electric quickwelder was enough to make her grunt. The auto-status check of the ship had told her what she already knew: her last repairs were not good enough for standard; she had to redo them before they arrived in Earth orbit and the docking crews red-marked *Starfire*'s license. Which told her what she'd be doing for the rest of the month-long passage. That also meant that she'd have to spend most of the passage in free-fall without the artificial gravity of spin. She grimaced.

Jemi shook her head, and the thin veil around the lower part of her face billowed with the motion. Most of the free traders that had managed to survive the economic downturn were in the same kind of shape—it didn't matter whether the registry was Earth, Highland, or Salii. Even the naval ships were old; no amount of painting could conceal the weldspots on their hulls, and anyone who knew electronics could see that the instrumentation was well behind the current technology. She thought of the sleek, unbroken lines of the T'Raijek ships, those alien cruisers that could leap from star to star—everything humanity had seemed shabby and crude in comparison. She wondered at times if the continuing depression might not be due to a despair born of that comparison.

"Blame it on the T'Raijek," she muttered to herself. "They wouldn't care."

Jemi spun around until she was upside down to the docking configuration of the ship. She pulled herself "down" until she could see the underside of her spare thruster relay, looking for one of the old welds. What she saw made her cry out, as if she were in pain.

It wasn't much—a stuffed toy, a furry thing with blue and yellow fur, the snout of an elephant and the rotund body of the usual teddy bear. Beneath the relay, it was snared between the support strut she'd welded in to hold the last set of hull repairs and the underside of the panel. The toy floated accusingly in its ugly, scorched-metal cage.

Kenis must have put it there.

The thought constricted Jemi's throat. She couldn't breathe, staring at the plush creature. Searing tears gathered at the corners of her eyes. She took a sobbing breath and slid the upper curtain of her k'lyge, the Highland veil of discretion, over her eyes so that her pain was masked. That gesture had grown to be automatic in the last three months.

"Holder Charidilis, what's wrong?"

Jemi glanced toward the voice. With the ship in free-fall, the motion gave her a slight spin; she placed a hand on the relay to steady herself. Through the sheer cloth of the upper veil, she could see her vivicate Doni as if through a thin haze. The vivicate sat in the pilot's chair, the thick cord of the umbilical to *Starfire* trailing from his spinal sockets. He twitched spasmodically. The muscular glitches were the legacy of Doni's rekindled life processes.

"One of Ken's toys," Jemi answered. She could hear the emotion throbbing in her voice as she reached around the strut and retrieved it. She hugged the furry thing to her as if in doing so she could recapture some feeling of Kenis. The ivory beads sewn along the jawline of the k'lyge rattled—the death beads, the mourning beads. "Damn," she muttered. She thought she could smell Kenis on the toy, and that brought back the memories.

"Holder?"

"Shut up, Doni." Jemi turned away from him, her shoulders heaving. She put her head against the cool hull of the ship.

"See you when you get back, Mommy," he said. The crèche-mother held his hand as he tugged to go after Jemi. "Don't be gone too long, please." He always sounded so old for four, so mature. He frowned at her, his lower lip sticking out in that round, fair face, his green eyes looking just like Harris's—it was the only thing she didn't like about Kenis, but time would scab over that particular wound.

"Give me a hug," she told him, and he did as she bent down to him, his arms surprisingly strong around her neck. She kissed his neck, smelling the faint odor of the shampoo she'd used the night before, and another, sweeter scent that might have been Doni's cologne. "Know what?" she asked him, holding him at arm's length.

His face scrunched up at that. "I know already," he said. "You say it every time, Mommy. I love you, too."

She laughed and let him go back to the crèche-mother.

"I won't be too long, hon," she said, waving to him. "I just have to make sure that the ship's loaded and fueled. About two hours," she added, more to the crèche-mother than Kenis. Both of them had nodded.

"Make it quick, Mommy. Doni told me he'd show me something we found."

"I'll make it as quick as I can, Ken. You be good, okay?"

"Promise."

The next time she'd seen Kenis, he'd been a crumpled, bloody, unrecognizable form under a blanket.

"Damn it, Doni," Jemi blurted out. "I thought you got all of Ken's things out of here." She didn't want to be angry, and she knew that Doni was only a convenient target, a catharsis from the memories. In the three months since her son's death, she'd swung from hysteria to depression; every time something happened to tug at her emotions, she reacted too strongly. She wanted to apologize immediately, clutching at the toy with fingers gone white from pressure, but Doni just stared back at her flatly, a film of drool at the corner of his mouth.

"I'm sorry, Holder. I thought I had." He closed his eyes for a moment, his hand twitching once, then sinking back to his lap, trembling. "Holder," he said softly. "We all have to die. It was an accident. There was nothing you could have done."

That brought the tears fully, and with them came anger and disgust—anger that Doni could provoke the tears so easily, and disgust that she could not hold them back. She glared at Doni from behind the veil of the k'lyge, wondering what he had been in his first life, wondering if he remembered any of it. "I bought you to help run the ship, not to give me platitudes, Doni," she snapped. "If you can't do that, I'll sell you to someone else."

"I'm sorry, Holder," he said, and she could not tell with his flat inflection and the slurred vivicate accent, whether there was sarcasm in the voice or not. He closed his eyes then, putting all of his senses into the ship.

Jemi looked from Doni to Kenis's toy. A tear had dropped from under the veils onto the colorful fur. There, the blue had gone dark and matted.

They were a half-day out from Highland, well outside the orbit of Mars and heading inward to Earth. It was going to be a long trip. When she'd dumped Harris off the ship, over two years ago now, she'd only felt relief that a bad relationship had ended. Now, without the child that they'd given life to, the ship seemed like a tomb, small and dark and shabby.

Jemi took a deep breath. She cradled the toy in the crook of her arm and pushed away from the wall, floating down the corridor of her tiny, dilapidated cargo ship toward her room.

At first, in her dream, she seemed to be outside the great spidery wheel of the colony. Then, just as abruptly, she was inside with the discolored streets and the buildings that were falling apart faster than they could be repaired. She glanced up at the dayscreens and saw the speck in the artificial sky, a pinwheeling figure. The arms waved in a soundless terror.

She knew who it was. She knew, and she wanted to scream, wanted to do anything, but she was caught in the grip of the nightmare now—unable to act, unable to move. She could only watch. She could see Kenis falling toward the curved rim of the worldlet Highland, moving ever faster and faster as he drifted farther from the towering linktube. She could see all the details with frightening clarity. His mouth was open in a scream torn away by the rushing air, his green eyes wide with panic, his pudgy arms flailing desperately, helplessly. The shabby buildings of Highland seemed to rise up toward him with terrifying speed, until he was smashed against them. Jemi could hear the impact, and in her mind she saw it again

. . . and again . . .

. . . and again . . .

"Kenis!" Jemi Charidilis woke with a start, her throat raw and dry, her heart pounding with the terror of the dream. Every time she slept, every time she plunged into those horrible nightmares, Kenis was there.

This time she whispered the name, shaking her head with her eyes closed: "Kenis."

Then something pounded against the ship, jolting the bed beneath her.

It was wrong, it was all wrong. This *was* her cabin, yes, but the emergency lights were on, emerald green. Around the lights smoke hurtled past as if caught in sand-laden winds, yet all was caught in an eerie silence. Jemi pulled up her k'lyge, touching as she always did the beads she'd sewn into the hem after Kenis's death. Adrenaline banished fatigue. She knew, suddenly, that she was alive only because the failsafe shield of her bed had gone up and because she'd strapped herself to the bed even though she'd put spin on the ship for the night—she could feel herself floating free against the straps and her skin tingled with the prickling of the shield's static. The silence, the swift smoke: all told her that *Starfire*'s fragile hull had been breached and torn. Jemi cursed, adjusting the crown strap of the k'lyge firmly. She unbuckled the bed restraints and reached for the pressure suit hanging above the headboard, fumbling clumsily in free-fall. Pulling the suit from its rack, she knocked aside Kenis's toy, velcroed to the headboard. The colorful animal tumbled past her, spinning wildly—as Kenis had in her dream.

Even before the seals were in place, she could hear the yammering of the suit's alarm. "Doni?" she said. The hooting signal died, then Doni's voice screamed, "Get *up* here, Holder."

"I'm coming now," she said, trying to shake away the last

remnants of the nightmare. Damn the vivicate for being so panicky . . . Doni was usually trustworthy. "What's happened?"

"We've been holed, damn it! There's another ship— Please get moving. I—the ship's been hurt badly."

His voice trailed off and she felt a surge of acceleration, a lurching roll that made the hull's ceiling seem wrongly *down*. Jemi slapped a palm over the shield contacts, felt her suit suddenly balloon around her. "On my way, Doni," she said.

Starfire's corridors were a nightmare, awash in the sea-light of the battery lamps, filled with flying rubble that shifted as the ship spun erratically. Jemi passed a long, blackened tear through which she could see a lumbering, tossing starfield. The edges of the hole still glowed with heat. Jemi swallowed hard, forced herself to move carefully toward the navigational compartment in the interior of the ship. She was twisted back and forth with the ship's yawing movements. The hallways of *Starfire* were in chaos, nearly useless with the ship's insane rotation. She pulled herself from handhold to handhold, cursing the entire time. She found herself thinking, oddly, how difficult it was going to be for her to repair all this damage.

If you live through this, you'll never see her repaired: you can't afford it.

At least the navigational compartment was still airtight—the pressure suit flattened again as she cycled through the lock. Doni was in his seat at the center of the room, the ship's umbilical snarled around him. The vivicate was on the edge of panic. His eyes were glazed and wild, his mouth working soundlessly as he turned to her, spittle laced with blood flying from torn lips—he'd bitten himself. He'd not disconnected—through the sockets, he *was* the ship, and the ship was terribly wounded. If he survived this, he'd be useless to her afterward. *It was so hard to find one that had anything close to a pilot's reflexes, and I paid so much for him* . . . It pained her to see the mad eyes and flailing limbs of the man who had already died once before. "Christ, Holder, they're killing us! We're holed in three fucking places, and I can't outrun them. They won't answer."

"*Who*, Doni?" Jemi shouted, trying to get past his fear. "Who?"

"You won't believe—" Doni closed his eyes momentarily and

an LCD monitor lit on the control panel before him, shimmering with static. Doni flung a spastic hand toward it, pointing. "Look!"

Jemi's eyes narrowed. "My God," she said.

She had time to say nothing else. The walls buckled suddenly; a great, rushing silence slammed her from her handhold and Doni began a scream that he never finished. *Starfire* shuddered in its death throes.

Jemi saw her lost son Kenis as the chaos of the control room faded from her sight. He smiled the wide grin that she remembered too well, and she reached out a hand for her child. "Come to Mommy, love," she said.

Only within the navy is there still the pride that mankind once had. You are the future, all of you. You hold the foundations of the UCN. You work to accomplish your dreams while your brothers and sisters slumber at home.

—from Admiral Strickland's address to the graduating class, Naval Officer's Training School, 2167.

CHAPTER TWO

She remembered a dream, a child falling and falling who looked achingly like Kenis. But it wasn't Ken. It couldn't possibly be her son, for Kenis could never have climbed a linktube.

Kenis was only two. He'd spent too little time in full gravity, though she kept spin on the ship as much as she could: he was still just beginning to learn to walk. It wasn't Ken. It couldn't be Ken. She wouldn't let it be Ken.

The bearded face above her was not unkind in appearance, but it was unexpected. Jemi started, trying to turn on the bed. She groaned with the effort; she could hardly move. Her muscles were stiff and aching. A hand—the sleeve cuffed with the twin starbursts of the United Coalition of Nations Navy—gently pushed her back down. "No, please. You can't get up yet. Your injuries . . ."

His breath was warm on her naked face. Jemi, trembling, touched her cheeks and found not the cloth of her k'lyge, but skin. She turned away from the man hastily, burying her head in her pillow. Tears of shame burned in her eyes. *Seen. Seen by a stranger with all the emotions open. No one except Kenis has seen me that way since I tossed Harris off the ship.* "The k'lyge," she breathed. "My veil, please."

The man seemed startled. He touched her again, not comprehending her distress and insensitive to her feelings. Like most naval people; like all Earthers. A Highlander would never have let her wake up in so compromised a position; a Highlander would have cared about her privacy. If Highland ever rid themselves of the UCN's shackles, as the colony of Salii had done, it would be because of that uncaring arrogance. It would be their own fault. "Just a moment!" Jemi listened to his footsteps crossing the room. She heard a drawer open and close again with a soft thud. Familiar, soft fabric brushed her hands. "Is this what you want?"

"Thank you." She could hear the shakiness in her voice and hated the fact that she wasn't able to control it. Hastily, Jemi adjusted the forehead and crown straps, moved the nearly transparent eyeveil aside and pulled the lower curtain over her nose and mouth. Her breath was moist and comforting against the azure cloth. Ivory beads swayed along the jawline. She could feel the man's stare on her.

"You're from Highland." His voice was professionally gentle.

She nodded, still facing away from him.

"I thought that you were. We had an engineer from there shipping with us on one tour. He wore one of those—what'd you call it?"

"K'lyge," Jemi said. She turned back to him, smoothing the veils. There was a strange smell to it—like smoke or burnt plastic. Her fingertips brushed the lower hem and found beads there that she didn't remember. She read the incised lines there with her fingertips, wondering if this was the betrothal k'lyge Harris had given her. Her fingers stopped; she gasped. These were mourning beads.

Death beads.

Jemi inhaled sharply, suddenly frightened, realizing abruptly that she didn't know where she was, didn't know this man in the white naval uniform, that any calmness she possessed was only the lethargy of medicines. The man wore a familiar symbol on his chest: twined serpents. He was a doctor, then, and that explained the aloof friendliness in his voice. Fear hammered at her, and Jemi drew the eyeveil across so that he could not see her panic. She remembered the dream all too well. *Harris. Let it be Harris; I might have mourned for him too, simply because of what we'd been. But not Kenis. God, it can't be Kenis.* "Where's my son? Where's Kenis?" She could hear the rising panic in her voice, the rush that revealed her concern. She forced herself to breathe slowly, to be patient—she could tell by this one's unhidden eyes that he would speak only in his own time.

The doctor's smoke black pupils stared at her through the thin haze of the eyeveil. "When did you pick up your cargo, Holder Charidilis?" He used the polite Highland form of address, but his accent was European.

"Last week, from the Outer Mines." She could not understand the stupidity of the man's questions—what possible difference did the timing of her cargo matter? "Where's Kenis? Please . . ."

Underneath the beard, she saw muscles working along his jaw—he was keeping something back. A dread certainty stabbed at her, a blade of ice. "This question is going to sound ridiculous to you," the doctor was saying. "You must believe me when I say that your answer's very important. When you loaded that cargo—what year was it?"

Jemi hesitated. Behind the k'lyge, her eyes narrowed. Her lips were dry, she licked at them with a tongue, trying to shake away the fog of the drugs. "'Sixty-eight," she said impatiently. "Look, any idiot knows what year it is. Listen to me—you must tell me where Kenis is. I have to know—" Abruptly, she fell silent. Jemi could see the fatal, unspoken words even under the semi-veil of the doctor's beard. His mouth began to open; then he shut it again. He blinked slowly.

"I have orders to inform Admiral Strickland that you've awakened." He was trying to placate her now, all his words overinflected with heartiness. Behind it, like a shield, was an underlying, impersonal efficiency. "It'd be best if you waited to speak with him."

Worry and fright banished the stupor of the medication. Jemi rose to an elbow, feeling muscles pull and tear along her side. "You ask me stupid questions, and then you expect me to wait to get the important one answered?" she raged. "*You tell me now!* Where's Kenis? What's happened to me?"

The doctor retreated a step, put his back to some machine that was attached to a curving wall. Amber lights winked behind him. She could see more of the room—the floor curved upward like a bow at an odd angle, empty beds bolted along the rise. She seemed to lie at the bottom of a bowl—a ship, then, under spin. "If you'll wait a minute, Holder, I'll call for the Admiral."

"Damn you, give me an answer, not more evasions. Why are you so cruel?" Jemi tried to sit up, then lay back once more as muscles spasmed along her spine. "Oh, Jesus!" Her teeth gritted against the intense pain, her hands clawing at the sheets. She could not hold back a grunting cry.

"Holder—" The doctor rushed forward and reached for her. She felt a pricking in her arm and a shadow fell over her veiled face as he moved equipment over her bed. "Keep away from me," Jemi whispered, gasping. "Just give me my son." She struck out at the man, feeling her nails dragging against skin. She lashed again, clawing, and found only air. The man backed away from her bed, cradling his hand against his chest.

There was suddenly no kindness at all in his gaze.

"I can't give you your son." His voice was harsh. He looked at his hand, and Jemi could see the blood she'd drawn. "No one can, unless you want him as a vivicate." Then his eyes widened with guilty sorrow, his lips twisted with remorse. "Holder, I'm sorry. I didn't mean—"

But Jemi wasn't listening. She screamed.

She screamed because she knew that he told her the truth, because she knew that Kenis was gone and yet she had no memory of his death at all. In her mind, it had been but a few hours since she'd put Kenis in his bed aboard *Starfire*. She screamed, not caring that her sorrow and fear rode for all to hear in that keening, banshee sound. She was still screaming when something intensely cold pressed against her arm and flung her back into muffled darkness.

She floated for a time in that darkness. There, a strong, dark voice spoke to her, its subtones all compelling her to trust it. Again and again the voice repeated the words: "You have lost two years. The year is 2170, not 2168. You've been hurt; you've forgotten much. Kenis is gone. You will mourn your son because you must, but you will be calm. You will be calm. You have lost two years . . ."

She listened. She heard. But she was not certain she could believe.

Admiral Strickland had a look of benign and secure authority: silver-gray hair cut in the usual short military manner, a ramrod-straight back, and steel blue eyes caught in folds that crinkled sympathetically at Jemi as she entered his office. The walls were a surprising pastel blue totally unlike the drab of the corridors, though paint was peeling in long strips from a corner. Strickland smiled at her and a slow sadness touched his lips. He bowed to her in a manner that she imagined her great-great-grandmother might have seen, and waved a large, stubby-fingered hand toward a scarred wooden chair bolted before his desk.

"Have a seat, Holder Charidilis," he said, dismissing the nurse who had accompanied her. "Rest yourself, please. Dr. Miles tells me that you're coming along fine, but that you're still weak." Strickland cleared his throat—it seemed to be a nervous habit. "Tea or coffee?"

"Nothing," Jemi said. Then, belatedly: "Thank you, anyway." She blinked heavily. Her thoughts were slow and wandering—the doctor had given her an injection before she'd been allowed to see the Admiral.

Strickland nodded, smiled again, and poured himself a cup from a silver servette beside the desk. Jemi watched him. The Admiral moved slowly, carefully, as if at any moment the ship's living quarters might lose spin and the false gravity collapse—she supposed that it might have happened before to him—she could tell by the layers of paint that the ship was old. Turning the handle of the dispenser, measuring sugar, stirring: everything was done meticulously and without hurrying. He said nothing to Jemi until he'd placed the steaming cup in the exact middle of his desk. "You must be tired," he commented at last. "You've been several days recovering."

He stared at her without seeming to notice the k'lyge's lower veil masking her face. The corner of his mouth lifted in a faint smile. And he was right, as well—Jemi *was* tired and the medications hung like a mist over her thoughts. She shifted in the chair and grimaced behind the k'lyge at the resulting quick tug of pain.

The Admiral shook his head in sympathy. His massive hands cradled the mug as if for its warmth. "Holder, you've had a terrible experience. Believe me, I can understand both your confusion and your concern. I hope I can alleviate some of that for you."

There was one thought before all the others in her mind. She spoke it more gruffly than she intended. "Where's my son?" Jemi fingered the death beads on the k'lyge, praying that the answer would not be the one she feared, the one the dark voice had foretold in the dreams.

Strickland glanced down at his desk. He cleared his throat again. His eyes were very sad, like a puppy's. "The doctor informs me that you've been told subliminally. Yet I dread having to be the one that consciously gives you the truth. Your son . . . Kenis . . . is dead. He was killed in an accident three months ago on Highland. You've gone through the grief once before, and it's unfair that you're being forced to endure it again. I've contacted Highland and asked that they forward the report to New York, where we'll be taking you, but I've been given the essential details. It was an unfortunate fall from an inner linktube. He'd been climbing . . ."

Jemi had drawn the eyeveil across with Strickland's first words. She heard them all—slow, deliberate, methodical, like everything the Admiral seemed to do, and she cried bitter, silent tears. She'd not thought that she could ever hurt so badly. Images of Kenis came to her: his smile, the joy of his first accomplishments, his first words. His laughter, bright and unalloyed, the feel of him suckling at her breasts—the memories were a thousand small knives, each taking their blood from her. "Three months ago," she repeated when she could control her voice. She lifted her head to Strickland. "And that was 'seventy? Is that also what I've been told?"

He didn't want to admit it. She could see it in the way he grasped the mug. "Yes."

"Admiral"—she had to stop, swallowing back the grief once more—"my last memory is of 'sixty-eight. In my mind, Kenis is two, yet you tell me that he was nearly four when—"

She couldn't say it. The words choked her. She swallowed again, feeling the wetness of her cheeks, glad this once of the imposed calmness of the drugs. "I've lost Kenis twice. He's not only gone from me, but half of his life's been stolen from me as well. Admiral, I want, I *need* to know what's happened. You've said, correctly, that I'd be confused. I am. Where's *Starfire?* Where's my vivicate, Doni? Where am I and why am I here? Your Dr. Miles wouldn't answer any of my questions." The sorrow overwhelmed her again and she bent her head, her shoulders heaving helplessly. She could hear the Admiral's loud breath as he waited for her to look up again. She could hear him lift his mug, set it down. He cleared his throat. Jemi took a deep, sobbing breath and raised her head.

"Captain Miles was following my orders," he said. "Please don't blame him. I'm afraid that you won't care for my answers, Holder."

He was staring at her, his mouth twisted in a dismayed grimace. If it was simply discomfiture, she could understand it—most people who were unused to the k'lyge found it disconcerting to see nothing of the face of the person to whom they spoke, to miss the intricate and detailed language of the mouth, the jaw: all the musculature of the face. That was the private speech that, by the customs of Highland, only intimates should share.

Finally, he simply glanced away. He *harrumphed* several times and his thick fingers toyed with the slick glaze of his mug. "It's difficult to know exactly where to begin," he said at last. "Let's start with the easiest things. You're aboard my cruiser, the *Strolov*. We were on a routine patrol when my communications officer told me that he'd picked up a distress beacon. We investigated." Strickland paused, almost too long. Jemi wondered if he were arranging words to his satisfaction; to spare her pain, perhaps.

"You found *Starfire?*"

He glanced back at her. He sipped his coffee, rumbled his throat. "We found *Starfire,*" he said. "She was gutted and helpless after an attack. We also saw something else, on the very edge of our sensor's range: a fleeing ship—from all indications, it was Condor class, something much like Salii would build. That would make it a Family Jardien ship. However, before we could run the entire analysis, the craft slipped away. With a newer ship, a better drive system, they would not have gotten away."

Strickland shook his head, looking down at his desk. He almost seemed to sigh. "This has been a constant guerrilla war between the navy and the Jardien pirates, as you know. And this is a good indication why it drags on, in the face of the fact that all mankind should be standing together now. The T'Raijek—" Strickland's head came up, twisted in a bemused expression. He smiled—a flicker of thin lips—then turned sad again. "I know that none of this concerns you at the moment. You must forgive an old military man his tirades, Holder Charidilis. The junior officers aboard can tell you that these speeches sometimes slip out. If you'd like to hear my old war tales, I'll gladly bore you sometime later. My apologies." He inclined his head.

Jemi nodded. Behind the k'lyge, a faint half-smile touched her lips. She thought that she might like this man, had they met under different circumstances. But her grief would not allow her to speculate much beyond the fact of Kenis's death. "I'll gladly listen later, as you say, Admiral. And I hope that you don't think me ungracious if I say that right now my only interest is in Kenis and my ship."

"I'd be surprised if you felt any other way," Strickland answered. Each word was precise, separate.

The Admiral swiveled in his seat. He reached to one side of the desk and touched a contact there, grimaced when nothing happened, and touched the contact again, harder this time: an LCD screen spat light on the wall to Jemi's right. There, like a model set on satin, rested the wreck of a ship. Torn and savaged as it was, Jemi didn't recognize it for a moment. "Not *Starfire?*"

"I'm afraid so."

"Christ," Jemi whispered.

She stared at the hulk. *Starfire* had been a large sphere linked to a box, the array of the mercury ion drive trailing behind it. Now, the ball of the living quarters was rent by scorched lines, the drive was a twisted, melted glob, the storage compartment hung by a few cables, askew and crumpled. Metallic fragments slid past the camera view, winking in the glare of *Strolov*'s spotlights.

"I know she looks bad," Strickland said. "But I've had my engineering staff go over her and they tell me that she's salvageable." His voice was soft, empathetic. "We have her under tow, taking her back to Uphill Port. You should have no trouble getting repairs authorized. I assume you're insured?"

"I am—I mean, I was . . ." Jemi's words trailed off in a whisper. She leaned her head back against the cushions of the floater and stared at the corpse of her ship. She closed her eyes once more.

Kenis, in free-fall in the tube leading back to storage, his arms and legs flailing as he tried to control his motions, bouncing from bulkhead to bulkhead and all the time giggling . . . Harris was there then, before I kicked him off the ship. We both watched Kenis—proud parents. Doni shot past us, the vivicate as dexterous here as he was awkward in gravity, and retrieved the blundering Kenis. Doni and Kenis both laughed, and Harris and I laughed with them.

The mourning beads were cold against her throat. "Admiral, I still don't understand. Why can't I remember any of this? Was I that badly hurt?" She still looked at the ship.

"The Jardien ship attacked you. In the time before we arrived, for some reason of their own, they wiped the last two years from your memory."

Always precise, each word dropping into existence like a gem. Impossible.

Jemi turned to stare at the Admiral. Through the fabric of the k'lyge, his features were softened, yet there was a hardness to the set of his jaw that made Jemi wonder at the calmness of the man's words. "That's not possible," she said slowly, half in defiance, half in disbelief. "It can't be done."

Strickland growled throatily. He seemed more nervous now than before. He picked up the coffee mug, set it down again without tasting. "Yet that's the only supposition that I can make, Holder. I can understand your disbelief. What I've just said is, by all that I know, impossible—at least with the precision we've found in your memory loss. But my people have examined you in every way they could. And you know that Salii's technology diverged somewhat from ours during their isolation on Mars." He shrugged, brushing imaginary dust from his desk top. "You show no trauma to the skull—so the memory wasn't affected by a blow. There isn't any subconscious suppression of the memory, either. I ordered you examined under drugs, using techniques our intelligence branch has utilized, and you still could not remember."

Now Strickland sipped his coffee. He made a face as if the brew were too bitter. Jemi wished that he would speak faster, yet at the same time she yearned for him to say nothing more. She didn't know how much more she could absorb. Everything that he had said hammered at her, making her want to dissolve into helpless panic.

"I can't see your face," Strickland said, "so I don't know how you're reacting to all this. Believe me, I ordered you tested in such ways only hesitantly. I felt I had to do it, for various reasons that I can't go into here. I'm relatively satisfied that you've faked nothing, that your attack and your memory loss are, for whatever reasons, genuine. If that makes me sound callous, I'm afraid that it's part of the job and not my lack of sympathy for another human being."

She couldn't summon the anger she thought she might have felt; not when Strickland was so empathetic, not when the death of Kenis weighed on her. "I couldn't fake losing my child," she said. "I couldn't. But I've never heard that it was possible to induce a memory loss such as mine."

Harrumph. "It's certainly possible—certain techniques, combinations of drugs and hypnosis . . . There are interrogative techniques, yes." Strickland glanced down at his hands as if they held the answer. "But none of them could have done this so cleanly, buried it so well. Your memory is sheared off, a clean slice somewhere during May 15, 2168. If we probed deeper, I suspect that we could narrow it down further to an hour, a minute. From that point on, your recall is simply gone. Vanished."

"You're telling me that what happened to me can't be done."

"I'm telling you that *we* couldn't do it." His hand came up to cup his chin; he leaned toward her. "Perhaps Salii has something that the UCN knows nothing about. And there is always the technology of the T'Raijek—an alien race with a stardrive could certainly have the ability to do this to you." He looked at her strangely, as if waiting for a comment. "I think we can discount Highland—your home could have nothing that I wouldn't know about." Then Strickland rose, walking with halting steps toward the screen. His right leg dragged as if from some old injury. He stared at the view there for a time, his hands locked behind his back. Jemi watched his fingers flexing, curling into fists: something bothered the Admiral deeply, something beyond what he'd said here. The man was not at ease with himself; some demon raked his soul from inside—his stance was too erect, the muscles too taut. He spoke to the screen, not Jemi.

"Let me state all this openly, Holder Charidilis. First, your ship was attacked. You are a small, independent trader carrying, according to your log, a shipment of bioelectronics from Highland, to be delivered to Uphill and ferried down to Tokyo from there. You were perhaps ten days away, seven days out from lunar orbit. And a Family Jardien vessel attacked you. Then they boarded the ship they'd gutted—just incidentally having destroyed the cargo in the attack—and they either find your vivicate, Doni, dead or kill him themselves. You, Holder, they torture—what else can I call this selective destruction of memory? Obviously these pirates were not after your cargo or money, but something that you knew or held. That's the only scenario that makes sense, isn't it?"

"If you're certain that my memory's been wiped, Admiral, then I can assume the question's rhetorical."

He turned to her and smiled. His laughter was genuine; it filled the room. Jemi suddenly wanted to see Strickland more clearly. She no longer cared that he saw her sorrow—these people had known her far more intimately than she wanted to admit; what would seeing her tears matter? She pulled the eyeveil aside and fastened it behind her ear, pushing dark ringlets of hair back. "I didn't intend for that to be amusing, Admiral. My sense of humor's entirely gone, I'm afraid."

He still smiled, but the set of his face hardened, as if he didn't enjoy his thoughts. He took a stiff-legged step toward her—his right knee didn't seem to bend. "Have you ever smuggled, Holder? Have you ever been tempted by the large profits a clever person can make shipping contraband?"

She had expected the question. It seemed obvious in the face of the incident he'd outlined. She willed her eyes to show nothing, and replied with as much calmness as she could muster. "I can tell by your face that you already have an answer to that. Why do you bother to ask?"

Strickland shrugged, though the smile faded. "You admitted to it under the drugs, yes."

"And that admission is illegal, Admiral. As a citizen of the UCN, you can't convict me with that."

He waved aside her protest, his demeanor pained. He moved slowly over to his desk and leaned against it. Under the gray hair, his forehead was creased. "I'm not trying to shock you into an admission, Holder. Please believe that. I know that nearly every entrepreneur like yourself smuggles at one time or another. In poor times like these it's rather forgivable. I assure you that I don't care: I've no intention of using that information against you in any way. But you must understand why I ask."

His face sagged, his shoulders dropped, as if the Admiral had suddenly decided to drop his facade and show his weariness. He reached across the desk and picked up his mug once more. Again, he cleared his throat. "You're sure you'd like nothing?" He pointed with the mug to the servette.

Jemi shook her head.

Strickland moved over to the servette himself and carefully warmed his coffee. He spooned a small amount of sugar into the liquid, stirred. "The conflict between Earth and Salii is going to drag on for decades, Holder. Year upon year. There will be some other tired old man commanding this cruiser when the treaties are finally signed. Neither side can move freely. It's like a pawn-dominated endgame: we all make slow, careful moves, always watching the other side. None of those moves by itself can cause mate. None of us can be entirely independent of the other."

He sipped his coffee, made a face again. Jemi waited. "Oh, yes," he continued, "the Family Jardien and Salii are legally free of all ties to Earth, but, damn it, Earth *built* that colony." Strickland shook his head and his gaze traveled back to the screen and the hulk of *Starfire* once more. "I need to find out why this happened, why the Family Jardien would attack you. It must be important."

"I can't tell you why."

He sighed. She could hear a wheeze in his breath. "I know you can't."

"Admiral, what could I possibly have smuggled that would be worth the Family Jardien's time? The Saliian pirates go after cargo that they can use—they don't destroy ships. Even if I *did* have something aboard, why not just kill me rather than going to the trouble of wiping my memory? By any logic I can conceive, I should be dead. I should be with Kenis." She could feel the tears gathering again at the mention of his name. She spoke through their shimmering. "Damn it, Admiral, what do you want from me? I've lost my child, two years of my life and his, and I don't remember anything that can possibly help you." She would have said more, but forced herself to stop.

Later. You can be angry later, you can mourn fully later. For now, wait. Be calm. Harris used to say it: "Jem, you're too damned quick-tempered. That's why you and I never seem to get any close anymore." It was too like Harris to put the guilt entirely on her rather than sharing it himself, but there was some truth in what he said—and that had made her even angrier.

"Perhaps you were working for the Family Jardien."

He didn't believe that himself—she could see it. He wasn't even looking at her. His gaze was still snagged on the wreck of her ship. There was no inflection of suspicion in his plodding voice. "You drugged me and looked into my mind, Admiral. I'm sure that you have sources to uncover my past movements, as well. I'm positive you've already formed an answer to that question."

"You're right," he admitted graciously. "I won't bother to ask again. Frankly, I'd be most pleased if I thought you were an agent of the Family Jardien: I'd no longer be so concerned over the affair. It might make sense: an internal squabble . . ."

"Admiral Strickland, what happens to me now?"

He said nothing for a minute. Limping over to his desk, he seated himself once more, sighing and wheezing with a rumbling of mucus in his chest. He touched the screen's contact. *Starfire* vanished, the room lights brightened. "We'll take you to Uphill and then New York. At the moment, we're two days out, inside lunar orbit. You still have some recovering to do; I'll leave you to the ministrations of my medical staff for the remaining time aboard. You'll have a private cubicle where no one need disturb you—I've commanded Highlanders before, and I know your needs. I'll ask you to verify my report and give a statement of your own, but . . ." He spread his hands wide, then brought them back around the mug. He smiled gently at Jemi, the folds lifting around his eyes. "You'll be free to go. I'll see that the report on your son's death is given to you. From that point, you may do as you wish."

He wasn't finished. Jemi saw his eyes suddenly narrow, his back straighten. He spoke with more force than before, with an edge to his voice that Jemi didn't understand. "There's one provision to all this, Holder Charidilis. You *will* contact me personally if you learn anything more about this incident, if memory begins to come back to you, or if you stumble across something that you think might interest me. Contact my office at Uphill Port. If I'm available, you'll be put through; if not, leave word where you can be reached, but give no one else the information. Frankly, there are people within the UCN and the navy whose sympathies are more with the Saliians than the UCN. Holder, I want to see this long war ended, and you may know something that will help in that. It wouldn't surprise me if a message for my eyes only was intercepted. Please, contact *only* me. Is that acceptable?"

Jemi shrugged, pretending nonchalance. Once away from Earth, back on Highland where the nearest naval base was a week or more away, she intended to forget Admiral Strickland entirely. "That's as acceptable as anything I could wish, Admiral. I feel invaded. Raped. At this point, I'd do anything to know who stole Kenis from me, and why. I assure you, I'm on your side in this." Jemi stood. The beads of her k'lyge clashed percussively. "I won't take any more of your time, Admiral." She was tired; she wanted to sleep, to have time to think out all of this. Her mind was numb; she could only think about Kenis—it didn't seem possible that he wasn't in his bed on *Starfire*, waiting for her.

"I hope you hold no grudges against me for the way you've been treated."

"Admiral, you saved me, saved my ship, and healed my wounds. The rest you did because you had to. I understand that."

Strickland nodded and smiled. Jemi turned to go. She was almost to the door when he spoke again, and hidden emotions twisted his voice: "I'm very sorry about your son, Holder. I lost a daughter myself to an accident, and I can understand how you feel. I wish I could help you with your burden. Whoever did this to you should not have stolen your remembrances of Kenis: that was the unkindest thing done to you. No one should be forced to mourn twice."

"Admiral Strickland," Jemi answered, "I'm sure I never *stopped* mourning."

She slid the eyeveil back over her face as she turned away from him.

The cities were once humanity's finest accomplishment. After the World Depression—the Bust—after three decades of utter neglect and with few resources left, the cities had become old, filthy, and dangerous. That they still stand, that they can still evoke feelings of awe in us, only makes their decay more pitiable.

—introduction to "Cities" by R. M. Jordan, UCN Geographic, May 2169.

CHAPTER THREE

Karl Shiolev had never seen the Director. That fact made meetings with that official all the more terrifying. The rendezvous changed location every time, from a shabby tenement apartment in New York to here, an underground car garage in Paris. The garage was abandoned; with the oil supplies nearly depleted on Earth, far fewer people could afford to run groundcars. This place was as safe as any other.

There was only one constant to the encounters. There would bc a backlit screen on which Karl could see a bulky, moving shadow of a head and torso. He would hear a voice that was too filtered and synthesized to be recognizable. For that matter, he didn't know if the silhouette of the Director was real. He knew nothing about the person at all, whether the Director might be tall or short, fat or thin, man or woman. There was only the shape on the screen, the unreal voice, and the feeling of eyes peering at him.

He sat on a plain wooden chair and tugged at his sleeves, uncomfortable. He touched the scar where a tube had once pierced his nostrils—where the oxygen tube used by the Families on the surface of Mars had once gone.

Shiolev was on one of the ramps, the screen filling the area before him. He cleared his throat, hearing the sound echo through the concrete structure. He would rather be back in space, back on Salii again with the Director's money in his pocket and Mars turning slowly underneath him. This last bit of business had been distasteful—having to share the rebuilt Condor ship with that witch of a psychologist, having to fire on a helpless freighter. But there were the debts to pay if he ever wanted to return to Salii and Mars, and the Director had promised that all the notes would be torn up afterward. He would talk with the apparition one last time and see the notes destroyed. Then he would go home and try to forget it all. He would go home a hero, having helped Family Shiolev and the influence of Family Jardien on Martian society.

His butt was getting sore, sitting on the hard wood. He shifted his weight even as the screen lit, flooding the ramp with blinding light. Shiolev shielded his eyes momentarily against the glare.

"Quit fidgeting, man," the voice said. It arced and buzzed, as if imbued with a snarling energy. "Tell me, what did Maria use on the woman?"

"Scloramine. Not many people know about it—she told me that it's a psycho-suggestive derived from natural organics. The stuff is purified orbitally on Salii, and its use classified—I know that the UCN got hold of the formula, though. HeadFather Shiolev said that a Saliian turncoat gave it away to the UCN a year ago in return for amnesty."

"A turncoat like you, eh?" The voice screeched laughter. "Charidilis talked freely?" the Director rasped then, a growl with high overtones.

"We took what we could before the navy got there." Shiolev shivered, remembering the scene in the little portable shelter they'd rigged in the middle of the ship's rubble: the wide-eyed Holder yammering about her life, her son, reliving all the emotions before his eyes. The witchwoman laughed half the time, not caring that Charidilis was emptying the vessel of her memory forever. "The stuff's really amazing—Charidilis babbled on non-stop, with all the detail you could ever want. At your suggestion, we started with the most crucial time period and moved back from there. We'd gotten a little earlier than the most critical parameters by the time we had to leave."

"And you say you got nothing? *Nothing?*" The last word was overloaded, distorted, and the man jumped in his seat.

"I'm sorry, Director. Maria claimed to be one of the best people in her field. That was corroborated by others we contacted. She said that Charidilis had nothing to tell us."

"Could she have been mistaken?"

"According to her backup, it's possible. Under Scloramine, the subject must be led or you get too much trivial information. If we could have taken the time to do it slowly and sift through everything, we could be more certain. As it is . . ." He shrugged, watching the slow movements of the shadowy figure behind the screen. Was the head bald, or did the Director wear a skullcap of some sort? "We can't be entirely certain, no. But the chances are small that Charidilis could have withheld anything."

"Or our time frame was wrong, which is also possible," the Director added. "We know that the T'Raijek used her ship to transport the crystal. If the crystal wasn't passed to its contact, then it was hidden on the ship. I find it hard to believe that she couldn't have known."

"What do you want me to do, Director?"

"Nothing." The distorted shadow of a hand flickered over the screen. "You can leave. I'll take care of the rest."

"Director, I hate to suggest this, since it appears that the woman was entirely innocent, but she is a loose end."

"Yes, and we hate loose ends, don't we, Karl Shiolev? You enjoyed getting rid of Maria, didn't you?"

Despite the filtering, there was no mistaking the amused sarcasm in the Director's voice, and Karl smiled wanly in response, straightening his back against the chair's unrelenting spine. The chair legs scraped loudly against the oil-stained floor of the garage.

"I don't deny that Maria and I were at odds most of the time, Director. I didn't enjoy killing her, though; I'm not a monster. But I'm just as glad she's gone. For the same reason, we're both safer if Charidilis is gone. I'd prefer not to be the one to have to do it, but if you insist—"

"You're probably right, Karl. But you needn't concern yourself. I'll take care of it."

Shiolev rose with an audible sigh of relief. "As you wish, Director." He brushed his hands over his pant legs; his palms left a smear of moisture. Already he was thinking of Salii, of the welcome he'd get from HeadFather Shiolev. "Director, there's the matter of my debts."

"More loose ends, Karl?"

"Just my payment, Director." He gave a weak grin in the direction of the screen, his hands fluttering out like moths. "I deserve it, I think."

"Probably you do, Karl." The shadow moved on the screen, became smaller and sharper. Shiolev could distinctly hear footsteps, as if from leather soles. The screen itself seemed to shiver with a breath, and then it was held aside by a hand—a fisted hand that held a short-barreled gleam of metal. The light flared out behind the Director, pinning Shiolev in its shadow. Without the veil of the screen, Shiolev could recognize the man. He knew him. He'd seen the face before. And because of that, he knew what the gun meant as well. This man would never have let Shiolev see his face unless—

He stepped backward involuntarily; the chair clattered to the concrete and Shiolev stumbled over it in his haste to get away, falling heavily. "No!" he screamed, his face down on the ramp, afraid to turn around. He thought he could smell decades-old fumes from the cars. "Not me, not after all I've done for you!"

"You're a loose end," the voice said, still filtered, still alien. "You know what we have to do with those," the Director said.

He pressed the trigger. There was the faintest pop of compressed air. Shiolev's body jerked once, a tiny circle of red appearing in the middle of his back. Then he lay still.

When the body was found several hours later by the street people who sheltered there, it was as cold as the concrete on which it lay.

New York.

The streets near the East River catered to port workers, transients, and the businesses dealing with interworld commerce. In a time when the United States's influence on the world had been usurped by the establishment of the United Coalition of Nations, New York still managed to keep a stranglehold on her position as a center for finance. Her lines of influence ran both from the lofty offices uptown to here, where dank, grimy warehouses crowded the waterfront. To this sprawling place came much of the cargo offloaded Uphill—at the orbital stations. Shuttles shrieked overhead through an overcast composed equally of cloud and pollution. They landed at the new strips built on ground laid waste half a century ago by a Saliian Family Jardien pirate who had strafed the city. Seagoing ships waited patiently at their moorings.

Earth was still the great consumer for humanity—the electronic products of Highland, the raw materials from the mining platforms out beyond Mars, even some of the goods of Salii: all made their way back here. Even the alien T'Raijek, in their ships that could leap between the stars, even *they* had come to New York first.

The burrough that had once been called the Bowery seethed with a vigorous and sometimes dangerous life. The streets were dirty with rubbish, stained by time. A constant drizzle left pools of oily water in every depression; the very buildings seemed to exist only to cast a darkness on the alleys between. The place collected filth.

Jemi had always enjoyed her visits here.

But not this one. Her mood had been too darkly stained. Strickland had given her the report on Kenis. The pages of cold type had told her nothing. They had evoked no memories; even the pain she should have felt was blunted by the technical, dispassionate language of bureaucracy. The "subject"—that's who Kenis was to them. The "subject."

The subject had been left in the care of a crèche while his mother was involved with loading her ship. The subject had wandered away from the crèche and been seen climbing the outside of a linktube between sectors of Highland, where the lessened spin of the colony produced a lower gravity. Before anyone could get to the subject, he had fallen; slowly at first, then ever faster as he came nearer the rim of Highland. Propelled by the colony's spin, he had slammed into the buildings there. He had been dead when the medical team reached him. The crèche-mother in charge had been cited for negligence and jailed after the investigation, but the subject's death was termed accidental.

Jemi had read the report. Read it again. It brought only tears and frustration. Finally, she'd fought off the misery and (with Strickland's aid) arranged for *Starfire*'s repairs. Then she'd attacked the small mound of paperwork: Strickland's report; a letter to her uncle on Highland, giving him an unexpurgated version of the story; a note to Vivicate Corporation, informing them of the termination of Doni Rowe; a call to her client's representative in New York, to tell her of the loss of the cargo.

It had taken all her energy to get herself ready to leave the hotel room in the Marriott, uptown. There was little enough to gather—she had only a change of clothes given to her on *Strolov* and her k'lyge. Strickland had arranged for her to be given a loan from a victims' aid program until she could transfer some of her own funds from Highland—he must have known but had not mentioned that Jemi had no savings. She'd borrowed a boot-knife from one of the crewmen before leaving Uphill: that she was going down to New York had been enough explanation. The crewman had smiled and tossed it to her.

Evening found her, sullen and depressed, in a tavern off South Street. Jemi adjusted the k'lyge as she took a seat in a far corner, crossing the lower folds with the white underveil; a sign on Highland that she wished no company. She'd brought a paper with her from the Marriott. All the news was unfamiliar to her: different names and different faces staring back from the holos. New problems in new locations. She didn't even recognize President Hughes, who leered at her from the front page:

PRESIDENT OFFERS CONCESSIONS TO UCN

She turned quickly to the local section to escape the confusion she felt at the headlines. There was a one–column-inch mention of *Starfire*'s attack, sandwiched between two other stories: New Mayor Celebrates and T'Raijek Found Dead, State to Investigate. The story under Highland Freighter Attacked included a quote from Admiral Strickland, but there was no mention of any Family Jardien vessel. Strickland spoke only of an "as yet unidentified ship.'' Jemi shook her head. She set aside the paper, dialed a drink on the table's menu—Glenfiddich. There was nothing comparable to that, and such luxuries were far too expensive on Highland. She had more than once smuggled bottles of scotch back home.

As she waited for her order, Jemi glanced about. The place wasn't much, but then, few places were anymore—plastic beams molded and stained like wood straggled across the roof, ostensibly to give an aura of age to the tavern but instead jarring her with their artificiality. The tables were battered and scarred by years of use, a dark sludge having accumulated in the grooves. The glass over the menu selector was scratched, almost translucent in spots. Graffiti spilled over the plastic planking of the walls. Near the back of the bar was an alcove for vivicates, discreetly set away from the main area of the establishment. Despite the fact that the place was crowded with workers and the tables were filling up at the shift-change for the port, the vivicate alcove was empty. Even on Highland, the vivicates seemed to avoid public places. It was just as well; most people were disgusted by the vivicates' stumbling, slobbering reflexes.

To one side, near the bar itself, there was a table of fellow Highlanders. Jemi glanced at them; they had seen her as well. They nodded, their own k'lyges swaying, but with her veils bespeaking her desire for privacy, none of them bothered her further.

Her table chimed dully and she took her scotch from the center cabinet. As she lifted the k'lyge to sip the smoky liquor, she saw a T'Raijekian alpha male come through the tavern door. She recalled the headline in the paper and marveled that New York could have two of the aliens at one time, especially the alpha males. From what Jemi understood, the alphas were the rarest of the tri-sexed T'Raijek. She'd heard that the T'Raijek sometimes used the free traders for in-system transport, though she'd never ferried one of the aliens before—unless, she reminded herself, it had happened during the previous two years.

The thought made her sullen; she stared at the T'Raijek, wondering if he'd come here looking for a convenient ride. The alpha male was stocky, short and squat, not like the tall and regal omega males she'd glimpsed around the Highland embassy. His head was bald, the skin golden with a distinct orangish cast, though a dark fur began at his cheeks and continued until it went under the powder blue tunic he wore. The face itself had the barest suggestion of a snout, the cheeks and nose thrust out. Two six-fingered hands with double opposable thumbs were hooked into a large silver belt; below, his penile sheath bulged grossly under tight pants. Around the room, people tried very hard not to stare. Jemi followed the path of the meter-high creature until she lost him in the crush around the bar.

"Do you mind company, Holder?"

The voice startled her. Jemi turned to see the face. The man who'd spoken had short, dark hair, pleasant and large green eyes, and a mouth whose smile twisted around a small scar dimpling his left cheek. Tall and thin, he seemed confident, standing easily beside her table. At another moment, in a different place under different circumstances, she might have been intrigued.

Not tonight. Not when the unknown ghosts of the stolen memories crowded her. Harris, her former husband, had also been tall, dark and confident, and Kenis would have grown to look much like his father. Jemi glanced away from the man and placed her glass back down on the table. "On Highland, a person would have been able to read my veils and wouldn't have disturbed me." When she glanced back up, he was still smiling, one side higher than the other.

"This is New York, Holder. Home of all humanity and all customs. I can't read the veils at all. I only saw someone who looked interesting. I'm sorry if I offended you, but you still haven't answered my question. Would you mind some company?" He shifted his weight from foot to foot. Jemi thought that he must be a man unused to failure. "It can be lonely sitting by yourself in a strange place," he said, and there was a sympathy in his voice.

Jemi made no effort to smile falsely, as a veiless one might have done in the same situation. The k'lyge made such lying gestures pointless. She simply gazed at him. "No," she said. The words were a warm breath against the cloth. "I'd prefer to be alone tonight. For my own reasons," she added, not wanting to be too abrupt.

The man shrugged, gave that twisted smile again. "I *listen* well, too, if that's what you need."

"No," she repeated, more firmly this time.

He hesitated. Jemi could see him balanced between continuing the effort and acknowledging defeat. Finally, he turned back into the crowds with a sad wave. Jemi glanced back over at the table of Highlanders. One of them nodded slightly; he had noticed and sympathized.

She picked up her drink once more, glancing about the room. The T'Raïjek was gone or hidden in the throngs. The tavern, the night, the city had all begun to cloy on her, though she sat a half hour longer. There was too much false laughter, too much loud conversation clashing with the rumble of canned music, too much animated, artificial friendliness. Jemi felt lonely; worse, she knew that she was feeling sorry for herself. She wanted to cry, wanted to be *with* someone, if just for the temporary solace another human being could give her. She would have readjusted her k'lyge and gone over to the table of Highlanders, but they had finished their drinks and left. If Kenis were still alive, she could have cuddled the boy in her arms, smoothing his unruly hair—

And that thought sent her skittering through what memories she had of such moments with her child, and they seemed tragically few. All the rest of them were gone.

Taken.

People chattered happily around her. It seemed hollow and unreal. For all she knew, she might have met some of those here tonight, might have seen them in her last two years of travel. One of them might have been a lover and she would never recognize him or her.

Abruptly, she pushed her chair away from the table and left the tavern.

The night was sultry, muggy with the drizzle, and noisome. Shuttles howled at the city with banshee cries, steam rose from the puddles. The clouds were infused with a green glow from the lights of downtown Manhattan to the west. Jemi strolled aimlessly down South Street and into the warren of streets along the East River, past the bars and the crowded houses, past pilots and dockworkers, past whores of both and indeterminate sexes working the restless night. Jemi sought out the less inhabited areas of the sector, near the warehouses ringing the landing strips for the shuttles. She wandered between long, low buildings, her boots scrunching on blacktop. One by one, she tried to conjure up the lost months—they were gone. Gone. One of her last memories of Kenis was of a scolding. She'd become angry with him because he'd refused to pick up his toys.

"Damn it, Kenis, do what I tell you. Pick them up." He giggled at her, either not seeing or not caring about her irritation, and toddled away with an unsteady swagger. "No," he insisted, using one of his few words. That made her angry enough to shout at his retreating back. "Young man, you have three seconds to get back here. One, two . . ." In the end, she'd had to chase after him. She spanked him, and then scolded him again when he wouldn't stop crying. She'd apologized immediately, knowing that she was punishing him for something he didn't understand. She'd hugged him fiercely then, crooning to him, and helped him pick up the toys as he sniffled alongside her. That was nearly the last time she remembered being with him.

Jemi turned a corner and didn't realize that she was nearly at the end of a cul-de-sac until a building had reared up to block her path.

There was the scrape of a footstep behind her.

She'd not expected to see that face again. Certainly not here. He smiled that tilted smile, the scar white in the glare of spotlights along the building's roofs. He flipped a long knife from hand to hand as he stared at her.

"Hello again, Holder," he said. "You should have taken me up on my first offer—you made it difficult for me to get you alone, and that can make me very angry."

Jemi was stunned for a moment. She hesitated, then reached down to draw her own knife from its leg sheath. "You don't want trouble," she said at last. "Just leave me alone. That's all I want. I don't have enough money to make this worth your effort."

"Don't want money."

Her lips tightened under the k'lyge. The veils swung. "You'll get nothing else."

He seemed almost jovial. He snickered. "I know what you're thinking, and you're wrong. Oh, I may have that anyway, afterward, but it's not the primary thing at all." He flipped the knife once more and took a step toward her, his hand tightening on the hilt. "You know, most people would use a gun," he said. "They don't want anyone to struggle, to fight. But *me*, I enjoy that. Guns are too impersonal, don't you think?" His smile was gone now, his lips pressed tightly together, the scar standing out against flushed skin. His voice had the same warm sympathy she'd heard in the bar, only now it seemed eerie and cold. Jemi retreated, crouching, feeling the weight of her knife. It had been a long time since she'd used a knife, and that time had only been a bluff, one luckily not taken. She had a sudden intuition that she would die here. The man was quick and sure of himself; her own street tricks were few. If he was at all good with that weapon, she knew that she would feel its edge.

He came at her slowly, then in a sudden rush. She brought her knife up, grunting, felt it slither along the length of the man's blade as she kicked at his groin. He back-stepped, untouched, not giving her the opportunity to run. He grinned, a feral smile. "Now, that won't work at all," he taunted. Jemi didn't answer. She was breathing fast, panting, her back to the wall that trapped her. The man stared with emerald eyes, shook his head.

He smiled.

He took a step.

He fell.

As Jemi stared, a T'Raijek alpha, either the one from the tavern or an identical alpha male, stepped into view from the mouth of the alleyway. He was pocketing a gleaming device in a pouch hanging from his belt. He strode up to the body with a side-to-side rolling gait and examined a small, bloodless discoloration in the back of the man's shirt. Then he looked at Jemi.

It was an old face, hidden behind the luxuriant growth of facial hair. Pupils like dull dark chocolate were webbed in a hundred folds—those eyes stared at her. "You going to a masquerade or did you plan to rob a bank?" he said to her.

His voice sounded like two rocks arguing, and the accent was guttural, almost Germanic. Jemi stared from the alien to the body of her attacker. When she didn't speak, the T'Raijek growled low in his throat. "You could try 'thank you,' or does the mask mean that you can't talk, either?"

"Umm, thanks," Jemi said at last. She wrenched her gaze away from the man. "He's dead?"

The T'Raijek visibly bit back some comment. "Yes, that was the basic idea," he spat out. "Would you rather I'd politely asked him to leave you alone?"

"Not exactly." Jemi realized that she was still holding her knife. She began to sheathe it, then thought better of the idea—too much had happened in the past few days, in the past hour. Too much coincidence. First the scarred man, then the T'Raijekian . . . she couldn't believe that any of this had been accidental. She kept her hand at her side, but tightened her grip on the hilt. "Who are you? What do you want with me?"

"Forget the bullshit. I just saved your fucking life."

The obscenities, coming from the alien, almost made her laugh in shock, and she realized that she was giddy from the adrenaline surge. She inhaled deeply, not caring that the air stank. She leaned back against the wall. Cool moisture seeped through the fabric of her blouse. "I'm sorry. I'm very grateful to you and I'm glad you showed up when you did, but it doesn't make any sense."

He smiled, a mirthless grin that exposed wide, flat, and crooked teeth. "I do good work, huh? Just like you apes." He prodded the body with a foot, and Jemi noted for the first time that he wore no shoes. His toes were long and big-jointed. They looked as if they could do well as hands. He stared back at her in turn, with a look almost of defiance.

"Am I supposed to know you," Jemi asked. "You keep looking at me . . . Have we met before?"

"How would I know that? Take off the veil so I can see your face and I'll tell you."

Jemi's intake of breath was a hiss. "You're impudent. On Highland, comments like that wouldn't be tolerated."

"People who are in other people's debts should be *very* tolerant, I'd think," the T'Raijek replied. He prodded the corpse again for emphasis. It moved limply. "You can call me Ardent.

Now, I'll admit that this has been a charming conversation, but it'd be better if we continued it somewhere away from the evidence, don't you think? You owe me a drink."

"I do?"

"Absolutely." Ardent's gaze was steady—Jemi began to wonder if the alpha males ever blinked. She crouched down, the beads of her k'lyge swinging. She quickly went through her attacker's pockets. Touching the body brought on a sudden nausea; Jemi sat down on the pavement, breathing heavily, trying to control her stomach. "Looking for money?" Ardent inquired. There was no mistaking the sarcasm in his voice. He leered at her, closer to her than she liked.

"Can't you ever be quiet?" She swallowed heavily.

"You wear a mask, I talk. We all have our faults."

Jemi shook her head, and turned back to continue checking the body. Scarface had no papers, no identification at all, only a few loose bills of low denomination. There was nothing to place him or to indicate why he might have chosen her as his victim. Jemi thought of Strickland, of his instructions to inform him of anything out of the ordinary. She knew that she should contact the admiral, yet something held her back. *You can always do it later. It hardly matters now, after all—it was probably just a random attack. You'll get caught up in more paperwork, more questions. Highlanders know the Earthers all too well—just get away from here.*

She found it easy to convince herself. She rose, feeling the ache of muscles only recently healed, and glanced down at the T'Raijek. Her stomach still roiled, and she could not bear to look at the corpse again.

"Let's get your drink," she said. "I need one too."

"You could use another pilot to help you, and you need an ally. You need me."

They were in another bar, drinks pooling rings on the tabletop. Ardent's thick hands were wrapped around a glass of water, which he sipped as carefully as the scotch that sat before Jemi. The tavern's patrons stared and goggled around them, but stayed well away. Ardent's black, intense gaze was fixed on her once more. "You haven't answered me," he said when Jemi didn't answer him.

"You're joking," she said. "You must be." This was her third shot; the first had gone quickly, as if she could obliterate death with the liquor's fire. Then she'd left the T'Raijek briefly to phone the local police, to tell them about the body. The stress of that anonymous call had gone into the second glass.

"I'm serious," the T'Raijek insisted. "The last thing you want is another vivicate, some zombie that can't even walk well."

"Without the vivicates, Highland would die. Earth would die—they use them almost as much as we do," Jemi insisted. "We need the manpower. The UCN advocates their use—"

Ardent waved the comment away. "I'm offering you a chance and you keep babbling nonsense." He took a sip from his glass and then wiped at his beard with the back of his sleeve. "I have piloting credentials—all UCN-certified. You want to see them, or do you think you might trust someone who's taken a ship between the stars?"

Jemi could sense the scorn in his words. Perhaps because of that, perhaps because too much had happened to her too quickly, she found her irritation rising. "I'll see them," she told him, holding her hand out.

Ardent's beard twitched around the ancient mouth, the coarse, thick strands moving over the pushed-out face. For a second she thought that he might refuse—what little she knew about the T'Raijekian alpha males said that they were proud and touchy, perhaps as a legacy of their rarity; Ardent seemed to fit that mold well enough. The T'Raijek had entered human history only a scant half-century before, affording humanity a glimpse of worlds beyond their sun, but even those who had made a study of them knew very little of their society, nor had the T'Raijek volunteered much.

Yet this one had saved her life. If Jemi wasn't sure that she could entirely trust him, she did owe him that. On Highland, where death meant that one's body might later be sold as a vivicate, your mind trapped inside a twitching, altered face, a life debt was not one easily cast aside.

Ardent had dug into the pouch that covered his codpiece. Jemi caught a glimpse of rolled, thick flesh, and then Ardent pulled a holocard out from an inner pocket. He held it across the table to her, grinning when she was very slow taking it. "Strange place to keep things," she said.

"I get very few pickpockets," he answered, still laughing at her.

Jemi examined the card, read the testimony there. She slid it back toward him. "Fine. You're certified. I can still hire a hundred others here on Earth or buy another vivicate. Why should I bother with you?"

"I'll work for five hundred a month."

Jemi scowled, her forehead furrowed above the k'lyge. The alcohol fuzzed her brain. "That's half union standard."

"I'm not union."

"Then what *are* you, and why are you so interested in working for me?"

Ardent drained his glass. He slammed it down on the table. In the dim bar-light, his eyes glittered wildly. Around them, people turned to stare. "Hell, woman, the tale about *Starfire*'s all over the port. *Everyone* knows you'll be looking for a pilot."

Jemi shook her head, lowering her voice deliberately. "So you just happen to go to the bar I'm in. By chance, you're walking by when someone *else* who was by accident in that same bar attacks me. Luckily, you're flat broke and willing to work for half-scale even though you're certified and as a T'Raijek the UCN'd gladly foot your bills for a while. That's a whole lot of coincidence to swallow."

"The T'Raijek believe in a God of Oddities."

"I don't. I'm having trouble with it."

Ardent shrugged at that. He plucked his card from the table with his long, oddly jointed fingers and stuffed it back in the codpiece. Muscles bulged in his thick neck as he shook his head at Jemi. "I went looking for you, yes," Ardent said. "You're not exactly hard to trace, not with the k'lyge, not with your current notoriety. I went into the tavern to see you, but I'm lousy in crowds—they always want to see *me* and get in my way. You're all too tall—I saw a lot of stomachs. When I noticed you at last, you were already at the door. By the time I fought my way outside again, you were halfway down the street, strolling along without a care in the world and totally oblivious to the man following you, who was obvious enough that he could have been wearing a fucking sign. So *I* followed *him*. I was curious. And I'm not without funds of my own; no T'Raijek ever is."

"That almost sounds plausible so far."

Ardent inclined his head in a curiously human gesture. "Why, *thank* you. And to think that I was beginning to feel that you were as gullible as an omega."

"That doesn't mean that I trust you."

"Yes you do." Ardent's furry beard lifted as he raised his head, defiant. "Anyone else would have stayed in the area of the attack, would have called the authorities immediately, not later. *You* went with me."

"I was shaken," Jemi said. "I'm supposed to contact Admiral Strickland if—"

"Strickland has his nose up his ass," Ardent interrupted, his voice too loud. He seemed strangely fierce and dangerous for a moment, then he smiled again. "And why would the Admiral want to be bothered about a mugging in New York? They happen all too often here."

His mocking tone gigged Jemi's irritation. "What I tell the Admiral, and why, is my own business."

Ardent said nothing. A finger circled the lip of his glass. Then he shook his head as if to rid it of a thought, and his voice was gruffly cheerful again. "You're right in that, Holder. Absolutely. You'll learn that we alphas are sometimes too forward for our own good—ask any omega. So . . . when do I get to see this ship?"

"I haven't said that I'd hire you."

"More important, you haven't said that you won't, and you don't look like you're leaving."

"Aren't you afraid that I'll say no just to prove that your confidence is mistaken?"

"You're not that easily manipulated, are you?"

Despite her suspicion, despite the irritation, Jemi was enchanted with Ardent's banter and intrigued by his insistence. *Send him away and you'll never know anything about him. He saved your life when he could as easily let you die. And no independent worth her ship ever completely trusted the navy. If you want to find out about the attack, about Kenis, you'll need help.*

There were a thousand objections to that logic; she ignored them. Her final decision was impulsive, intuitive. She fingered the death-beads of the k'lyge and remembered how fascinated Kenis had been by pictures of the aliens—the regal omega males; the dangerous-looking, elusive females; and the squat, dwarfish alphas, almost comically endowed. Kenis would have been tugging at her sleeve. Behind the veils, a corner of her mouth lifted in a smile. "You're damned clever, aren't you?"

"Yes," he answered, staring directly back at her with those ancient eyes. "When do I see *Starfire*?"

Jemi picked up her glass. She swirled the amber liquid in it, lifted the hem of her k'lyge, and sipped. For good or ill, the decision had formed in her mind. At last she set down the glass and looked across at Ardent.

"In the morning," she said. "We'll go up in the morning."

The T'Raijek came at exactly the wrong moment in mankind's history. Without them, perhaps we might have climbed out of the morass. With their strangeness and their technology overshadowing our own stalled progress, we collectively shrugged our shoulders and wondered: Why bother? Let the rest of the universe come and find us.

If that sounds like a portrait of wounded vanity, well, maybe that's an accurate mirror we're looking in.

—from the preface to the *Time* magazine
Special Issue: The Half-Century Mark;
January, 2150.

CHAPTER FOUR

There was no clear, cold light in the morning to change her mind. In fact, the day presented outside the Marriott's weatherscreen was hot and damp, with billowing clouds lumbering across the East Harbor to be snagged on the city's tall buildings. Yet she had indeed changed her mind.

Jemi's mood matched the gloomy morning. She rolled naked from the bed and padded about the room, her arms crossed under her breasts, muttering. She kicked at her pile of clothes and sat down heavily in the room's one chair, one leg over the worn upholstery.

Before her floated the image of the man the T'Raijek had killed. The blood was very bright and very real, and a gaping, stunned terror was fixed eternally on the scarred face. Somehow, in the adrenaline rush of the night, she had been able to ignore that image. The death had sickened her, but she'd walked away from it. She'd even gone to *drink* with this Ardent, who could so casually kill a person. It all seemed surreal to her now—the whole night. It didn't make any sense. It wasn't her, it couldn't have been her. Her stomach churned at the memories, and she closed her eyes to stop the sudden queasiness.

"You're an ass, Holder," she said aloud.

She sat there for a few moments more and then called out loudly: "Room Service."

"What can we do for you, Holder?" a voice responded after several seconds. The ancient speaker crackled; she could hardly understand the query.

"A newspaper and coffee."

"Yes, Holder."

The order was delivered within ten minutes by a bored-looking young man. In the meantime, Jemi had dressed and donned her k'lyge. The busboy's jacket reflected the malaise that gripped humanity: worn, spotted with old food stains that no amount of washing could have erased. Jemi overtipped the teenager with Strickland's money, and sat down to leaf through the paper. Fifteen minutes later, half the pot of coffee gone, she threw the paper down.

There was nothing in it.

Nothing about a man killed in the East River district. She hadn't expected that to make the front page, but she'd gone through every column of the local section and found nothing. She couldn't believe the body hadn't been found; not when it had been left in plain sight near the warehouses, not after she'd phoned. Even if the police had somehow missed the body or thought her call a crank, at shift-change before dawn this morning the area would have been swarming with people. An obvious murder, no matter how unimportant the victim, would have gotten *some* press coverage.

And it was important to her. She'd never been party to death before. Yes, she'd been on the edges of society's laws. She'd smuggled, she'd cut corners that shouldn't have been cut, she'd even been in physical confrontations before, situations fraught with danger. Yet none of them had come to such a bloody and final conclusion. Her attacker's death left her shaky, thinking of it—she couldn't believe her calm of the night before. That had been false emotion, a numbness caused by all that had happened to her in the past several days.

She remembered pawing through the scar-faced man's pockets,

remembered the heavy limpness of his arms when she moved them. Her stomach heaved with the thought.

Jemi ran into the bathroom, barely making it before the coffee came back up.

Sitting on the cold, broken tiles of the bathroom, hugging her knees to her chest, she was suddenly very afraid. *You touched him. You must have left fingerprints all over the body. They couldn't miss them . . . You've got to get out. You've got to leave.*

Jemi remembered telling the T'Raijek that she would hire him. She remembered that she was supposed to meet him back in the bar where they'd met the night before and go from there to Uphill to see her ship. Jemi no longer wanted to see the alien. She wanted nothing to do with last night; all she desired was for it all to go away. She stood, her decision made. She would leave her room here and go directly to Uphill. She'd stay aboard *Starfire*, wouldn't see anyone. She wouldn't mention the attack, the death, the T'Raijek alpha male named Ardent. None of it.

She had nothing to pack. She plucked the keycard from the dresser and left the room. Down in the lobby, she tossed the card to the clerk and signed the bill. She turned away from the desk, ready to board one of the transports to the Uphill shuttles.

She nearly walked into Ardent.

He grinned up to her. " 'Morning, boss," he said. "You don't have to worry about avoiding me—there wasn't anything in the papers at all, was there?"

"Do you always know what people are thinking?" The question was only half in jest.

"Not always," he answered, the grin still splitting the hairy face. His teeth were broad and wide-spaced. "I just know how I'd react if the situation were reversed." Around them, people stared at the T'Raijek, and Ardent gestured at them. "Anyway, it's too late now. You've already made the association with me. I'm not exactly the type that people will forget seeing, eh?"

Jemi took a deep breath. She felt hemmed in, trapped, lost in a web of circumstance that she didn't understand. *Uphill. Starfire.* Those were her only thoughts. Get back to the ship, to the familiar. "I'm going Uphill," she said, tersely. Her k'lyge billowed with her breath, the death-beads chattering like teeth. "Come along if you want to."

* * *

Starfire hung in a webbing of monofilament lines, the firefly sparks of welding torches playing around her. She was beginning to look like a proper ship again, but parts of her hull were still scorched and a great rent in her cargo hold was still open, the steel plating curled back like blackened orange peel. Still, Jemi could look at her limned in blue-white earthlight, and see she was restored. That was good—she'd wondered if she'd ever be so lucky, after the sight of the wrecked ship in Admiral Strickland's screens.

Under her k'lyge, she smiled despite herself. She switched off the screen that showed the outside view.

At her side, Ardent growled. "You people get too damn attached to machinery. You'd think you used a hammer instead of semen to make babies."

"That's crude," Jemi told him.

"It's true."

They were in the pilot's compartment, where most of the cosmetic repairs had been done. In the room, workers still huddled before open cabinets, repairing the wiring relays to the rest of the ship. One, a petite woman, hung upside down near the ceiling, her head poking into an access duct. Ignoring Ardent, Jemi floated gently over to her. "What's wrong in there?" she inquired.

The woman's body jerked, and the head came quickly out from the duct. Her startled dark eyes were impossibly wide. Then the woman laughed, though the amusement sounded forced, as if Jemi made her uncomfortable. *The k'lyge,* Jemi thought.

"Holder," she said. "You surprised me. I was checking for a blockage in the duct. I was told—"

"There can't be a blockage or we'd all be dead. That's the main air supply duct—I know my ship, after all."

"Yes, Holder, but—"

"I wouldn't argue with the Holder. You won't find anything in there, believe me," Ardent drawled behind them. His words were tinged with an amusement that Jemi didn't understand, and the worker's eyes went wide again for moment. "This was the Holder's first child," Ardent added. As the worker drifted off toward the knot of other laborers, Jemi turned on Ardent, raging.

"You've no right to say anything like that, bastard," she hissed tersely.

"You're wrong, Holder. I can say whatever I like to you—we've a dead man in common, remember?" His words were a soft threat, and then he shook his head, sighing. The small alien hung in the chilly air like a stormcloud, one hand clutching the back of the pilot's seat. He toyed with the ends of the umbilical, the joints of his fingers looking arthritic as they bent strangely to the side. "Look at this crap," he said. "This'll rust out in a decade. Less. Inferior materials."

Behind the mask of the k'lyge, Jemi frowned. "She's mine. She's my home even more than Highland. I put years of myself into her. I raised my son here. Inferior materials or not."

"I'm awfully impressed," Ardent said dryly.

"The ship is Kenis. The ship is the years I spent paying for the freedom to work for myself. It contains my life—do you understand that?"

"I can understand it," Ardent replied. "I just think it's a little sentimental. It's steel and plastic: it's not real—not flesh and blood. Well, not most of it."

He pulled himself downward a little, prodded the cushion of the seat with a thick-padded fingertip. Jemi watched him, and saw the stain there, an irregularly shaped blob, ugly reddish brown in color. That made her inhale sharply. She looked away abruptly. Ardent made a sound that she couldn't decipher, almost a half-laugh.

"I don't find it funny," she said. She pretended to study the repair work and saw nothing of it. She let herself drift in the air-tides of the room, and turned her head back to glance at him. The beads clashed together on the k'lyge, a soft percussion.

"It's not your blood. What should you care?"

"I liked Doni. He was a good pilot. He was part of the family."

"He was a vivicate," Ardent scoffed. "I thought Highlanders considered vivicates somewhere above dogs and below small children. He was a possession: you *owned* the man."

"He could pay off his life-debt. Then I wouldn't have had any legal right to his body." It was an old argument, one that always was raised when talking to non-Highlanders. They didn't understand the economic realities of Highland—they needed all the hands they could get: to mine the ore, to keep Highland together, to do everything that had to be done. Without the vivicates, there wouldn't be enough people to do the menial labor, the basics. You died, and you left your body. If it could be revived, then it was only fair that you have to pay off the corporation for bringing you back. You had to pay your debt to Highland. And most vivicates could not remember their past lives, anyway. Doni had been a good companion but he hadn't been entirely *human*. But you couldn't just say that to someone—they had to experience the vivicates and live with them to know.

Kenis liked Doni. They were the best of friends, I think. Ken would go to Doni as much as to me or Harris. Like the rest, the thought seared her mind as if someone had poured molten lead over it. She could feel the burning in her eyes as well, and she let herself drift away from the chair, away from Ardent.

The sharp, acrid smell of welding came to them and the air currents suddenly pushed her toward the ceiling of the room. One of the interior doors opened and someone floated through, a pressure suit and visor hiding the face despite the fact that the hull was airtight. "Holder Charidilis?" A man's voice. He pushed against a wall, turning his body. Jemi could see the insignia at his breast then: two stripes over an eagle's claw: UCN security.

"Here, Corporal," she said.

"Commander Nys would like to see you in his office as soon as it's convenient, Holder." The glossy expanse of the visor glittered as the soldier's head swiveled to regard Ardent. Without the facial expressions, Jemi could not be certain, but the man's stance seemed to indicate hostility. To be able to read emotions from stance and attitude was a social skill on Highland, where the faces were camouflaged behind the k'lyge. Jemi wondered at the distaste the man showed, but if Ardent noticed, he only smiled.

"Does *convenient* mean right now?" Ardent asked.

"The Commander didn't say."

"He probably thought he didn't have to," Ardent said before Jemi could speak.

"That would be my assumption," the corporal answered. Through the pressure suit's body-speaker, his voice was professionally bland.

"Tell Commander Nys that I'll be right there," Jemi said, interrupting them quickly. Irritation with the T'Raijek burned at her, banishing the pain of memory, turning her neck scarlet under the shield of the veils. She stared at Ardent, who shrugged his shoulders innocently.

When the corporal had gone, Jemi turned on him. "What the hell right do you have to speak for me?" she demanded. "I *hired* you. If you're going to do as you damn well please anyway, then you can get off my ship now. You can tell anyone about anything you damn well please. I won't be blackmailed by you or anyone." With another Highlander, she might have pulled down the upper veil to take the edge from her rage. But she let him see the fury glittering there.

He didn't seem to care.

He bowed deeply in the middle of the air, hanging before her like a ludicrous puppet. His deep, gravelly voice intoned, "Yes, mistress," with such oversincere apology that she could say nothing more without displaying her anger to all the workers.

Then he seemed to collapse, all his barriers suddenly down. When he spoke again, his voice was utterly sincere: "Holder, about my saying that the ship was your first child—I didn't think before I spoke. I didn't intend for that to hurt you as it did." There was a vulnerability in him that she'd never glimpsed before, an openess to that old-man gaze.

It took the fire from her anger. "I have to see the Commander," she said.

Jemi turned and left the ship, leaving Ardent to follow if he wished.

He didn't. He stayed aboard the ship.

Commander Nys was Oriental. His office reflected his ancestral past, hung with ink and watercolor landscapes. Jemi recognized one as a view of Fujiyama, with delicate trees etched before the brooding mountain. A flat, black-and-white photo hung on the wall behind him—two people in white martial-art uniforms with what looked to be black skirts. A man recognizable as a young Nys was captured in the midst of throwing another. Nys's opponent was blurred by motion, upside down and perhaps three feet off the floor. Jemi wondered how the man could have possibly hit the ground and survived.

The other furnishings were few—a desk, two chairs, a low

table on which sat a vase with blue flowers and vines on a white background. Nys himself was small and dainty, his hands and face as finely drawn as the details in the landscapes. He didn't look as if he were capable of throwing anyone at all. He bowed to them as he opened the door to his office, smiling.

"Holder Charidilis," he said, his alto voice tinged with a light accent. "Please come in. I can offer you tea, or something stronger if you like. Whatever your pleasure."

"Nothing for me, Commander," Jemi answered. She took the seat before his desk, and Nys eased into his own chair, folding his hands on the desk's highly polished finish. A reflected Nys seemed to gaze at her upside down.

"Your ship's progress satisfies you?" the Commander inquired softly.

"Yes and no," Jemi answered honestly. "I won't be totally satisfied until she's completely repaired. I'm impatient to see the work completed. But yes, I think the work being done is fine."

Nys steepled his hands before thin lips, nodding his head almost imperceptively to her words. "Most of the ship's sealed now, and the circulation system's completed. I understand that some of the drive controls still have to be traced down and replaced, but you should have *Starfire* back to you within a few weeks. What will you be doing then?"

"I've already made some contacts here—there's a company that has wheat to be hauled to Highland. I think I'll contract to take it up, though wheat's not very profitable. It'll be something, though, and I want to go home first. There're things I need to know there."

"About your son?" the Commander prompted. His expression was impassive. Jemi couldn't tell if the man was sympathetic or not.

"About Kenis," she agreed. "About the two years of life we've missed. About Harris, Ken's father, too. There'll be answers there."

"I hope you find them," Nys answered, but there was no warmth in his voice at all. He blinked, the epicanthic folds at the corners of his eyes prominent. He was looking away from her now, his gaze focused on one of the drawings, though he continued to speak. "Are you considering hiring the T'Raijek known as Ardent as your secondary pilot, Holder?"

Jemi had never cared to deal with Earthers in general or the military in particular. They asked questions too bluntly; they were rude and all too convinced of their own right to treat other people in that manner. To that extent, Jemi could understand Salii's continuing war with the UCN. Being forced into this type of confrontation always brought to the surface a latent paranoia. Nys's question sparked that reaction and Jemi found herself answering with a question of her own. Her voice sounded hostile, and she struggled to keep the tone neutral. "Is there a problem with that, Commander?"

Nys blinked again, still looking away from her in that disconcerting manner. "Not necessarily, Holder. There's no regulation that says you can't choose whomever you wish, though one might wonder why a Highlander would hire a pilot rather than buying the services of a vivicate. And the T'Raijek alpha is of Clan Hlidskjalff, not Njialjiad. His people are not in favor even among the T'Raijek at the moment. A vivicate—"

"Vivicates are damned expensive on Earth, for one," she interrupted. "Earthers don't regard the dead in the same way as Highland. And I still may do that, once I'm back on Highland. That's an advantage to hiring—you can always fire the person just as easily. I'd have a lot more invested in a vivicate; I couldn't dispose of it so easily. Ardent is qualified, isn't he?"

A faint nod. Nys pulled his attention away from the painting. His gaze found her eyes for just a second, then dropped to the part of her face hidden by the k'lyge. He watched the swaying of the beads along the hem, the faint image of her mouth behind the cloth. "He's qualified, though this is the first time that any T'Raijek has deigned to be employed by a human. Odd that he would pick you, isn't it?"

The Commander's gaze came up, and the stare was far more intense than she expected. Jemi found that she had to consciously avoid looking away. Her feeling of paranoia increased; she didn't know what the man wanted her to say. "I resent the implication I think I hear, Commander," she said at last. "If you're hinting that I'm hiding something from you, you're wrong."

"I didn't mean to imply that, Holder," Nys answered. "Though I always find quick protests fascinating. They make me wonder what the person has to hide."

If she felt that she could, Jemi would have left then. But she couldn't, not with *Starfire* here in the docks of Uphill, not with the help that Admiral Strickland had given her. The Commander, at least, had been helpful. When he had questioned her, she had felt the sympathy in his voice at the necessity. She remembered his warning about others within the navy, as well. "I've said what I've needed to say, Commander," Jemi answered stiffly. "Admiral Strickland had asked me to report only to him, and that's what I intend to do. If I have anything to say—and I don't, at this point—I'll give *him* the information, not you."

Nys smiled at that, showing small, even, white teeth. "I'm currently the ranking officer on Uphill, Holder," he said. "Admiral Strickland is aboard *Strolov*, now somewhere outside Luna, I understand. And, of course, anything you say to me will be passed along to the Admiral."

"I have nothing to say," she insisted. Nys was hiding something. Jemi could feel it. There was an arrogance to his face that told her. His eyes had a dead, dark blankness, but she could see the mind working behind it. He was waiting for her to make a wrong move, stalking her like a patient cat.

"You don't find it curious that a T'Raijek would come up to you while in New York and offer his services as pilot, Holder? You don't think that strange? You don't wonder at the fact that this would happen after your ship is so mysteriously attacked by a Family Jardien pirate and your mind altered? You don't find it odd that a Salii agent would be murdered in New York yesterday as well?"

Jemi was glad for the k'lyge, glad that she had seen the thrust coming, even if she'd not known exactly what information Nys was holding back. *The scarred man. The one Ardent killed.* She knew who Nys referred to with a dread certainty, and the questions hammered at her while she forbade her eyes to reveal anything, while she held her body in check lest it reveal her shock. She longed to pull down the upper veil of the k'lyge and hide entirely from Nys's inspection, but knew that she dare not do that. She took a shallow breath and spoke as calmly as she could.

"I wonder at everything but the last, Commander. Anyone with intelligence would do the same. But I'd've had to hire someone as pilot, in any case. I consider myself lucky that someone was so quickly available, and I can understand someone—even a T'Raijek—wanting to get away from Earth. And I'm sure that I never *asked* that my ship be attacked, Commander. These things just happen; ships have been attacked before by Family Jardien pirates, as you know. I'm certain that I was as surprised as anyone." Jemi took a deep breath, dimpling the fabric of the k'lyge. "As for the Salii agent, I don't know what the hell you're talking about."

"Her body was found near the area you were in last night."

Her body? She almost spoke, then saw the cant of Nys's head and the lie he'd just spoken—he was waiting for her to correct him, to make any comment that revealed surprise or relief.

"I noticed several women in the area last night," Jemi said. "I hope that's not a crime."

Disappointment creased the man's face. She saw the slight relaxation in his shoulders; he slumped back in his chair a touch. "Not a crime. Not at all," he answered. He frowned, staring at her, and then his gaze left her once more. "I'd advise you not to hire the T'Raijek, Holder. I, for one, wouldn't put my life in the hands of someone I didn't trust."

"I can well understand that, Commander," Jemi said. She rose to her feet and went to the door. "That's why I'll be quite happy to get *Starfire* repaired and away from here."

She thought that would get a reaction from him, but she was disappointed. He regarded the painting to his left as if the delicate leaves of brushed ink held his fascination. In the drawing, a crane was spreading its wings to take flight from a pond. "For your information, Commander, I'd nearly changed my mind about Ardent until I talked to you just now. Your anxiety to get him away from me makes me want to retain him instead."

"It's your choice, Holder," Nys replied blandly. His thin, sallow cheeks were hollowed, as if the words tasted sour in his mouth. "I would only remind you that Highland and Earth are on the same side of this battle. You are a citizen of the UCN, as I am. We all oppose Salii and her pirates, and none of us knows on which side the T'Raijek might be. Still, I suppose you should consider yourself lucky to have the alien, as you say."

"I suppose so, Commander Nys," Jemi answered. "When it comes to my ship, I tend only to think of *my* side."

"Ardent?"

The T'Raijek was still in *Starfire*'s navigational section, though the work crew had gone elsewhere in the ship. Jemi had put on deck boots, keeping her on the "floor" of the area; to her orientation, the alien seemed to be standing on his hands across the room, his head poking into the ventilation duct where the worker had been earlier. The view made her momentarily dizzy.

His voice came to her muffled. "You know, if I were going to hide something, it wouldn't be here. It's too obvious." He leveled himself out of the duct and hung floating in the middle of the room, grinning at her. "It's clean, though—they're doing a good job."

Jemi ignored Ardent's clowning. "Can you really pilot this?"

His grin faded. "Easily. It's a toy," he said, and he tugged at the fur on his chin with long, slender fingers.

"Then you're hired."

"I never thought there was a question about it."

"There was before. Not now," Jemi answered, her voice taut. Ardent sensed her distress, for he grinned again and tumbled slowly in midair until he hung upside down before her. "I love people who make decisions from logic and not emotion," he said. And he spun away from her before she could retort, wondering how much he knew of what Nys had said to her.

Jemi felt trapped. She could feel the presence of unseen walls. She could not see an easy way past them.

So she'd wait. She'd wait. She watched the dwarfish alien dart about her control room and thought of Kenis, of the life she'd lost in an attack she could not remember.

They think I'll do what they say. They think that they can ask questions and not make me wonder. They think I'll mourn and forget about this.

She knew that they were wrong.

Of humanity's accomplishments, Highland should have been one of the grandest—a city wheeling its way through space without being anchored to the overwhelming presence of a parent world. We should have made it a marvel, a wonder, a fantasy. Instead, we succumbed to economics and utilitarianism, foreshadowings of the Bust. We made Highland drab.

We wanted a monument to our future, yet we took the uncut marble, set it on a plain base and said: "This must suffice."

Small wonder that Highlanders are considered to be so private and sour.

—from "The Aesthetics of Poverty" by
William Salchow, in *Architectural Digest*, Fall 2170.

CHAPTER FIVE

For two weeks, Jemi fretted over *Starfire* as she had over Kenis when he'd been ill. She moved into her old rooms aboard the craft despite the protests of the work crews, commandeering the cabin as soon as it was airtight and sealed. Ardent remained at a hotel in the tubes of Uphill. He was with Jemi for a few hours every day, going over the progress with her. His presence seemed to make the workers edgy; Jemi was happy that Ardent didn't seem compelled to stay longer than he did.

Nys avoided her, which also pleased her. As for Admiral Strickland, she heard nothing from him personally, though on the day that *Starfire* was handed over to Jemi fully sealed and ready to be released from dock, a package arrived for her from the Admiral's office in Uphill. In a nest of packing was a k'lyge of raw, ivory-colored silk. The attached note said simply: *For better times*. Jemi smiled, holding it up. Then she touched the death-beads along her own k'lyge and put the Admiral's present back in the box.

"Thank you, Admiral," she whispered. "But I'll save it for later." His thoughtfulness made her suddenly optimistic. *In two months you'll be home. Back on Highland you can begin to put all this behind you. You can find out about Kenis, you can begin to pick up the threads of your life again. It will all be better then.*

Two months, a little more or less. Jemi did not feel entirely comfortable until Uphill and Earth were dwindling behind her back.

She had to admit that Ardent seemed to be as good a pilot as he'd boasted. She let him take *Starfire* out of the dock. If he was not as adept as he claimed, it would be better to know immediately while *Starfire* was still near the repair docks. But Ardent adroitly and delicately nudged the ship away from Uphill, looking like some ugly, orange wolf-child in the human scaled pilots chair. When they had made the orbital shifts and were away from Uphill, he set the ship's nose directly on the course bearings to intersect Highland's position in the Belt, and then he sat back. He leered at Jemi without saying anything. His smirk was message enough. Jemi nodded to him and went to her cabin.

Three weeks out from Earth, as Jemi was taking her daily shift in the pilot's seat, checking the status boards, Ardent spoke to her from across the room. "This is about how far you were when you were attacked, isn't it?" Jemi had taken spin off the ship to readjust the ailing, old gyros of the ship. He was gliding through the compartment, a food-sphere filled with some pasty green mess floating along before him. He cooked for himself in the galley, professing to detest human taste in cuisine. It was another indication of how little Jemi had come to know the alien in the time she'd spent with him. She'd found the T'Raijek to be solitary, not wanting to be disturbed when he was working, and keeping to his own cabin when he was not. She had thought they would talk, had thought that she might come to understand some of the shadowy relations of the T'Raijek—how the great Clans formed their alliances among themselves, or even the way the three sexes merged and mated. Yet Ardent volunteered nothing, and Highlanders were taught to respect privacy—it was as much a part of her as the rituals of the k'lyge.

She told herself that it was just as well. Had they become friends, she would have had to talk about Kenis, and she didn't know if she could do that yet. There were times, moving through *Starfire*'s corridors, when she thought she could hear Ken's giggle, and she'd turn, expecting to see him.

He was never there.

"I don't know where the attack took place, exactly. It's in the computer but I haven't checked," she said finally, realizing that Ardent was still waiting for her answer. "I don't remember."

If he heard the sarcasm in her voice, he didn't respond. "They hit you at precisely this distance out from Earth," he said. "I checked Strickland's report and it's in your navigational records."

He caught a stanchion as he drifted, pulling himself to a halt. The food-sphere bounced against the far wall and rebounded back toward him.

"Do you expect me to stop and look?" Jemi asked him. "Even if this were the exact area—and it's not likely to be anywhere near it—it wouldn't look different from any other. There's not much in the way of landmarks out here, you know."

Ardent caught the sphere as it slid by him. His bearded face turned to Jemi. "A Jardien ship would have come from Salii and Mars. I just wonder how far we are from Mars orbit, and where the planet was located when the attack occurred."

"I don't know," Jemi said again.

"Aah," the alien replied, nodding. Long fingers curled around the sphere, slid the opening back and dipped into the viscous mess inside. He pulled the finger out, the gellid stuff clinging, and licked it clean. "Not bad, if I do say so myself. Want to try some?"

"No," Jemi said. Under the k'lyge, she frowned.

"Didn't think you would. No sense of adventure. You judge too many things by appearance." With that, Ardent kicked off again, leaving the room.

Jemi sat there for a moment, the blinking lights of the status boards hanging before her eyes. With a stab of her finger, she canceled the display and called up the ship's com-system. "Query," she subvocalized. "Give me the coordinates of Mars relative to ship's position when we were attacked. Do you know the date?" A green light flashed before her eyes. "Good. Visual display."

In a moment, a shimmering image of the solar plane hung before her, viewed from above. Highlighted in bright red was the fourth planet. The area of the attack was a yellow dot. A glowing line connected the two, cutting across the orbital planes and grazing the circle that represented the sun. Figures were printed there: ***2.42 A.U. (3.61 X 10^8 kilometers).*** The colony of Salii, circling Mars, had been nearly in opposition to the attack, which had taken place well outside that world's orbit.

Jemi stared at the display. Her jaw clenched. "Query," she said tightly. "Practical range of Condor class ship."

The display shimmered, dissolved. A new set of numbers gleamed in its place: ***2.5 A.U. (3.73 X 10^8 kilometers).***

Jemi found herself holding her breath. *It's possible, but it's cutting it so close. So close. No Family Jardien pirate would be sitting there waiting for a random freighter to pass by, not when Salii was so near the edge of its range. If it was Jardien, they had to have good reason to be waiting. It couldn't have been random. They wanted me. They wanted* me. *Me and nobody else.*

"Why?" she whispered aloud. "What did I have? What did I know?"

She had no answer for that.

She wondered why Ardent had hinted so heavily concerning the point.

For the next few days, she waited for the T'Raijek to bring up the subject again, but he never did. He performed his tasks. He made polite, if edged, conversation with her when they passed, but he never gave her an opening, a way to lead the conversation toward his comments about the attack.

Jemi, for her part, found that she couldn't bring it up herself. Something held her back, an unvoiced distrust in the T'Raijek. *He saved your life. Kenis would have liked him; he always liked hearing about the T'Raijek . . . You even gave him a book about them. Talk to him.* Yet she didn't. She told herself that she would replace Ardent when they arrived at Highland. She would buy another vivicate. She would get rid of Ardent because he was connected with this strangeness. *Get rid of him and this will all pass,* she told herself. The voice in her head wasn't overly convincing.

It was a long two months.

* * *

Highland was a wide, dirty white ribbon looped on end, glowing in the darkness with a myriad pinpricks of light. Here, in the asteroid belt, the sun was a paler, distant disk that sent sharp-edged shadows rolling along the spokes of the linktubes. Jemi set *Starfire* spinning in concert with the colony's inner hub, until the huge wheel of Highland seemed to stand still while the stars spun around them. To one side, a fleet of mining ships gnawed at a captured asteroid; to the other, a processing platform blazed, a stream of waste spewing outward from it into the depths of space. Highland itself looked handsome until one examined it more closely and saw the stains, the repairs, the signs of age on the huge colony. Some of the warning lights were out on the perimeter, one of the docking doors was buckled and warped by an old collision—it had been that way in Jemi's memory as well, two years ago.

Highland, like Earth, like Salii, did what she needed in order to survive. Repairs that could wait, did.

Jemi was in the pilot's chair. Ardent had buckled himself to a temporary seat beside her, watching. With the ship's spin, the corridors of the ship coalesced into definite ceilings, floors, and walls. Ardent looked unhappy. He stared at the flatscreen in front of Jemi and scowled. "Don't your people ever get tired of garbage?" he muttered.

"The processor?" Jemi asked, her voice light. *Home. Not even the damn T'Raijek can make me irritated at this point.* "You think it's going to fill up the solar system before we find a way to get rid of it?" she scoffed. "If the T'Raijek are bothered, why don't you tell us how to refine the ore without waste—I'm sure we'd appreciate the information."

Ardent looked as if he were about to retort, but the flatscreen shimmered and a translucent face materialized in the air before them: a dark-haired man, a k'lyge fringed with metallic flecks covering his face from the bridge of the nose to the jawline. Cloth swayed with his words. "Hello, *Starfire*. This is Highland Port, Comptroller Tyler speaking. How was your flight in, Holder?"

Jemi recognized the man, one of the usual controllers at the port. Jemi keyed on her visual link and nodded to him. "Perfectly ordinary, Comptroller. And it's good to be back."

"Good," the man said. His voice was flat, expressionless, though the eyes seemed somehow angry. "I've been told to instruct you to move to Examination Sector Five. A Customs crew will board your ship."

"What?" Outrage filled Jemi's voice, and she struggled to hold it back. "Comptroller, Customs should be aware that I ran empty on this trip out. *Starfire* was attacked and I've just had repairs—"

"Customs is aware of your situation, Holder," Tyler interrupted her harshly. "I'm just relaying my orders. If you wish to protest, I'll put you through to the Customs office."

His voice told her that the situation was hopeless, but the sense of unfairness still fueled her irritation. She shrugged at the heavy weight of the nervelinks draped across her shoulder, leaning forward as if she could physically confront the man. "I don't want the office, Comptroller. I just want to be treated like any other citizen. Since when does Highland search a Holder's ship when they damn well know she deadheaded it?"

"I'll put you through to Customs," he repeated, more sharply this time. Sparks of silver light glinted from his k'lyge. "In the meantime, Holder, your ship is delaying traffic. Please move to Sector Five. My vivicate will give you coordinates." Tyler glanced down, and his shadowy image dissolved. After a moment, another face coalesced in front of Jemi—under watery grey eyes, the aquiline nose, thin mouth, and bearded chin seemed naked without a k'lyge. There was a slight sheen of drool at one corner of the mouth, and the eyes blinked too rapidly: Tyler's vivicate, waiting patiently for Jemi to acknowledge him.

"Damn it," she muttered.

Ardent had said nothing during the exchange, but now she heard low chuckling and turned in her seat to see the T'Raijek smiling. He cocked his head at her. "Home sweet home," he said softly, still laughing.

"Do you know what's going on here, Ardent?" she demanded. "Why do you find this so funny?"

"I'm simply amused by the wonderful show of trust among humans," he answered. "And as to what's going on, you'll have to tell me, since *I've* never been here before.'' He gazed into her glare with affected innocence. ''Surely you know the answer, Holder?''

''No, I don't,'' Jemi said. ''But I'm damned well going to get it.''

It took three hours for the crew of five to go over the ship. Jemi fumed, pulling her upper veil over her eyes because she knew that they could see her anger too visibly. She hid it especially from the crew supervisor, a woman who sat in the pilot's compartment with Ardent and Jemi, sipping the bitter Earth tea that Jemi had offered her. Her k'lyge, inset with the tiered-wheel symbol of Highland, also covered her entire face—as was proper in the situation: those in sensitive positions did not show their faces. When the last of the crew had bowed to her and left the deck, the woman set her cup down and nodded to Jemi. ''Thank you, Holder Charidilis,'' she said. Her voice was professionally warm, a contralto. Jemi could just see the outlines of round cheeks and a full mouth behind the thin cloth. The eyes seemed dark and large; a face that would match the plumpness of the hands. ''I'm sorry for the inconvenience.''

Jemi knew that the woman was waiting for Jemi's own apology, and Jemi took a deep breath. ''I'm sorry as well, Holder Weber. I hope you and Comptroller Tyler will forgive my irritation, but I think you can understand the reasons. Does Highland now search all ships for contraband?''

The woman's veils swayed with the faint shake of her head. ''No, Holder. But we've always made spot checks of freighters. You've encountered them before, I'm sure. This was just a random search.''

Politely. Always politely. Yet Jemi could hear the hardness behind Weber's voice, and that told her the woman was lying. Yes, Jemi had been searched before, but never this thoroughly. *They thought I had something, but what? What?*

Ardent never gave her the chance to ask that question, even had she wanted to do so. He sniffed loudly, causing the two women to look at him. ''Are we done now?'' he growled. ''I'd like to go breathe air that's a little less tainted than this.''

Weber's veiled head turned fully to the T'Raijek—Jemi knew

that the woman stared. "The air here seems fine to me—" She hesitated, a breath, as if she didn't know how to address the alien.

"Call me Ardent, or if you insist on Highland propriety, use my Clan name: Hlidskjalff." The name sounded vaguely Germanic or Norse, with deep gutturals. Ardent's eyes narrowed as he said the word. "That would translate loosely as Staff-That-Cuts. My ClanMother once was in residence at the embassy here."

"I've seen your honored Mother, before she was . . . deposed," Weber answered. The hesitation, so obviously intended to accentuate the last word, surprised Jemi.

"I'll be seeing the ClanMother Njialjiad as soon as you let us out of here. I'll convey your preference for ClanMother Hlidskjalff to her." His voice bordered on insult. "You *are* done, aren't you?"

For a moment, Weber continued to stare, her k'lyge unmoving. Then she glanced back to Jemi, and nodded once more. "I'm finished here, Holder Charidilis. You're free to move your ship to the cargo berths and disembark." Weber sipped again at her tea, draining the cup as custom dictated and then setting it down. "Thank you for your hospitality, Holder," she said, rising. "Enjoy your return home. And I hope you find a proper pilot for your next trip. Clan Hlidskjalff is out of favor among the T'Raijek now. Perhaps that's why they must beg for a vivicate's job."

Weber left the room at a slow pace. Before the door could close behind her, Ardent's voice spoke loudly: "Huh, I guess *I've* been put in my place." He snorted.

The door slid shut.

Jemi glared at him. "You don't *have* a place here. Not anymore. I want you out of here—all you get me is trouble."

Ardent snorted. "You mean you're letting that bitch intimidate you? I saved your damned life."

"And I gave you a job. That'll have to make us even, T'Raijek. You're fired."

"You're making a mistake, Holder."

Bright spots of color flared high on Jemi's cheeks. She pointed, overdramatically, at the hatchway through which Weber had disappeared. "Out."

"Out it is," Ardent repeated, spreading his hands wide. "But don't say I didn't warn you. If you change your mind, I'll be at the embassy, sucking up to the new ClanMother."

Tari Harris knew that Security Adjunct Michaels was a pleasant enough fellow—a man of later years whose body showed much time spent behind a desk, much of it in the lowered gravity of the Inner Hubs. Harris doubted that the Adjunct could walk more than a few meters along the rim of Highland without becoming winded. The portly old gentleman greeted Harris, dismissing the secretary who'd ushered him in with a wave of a rope-veined hand. The Adjunct wore a k'lyge that looked as if it had been in style when the veils had first become customary, back during the bleak time all of Highland referred to as "the Infection." The cloth was heavy and thicker than the polite and fashionable veil Harris wore, as if the Adjunct still feared the airborne virus that had killed a good portion of Highland's already low population six decades before. He gestured toward a plush chair. "Sit down, Provost Harris. Pull that thing over here a bit so we can talk easily. Drink?"

"No, thank you, Adjunct."

The Adjunct's eyes smiled over the lower veils, bushy white eyebrows drooping over the baggy lids. "No need to stand on ceremony, Tari. I'm not given to unnecessary politeness. If you want a drink, say so. I'm going to have one myself."

Harris laughed, a little too harshly, he thought, and forced himself to cut the laugh short. *Don't make him think you're a fool—how often does a Provost get summoned to see the Adjunct? He's used your first name: that's a good sign.* "Thank you, Adjunct. I will, then."

"Scotch do for you?"

"It would be a great pleasure. Good scotch is too rare up here."

"Unless you can afford it on the black market, eh, Tari?" The question sounded innocent enough, and the Adjunct wasn't looking at him, yet it confirmed Harris's suspicions about the subject of his summons. He'd known that it must have something to do with Jemi. Like the rest, he'd seen the news reports about the attack on *Starfire*—he'd even been interviewed once or twice himself during the day or two that the news was topical, and he'd seen the small report in the Highland faxsheet that said she was on her way back to the colony. The Adjunct poured them each a small glass of amber liquid from a small stand near his desk. He slid Harris's glass across the slick desk top—in the reduced gravity of the Inner Hub, it seemed to drift lazily. Harris reached for it clumsily, nearly spilling some of the scotch. He clutched at the glass nervously, looking up to see the Adjunct watching him, his own glass now hidden behind the k'lyge as he sipped.

Harris lifted his veil and sniffed at the scotch. He took a sip; the smoky liquor seared his throat satisfyingly. "That's excellent, Adjunct. Thank you."

"One of the perks of my job, Provost," the Adjunct said jovially. "I never lack for material niceties. You'll learn that yourself, I think. You're a rising young man yourself, as I was once. Maybe one day you'll sit here, eh? Sit here and get to watch Highland spin below you."

"I don't aim quite so high."

The Adjunct shook his head, setting his scotch down on the desk and leaning back in his chair, his hands laced behind thick gray hair. "I think you do. And ambition is fine, Tari, so long as it's well directed."

As Harris hesitated, wondering how to reply to that, the Adjunct let the chair come forward again, fixing Harris with his intent stare. "I could use your help, Provost."

"I'd be happy to oblige, Adjunct. What is it?"

"You were married to Holder Jemi Charidilis for a time."

Even having expected the words, they still stung Harris like an electric shock. He felt suddenly and ridiculously guilty, as if having been with Jemi for that short time had somehow contaminated him in the Adjunct's eyes. He hoped the k'lyge hid the heat he could feel in his cheeks. "It seems like a long time ago, Adjunct. It's been, what, nearly three years or more since we split up. It was a poor match, and we both were glad when it was over."

"You've had no contact since?"

The blush rose, and Harris fidgeted in the thick embrace of the chair. He sipped again at the scotch, then held the glass in his lap, his fingers stroking the smooth surface. "We had a son, Kenis, as you probably know, and so we saw each other occasionally. Once, a year and a half ago, we—" Harris stopped; the memory was painful. "We spent a night together. Mostly we found out how much better off we were alone."

Talking about it had brought back vivid memories; lost in them momentarily, Harris was startled back into reality by the Adjunct's words: "That's a pity."

"Sir?"

The mane of the Adjunct's eyebrows lifted and gathered. The lower veil swung lethargically. "Has she contacted you at all since her ship was attacked?"

"No, Adjunct, she hasn't. There wasn't any reason to, I guess."

The Adjunct nodded. He seemed to sink into his own reverie, and Harris waited, wondering where the man was leading. He glanced down, noticed the scotch, and drained the last bit of it from the glass. He set it down on the edge of the desk.

"She had an unfortunate experience, your Holder Charidilis," the Adjunct said at last, his voice a low rumble. "I'm not at liberty to say much here, Provost. In your capacities, you've come to understand some of the precariousness of Highland's political situation. You know that we tread a delicate balance between placating Earth and pursuing our own eventual independence. As Provost, you've no doubt seen how close we sometimes come to overbalancing: it's only through hard work and the exploitation of all our resources that Highland manages to stay even partially self-sufficient. We need the ore, we need our people, we need the vivicates that the Corporation provides. We can't afford to antagonize anyone—not Earth, not the T'Raijek embassy here, not even the bastards of Salii—for fear that one of them might withdraw their support of our economy and cause that fatal imbalance.

"Most of my job as Adjunct is to see that the interplay between those factions doesn't affect Highland. I'm afraid that your former mate has become involved in a political situation—mostly by accident, I'm convinced. I was hoping that perhaps you could convince her that she would do well to be less curious about certain things. There might be repercussions if she persists. We might be forced to take actions I'd regret."

"Persists? Actions?" Harris almost laughed, shaking his head. "Are we talking about the same person, Adjunct? Jemi—Holder Charidilis—might have a temper, but she's not the type to lift her k'lyge unnecessarily. She'd prefer to avoid trouble if she could. I have trouble seeing her in the midst of an intercolony situation. She can barely afford the fuel for the damn ship she runs."

"That's not what certain people within the UCN navy seem to think. But perhaps it's the company she keeps, Provost. For instance, she's hired a T'Raijek pilot, of the Clan Hlidskjalff. As you might know, the Clan Njialjiad has newly taken over the T'Raijek embassy here. I don't know exactly how the T'Raijek operate, but I do know that the Hlidskjalffs are barely tolerated now. We also know that T'Raijek bodies were taken from the embassy and placed aboard one of the star vessels to be returned to their home world. Humanity can't afford to offend a race that has the capabilities of the T'Raijek—we need their technology if we're ever to get out of our own solar system.

"And there's the admitted mystery concerning the attack on her ship," he continued. "Tari, I've heard rumors concerning that attack from Admiral Strickland himself. If she's hiding something, you'd do well to convince her to bring it out in the light here, where people understand her. If she's innocent, then you would be doing us and her a service by convincing the Holder that there's nothing further to learn about her amnesia."

"She was always devoted to Kenis. However she and I disagreed, Adjunct, we were alike in that. I can understand how she'd be upset at losing half of her life with him."

"I know, Provost, and you both have my sympathies at losing him—I know how I'd feel if I lost my own children. And that's where you can help: give her the support she needs, give her what you can of Kenis, of the past she lost." The Adjunct nodded, as if to some inner voice. His fingers, like sticks in loose bags of skin, drummed the desk top. "I can assure you that your efforts in this would be appreciated, Provost. From me, and from the UCN."

Harris could hear the warm promise in that voice. *Jem, I never thought you'd ever do me any good. It looks as if I might have been wrong*. "Then tell me how you'd like me to proceed, Adjunct."

The Adjunct's smile, hidden, could still be seen in the folds around his eyes. "All you need do is keep her out of trouble, Tari, or inform me if that looks to be impossible. Tell me, Provost Harris, do you still love her?"

"Adjunct, I don't think I ever did. It was just one of those strange attractions. We're incompatible. Had she died in that attack, I would have been sad, yes, but I would have gotten over it quickly. She's not a part of my life anymore, especially since Kenis has died."

"That's what I thought, Provost." The Adjunct nodded. "That's what I thought, and that's what I'd planned on. That's good, that's good." The Provost lifted his k'lyge slightly and quickly drank the last of his scotch. He put the glass down with a loud thump and smacked his lips. "I'll count on your cooperation then, Provost. We all want what's best for Highland and for ourselves, eh? You won't be sorry that you decided to help."

What do we know about the T'Raijek after their three-plus decade presence here? Very little beyond the fact that they are tri-sexed, the female of the species is dominant, and while mammalian, their ancestors were more similar to our own canines than apes. We have a smattering of knowledge about their society, their technologies, their way of life. We know even less about the other races that dwell beyond our sun—the T'Raijek acknowledge that they exist but give no details. For those who read and believe stories such as "Alien Monster Born to Unwed Mother Is Reincarnation of Mozart," such things might lead to a certain paranoia, but frankly, their secrecy makes a certain amount of sense. Would you teach your two year-old child how to start your car or to operate a vibrosaw? Of course not.

—from news holocast editorial, UBC,
New York, June 21, 2170.

CHAPTER SIX

"My name is Holder Jemi Charidilis. I'd like to apply for permission to speak with Ruth Diesen."

The man to whom Jemi spoke glanced up. Above his smoke gray k'lyge, one pupil gazed back in pale blue. The other flickered greenly, tiny characters scrolling across the lens—a terminal implant. He blinked slowly and constantly, rubbing pudgy fingers over the transmitter plugged into his wrist socket: the transmitter's steel surface was polished to a worn, satin sheen. Jemi could smell an unsubtle cologne.

"Are you a relative of the prisoner?" he asked.

"No, I . . ." Now that she had begun, Jemi didn't know how to tell the man the story—it was all too complicated. Ruth Diesen had been the crèche-mother convicted of negligence in Kenis's death. Like all prisoners on Highland, she would be here in the Ministry of Justice, behind the forbidding walls and performing "social work." For most prisoners, that meant supervising one of the teams of vivicates owned by the government. "I have business to conduct with her," Jemi told the attendant. "Personal business." There were perhaps ten of the jail supervisors in the room, all the desks separated by cubicles. To her left, she could hear someone else's muffled voice. *I want to talk with her. I want to ask her about that day, that's all. I want to see her; I want to see the person who let my child die. I want to ask her why and look at her face as she answers.*

I want to see pain there.

A blink, a caress of fingertips over the transmitter. "And what might that business be, Holder?"

"Forgive my impoliteness, Holder, but that's between the two of us. Is one Highlander not allowed to see another, even when one's social responsibility is being corrected?"

The man sniffed, but the way he sat behind his desk seemed to indicate boredom more than anything else. He closed his eyes momentarily, and tapped at the transmitter with a fingernail. "That would be up to Holder Diesen. I would think—" Bright letters flowed across the emerald eye. His eyebrows lifted, the lower veil of the k'lyge billowed with an exhalation. Jemi caught a glimpse of pursed, fat lips behind the cloth.

"You wish to speak with Ruth Diesen? Formerly crèche-mother of the Port Crèche?" he asked, peering at her again.

"Yes, that's the one. Is there a problem?"

He chuckled softly, and his amusement confused Jemi. "You might say so, Holder. Ruth Diesen has been dead a year and a half. If you want to talk business with her, I'd seek out her heirs. If you want to be social, my records tell me that Vivicate Corporation bought the body—if you *like* to play around with the Rekindled, you might go ask them what her name is now, and who bought her."

He stared at her: weak blue, brilliant green. She knew a sneer was there, even if she couldn't see it.

She might have left then. Evidently it was what the attendant expected her to do, for he looked away after that slow examination and shuffled papers on his desk. Jemi began to rise from her chair, then sat again. *You can't get answers that way. If you want to know, you'll have to ask.*

"What happened to her?" Jemi knew immediately that the question had been a mistake. The attendant looked back up, and lines had appeared in his forehead. The k'lyge lifted slightly with whatever emotions were twisting his face. "What does it matter, Holder?" he replied, his voice no longer neutral. It held a distinct undertone of menace. something in the terminal eye flared and died. "She's dead. She's a vivicate—she has no rights except the right to privacy."

"She killed—her negligence killed my son. She was the crèche-mother." The words choked her. The explanation died as Jemi swept the upper veil across her face to hide her eyes. *You still can't say it. You still don't believe that he's dead. How can you believe it when to your mind it was only a few months ago that you held him or changed his diapers?*

As most Highlanders would have done, the man looked away from the display of grief, allowing her privacy. He slid papers, blinked. "Ruth Diesen was attacked by another prisoner—an accident. He went berserk one night in the exercise yard, took out a knife filed from some metal bar he'd managed to pilfer. She was just one of three. Fate, Holder: that's all."

"It doesn't make sense—"

"Holder." His voice was an admonishing bark. "There's nothing you can do about it. I'd advise you strongly to leave it alone. This is Highland, not Salii. We all have our responsibility to do what's best. I'm sure everyone here did his job. There're some things you can't help."

Jemi stared at the man, his features blurred by her eyeveil as an inner fury welled in her, fueled by grief and frustration. "He was my son," she raged back at him, not caring that her voice sobbed with her anger. "How can I forget him? Every time I try to find out what happened to me, every time I try to get back to Kenis, someone blocks me. I want to know why, Holder. I want to understand."

But he wouldn't answer, wouldn't reply at all. He simply stared at her, stared as if she were a madwoman, stared at her until she finally turned her back and fled the cubicle and the hall.

Behind her, when she had gone, he spoke softly into the steel gray box confining his wrist.

She stood there in the middle of the walkway with tears tracking slowly down her cheeks. Jemi's weeping was silent and hidden behind the k'lyge, but those that moved around her could see her slumped shoulders and her lowered head.

The spot looked ordinary. There was nothing to show that only six months ago a four-year-old boy had died here. It was just a *place*, a section of concrete as anonymous as the next one up the street. Jemi could not even be sure that this was exactly the spot. There were no markers, no signs, no trace. There was only the plasteel and concrete of Highland's walkways, wavering behind the shim of the k'lyge and the tears that filled her eyes.

It should have been a special place. It should have spoken to her soul. Instead, it was simply another noisy space in a loud colony, scuffed and coated with the dirt of a million shoes. The buildings around her were dingy, the light facades grayed with age—Highland was nearly two centuries old, and parts of the artificial worldlet were beginning to deteriorate. There were never enough funds to repair them, to finance the upkeep that should have been done. Highland's leaders shrugged and said that even the colonies of mankind must have slums.

Kenis had pinwheeled down from the linktube into a slum of Highland.

She cried as much for that as for her own loss.

Jemi looked up, taking a deep, sobbing breath. One always seemed to be looking up here. With gravity replaced by simple centrifigual force, a person stood in an eternal, moving valley with Highland looping up before and behind. Above, she could see the maw of the linktube where Kenis had been climbing, well to spinward. It seemed faraway and insignificant. She brought her gaze down again, to the graffiti-scrawled walls that hid Center Park and Kyle's River. Garbage pooled around the central curb. To those coming here from Earth, Highland stunk, no matter where they were inside the colony: even near the port, in the high-class hotels that glittered around that fashionable area, no filtration could disguise the stench of humanity, cycled and recycled endlessly. For them, it was a nagging odor, a reminder of man's presence that one never quite got used to.

To Jemi, to all Highlanders, it was simply the way a world should smell. She only noticed its absence when she was away. Nearby, a vivicate wheeled a cart and broom, slowly gathering the worst of the debris. The vivicate was female—it could have once been Ruth Diesen, for all Jemi knew. She watched the vivicate continue down the street as she tried to rein in her emotions once more.

Around her, veiled Highlanders judiciously ignored the woman standing in the middle of the busy lane. The manner in which her k'lyge hid her face told them enough.

What do I do? How do I make a start at this? She took a slow breath, feeling very alone among the crowds. It was Highland's evening. The lamps overhead were beginning to dim; in a few minutes, the dayshields would slide back, revealing the transparent canopy and allowing the remote suns to peer in—dispassionate observers hidden behind the veils of distance. She'd spent the day trying to uncover more information concerning Kenis's death.

After leaving the Ministry, she'd tried to contact Harris—he'd not been in his apartments and she found herself unable to leave a message with his vivicate. She'd called Harris's parents then—they'd been cool and distant toward her, as they'd been since she and Harris had parted ways. If they'd heard what had happened to her, they said nothing, and she quickly terminated the conversation. In the nearest library, she'd looked up the same news articles that Admiral Strickland had given her, finding that he'd given her everything that seemed connected to the incident with the exception of Diesen's killing. Her own parents were dead, her brother had returned to Earth a decade earlier—she'd never felt close to him in any case. She wasn't friendly enough with the rest of her family to feel like contacting them.

She felt more lonely than she'd thought possible, here in the place she called home.

"The crèche-mother was killed while awaiting trial. Another prisoner went berserk. He had a knife that the guards had overlooked."

Jemi knew the pleasant voice, the tone that always seemed on the edge of laughter no matter what the subject. Harris. He spoke her thoughts. She didn't turn around, but stared up at the roof as the long tubes of sunlamps went out completely and the shields petalled back. "They turned her into a vivicate," Harris continued. "Isn't it nice to know that someday you might hire her to do your housecleaning?"

His jocular manner made her want to turn and rage at him. That feeling banished the sorrow at last, hiding it behind anger. *Same flip bastard as always, eh, Harris? Figured out yet that that's one of the reasons I came to hate you?* "I couldn't reach you, Tari," she answered, still looking away from him. Her voice was shaky yet; she paused for a moment before continuing. "I thought maybe you'd gone to the Outer Mines on business. Your parents didn't want to talk to me." Overhead, sunlight sent fingers of shadow to stroke the bow of Highland's far side. "How'd you know I'd be here?"

"Connections," he answered. "I'm Provost for my district now. I can find out things. I could also guess where you might go, Jem. You were quite a news item for a day or two; I figured after what happened that you'd want to see everything. As for my parents—well, after the row last time, what'd you expect?"

"The last time I was here—at least, the last time *I* remember being here—we got on well enough. I let Ken stay with them against my own better judgment while I took a shipment to the Outer Belt," she said wearily.

Behind her, there was a lengthy silence. She heard him shift his weight, felt the warmth of his presence move slightly away from her. "You had a large fight with them last time. They thought you should have had Kenis stay with them instead of at the crèche. You hadn't wanted to do that. You told them that you felt they tried to turn Kenis against you. They said that if you'd left him with them, he wouldn't have died."

Jemi closed her eyes, took a deep breath as a quick vertigo seized her. She opened them again and turned. Harris stared back at her, his eyes gray over the rim of his k'lyge, the lower veils imprinted with the insignia of the Provost office. He wore a suit, as usual, cut in a more modern style than Jemi remembered his wearing before. She wondered who he was seeing now that made him dress that way—left on his own, Harris had no taste in clothing. "I don't remember the fight, Tari," she told him. At another time, she might have shouted her reply, but her mourning had left her simply tired. "But I can imagine it, if they said something as unforgiving and cruel as that."

"They didn't mean it the way it sounded," he told her. His thick, dark eyebrows wrinkled with his reprimanding look. Jemi could imagine the thin-lipped mouth behind the veils, one side turned down. "They never tried to turn Kenis against you. They were only trying to correct the bias that Ken seemed to have against me."

"Still an apologist for your family, Provost?" Her tone was sharp, and she started to blunt the edge with some other remark, but bit back the words. *No, it never changes. Even with two years of your life lost, it hasn't changed. You can start in with the arguments as if you'd never left here.*

"I loved Kenis, Jem. I didn't like him looking at me like some vaguely remembered uncle."

"You *endured* Kenis, Harris. How did you phrase it? 'He's hurting us, Jem. He's coming between *our* relationship.' Yes, you were such a good father." Jemi wished that he'd not accosted her here, in public, in the open, in this place. He soiled it worse than the dirt in the street, and her tears threatened to come back.

"You remember it worse than it was," he insisted, his voice a little louder, the eyebrows knitted together now. Around them, a few people stopped to stare—public arguments were rare in Highland. On a world the size of one of Earth's larger cities, it was already too easy to know everyone else's business.

"Harris—"

"I mean it, Jem. You're twisting my words, making it sound like more than it was—you did the same thing with my parents. All they wanted was a chance to help raise their grandchild."

"Tari, please." There were furtive glances in their direction now, people pretending to stop and gaze around them as an excuse to eavesdrop on the confrontation. A shirtless man in a tattered, slate blue k'lyge and stained black pants actually took a step closer with gross rudeness. "Come with me, Harris," Jemi said. She began walking away.

"Where?" he demanded.

"Does it matter? Tari, *please*. Let's try to talk. You wanted to see me," she said again. *Damn you, Harris. Just get off the streets. We're making a scene.* "If you want to know what I've done, talk to me where we can be more private."

Finally, he loosed an exaggerated sigh and went with her down the street toward the glow of a hoversign: DINO'S. The gaze of the crowd followed them. Jemi ducked into the restaurant. As with all Highland public houses, there was no common dining room. The building was divided into small private rooms, with a tiny public tavern in the center. There seemed to be no customers in the place. A waiter showed them to a vacant cubicle. In a better establishment, the waiter would have been professionally bland; this one stared rudely at them, with open boredom. The man threw the menus on the table and left them to seat themselves. "Your server will be here in a minute," he said tonelessly. The door clicked shut behind him.

Harris tried to turn it into a joke: "You could always choose a good restaurant." Neither of them smiled.

Here in private, it would have been permissible to open her k'lyge fully, but she left both veils shut; she knew her eyes would be red and puffy from the crying, and she didn't want him to see that. "Why did you come looking for me, Tari?" she asked without preamble.

Harris squirmed slightly in his seat, toying with the raveled plastic edges of the menu without looking at it. "I thought I'd see what you remembered," he said. "I thought maybe I could help."

"When did you become so altruistic?"

He flinched at that, leaning back in his chair and running his fingers through stubbly brown hair. "You lose your manners every time you go off Highland," he said. "That's what I always hated about seeing you leave in that damned ship of yours."

"At least I don't stand in the middle of streets and argue," she retorted. Then, realizing that the conversation would just deteriorate into another argument, she cut off the rebuttal. The death-beads clattered along the hem of her k'lyge as she shook her head. Harris's gaze followed the movement, snagged on the beads. She sniffed, wishing she could move the eyeveils aside and wipe her eyes but not wanting to let Harris see her. "Harris, I'm sorry. I'm sorry this happens every time we see each other."

"Not every time," he said. His voice was a shade too soft, too low.

"What?" she prompted when he said nothing else.

"You don't remember, Jem? Damn, I must be losing my touch."

His voice mocked her, an undercurrent of distaste that told her. "We haven't been to bed for a year, at least not that I remember. God, Tari, are you saying that I made *that* mistake again?"

He gave a quick, bitter laugh. "We *both* made the mistake, Jem. It wasn't very good, for either of us. I'm actually glad that you don't remember; it started out so well—" His hands slashed air.

"Then I'm sorry for that too, Tari." She could not put any sincerity in her voice, but he nodded as if he hadn't noticed the lack.

There was a soft knock on the door. It opened slightly and a server tilted her head into the room. Her features had the bland, neutral smoothness of the vivicate, that undistinguished plainness that was the stamp of the revived dead. Her face was naked, and there was a twitch to one side of her face that made viewing the woman an uncomfortable experience, like staring at a crippled person. She would have been cheap, this one; that, as much as anything, spoke of the fare likely to be found here. "Coffee," Harris snapped at the woman. The vivicate nodded, though Jemi thought she saw irritation in the woman's phlegmy eyes. Then the server's flat gaze swiveled around to Jemi, staring at her too long. "The same," Jemi said. "Thank you."

"I'll bring it right in, Holders," the vivicate said, inclining her head. Her speech was slurred, imperfect.

As the vivicate left the room, Harris muttered in disgust, "God, that one should have been scrapped. Jemi, do you know that a group of vivicates actually had the gall to challenge Vivicate Corporation? They tried to sue for wages and compensation, as if the company should provide its services for free. They've forgotten that they owe their existence to the company and Highland. There's actually talk among them of striking, of demonstrating for what they call their rights. How you managed to live with Doni—"

"I liked Doni, most of the time," Jemi answered. "It wasn't

his fault that he'd died. Highland's always been too intolerant of the vivicates we create."

"You're away too much, Jem. That's your problem. You don't see things like a Highlander, half the time. You don't own your body after you die—that's basic to Highland's existence. Sometimes you sound so damned self-righteous."

"Is that another thing you hate about me, Harris?"

He sighed at that and his tone changed, hardened. Jemi told herself that she didn't care. "Okay, Jem. Have it your way—you've been given a chance to remake the last two years of your life. Throw away the chance if you want."

"You mean throw away the chance to come back to you."

He stared at her over his k'lyge. "Yes," he said flatly. "Yes, I do."

Jemi felt her nerves souring her stomach, the bile rising in her throat. She swallowed it back. "All I want from you or your parents are things that I lost with the attack on *Starfire*—pictures of Kenis, for instance, recordings of him: I lost all that when *Starfire* was destroyed." Her voice wavered; she plowed on despite it. "Give me that much, and I'll be happy, Harris. That's the only part of those last two years I regret losing."

"I can give you that," he answered, but something in his voice made her glance at him sharply.

"What are you going to charge me for it, Harris? What's the hook you have buried in this? You're not the type to be charitable."

He tapped his fingers on the table, staring at her. "You went to see Ruth Diesen today," he said slowly.

"She's dead. Like half the other people who are connected to my past."

"Then let her stay dead," Harris continued. Under the k'lyge, he cleared his throat. "I'll get you the pictures, the recordings; I'll get you everything I can. But after that you'd be best leaving Kenis's death in the past."

The words, the tone of voice, his obvious nervousness: they all told her that there was something deeper here. Jemi felt a slow burning in the back of her throat, and she knotted her hands into fists on the table. *What is going on here? He's trying to hide something for someone else.* "That sounds like a threat. It also doesn't sound like *you,* Harris. Who's talking through your dirty little mouth, and why?''

He shook his head, the surprise coming into his eyes a fraction too late, alight with falsehood. ''You make it more than I'm saying. It's for *your* good, Jem. Your mental health. It's happened, it's over, there's nothing you can do to change it. You've grieved once and gotten over Ken's death, and I know how hard it must be to have to do it again, but you must. You have to put the grief aside.''

''I don't believe you, Tari. These aren't your words—you're just parroting a speech you've been given. What's so important about this that you're getting pressured into making this overture to me?''

''Jem—''

''I want to understand what happened, Harris. That's all. And every time I make a move, it's beginning to seem like there's a boulder right in front of me. I don't like that—I'm wondering what's being hidden. I'm wondering who's trying to crawl under the rocks I seem to be turning over. I want my *son* back, that's all. It doesn't seem like too much. If it is, that's just too bad. I'm not going to stop looking.''

''You've a paranoia complex, Jem. You've always blamed your troubles on other people. When you and I had problems, it was always *my* fault, never yours.''

A sobbing rage filled Jemi; she rose to her feet, slapping the table as she leaned forward toward Harris. ''*Paranoia?*'' she cried. ''Is that what you think?''

''Jemi, listen to me. I'm only trying to help. You have to believe that. I'll do what I can as Provost for you. I'll do some digging myself.''

''You'll sit on your ass, Harris. You'll do what whoever's pulling your strings wants you to do.''

The door opened; the vivicate entered with a tray. Both of them fumed, tight-lipped under their k'lyges. Then, with a choking gasp, Jemi whirled around and left the room. Harris shouted after her, the vivicate gaping. Jemi did not stop until she reached the crowded streets again.

In the central tavern of Dino's, a shirtless man watched her leave. He waited a few seconds more after Jemi had stormed from the establishment, sipping at his drink. Then he set the drink down hard on the bar and rose. Harris came out from the private room. He shrugged, nodding to the man, who returned the nod and left.

On the street, he could see her, to his left and moving away at a half-trot. He pushed himself into a casual lope and followed.

The ClanMother Njialjiad lay half-submerged in the nutrient pool, deep within the maze of twisting passages that was the T'Raijek embassy on Highland. There were perhaps twenty of the blind younglings in the pool with her, chasing each other around her floating body and occasionally coming up to suckle at the long rows of teats dotting the front of her sleek, furred body. An infant omega male was there now, and she cupped a large hand around his head, smiling and rolling over on her back, floating. The ClanMother's narrow face, like that of a long-muzzled, earless fox with startlingly large and expressive eyes, looked over to the curtained entrance of the room. The curtains were still swinging—Lurief had arrived at her summons. The large oval tympana of skin at either side of her neck vibrated with the sound of his breathing, and she throated out a rumble of greeting.

"He sucks like you when you last had me, Lurief," she said to the omega male standing near the side of the pool.

Lurief inclined his well-groomed head to the ClanMother, smiling in return. Tall, slender, he bowed to her. "Then perhaps he's mine, Mother. That thought is most pleasing."

"I think not," she replied. "That one is from two seedings ago, before I allowed you to partake." The racket of the younglings was constant, echoing in the vaulted ceiling of the room as they splashed and shouted. The light was ruddy, the room deliciously warm, the nutrient pool almost gelatinous with microscopic life. Two more younglings swam over and took nipples—alphas this time—the precious rare ones, with wide, heavy bodies that moved clumsily in the thick, salty Waters-of-Peace. "You've confined the alpha Hlidskjalff to his room?"

A slow, frowning nod. "Yes, Mother. He awaits your decision—should I ready the DeathMaster? The Hlidskjalff should freshen the Waters as did his ClanKin."

"No, Lurief." The ClanMother smiled at the obvious disappointment that crossed Lurief's face with that pronouncement. "You're too eager, Lurief. That's why you're still Third Tier when someone with your skills should be Second or First. We still have need of this Hlidskjalff, and he is an alpha. The YoungBearer Charidilis is here as well, and I expect that she will come to see our Hlidskjalff in time."

"The ape tired of him. She sent him away," Lurief persisted. He waved a long, thin arm in protest.

The omega infant blinked at the ClanMother and let go his nipple. He paddled away from the ClanMother as she stroked his fur lovingly. A female, her eyes just beginning to open, came up to take his place. The ClanMother crooned to it. "Softly, softly, darling," she said as the infant began to suck. "Charidilis will think that a mistake," she told Lurief. "She's too intelligent not to realize that the T'Raijek are a part of all this, and she'll come looking for answers."

"We can't let him go. He's a danger to Clan Njialjiad."

"We *must* let him go if she wants him, dear Lurief. First, he'll claim to follow the death-oath of the old ClanMother Hlidskjalff. Second, Njialjiad must recover the crystal that was lost—that's imperative. The information can't be given to the apes—that's our order from GreatMother Ktainias. Fail in that, and Clan Ktainias will do to us as we did to Hlidskjalff. Ktainias is already having to fend off questions from the Overlord about our interests with these apes." The ClanMother made a face. "If those bastard Traal ever find themselves in a war with us, if they ever realize what Hlidskjalff did . . ." The ClanMother sighed, her face bleak. She sunk lower in the water. The younglings, protesting, squirmed to stay with her, and she hugged them to her furiously. "Can you imagine our world as a blackened, barren wasteland, Lurief? I can. I can see it all too well. I saw the holos of the ships that first met the Traal. The Traal frighten me, Lurief."

The ClanMother sank so that only her muzzle and eye ridges were out of the pool. "Let the Hlidskjalff go if she wants him," she whispered. "Let him go. I understand her. I know how she feels at the loss of her youngling—it would be like losing an alpha. That will drive her to find our crystal. She will come."

The ClanMother sank entirely below the surface of the pool. Through the murky waters, Lurief could see her shimmering form, stroking the younglings each in turn. Ripples chased themselves from one side of the tank to the other. When the ClanMother did not emerge from the pool after a few moments, Lurief sighed and bowed in her direction. Then he turned and left the room.

The Bust was a slap in the face of humanity. Ideologies and national borders crumbled with the realization that none of us are isolated. We were all indeed one people, even if we realized it only through suffering. All over Earth, millions starved, died in the rioting, froze to death in unheated homes, committed suicide. Billions were deprived of the simple luxuries they'd taken for granted. Salii, our foothold on the planet Mars, was given up for lost, with the thousands there flatly abandoned. The funds that powered Highland were cut off, and here our life was extremely difficult—thousands on our own colony succumbed to simple disease.

But perhaps it taught us a lesson. We know now that by each of us trusting the other, we can pull through. We know that those who point out the way have our best interests in mind. We who lead our society will never allow ourselves to be simple pragmatists. We must listen to all voices. What any one of us does today will affect someone else tomorrow.

That is a weighty responsibility. None of us can take it lightly.

—from a campaign speech by Tari Harris.

CHAPTER SEVEN

Jemi fumed as she left Dino's, blindly angry with Harris. Angry with nearly everything. In her fury, a suspicion clicked in her mind. She ignored the temptation to look behind her and turned toward the Inner Hub where the government buildings gathered. Moving from the poorer sectors to the business and administrative areas, anyone following her would be more conspicuous. Still, she saw nothing, taking furtive glances behind when it seemed safe. She tried to correlate the veiled faces behind her, but none of them seemed to be the same any two times. Eventually she gave up the effort, chiding herself for her paranoia. *You're home. Stop acting like a fool.*

As Jemi approached the Inner Hub, near the band of Center Park, waiting for a ground transport to pass, she happened to glance back a last time. She made sudden eye contact with someone a few meters behind her, who immediately turned away to look into a shopwindow, but not before Jemi felt a start of recognition. At another time, in another place, she might have simply wondered at him and passed off the familiarity as coincidence. But the day's events—learning of Diesen's passing, talking with Harris—had sensitized her. She turned quickly away with an inner gasp, hoping that she hadn't given herself away. The shirtless man where Kenis had died, and the glimpse of what she now realized was that same man in Dino's: it was him. He wore a flowered shirt now, but she was certain that this was the same man. His build, his height: they were all the same. That was the reason his face and k'lyge and brought on this feeling of strangeness.

Yet she knew that there was nothing she could do about it at the moment. *Go on, do what you intended to do. Let him give himself away. Just be careful.* The transport passed with a lurching rumble. She moved in a knot of people toward the park.

She turned right at Main Street toward the Port Authority. Entering the tall building attached by linktube to the hub of Highland, she went to the Records department and signed out the old loading slips for *Starfire*. It didn't take her long to find what she was looking for. She sighed under the k'lyge, and handed the flimsies back to the bored attendant. She went outside again, knowing what she needed to do. Adrenaline made her hands tremble. She made certain that she looked neither right nor left as she left the building. When she could, she stopped at a store window and used the dim reflection in the glass to look behind her, feeling foolish, like a child playing at spy. *It won't work. This isn't a vidshow drama. You're overreacting. He won't be there.*

Yet he *was* there. Yes, that was the same man, the same dirt-streaked k'lyge and shirt, two storefronts down.

Suspicion turned to cold fear.

Highland was always the same moderate temperature. Despite that, she found that she shivered. Let him watch, then. She would do what she had to do.

Jemi moved on. At the first corner she turned abruptly and found a recessed storefront. She put her back to the wall and waited. Her pursuer came down the street a few seconds later, his eyebrows knitted above the soiled k'lyge as he moved his head from side to side, walking quickly. Jemi stepped out in front of him, her anger overriding caution. She could feel her heart hammering against her ribs as she accosted him. "You," she half shouted. She pulled at the sleeve of his shirt. "What do you want with me? Why are you following me?"

His eyes widened, dark pupils in a light face. He gasped, throwing up his hands to knock her back. Jemi thought that he'd strike her, but the man turned and fled back the way he'd come.

"Damn you, leave me alone," she shouted after him. She started to pursue him, but thought better of it after a moment. Her breath was racing; she could feel her pulse throbbing at her temples. Around her, Highlanders had stopped to watch this odd confrontation. Now, with curious glances back to her, they started to move again. As they passed her, they stared from the corner of their eyes or through suddenly pulled eyeveils. Jemi hesitated, and her gaze caught that of the shopkeeper into whose doorway she'd stepped. He watched her from behind windows stacked with electronic equipment. His eyes accused, and Jemi pulled her own eyeveil over guiltily, dropping her gaze at the same time. The watcher was gone, at least; she'd gotten rid of him, even if the questions remained.

The storekeeper still peered through the windows. With sudden bravado, Jemi gave him an obscene gesture and moved on. Yet she'd not gone a block before she started shaking and had to lean against a building to steady herself.

Highland had changed for her in the past few hours. She no longer felt comfortable here. The walls, the ever-present ceiling were confining and threatening. She knew she could not stay here very long, and that if someone wanted to find her, she could not hide.

All I want is Kenis. Tell me what happened to my child and I'll go, she wanted to shout.

She took a breath, a tentative step. She began to move again.

The T'Raijek embassy on Highland was an anamoly, an ugly, rambling building that more nearly resembled a pile of boulders splashed with bright colors than the sleek, plastic, white lines of most of the Highland buildings. Set in the midst of one of the larger free plots of ground near Highland Center and backing onto Kyle's Park, from a distance the embassy appeared to be the rubble of a broken toy castle, with round-windowed minarets sticking out at odd angles. Harris had once told Jemi it was because the T'Raijek lacked "the tyranny of the right angle." She'd argued instead that the embassy reflected a preference for natural growth rather than constructed, artificial things: it looked more "grown" than "built." She may well have been right. Certainly none of the other various T'Raijek embassies—Earth, Luna, or Salii—were exactly the same, though all had the same basic structural basis. The place was a maze, a warren of rooms and corridors intersecting at odd angles and elevations. It was not a place built for human sensibilities, but then, its builders hadn't much cared about human aesthetics.

There were no guards at the embassy gates, which were swung back. On the grounds, a few Highland children, too young to be wearing k'lyge yet, played while parents watched and talked. The place might as well have been part of the park. The sight of the children reminded Jemi, as too many things did nowadays, of Kenis. To force her mind away from that path, Jemi concentrated on the building itself, wondering about the T'Raijek young and why they were never seen playing on the grounds.

The pea-gravel path she walked led into a bare wall. She stood under an overhanging lip of the building, one of the lopsided towers angling toward the distant roof above her. Out of the corner of her eye, she watched the park's entrance. With a shudder, she saw the thin form of her watcher slip into the park and wander toward Kyle's River at a discreet distance; there were two other men with him now, and Jemi felt the beginnings of an overriding panic. She turned her attention back to the embassy building, knowing that she had no choice now.

The wall was knobby and a bright, improbable blue. An irregular oval crack marked the outline of what might have been a door, but there was no one there, and no call buttons to push. Jemi hesitated, and was about to knock on the wall itself when a sibilant, pleasant voice called, "May I help you, Holder?" The question seemed to come from the air around her, with a disconcerting lack of focus.

"I've come to see Ardent," she answered. "Ardent Hlidskjalff." There was no immediate answer; Jemi wondered if she'd given enough information. *Ardent* would have simply been a name the T'Raijek had chosen to call himself, one that humans could say easily but that none here would know. "He's an alpha—"

"We know him, Holder," the voice interrupted. "A moment—will you place your right index finger in the small niche just to the side of the door, please?"

Jemi glanced there—she'd not noticed the smooth, concave depression before. She placed her fingertip in the groove. A bright light swelled around the finger, pulsed once, and was gone. "Holder Charidilis," the voice said, "please enter."

"Enter *what?*" Jemi began, but then the wall before her was simply gone. No noise, no flickering, no warning. An interior she'd glimpsed in pictures beckoned her, everything glowing like iridescent mother-of-pearl under a dimmer and far more reddish light than that of the sun that warmed Earth. Behind her, Highland children stopped playing to gape and point. Jemi stepped inside.

She knew that the wall snapped back into place behind her; she could feel the slight difference in pressure and her nostrils twitched under the k'lyge, suddenly lacking the scent of Highland. The hallway in which she found herself was humid and almost too warm. This place smelled like oily lavender; floral and a bit too sweet. It was as if Highland did not exist, outside. She wondered if this was the way the T'Raijek home world smelled.

She could not wonder long, for a shrouded form strode toward her from around a corner: an omega male. He was the antithesis of Ardent—slender, tall, and if too different to be called handsome, he nevertheless had a distinct bearing that translated as sophistication to Jemi. He bowed to her from a meter away, inclining his body from a waist that was set too low on the body. His skin seemed the same golden orange as Ardent's, but his head was entirely hairless, without the downy carpet that covered the alpha below the bare skull. The eyes were large and wide set, a little bulbous and turned to the side in a nearly reptilian fashion. The nose was a small mound slitted three times, the mouth a tight, lipless gash. The alien was clothed in a long gown that left his arms free but hid the thin body and the legs and feet completely, trailing behind him on the slick floor of the building.

"Holder Charidilis," he said, and his voice was the one that had spoken to her through the wall: soft, pleasant. "Welcome to the T'Raijek embassy."

"Thank you—" Jemi stopped, not sure how to address the Omega.

His mouth widened, opened in a brief smile. His eyes glittered with some inner amusement. "My apologies, Holder. I didn't intend to hold back the usual courtesies. I am Third-Tier Diplomat Lurief, of the Clan Njialjiad. Our ClanMother rules here."

Jemi nodded to him; he bowed again, with a precision strangely like an old-world diplomat of Earth. When Jemi had last remembered Highland, two years before, the ClanMother had not been of Njialjiad; Jemi was certain of that. Perhaps the T'Raijek simply rotated their representatives, or it reflected changing political situations back on their home world—anything. She remembered Ardent mentioning something, but she'd not really paid attention.

"Your embassy is more beautiful than the pictures I've seen," Jemi told him. It was true enough; the walls seemed to glow with their own fire, and shifting bands of light ran upward from the walls toward a shadowed ceiling. "Is it like your world?"

"Like parts of it, Holder," he answered. He inclined his head to the walls. "Our sun is older and would be dimmer to your eyes. T'Raijek eyes are sensitive to lower wavelengths of light than yours—to us, this place is fairly bright, and Highland itself rather too glaring and blue. For you, a lot of the light is felt as heat, perhaps; didn't you notice that it was warmer here than outside?"

"Yes."

"Our building's heat is also to some degree our light, though our world overall is colder than your home world. We are suprisingly similar despite our differences though, I think." Lurief gave an oddly human laugh, smiled, and offered her his arm.

"Would you come with me, Holder? I'll take you to a private room where you can meet with the alpha Hlidskjalff. He has been"—he gave a tilted smile and paused—"summoned."

His skin was cool and soft. Jemi found that she liked the feel of it. He guided her along the twisting passageways. After a few turnings, Jemi was totally lost. The intersections never met at right angles or with equal numbers of offshoots. The hallways sloped, rising and falling steeply so that she was no longer sure whether she was above or below ground. Lurief kept up a constant chatter as they walked, pointing out oddities of construction that she might have otherwise missed. He told her that the embassy was, indeed, grown. "The walls were once a living organism, perhaps much like the coral of your Earth, though the remains are much stronger than the bones of that animal. My ancestors once huddled in caves like this against the predators outside, Holder. As we evolved, we kept the housebuilder organisms and improved upon them. I'm afraid that if my people had to build a city the way you built Highland, we'd be lost. But we could grow it like a plant in airless space, twist it into the shape we needed and place all the mechanisms that hold the life inside—it comes to the same thing, I suppose, and we find our way easier. I suppose that's not surprising. There are stranger things in this little arm of the galaxy, I suppose."

"You've seen other races?"

Lurief smiled gently. "Myself, no. And there are some things it is better simply to avoid." The hairless face twisted, as if there were more to his words than she understood. "But strangeness can be found here, as well. We found it odd, for instance, that the alpha Hlidskjalff became your pilot."

The transparent change of topic nearly made Jemi laugh. "You weren't the only one," she said, glad the k'lyge hid her weak grin. "Were you less surprised that I fired him, or are all the alphas so rude as Ardent?"

"It's been my experience that most alphas tend not to know when they should be quiet. It comes of their being so few—they tend to think that no matter what they do, they are not expendable. Alphas are violent children who have never grown up. In addition, the one you call Ardent has the passion of his misplaced convictions."

"Misplaced?"

"He still mourns the death of his ClanMother and the omega Hlidskjalff who was betrothed to him, Holder. He is volatile and dangerous, I'm afraid. Distraught. You did well to rid yourself of him. You *are* rid of him?" The way Lurief said it made Jemi wonder if perhaps he suspected why she was here. She didn't answer.

They turned a corner into a small alcove set apart from the corridors by a hanging cloth of soft, bright silk. Inside, in a room dominated by what looked to be a large stringed instrument on a stand in the center, Ardent sat on a three-legged chair that appeared to grow from the floor. The omega bowed Jemi into the room but didn't enter himself. The glossy fabric of the curtain fell back with a swishing hush.

The bald-headed, bearded alien glanced at her with his aged eyes. "You show up in the strangest places. I thought you were done with me."

"I thought I was, too."

"Change your mind and come crawling back?"

"I still need a pilot."

"Buy a vivicate. You'd *own* him, then. You wouldn't have the overhead and expenses."

"You won't make this easy for me, will you."

Ardent grunted something that might have been a laugh and swung down from the chair. He went over to the device in the middle of the room and stroked the array of strings: a discordant, percussive trill shimmered in the room. "You're asking me back?"

Jemi nodded. "I am. You were a good enough pilot. I have a cargo that's due on board tomorrow. I could buy a vivicate, but that'd put me pretty deep in debt. I don't feel comfortable about that now, and you know the pilot's guild prices. You were . . . cheap."

Ardent snorted. "At least I have *some* good qualities." Then he canted his head back and spoke to the air, as if to an unseen listener. "You see, she asked me. I had nothing to do with it. I still claim a death-oath." He brought his head down again, and his mahogany, old-man eyes fixed on her. "Are you going to change your mind again before we leave, or can I assume I have the job?"

"A lot's happened to change my mind," Jemi said. "Too many strange things have happened to me. The woman who was convicted of Kenis's death is dead herself, and Harris—"

"I don't need to hear about your little troubles, Holder," Ardent cut in, almost angrily. His hand slashed air, the snout of a nose pushed out. "I'll help pilot your ship, so let's go see about your cargo." With a glare up at her, he began to move toward the entrance. As he passed her, he growled in a low whisper: "You should learn when to keep your mouth shut." Jemi could only follow him, angry herself at his attitude. But he was part of what was happening: she was certain of it, and she was not going to let this part of her past slip away. She followed.

As Ardent flung the curtain aside, they could both see Lurief standing in the corridor. The omega male bowed to Jemi as she passed, a strange expression on his face. "Hear anything interesting, Diplomat?" Ardent growled at him.

"You misjudge your importance, alpha Hlidskjalff," Lurief replied softly. "I was waiting to escort Holder Charidilis back to the entrance. Clan Hlidskjalff has an unfortunate history of incompetence and poor judgment of late. I had hoped to convince the Holder that she's made a mistake."

"It wouldn't be the first, Diplomat Lurief. But it's mine to make," Jemi replied, and Ardent laughed.

"You see, Lurief? I had nothing to do with it. Tell the Clan-Mother that." Then he turned his back to the omega and spoke loudly to Jemi. "Omegas think with their cocks, not their heads," he said. "When one of the Bearers cuts herself, the omegas bleed for her. He'd love to carry my seed to one of them and croon his little love songs while he puts it in her." Ardent grinned back at the tall, shrouded form of the omega. "Wouldn't you, Lurief? You'd love to have me bury myself in you, just once, so that you could impregnate your BearerMate with a decent set of genes." Ardent's fingertips flicked along the fabric of his codpiece, and he laughed when he saw that Lurief's eyes had followed the motion.

The omega's voice was polite but cold. "As I said, alpha

Hlidskjalff, you misjudge your importance. I assume that you'll be going with the Holder?"

"I assume the ClanMother has no objections to my voluntary withdrawal from the embassy? It was a request, after all."

"You're within your rights to do so, as you know. I'll tell her that you're going and leave you to escort the Holder out."

He bowed to Jemi, staring at her with an expression she could not decipher. In a person of her own race she might have been suddenly apprehensive, for there seemed to be violence in his gaze, but she could not be sure. The omega straightened and left them without another word. In a few steps, he turned aside into one of the twisting passageways and was gone.

"I don't understand," Jemi said, half to herself.

"You understand jealousy, don't you, Holder?" Ardent replied. "The T'Raijek aren't so different as that. Follow me; they'll have my bag ready at the entrance."

She almost told him of the three men waiting for her outside. But Jemi remembered his low warning of a minute ago. She only nodded. *They won't bother me as long as the T'Raijek's with me. They won't dare. They can't.* She tried to convince herself that she was right, but the reassurance seemed hollow. She had confronted them; she'd let them know that she knew—she didn't know how they might react now.

There's nothing you can do about it anyway. There isn't anyone you can be sure that you can trust. No one at all. The only one was Kenis. Only Kenis. And they took him too.

When they left the embassy, the three men were still gathered at the entrance to the ground. As Ardent and Jemi passed them, they openly stared over their k'lyges. Jemi avoided looking at them, but Ardent gazed steadily back. If he thought anything of them, he said nothing to Jemi.

Aboard *Starfire*, Jemi let Ardent put his few belongings in his room, telling him to meet her in the pilot's compartment, and then went there herself. She opened her locker and took out a gun that Harris had bought on their first trip together, an ugly, squat-snouted device that fired charged glass pellets with pressurized air. Harris had always taken it with him when they left the ship, but Jemi had never used it. She'd insisted that he show her how to use it, and when she'd kicked him off the ship in that final argument, he'd left it. She was almost surprised to find it still there, after all that had happened since. Jemi checked to see that the thing was still charged, then tucked the unfamiliar weight into her belt. She sat in the control seat and attached the umbilical of the support system. Closing her eyes, she let the readouts flicker across her mind: yes, the hatchways were all sealed, except the door through which Ardent would come. Once again, she reviewed this step in her mind, asking herself if this was really something she wanted to do. *Of course it is. What other options are open to you? Who else can you ask?*

When she heard him enter, she closed the hatch behind him and swiveled in her seat. She pointed the gun at him.

He tried very hard not to stare at it. The T'Raijek blinked heavily, drifting awkwardly in midair. "Something I said?" he asked in a soft voice.

"I've had enough jokes, and I've had enough evasions," Jemi answered. Behind the k'lyge, she licked dry lips. "I'm tired and very scared, and I'm going to ask you some questions whether you like it or not."

"That's nice. Is that supposed to get you answers as well?" Ardent gestured at the gun with a long, thick-jointed finger.

"I think it might," she answered. "You're part of everything that's happened to me. You're part of it all."

He blinked rheumy eyes snagged in wrinkles. He rubbed at the fur of his chin with a hand. "It sounds to me like you're a paranoid schizophrenic," he replied thoughtfully. "Maybe you should talk to someone in one of the psych-health clinics. It's a damn serious delusion when you think the whole universe is against you. Before you know it you'll be thinking you're the next messiah."

"It's *not* a delusion!" Jemi snapped, and the gun wavered in her grasp. Ardent sucked in a deep breath. "You're a bastard like all the rest of them," she continued. "But I know things that I wasn't supposed to remember."

His eyes narrowed at that, his lips thinned, and Jemi could see the sudden alertness. "Your memory's returned?" he asked.

For a moment she thought to bluff him, to say that yes, she remembered it all. But it seemed too flimsy a ploy; if he truly knew what was happening here, she'd be easily caught in the lie. "No," she admitted. "I don't remember any of it. But they didn't destroy all the records. I'm not stupid. I can check things myself. They didn't dare touch too much, or it'd look like the cover-up it was."

" 'They,' " Ardent repeated contemplatively and with a hard edge of sarcasm. He rotated slowly in midair; a hand grasped a stanchion to stop the motion.

Jemi ignored him. "I carried another T'Raijek in *Starfire*. Another alpha, another Hlidskjalff, needing transport from Earth to Highland. Six months ago. You may call that coincidence, if you like, but I think it awfully unusual. Ruth Diesen, the crèche-mother who should have been watching Kenis when he was killed, was killed herself while jailed here on Highland. Another coincidence, T'Raijek? My former spouse Harris meets me in the street today and as much as tells me that I'd be better off keeping my nose out of Kenis's death. Coincidence again? Then I'm followed around by a man, and when I confront him, he runs away. I see him and two others at the gate to your embassy—remember them, the three by the gate? More coincidence?" Jemi laughed bitterly, the gun lifting to center on Ardent's chest again. The weapon's sights trembled in front of her eyes. "Tell me again about my delusions, Ardent. Better yet, tell me some of the truth."

"I've nothing to say to you." Ardent's wizened face was crumpled, lined like an old piece of leather. Muscles clumped at the jaw under the short growth of hair.

"I'm getting desperate, T'Raijek. I'm getting frustrated." Jemi took a deep breath, swallowing hard. She touched the death-beads on her k'lyge, lifting them slightly to display them to Ardent. "I'm willing to take some chances now that I wouldn't take before. If I have to hurt you to find out something, I will." Her laugh was bitter, tinged with resignation. "All I'd have to do is tell them that it was the madness of a bereaved mother. Everyone knows what's happened to me; any jury would be sympathetic."

"I saw you in New York, remember. I saw you trying not to vomit because there was a dead man in front of you. You're bluffing. I still don't have anything to tell you."

"You do, you must." The words were ragged with emotion. A wild desperation seemed to fill her—she let the straps fall from her shoulders and pushed off from the pilot's seat, drifting slowly toward the alien.

She would shoot him, if he forced her to do so, if he would tell her nothing. She would, she told herself.

Rasping, she flourished the gun. "I don't want to do this, Ardent. But I will. Please, you must tell me."

He shook his head. Sadly, Jemi sighted along the short, stubby barrel. Not toward the chest, but Ardent's legs.

They were no longer there. Ardent shouted as his wide, short body twisted with surprising agility and kicked off against the stanchion. He caromed into Jemi, the impact throwing her back against the wall of the compartment and knocking the breath from her. She felt his fingers clamping on her wrist and twisting the gun hand. She cried in sudden pain, her fingers letting go of the weapon involuntarily. Then he moved away, halting with his back to the pilot's seat, facing her. She cradled her injured hand in her lap. She bit her lip to hold back the tears of pain and frustration that gathered in her eyes.

Ardent's face was a mask, unreadable, the eyes narrowed to dark slits, the long fingers wrapped awkwardly around the little gun. He was dwarfed by the bulk of the massive acceleration chair, looking like an overweight child but for that odd face. He began to speak, softly at first, then slowly rising to a shriek. "You seem to think you're the only one who's ever lost anyone," he told her. "Holder, you haven't the slightest idea of the scale of things. I've lost friends, Clan-kin, and both of my TriadConsorts. I saw my ClanMother dismembered—right in front of me. And for what? For *nothing!* For a failed attempt to bring you people out of ignorance. Because *they* thought they could trust *you*. And you think that I'm going to be impressed by your asinine stunts? You think that because you wave a weapon at me that I'll plead for my life and tell you things you've no right to know? You're wrong. You've got your head up your ass. It's more likely that I'll kill you—*I* wouldn't be bothered by conscience. I wouldn't hesitate and give you the chance you gave me. I wouldn't heave my guts up because I had to spill a little blood. The alphas aren't like the rest of the T'Raijek—we'll attack and not give you the warning of *aljceri* or *kinjtha*.

"I'll tell you this, Holder, and it's all you need to know: you're involved in this accidently, wrongly, and the best damn thing I can do for you is to tell you nothing. One other thing: you need to learn who you can trust and who you can't. Think again about who saved your fucking life. Realize that while I'm with you, your own people will be slow to do anything to you because they fear an interspecies incident."

During the tirade, Jemi could only stare, watching the emotions run across that old-man, wizened face. His barrel chest heaved, the cords in his neck stood out like thick steel cables.

"You apes are like children," he said at last, in that throaty rumble. "You threaten the very people that protect you. All you care about are your own interests." He shook his bald head with disgust. He snorted disgust. "And *my* people . . . my people are exactly the same. Sometimes I think we all deserve the deaths we look for."

He let go the gun. It drifted in midair, pinwheeling slowly. Ardent pulled himself over the top of the chair. Without a glance back at Jemi, he kicked against the cushion and launched himself toward the hatch. In a moment, he'd gone through.

The vivicate is the new nigger. The vivicate is an economic cipher, nothing more. To you, we don't have minds, we don't have rights, we don't have wills. We're ugly, misshapen blobs of meat you tolerate because we do the menial jobs. Vivicate labor does anything too dangerous, laborious, or mind-numbing for the rest of you to do. We're cheap—why put precious money and materials into a factory for robots when you can just buy a vivicate? Why budget for research funds for better Thanatos-Vivication when the flawed creatures that current technology gives you will suffice?

Damn you all! Don't you know how it hurts to see the rest of you? Can't you imagine the agony of having shadowy memories of a time when you too had not yet died? I tell you—when you die and wake again as a vivicate, you will wish you had listened now.

—from a suppressed pamphlet.

CHAPTER EIGHT

Jemi did not see Ardent for the rest of that day. He stayed in his rooms, and she made no attempt to draw him out.

The next morning, Jemi felt much the way she had when she and Harris had quarreled. There was a guilty uneasiness hanging like a curtain between the two of them, the specter of the argument. Jemi was already in the outer hatchway, making certain that the hatch lock was cycled and there was air in the linktube between *Starfire* and the port. She had on street clothes and wore the k'lyge that Admiral Strickland had given her. Jemi felt strange wearing a k'lyge without Kenis's death beads, but after the confrontation of the day before she thought it time to set aside the mourning k'lyge. Jemi wondered if Ardent noticed.

She turned away from the gauge and glanced at him, knowing

that each of them was waiting for the other to say something. Harris had always been that way, too, but he would have only paused a few seconds before opening up the wound again. Tari would have pretended to be joking as he ripped off the scab. The T'Raijek only stared at her until she shrugged at him and said " 'Morning."

He wore only pants, his feet and chest bare—the growth of dark fur that began at his cheeks continued on down his body and disappeared under the waistband. The feet were covered as well, though he looked to have pads like a canine's. Ardent scratched at his chest; Jemi noticed that he had no nipples. "Where are you going?" Ardent asked.

"Doni had a friend, a lover—another vivicate that lived in the Rekindled House. I thought I'd go see her."

"You're not giving up, then. You think that she might know something about Kenis."

Jemi shrugged. "I won't deny that's part of it. But I also thought she might want to hear about Doni."

"What are you going to be able to tell her that she doesn't already know? After all, you've forgotten the last two years." He said it more gently than he might have; it stung, despite that.

"I can tell her what Strickland told me. That's probably more than Vivicate Corporation or the news gave her."

"What about the people that followed you yesterday?" Ardent reminded her. "This time you won't see them, Holder. This time they'll be ready. It won't just be one person; they'll change shadows every few blocks so that you'll never know who might be watching. If they need another accident, they'll arrange it. Maybe they'll just arrest you, and let you get killed the way Diesen did. Is that what you want?"

"I thought you said that was all paranoia."

He grimaced at that; the expression somehow made her feel smug. Jemi turned back to the lock—the pressure was up. She could go through. She started to flip the switch that would open the hatch, but Ardent's hand caught her wrist. The ligaments he'd strained in taking away the gun the night before were still painful; Jemi gasped. She twisted around to find herself uncomfortably close to the small alien's face. She could smell a faint spice in his breath, not at all unpleasant. "You still don't appreciate what I told you last night, Holder," he said. "I meant it when I said that you need to know whom to trust. And it's also true that anyone who'd want to harm you will be slow to do anything if I'm also involved. You'll be safer with me."

"You wanted me to stay out of this, didn't you? I can't do that. I can't sit here, Ardent, not while I might still learn something here. If that's self-interest in your book, then that's the way it'll have to be."

"It won't do you any good to see her."

"You can stay here, then—I'll take my chances."

"You could ask me to go with you," he said.

Jemi took a deep breath. She looked down at his hand; his fingers loosened on her wrist and released it. For a long moment, they hung there, drifting slightly in the air currents of the ship. Then Jemi nodded. "Come with me, then."

Ardent seemed to smile. "Give me a minute to get dressed."

The Rekindled House was near where she had been the day before, well away from the better sections of Highland. The building was butted against Highland's outer walls, as far from the main passages as it was possible to be and lost in a maze of warehouses used to store shipments to and from the port. The squat, ugly structure of gray stone stood in an improbably open space, as if the nearby buildings declined to get too near it. That space had been turned into a small, well-tended garden in the center of which they could see a man kneeling, weeding with a trowel in hand. His arms swung with the jerky, erratic motion of the vivicates. He plunged the trowel into a small bucket of peat, began to lever the trowel up, and pressed too hard; dark earth sprayed. The vivicate sighed and scooped up the scattered clods, patting them into place around a small ornamental evergreen. He didn't look up as the two approached him, but remained kneeling, carefully mounding the dirt around the shrub's roots.

Standing over him, Jemi said, "I'd like to speak with Mari Coyle."

The vivicate didn't answer. His fingers, trembling with palsy and stained with soil, continued their slow work.

"I owned Doni Rowe," Jemi said. "He was a friend of Coyle's."

Slowly, still kneeling, the man turned his head to glance up at Jemi, then at the T'Raijek, nearly at eye level for him. For a long time, his gaze lingered on that alien face, then he looked again at Jemi. One smudged hand shielded his eyes from the daylights on Highland's roof. His face was a ruin, one side of it looking as if it had been wax melted in sun. The right eyelid sagged, that side of the mouth turned down in a perpetual, helpless frown. A trail of moisture drooled over the chin from a corner of the frown. His voice was slurred and slow. "You *owned* Doni, eh?" The emphasis was unmistakably droll, despite the blurred sibilance of the misshapen mouth. "He was *yours*. You did a good job by him, Holder."

Jemi blinked at the man's tone. "You've no right to talk to me like that, vivicate," she said sharply. She could feel the heat of her breath against the k'lyge.

He shrugged. "Why, Holder? You going to buy *me* too? And for your information, Doni and Mari weren't friends. They were *married*. They were lovers. No matter *who* owned them, eh?" He turned, giving his back to them and returning his attention to his gardening.

Jemi glanced at Ardent. He looked blandly back at her, silent. Jemi looked around—from an upper window of the Rekindled House, a face glanced out from curtains. A few people walked the narrow street near the garden; none of them seemed to be watching the scene unduly closely. "I want to talk to Mari Coyle," Jemi repeated at last, loudly and deliberately.

"She's in the house, Holder. Go on in. Who am I to stop a Holder from doing what she wants to do?" He would not look at them.

As they walked up the path to the door of the building, Ardent spoke, nodding his bald head back to the gardener. "Are they all that way?"

"No," Jemi answered curtly, then realized that her annoyance was all too visible. "Doni was nice, polite; a decent companion."

"What's the Rekindled House?"

"Vivicate Corporation provides it—a place for vivicates who have yet to be sold, or for those released from service for one reason or another."

"They've no money of their own? The vivicates can't stay where they please?"

"Their wages go back to the Corporation to pay for the rekindling. When that debt's paid off, they can apply for Holdership. Until then, no."

"Uh-huh," Ardent answered. "And it never, ever gets paid back, does it?"

Jemi knocked on the door. "You're wrong, Ardent. Sometimes—" The door opened. The interior was dim; a woman stood there. Behind her, they could see a reception hall, the furniture well used but clean. "Holder," she said. She ignored the T'Raijek.

" 'Your Shortness' will do for me," Ardent said. The woman finally looked at him; he grinned at her, showing wide teeth. A half-smile tugged at one corner of the woman's wide mouth, then disappeared. "What can I do for you?"

"I want to speak with Mari Coyle," Jemi said. At that, the woman's face went hard, her eyes cold.

"You here to buy her? Corporation send you?"

"I . . ." Jemi didn't want to say the rest, but she could think of no other way to say it. "I owned Doni Rowe. I wanted to talk to her, that's all."

The stony face nodded once, letting the door swing open. "Come in," the vivicate said. "I'll see if *she* wants to talk to *you*." Her voice had the same puzzling belligerence as that of the man in the garden.

Jemi bit back a reply, her hands fisted at her side. She wanted to strike back, to turn the woman's words back on her. Jemi stepped into the hall, ignoring the woman. She took a seat on one of the chairs. "I'll wait for her here," she said. She pulled her eyeveil across, hiding her face.

"Whatever you want, Holder." Her tone verged on insolence. Another nod, and the woman went through an inner door, closing it behind her.

"It stinks in here," Jemi said. Ardent closed the outer door and leaned against it, his muscular arms folded across his wide chest.

"It does now," he said.

Jemi's veils swayed as she turned her head. "I don't deserve this kind of treatment. Not from vivicates. I'll admit that some Holders treat them badly, but not me."

"They were once Holders themselves. They were just like you. Don't you think they resent being Rekindled and given this low status?"

"We all know that we might become vivicates. We need vivicate labor to keep Highland alive. And you lose your memory of your past life as a result of the process. They can't remember much." She knew what he would say then, heard it even before he smiled at her and whispered the words.

"How upset are you at losing some of *your* past, Holder?"

She had no chance to reply. Jemi recognized the woman who limped through the doorway; Doni had shown her holos of her. The dark, wild hair seemed more shot with gray than Jemi remembered, and the still pictures hadn't conveyed the assortment of tics and twitches that afflicted her body. She had been a poor job of regeneration; it was no wonder that, as Doni had mentioned, Mari had always lived at the Rekindled House. She might have once been handsome enough, though the Vivicate Corporation was careful to alter the appearance of the body to protect the sensibilities of those who might remember the person in life. Still, the bone structure was fine, the skin smooth. Mari had an undeniable presence, even as a vivicate. She hobbled to the center of the room, using a cane for support. Her gaze snared Ardent, then swept over Jemi's veiled face. Mari lifted her chin.

"Holder Charidilis," she said. "You killed Doni." The last word was a spray of helpless spittle.

That brought Jemi out of her chair. She spread her hands wide in denial. "That's not fair and it's not true. Mari, I came here because I thought it might be good for us to talk. I came because I knew Doni's feelings for you. I came because I liked Doni. Kenis loved him like an older brother."

"You liked Doni the way a person likes a puppy. He wasn't a person to you, he wasn't real."

"Then you never talked to him about me. He would have told you."

Mari tilted her head back and laughed, the muscles stretched in her thin neck. The laugh was harsh, a cackle. "I use his own words, Holder. Do you want to read the letters? Do you want to read about how much he hated his servitude to you?''

''He played with my son. They were friends,'' Jemi retorted hotly. She was glad for the k'lyge, glad the woman could not see her face. She knew that it burned with her anger and embarrassment.

''You son isn't you. Your son isn't a Holder who wears the k'lyge, who can't treat a vivicate as human because that's against society's rules. Your son's dead, same as Doni's dead,'' Mari spat. ''Tell me, Holder, how would you have felt if Kenis had been older when he died, if he could have become a vivicate like Doni? Would you have looked at us differently then, or would you have been like the rest? Knowing that you could never recognize him, would you have ignored us as you did before?'' Mari stood her ground, her palsied hands trembling as she leaned on her cane, her body inclined toward Jemi. Tears gathered in the dark eyes and slid down the curve of her cheeks; her voice ragged with emotion, she nearly screamed the words: ''I *loved* him, Holder.'' Mari struck her own chest with a fist. ''Just *me*. I'm the one who has to feel the grief. You, you can just take another pet from the Corporation's pound. Don't worry, you'll come to love him just as much as you loved Doni.''

''You're being unfair to the Holder,'' Ardent's gruff voice interrupted. Both of them turned to look at him, still with his back to the outside door. Jemi was surprised by the T'Raijek's sudden defense of her. ''The two of you are more alike than you think.''

''Are the T'Raijek experts on human psychology?'' Mari scoffed. ''Look at me.'' She indicated her frail body. ''Do I walk like the Holder? Does my body move in the same ways? I *died*, T'Raijek. I died and paid the price for death in this society. Holder Charidilis still owes her debt.''

''She lost her son, and she lost part of her past life,'' Ardent insisted, his bass voice low. ''How many Holders would have bothered to come to see you at all? Give the woman credit.''

''Give her credit? Credit for what? For having a guilty conscience she thought she could ease by talking with me? Doni died three months ago, and until today all I'd gotten was notification from Vivicate Corporation that your compassionate friend's last payment for Doni would be credited to my account.'' Mari turned back to Jemi. ''Would you want to embrace me, Holder?'' She spread her arms wide. The front of her blouse was splattered with tiny droplets, wet with the saliva that flew from her mouth. ''Should we weep together?'' Her voice was freighted with sarcasm; a hand jerked up spasmodically. ''I've done my weeping for Doni. All I have of Doni is a few letters, a holo or two, and a lousy paperweight he gave me the last time he was here. That's all he could afford out of your wages—the cheapest damned thing. Still, he gave me all he could, more than you'd believe. I don't want or need anything from you, Holder.''

''Then why did you even come downstairs to see me?'' Jemi asked. Mari's face went blank for a moment at the question; through the silken barrier of the k'lyge, Jemi could see the vulnerability and fright that lay behind Mari's anger.

The vision dissolved her own rancor. ''Ardent, let's go,'' she said. ''Mari's right. You're right. I didn't come here because of Doni.'' Jemi shrugged. With a deliberate motion, she pulled the eyeveil back, letting Mari see her openly. She wanted to complete the gesture, to take Mari's challenge and embrace the woman. Jemi even took a step, and then stopped, uncertain. She started to speak, and found that she could not. She had no words for Mari, didn't know what she wanted to say.

In that moment of hesitation, the mask of defiance slipped back over the vivicate's face, and Jemi knew that any chance of understanding was gone.

''Get out of here,'' Mari hissed. ''Take the dwarf with you and go. Doni hated you, Holder. That's the solace I'll give you. He once told me that he hoped you'd die on Highland so that the Corporation could do to you what they did to us. That's what all of us vivicates pray for, Holder. That's what lets us keep our anger inside when the firstlifers ignore us or spit on us or strike us. We laugh because we know that one day they'll be just the same as us.'' Her voice had risen again, shrieking. There was the sudden odor of sour urine; both of them could see the dark stream that soiled Mari's pants and ran down the legs. ''Oh, damn you! Damn you all!'' Mari shouted, and she fled the room, her cane loud on the tile floor. The door slammed behind her.

Jemi could feel Ardent's gaze on her. She swept the eyeveil

back over with a harsh gesture as Ardent chuckled dryly. "You people should spend less time hiding yourselves away," he commented. "Maybe then you'd know each other better."

Her veiled head swung toward him. "The way the Njialjiad know the Hlidskjalff, Ardent?" she asked. Unwittingly, she saw that she had struck a nerve with that. For a moment she thought that he actually might strike her. Ardent's ruddy skin darkened with a rush of blood, and long muscles bulged in the thick arms. "Ardent, I'm sorry. I didn't mean it—I'm just disappointed. I'd hoped for more." Jemi sighed. She wanted only to be away from here, to be back on her ship.

"You came here and got nothing," Ardent told her haughtily. "You can't make me feel guilty for that—it's your own problem."

He shoved himself erect with his shoulders, turned, and left the building without waiting to see if Jemi followed.

She caught up with Ardent within the yard of the house. The gardener was still there, though he didn't look up. She fell into pace alongside the T'Raijek, neither of them speaking. Ardent glanced up once at the glare of the daylights, but otherwise kept his head down, staring at Highland's floor as they moved through the perpetual valley of the colony, toward the more crowded streets near the park. They were only a hundred meters or so from the Rekindled House when two men and a woman stepped from a warehouse doorway directly into their path. Here, on the outer paths of Highland, there were no others around—the buildings were mostly for storage and unmanned.

"Holder Charidilis," one of the men said, nodding to her but continuing to block their path. "Is this the alpha male known as Ardent Hlidskjalff?" Jemi was frozen into silence—she could see the glowing dot of a hologram implanted above the left eye of each of the three: a circle enclosing a stylized sun—the sumbol of Highland's security force. Their k'lyges were thin and fashionable, little more than wisps of cloth barely covering the lower half of their faces, and the same circled sun insignia was printed on the sheer cloth. Behind it, faintly, she could see the grim, set lines of their mouths. Jemi's stomach knotted queasily.

"That's me," Ardent growled beside her. "Who are *you?*"

The man touched the hologram with a finger. "Highland

Security. We were sent to find you,'' he said, looking down at Ardent. ''The ClanMother Njialjiad has requested that you return to your embassy.''

Ardent looked at Jemi, who shrugged back to him, then at each of the security people in turn. ''It takes three of you to give messages?'' he commented. ''It must be great fun when one of you has to take a shit. Do you take turns wiping?''

The strip of k'lyge did nothing to hide the flare of color on the security man's face. He balled his fists and took a step toward Ardent, but the woman put her hand on his shoulder. ''Mark, no,'' she said urgently. ''Michaels'll have your job if you touch him without provocation.''

''Yeah, that's it, Mark,'' Ardent taunted. ''Put your machismo back in your pants where it belongs.''

''Shut up, T'Raijek, or we'll make sure that there's sufficient provocation in our report to explain your broken bones,'' the woman told Ardent before Mark could answer. Her hand stayed on the burly man's shoulder, and her other hand slid under the flap of her loose jacket. ''Just tell us whether you'll obey your ClanMother Njialjiad and return to the embassy.''

''What about the Holder?''

Mark's gaze flicked over to Jemi, and she felt the animosity boiling there. ''She's all grown up, T'Raijek,'' he snarled. ''But we'll make sure she gets home safely. You going or not, alpha?''

''Maybe.'' Ardent turned slowly around until he faced Jemi. He looked up at her, his wrinkled face blank, as effectively masked as if he wore a k'lyge. ''You have to tell me now, Holder,'' he said. ''You have to tell me whether you trust me or not.''

Jemi could feel the tension in the moment. She knew that she stood at a crux, balanced. Her thoughts raced uncontrollably for what seemed minutes, though she knew that it was only a second: the bitter words from Mari Coyle, the wheedling half-threats of Harris, finding that Ruth Diesen had died . . . Deep inside, Jemi had become afraid of Highland, afraid of her past. If Ardent was gruff and irascible, at least he seemed to genuinely care. She couldn't say that about Tari, about anyone else here.

The decision was easier than she expected. She simply nodded.

It was as if that gesture let loose chaos. Ardent roared a

challenge—''*Aljceri!*'': a startling bellow that froze the three security people for an instant. In that moment, Ardent kicked back and up, spinning. His booted heel caught Mark solidly in the groin; with a thin scream, Mark collapsed backward into the woman, knocking her to the pavement. Ardent had already turned on the remaining man, leaping up with surprising speed, fingers stiff as he shot his hand toward the man's windpipe. Choking, gasping, the man went down.

Jemi watched, her mouth and eyes wide with shock. She saw him strike Mark, saw him take out the other man before the security man could pull his weapon from under his jacket. She also saw what Ardent could not: the woman had recovered her balance, letting Mark collapse writhing to the pavement. On her knees, she pulled her stunner from its holster. She brought the weapon up, pointing it at the T'Raijek even as he began to turn away from her downed companion.

You have to tell me now whether you trust me or not. Jemi took her cue from Ardent.

She kicked the woman in the head as hard as she could.

The sliver of the gun's dart went arcing away, the stunner itself clattering across pavement. ''Nice,'' commented Ardent. He'd reached into his boot, pulling out a slender, crystalline blade.

''What are you going to do?'' Jemi asked.

''Kill them,'' he said matter-of-factly. ''We need time, and that'll give us the most.''

''No,'' Jemi said firmly.

''Dead people don't tell the authorities that the fugitives got away, and that's what we are.'' He gestured at the last man he'd downed, who lay silently with his hands cupped around his throat. His face was a dusky purple. Looking at him made Jemi want to retch, made her remember the man sprawled in the New York alley. She forced down her gorge and looked away. ''He's already dead,'' Ardent said. ''What's two more?''

''No,'' Jemi repeated. She inhaled deeply.

Ardent sighed. ''You got a better idea?''

Jemi picked up the stunner. Deliberately, she fired a dart into the unconscious woman, then into Mark, still curled into a moaning fetal ball. Mark relaxed slowly, his head lolling back.

"There's an access road there," Jemi said, pointing between two buildings. "The two I stunned will be out for hours. Dump them in there and we'll have the same amount of time as if you killed them." When Ardent still hesitated, turning the blade in his hand, she shook her head. "I've had too much death associated with me already, Ardent. It makes me sick—I don't want any more. Please. I trusted you. Trust me."

"I don't understand you, Holder." He grimaced, but he put the knife back in his boot. Together, they dragged the limp bodies to the access road, piling loose crates around them. At any moment, Jemi expected someone—a guard patrolling the area, perhaps, or one of the vivicates on the way to or from the Rekindled House—to come across them and raise an alarm. Miraculously, it never happened. As quickly as they dared, they walked away from the area. Jemi could feel a prickling at her back, as if someone were about to shout behind them and point them out.

"Back to *Starfire?*" Jemi whispered as they walked.

"Not much of a choice left, is there?" Ardent grumbled. "Do you think that you'd last any longer in jail than Ruth Diesen?"

"*You* could stay."

"Not now," he said shortly. "I'm a little too fond of living myself. We're leaving. And in our situation, there's only one place we can go."

Jemi knew. She gave him the answer before he could speak it: "Salii."

On *Starfire*, Jemi quickly made preparations to leave, strapping herself into the pilot's seat and hooking the umbilical to the spinal plugs. The status lights for the ship's functions danced before her as she made the checks, running quickly down the list. Ardent had pulled an acceleration couch from the wall, latching it down and fastening the straps. "We don't have time for this," he urged.

"They don't know about it yet," she answered. "We have time."

"Your confidence is admirable. I'll be sure to mention it to Highland security when they come through your locks."

"Shut up," she said, and was amazed when he did so. "Let

me handle it. Highland Port," she barked, opening the intercom link. "*Starfire* requests immediate departure vectors."

"This is Comptroller Tyler, *Starfire*. What's your rush, Holder?"

"My cargo's aboard, my relief pilot's here, and I've taken care of everything else. Why stay, Comptroller?" She tried to make it sound casual, hoping that the link's mediocre sound would mask her anxiety.

Tyler chuckled at that, and the sound eased Jemi's nervousness. "Fine, Holder. You traders are always getting itchy. Let me see what I have—give me a minute."

A wave of static hissed in her ears as the Comptroller cut the link. Jemi took a deep breath, glancing over at Ardent. The T'Raijek shook his head at her. "Don't give him long," the alien said. "He could be stalling."

A click midst the pink noise, and Tyler was back. "Got your vectors, *Starfire*," he said. "I've fed them shipboard." Jemi closed her eyes, opened the proper channels: green lines of numbers sped across the back of her eyelids. "You'll have to wait a bit, though," Tyler continued. "I've a UCN liner coming into dock now. You're scheduled for 09:54."

"That's thirty-five minutes, Comptroller," Jemi said. She could feel the tension pulling at her face, drawing lines across her forehead. "Can't you do better than that?"

"Christ, you are in a hurry, aren't you? Sorry, that's the best slot."

Jemi took a deep breath. Ardent's shadowed eyes would not let her go. "Thank you, Comptroller. We'll wait," she said. Then, to Ardent: "Well?"

"You think you'll like the jail here? Can you imagine what a knife will feel like slicing into your back? Are you looking forward to the time when you'll drool all over your blouse like Mari?"

"Tyler said there's a liner in bound."

"Right. And Highland Security's after us."

"Maybe they don't know yet."

"Uh-huh. And how long ago do you think that trio of clowns was supposed to check in?"

There was no need for Jemi to reply to that. They both heard the distant, metallic boom of the portside linktube hatch being opened, reverberating through *Starfire*'s hull. "Strap down," Jemi snapped. She leaned back in her seat. She closed her eyes again, opening the shipboard systems. A high whine began to cycle upward, followed by a low roaring. The ship seemed to strain for a moment, then they were both pushed back in their seats as *Starfire* began to move.

The ships docked at Highland port were tethered to the linktubes by magnetic cables. As *Starfire*'s main engines fired, the cables tautened, straining. The linktube to the ship began to buckle: throughout the port, alarms began to shriek and the board before Comptroller Tyler flashed red. "Shut down!" Tyler screamed into the intercom. "Damn it, *Starfire*, shut down!"

Only ten minutes ago, Highland Security had called to order him to stall Holder Charidilis. Tyler didn't know what was going on and didn't much care—he knew that Security had sent a party to board the ship. He assumed it had something to do with smuggling—that happened often enough. He'd never had anyone crazy enough to try taking a ship out while still docked. He stared at his screens in utter bewilderment and a morbid fascination, half convinced that everything the screens told him *had* to be wrong.

The cable tethers were designed with such an emergency in mind: a ship leaving the docks with the tethers still attached could conceivably cause great damage to Highland simply by altering the rotation of the colony. They'd never had to use such precautions before; the releases were simply a safety measure built in with the expectation that they would never be used. When the pressure on the cables reached a certain parameter, explosive bolts fired, releasing the ship. Everyone in the port heard the horrible *thwang* as the cables parted from *Starfire* like guitar strings under too much tension. In the viewing screens, they could see the ship drifting away, the main engine pulsing brilliantly, the sparking cables flying away like long, coiled serpents. The cables lashed once against the port hull; the linktube to the ship broke apart, sending debris careering among the docked ships and dropping the air pressure in the port momentarily before fail-safe shields went up. "Jesus!" Tyler shouted.

"Get a crew down there *now!*" His ears had popped; he could feel blood running from his nose behind his k'lyge.

"She's fucking crazy," he screamed. In the viewscreens, *Starfire* began to pick up speed. The heat from her engines washed over the docking stations—more lights went amber, then red. The ululating sirens continued to howl, joined now by others, as the phone to Tyler's station began to ring insistently. Tyler keyed the line open absently, his attention still on that impossibly moving ship. "Yes, sir," he said to the shouting voice in his ear, "I did try to stop her . . . No, sir, I don't know why she did that . . . Yes, I'll contact the navy, but there're no cruisers in dock at the moment. There's not a thing I can do . . . Yes."

Absently, while his supervisor's voice went on insistently, Tyler collapsed back in his seat. *Starfire* had turned. Her engines pointed straight back at the port as she moved away. Their brilliance overloaded the screens.

"The woman's stark raving crazy," he muttered to himself. "Absolutely insane."

Most of the women I seem to come across have the same qualities as our energy resources. They're either beyond my means, dangerous, or used up.

—from a comedy routine.

CHAPTER NINE

For long hours, Jemi stared back through the rearward screens to the dwindling wheel of Highland. When it was certain that there had been no naval ships near Highland and that pursuit was futile, she turned her attention back to the ship. She plotted in a course for Salii that would evade the patrol routes of navy ships. Luck was with her there as well, for Earth was on the far side of the sun from Salii. Even a ship dispatched to intercept them would deplete its fuel reserves before they made Salii. An unmanned missile under enormous acceleration might be able to reach them, but that was unlikely—Jemi could not imagine their being that important. It would do no good to worry over that possibility. There were a few small naval bases between the orbit of Highland and Mars, but most of them had no ships, being only tracking stations.

The course fed into the navigational systems, there was little else to do. She rechecked the status of the ship and found no structural damage resulting from the hurried departure. The bay cameras revealed that the cargo of raw ore was still lashed down, though it would now never reach its intended destination. Salii was a short jaunt from Highland at the moment; Jemi shut down the engines, putting them into free-fall. She would have put spin on the ship, but she was too drained to flick the toggle to do it.

Jemi closed her eyes, taking a long, deep breath as her body drifted upward against the embrace of the straps. Her head lying back against the cushion of the pilot's seat, she looked over to

Ardent. The alien seemed lost in a trance, his hands folded in his broad lap as he reclined in the acceleration couch.

"You have to tell me now," she said. After the shrill bellowing of the thrusters, her voice seemed small. "You don't have any excuses. Not anymore."

He didn't look at her. His eyes were still shut. Only the mouth moved. "I suppose so. What do you want me to tell you?" He sounded resigned, almost sad.

"The truth would do." The k'lyge veil drifted upward with her breath; she brushed it back down and secured it.

"I'm not sure I know it all. And that's the truth."

"Do you know what happened to Kenis?"

He shrugged. "Maybe. Some of it. Not all that you'd want, I'm afraid."

Her silence was an invitation. "Single-minded, aren't we?" he muttered, and then he shrugged again. "Fine. I'm just not sure where to start."

"With Kenis. That's all I care about."

The comment sparked anger in him. His eyes opened; glistening, narrowed. "It can't be that way anymore, Holder. Not after what you've done. There's much more involved."

"Start there anyway," Jemi insisted. *He can't give Kenis back, you know that,* she cautioned herself. "Then you can tell me whatever you want."

Ardent unfastened the couch straps. He pushed himself into the air and drifted until he hung in front of Jemi. He gripped the arm of her seat with strong fingers, holding himself still. His dark, gold-flecked pupils were level with her own; they seemed to penetrate the gauze of the veils. When he spoke, his voice was low, a stony growl.

"The T'Raijek alpha that was aboard *Starfire* on your last trip to Highland was Cardik Hlidskjalff," he told her, then he shook his head. "No, that's not where I have to begin. I have to sketch out the background for you, Holder, or you won't understand at all. At that time, the ClanMothers of Hlidskjalff held the embassies: Highland, Earth, Salii. The government of Earth had been badgering the GreatMothers on our home world via the ClanMothers."

Ardent laughed at the remembrance, scoffingly. "They wanted

the technology for extrastellar flight, they wanted us to tell you how to fold the space-time continuum. The GreatMothers said no, but my ClanMothers, in their folly, had decided to give humanity those plans. But they weren't going to give them to the UCN. For several reasons, they had decided that Salii was the better choice.'' His fingers lost their grip on her chair; he began to slide away from her and up. ''You see, Holder—I try to talk about Kenis and end up at the beginning. There's no other way. You're going to have to be patient.''

''Then go on with it.'' Despite herself, she found this preamble compelling; it gave her a glimpse into the lives of the T'Raijek, which had only been speculation.

''The T'Raijek are no more peaceful than humanity,'' Ardent continued. ''We fight among ourselves just as you do. Perhaps that's why the GreatMothers of Clan Ktainias chose to reveal our presence to you and open the embassies. For myself, I think it was a mistake, considering what's happened since. It doesn't matter, though—the Clan Njialjiad betrayed us, and whispered to Earth of our plans. By that time, Cardik was already on his way to Salii with the information, locked in the matrices of a crystal infostone. He sensed that something was amiss. He'd been intending to take a normal liner to Salii—there was still some casual traffic between Salii and Earth then. I suppose that he couldn't take one of the embassy crafts because the ClanMothers Hlidskjalff were afraid that Njialjiad would suspect something—they didn't know that the BeastClan was already aware of it. In any case, he sought another way; he went to a trader craft that was in Uphill at the time. He went to *you*, Jemi, and paid for passage.''

''He put Kenis and myself in danger, without telling us? Or are you saying that he told me and I agreed?''

Ardent scoffed. ''You? You wouldn't have been willing to take him if you'd known. Until your ship was attacked and you lost your memory, you were like the rest of the apes, hiding behind the veils of your fears. You were like the UCN, wanting to gain knowledge without having to pay for it, as if simply by your existence you deserved it. That's bullshit. You wouldn't have taken Cardik knowingly.'' He paused, as if waiting for her to retort, but Jemi said nothing. After a moment, he took up the tale again.

"I don't know what happened to Cardik. All I can tell you is what happened on Highland about that same time. Our embassy became a battleground, first in words and then in fact. ClanMother Hlidskjalff Highland was formally challenged by BearerMother Njialjiad. That's what we call *aljceri:* equal combat. I watched them fight in the Deep Pits, and I saw Njialjiad tear out my ClanMother's throat in a gout of blood that sprayed and discolored the lower seats. Many of my kin refused to swear allegiance to the new ClanMother and died in the Pit that day. Others were purged in the weeks that followed for small infractions of Njialjiad rules. Most of the rest of us knew that we would suffer the same fate we've all expected our time would come. We heard from the Earth embassy that Njialjiad had won there too. Only the Salii embassy was still Hlidskjalff.

"Cardik arrived on Highland three days after our ClanMother died. He was immediately arrested and questioned. Before he died, he told Njialjiad that he'd hidden the crystal, suspecting that Njialjiad would declare *aljceri*. Njialjiad never intended to give Earth the contents of the crystal—the information they'd leaked to the navy spoke only of 'important technical information,' though I don't doubt that some suspected. Njialjiad was in agreement with the GreatMothers. They wanted to quickly recover the crystal and thus bolster their clan's standing on our home world. Failure to do so would indicate a weakness. I don't know how much Earth knew of what had happened, but I would assume that *Starfire* was heavily searched by Highland Customs, ostensibly for smuggling, and that the crystal was to be handed over to Njialjiad in return for other favors. They didn't find the crystal. It wasn't where Cardik had said it would be—I heard the new ClanMother's screams of anger when she was told. You were aboard the ship; you were searched as well, I know. The crystal didn't seem to be anywhere on the ship.

"Your son died that afternoon, Jemi. Probably no more than four or five hours later. The conclusion's obvious that his death was somehow tied with this, though I can't say what happened. The T'Raijek had nothing to do with it—Earth and Highland authorities were involved."

"Kenis was *four*." Jemi's voice was shrill, keening with the pain that Ardent's words gave her. Her voice trembled. "He was still a *baby*. Why would they kill him?"

"I can't answer that, Holder. I don't know how it happened. It could even have truly been an accident, as much as I doubt that. I don't know."

"And the attack on *Starfire*—that was because someone thought the crystal was still aboard. They thought they'd missed it, or that I'd hidden it aboard."

"I'd suspect so."

"They'd have killed me to find it."

"What's one life to the freedom to escape the trap of this solar system, Holder? You know now that the resources here are finite. You've already nearly ruined your home planet, and you're plundering the rest. It's costing you so much to do that that you've wrecked your economy, stuck in an endless cycle of depression and inflation. Some of your people starve. You know that there are other races out there in the vastness that you can't reach. You know that there are riches enough for everyone and that if you wait too long, you'll die here, another species like the millions in your own past that could never make it past the next state of existence. To many, that's worth one death—worth a thousand or a million deaths."

"They killed Kenis for it."

"I don't know that. Not for certain."

"I do," Jemi said flatly. "I do. And I hate them for it."

Ardent stared at her strangely, with an odd, almost violent pity in his eyes. "You know," he said, "I wish you'd stop feeling so damned sorry for yourself. It makes me want to gag."

She gaped at him, incredulous. "I lost my *child*," she told him.

"You act as if you were the only one to have lost anything." His words held a challenge, and Jemi reacted to it, stung.

"Where in the hell do you get the right to criticize me for that?"

Ardent thumped himself on the chest; the motion made him drift further away from her. "I get the fucking right because *I've* lost as much or more as you. *I* lost Csaal, the omega male who was my lifemate; he was one of those purged in the Highland embassy. I lost children of my seed as well—I don't know how many, since Csaal was one of those omegas who was always with more than one BearerMother, but I know that our merged seed had given life to at least a few of the Hlidskjalff younglings at the embassy. I never knew exactly which children might have been ours—that's not the way of the T'Raijek. I simply loved them all, because any one of them might have been mine. And I loved Csaal, Holder. I loved him as much as you loved Kenis, and I lost him. I don't weep for Csaal anymore, though. I'll do that after I've done something to pay his blood-debt. My own life doesn't matter unless I throw it away uselessly. That's the way I would feel if I were you, Jemi Charidilis."

Jemi could see the pain in Ardent's face. He didn't bother to hide it. A Highlander would have pulled the k'lyge over his face, an Earther might have turned away so that she wouldn't see the range of emotions that tugged at him. He let her watch. Let her watch as the tendons of his jaw knotted under the soft fur of his face, let her watch the dry-eyed rancor that pulled down his mouth and plowed deep lines in his forehead. His hands were fists clenched at his side, trembling with the force of his words. She did not care for his lack of understanding toward her own emotions, but she understood. She understood and forgave.

"Now what do we do?" she asked him.

Slowly he relaxed, and his usual sarcastic smile returned. The fingers uncurled, though she could see the six prints of his nails in each of his palms. "There's only one path left to us, Holder. The UCN isn't safe. We go to Salii."

"And talk to Family Jardien," Jemi added.

"Exactly. If they don't just kill us on sight."

Salii should not have existed. It was an anomoly. Salii proper was an orbital platform crossing the Martian poles just inside the orbit of Phobos, 9,000 kilometers away from the planet's surface. The original inhabitants of Salii—named after the Roman priests of the war god Mars—had been a multinational scientific/exploratory crew sent to determine what resources the fourth planet had that Earth could steal. They had the station, mining equipment, several fairly sophisticated laboratories, and shuttle craft—state-of-the-art equipment for that time, and better than what might be found in a comparable situation now. They also had a fair amount of determination, for the men and women of Salii knew that with worsening conditions at home, they might never make it back to Earth unless it was worth Earth's while to come and get them. Their diaries reveal that the majority of the team felt that Earth would be engulfed by war and famine. Some of them thought Earth would die entirely.

It was 2050 then, and the first signs of what would be called the Bust were just beginning to appear. The Great American Drought was in its third year, and the new dust bowl was encroaching ever further over the plains. Europe was caught in what was called the Endless Winter, when show fell through June in the south of France and the mountains never lost their snow peaks. The Soviet Union was dealing with its own internal rebellion as the masses slowly starved.

By '55, Salii had been left to its own devices, though Earth still kept contact with Highland and thus their mining factories in the Belt. They remained in radio contact with the colony and a few unmanned ships were sent with supplies. The U.S. offered to take the people of Salii back to earth on one of the ore ships coming from Highland. When that offer was flatly (and, frankly, rudely) rejected, Earth gave a mournful shake of its collective head and made no further attempts.

It was expected that Salii would die. Those who had begun the project would say that the failure wasn't their fault: it had simply been the economy that killed the people there—something that couldn't be helped. It would be sixty-four years from the last direct contact until the next, after the establishment of the United Coalition of Nations gave Earth its first halfway effective global government.

In those six-plus decades, the Families of Salii arose. Salii did not die. Salii, with bullheaded stubbornness, flourished. If Earth was lost to them, they would take the planet that sat under them: Mars. They dug into that stony, gritty soil; they braved the 200-kilometers-per-hour winds; they dug into the subsoil to find the trapped water and tapped the water ice that lay under the frozen carbon dioxide of the poles. Knowing that they needed more hands to help with the work, they abandoned the social mores of home. The children born of that new order grew up quickly, grew up hard and serious, grew up strange.

Salii gave itself the long task of making Mars a new home. The underground outposts on the Martian soil became small, domed towns poking cautiously above the ruddy soil. They found deposits of iron and began making steel. They built factories and laboratories. Clean thermonuclear devices were manufactured and set off in the polar regions, melting the caps and bringing on a rise in temperature and atmospheric pressure. They made machinery to break up the Martian rock and release the carbon dioxide trapped there. Mars began to change under their hands.

Salii, the orbital station, remained the center of government, but now there were six cities on the face of Mars under Salii's control. They were not named with the same classical fervor as those who had christened the original laboratory, but with the raw, gruff humor of the Families: Hard Work, And Taxes, Foul, The Pits, Underneath, and (ironically) Xanadu.

In 2119, the T'Raijek came. They contacted Earth and the UCN; they also contacted Salii. When Earth said via the T'Raijek that they were sending a representative to explain to Salii its duties to the UCN, then-Governor Wallace Jardien said that Salii owed Earth nothing, that Salii and her cities were independent of Earth and the UCN, and if Earth insisted on sending a representative, Wallace would send back only selected portions of that representative.

He made good his promise, as well. All that returned of the representative was the right hand, all the fingers closed in a fist but for the second one, which stood straight up in an ageless symbol of defiance. That act began the erratic, sometimes violent conflict between Earth and Salii.

Which was, of course, entirely the other side's fault, depending on who you asked.

Salii contacted *Starfire* when they were still two days out from the red planet.

Ardent was in the pilot's chair, taking his usual shift, as Jemi frittered about the navigational compartment. The static-filled broadcast hissed in the ship's speakers: "The border is once again closed, people. Turn your ship around. If you're UCN

Navy, we ain't afraid of the big bad wolf, so huff and puff all you want. You've an hour to comply with our request, at which point it won't be a request.''

Ardent looked at Jemi, who shrugged back at the alien. ''This is the free trader *Starfire*, out of Highland via a slightly hasty departure,'' Ardent growled. ''The owner's a fugitive, and the other person on board is a T'Raijek alpha—Clan Hlidskjalff, which should mean something to you if you've half a brain.'' Jemi frowned at that, shaking her head at Ardent. Ardent scowled and continued. ''We can't turn around, Salii. There's nowhere for us to go.''

There was a lag of a few minutes, most of that due to distance. Then the drawling voice crackled again. ''That just about breaks our hearts here, *Starfire*. Are we supposed to be impressed or are you just counting on our goodwill? By the way, you still have, oh, fifty minutes or so to comply with the turnaround order. It's hard to read the clock with only half a brain—you might have less.''

''Ass,'' Ardent commented to the air.

''Tell him that we've a cargo of iron ore,'' Jemi said. ''It's theirs for docking permission.''

''You want to bribe this idiot?''

''Is there a choice?''

''No.'' Ardent gave the man the information, then keyed off the transmitter. Neither of them said anything in the long wait for an answer.

''Plenty of ore on Mars,'' Salii said. ''Forty minutes.''

''Let me talk,'' Jemi insisted, seeing the tight fury in Ardent's face and fearing what another of his outbursts might accomplish. She leaned over the transmitter. ''Salii, this is Holder Charidilis. Tell the HeadFather of Family Jardien that I need to speak with him. Tell him it's about the T'Raijek crystal—tell them that.''

Jemi let go the switch even as Ardent's hand swept up to knock it away. ''Are you crazy, Holder?'' he raged. ''You think that the navy isn't listening to this, or Jardien, or my embassy back on Highland? Are you trying to set off an interworld incident? If Njialjiad thinks I have the crystal—''

''It's a bluff we had to take. Where else are we going to go? What other way is there for me to find out what's going on?''

"You're bluffing in a high-stakes game, woman, and you don't have crap in your hand."

"I don't have any other way, and nothing in the pot to lose."

"Just our lives."

"My life's my own, and you said that you didn't care about yours."

Ardent shook his bald, wizened head. The thick joints of his fingers flexed on the arm of the pilot's chair. "You've more gall than I credited you with," he said grudgingly. "I just hope they make it quick when they turn us into a meteor shower. If we get lucky, we might even look pretty when we—"

The speakers spat; the familiar voice hissed at them. "You've permission to dock at Salii, *Starfire*. HeadFather Gavin Jardien will meet you there." There was a pause, though the white noise pounding the speakers told them the line was still open. "Better make it a good approach, Holder. If anything looks even vaguely wrong, we'll take your ore from the pieces of your ship."

"Just stick your butt out the port window so we'll have a good target, Salii," Ardent said before Jemi could respond. He grinned at her as he cut the transmission lines. "Only a bluff, Holder," he said.

The BearerMother Njialjiad came into the room with a casual insolence that ClanMother Hlidskjalff Salii could barely tolerate. If she thought that she could have enforced it, she would have ordered the BearerMother to drown herself in the Waters. But this Njialjiad would only have smiled and called for *aljceri*, and ClanMother Salii knew that she could not win this time, not so soon after the last fight. For as long as she could, ClanMother Hlidskjalff ignored the Mother's unbidden presence, pretending to be listening to the stringclaw music that wafted through the room's sound system.

The piece was the "Solace of Time," the favorite piece of GreatMother Ktainias, who had composed it after her ascension battle. ClanMother Salii saw the smile on the Njialjiad's face, and wondered if she was merely amused at the choice, or whether this was the time when Clan Njialjiad would issue another challenge.

The Njialjiad smelled of Water oils, and ClanMother Salii

knew that the BearerMother had been nursing her younglings in the nutrient pool. The ClanMother's own offspring were in a nursery pool in one of the hidden passages of the embassy, guarded by four Hlidskjalff omegas. That was more a ritual precaution than anything else. ClanMother Salii was well aware that Bearer Njialdjiad would follow the customs to the letter, as her predecessor had done. ClanMother Salii's sides still ached with the deep cuts that the old BearerMother Njialjiad had gouged out when they fought in the Deep Pits before all the embassy. The scabs matted her fur with a discolored brown and pulled at her sides when she moved. She forced herself to remain still in her couch and growled a barely civil greeting to the Njialjiad.

"I'm sorry to disturb you, ClanMother," the BearerMother purred. "But I wondered if you had composed a reply to ClanMother Njialjiad Highland concerning the alpha Hlidskjalff who is with the renegade ape Charidilis. They will be here shortly, you know."

"I receive the reports well before you, BearerMother," ClanMother Salii answered as haughtily as she dared, and was pleased when the Njialjiad bowed her head in apology.

"Forgive me, ClanMother. I did not wish to appear so stupid. Still, ClanMother Highland wishes to know if you will order the alpha to return to her embassy. He is of Highland, and under her rule."

ClanMother Salii lay back on her couch, closing her eyes for a moment and listening as the stringclaw wailed and trembled. *Of course I won't do that. I can't, and ClanMother Highland knows it. This is only to give an excuse for the second challenge.* ClanMother Salii opened her eyes again. She looked at the BearerMother before her, seeing the sleek fur and the strong, young muscles rippling underneath the sheen. She saw the tips of the curved, retractable claws masked under the satin fur of her fingertips and wondered how they would feel as they slashed at her, laying her skin open and taking her life.

This time you'll die. This time you won't be the one that walks from the Pit. All for the decision of GreatMother Hlidskjalff . . .

"He knows to come here," she answered.

"That is the answer you give?" The Njialjiad said it as gently as she could; both of them knew the comment for what it was.

You will die when you finally defy us openly, the BearerMother was saying. *Your Clan has made its choice, and it was the wrong one.*

"That is my answer for the moment, BearerMother," Hlidskjalff said sharply. She thought that the Njialjiad would withdraw then, but the Bearer only nodded and rubbed her muzzle with a hand.

"All alphas act so impulsively—they can't be trusted. They ignore customs," she said.

"That is their gift, BearerMother," ClanMother Salii replied tiredly. The stringclaw recording sobbed like a lost thing. *The old argument again.* "Perhaps if we had listened to the alphas among us when we met the Traal, we might not have lost that fight. The alphas said that the Traal would ignore the rituals of war, and they did. That is why so much of T'Raijek resources have gone into finding ways to hide from the Traal."

"The Traal are beasts. The GreatMothers have declared them nonsentient. There's no shame in our defeat to beasts, and the next time we meet them, we'll not be bound by the rules of *kinjtha.*"

"There's shame if we ignored counsel that would have turned defeat into victory."

"Ignore our customs and we are lost, ClanMother. When we disobey GreatMother Ktainias, we destroy all that we are."

The ClanMother closed her eyes tiredly, expecting the quiet lecture to continue, but the Njialjiad's voice drifted off. She knew then that Njialjiad was tiring of the game, that the challenge would come very soon. She hoped that there would be a few more days at least, a little more time to heal and rest. Maybe she could even begin to feel some hope.

"Why did GreatMother Hlidskjalff trust the apes?"

The question, unexpected, brought ClanMother Salii out of her reverie. She opened her eyes to look at the Njialjiad, expecting to see defiance in the Bearer's stance, but there was only curiosity there. The ClanMother shrugged. "It's not obvious? She saw in them some of the traits of the alphas. She saw hope and an ally."

Njialjiad scoffed. "The apes can barely move within their own system. They scrabble in the dirt and fear the night. What good are they?"

"Perhaps none. But look at Salii—look how they managed to

survive when they should have died. They have managed to move forward while the rest of their race stagnates. Look at this Holder Charidilis—you or I, BearerMother, would have obeyed the rules of our society. We would have bowed our heads and submitted—but she struggles against that. And she has learned more than you or I would have learned."

"You deify stupidity."

"I don't agree."

"Then you think your GreatMother correct?"

"I think she made a valiant, courageous decision," ClanMother Salii said, "one that you or I would not have made. When the moment comes that you challenge me, BearerMother, we will both obey the customs and do as we must. Maybe if we were less predictable, we might *both* survive."

Njialjiad shook her head. "GreatMother Hlidskjalff more likely has made a choice that could destroy T'Raijek *and* the apes. If the Traal think that T'Raijek would plot and scheme behind their backs, they will retaliate. It will have been your clan's fault, but they won't care. They won't differentiate between Hlidskjalff and Njialjiad, T'raijek or ape. I don't find that a pleasant thought."

"I know you don't," ClanMother Salii replied softly. "Leave me for now, BearerMother. You'll want me strong enough to give you full challenge when we meet in the Deep Pits."

At that, the Njialjiad smiled and bowed. She withdrew from the room as the mournful sound of the stringclaw trilled a soft lament.

The only one that objects to a necessary pruning is the cut branch.

—Saliian proverb.

CHAPTER TEN

Salii was far smaller than Highland. The four-spiked wheel of the base had facilities for barely 50,000 people. Still, the silvery framework of that structure looked over a much grander scene than Highland. Mars was a red-faced giant, pockmarked with craters in the southern hemisphere, riddled with old lava flows in the north. Olympus Mons, the tallest known mountain in the solar system at thirty kilometers and a still-active volcano, lay there under the haze of new clouds. Argyre, a mammoth crater holding the city of Hard Work, slid under the band of the day–night terminator as *Starfire* made its approach to Salii. By the time they had completed docking, Vallis Marineris, a canyon gouged in the giant's cheek that would have stretched from San Francisco to New York if placed on the Earth, lay directly underneath.

Jemi had been to Salii only twice before. That may have contributed to the fact that, while Earth was a spectacular view itself, she felt somehow Mars was exotic, grander. The sight almost made her forget, for a moment, the events that had driven her here.

Jemi and Ardent had no trouble recognizing Gavin Jardien when they emerged from the linktube into Salii proper. Jardien himself was not an imposing sight: short and greatly overweight, his hair receding well back from his sallow forehead. He wore the bulky, synthetic furs of the Families, his gray-bearded face half buried in the fluffy pile, and his hawk nose penetrated by the thin loop of his oxygenator. Weak, colorless eyes squinted at them myopically.

What made Jardien imposing was the quartet of guards around him, two men and two women, all quite muscular underneath their furs, and all with close-range automatic weapons pointed directly at Jemi and Ardent. There was no one else in the area—this section of the port was conspicuously deserted except for the seven of them. "You have a crystal that belongs to me," Jardien said without preamble. "I would like it."

His voice was nasal and high. His eyes did not blink, and were far more powerful than Jemi had thought initially. His flat, arrogant stare made her want to drag her eyeveil over and hide. She did her best to ignore the guards, confronting Jardien directly. "I don't have the crystal," she said.

Jardien's reptilian gaze moved slowly from Jemi to Ardent and back. "Then you made a poor choice in coming to Salii. Liars die here, and only fools would have mentioned such a thing openly. Everyone has enemies, even Family Jardien—even here among the Families. You wasted my time and put me and my people at risk." Jardien looked down at Ardent. "And T'Raijek promise what they can't deliver. They become beggars in their own embassies." He began to turn away, his guards grinning, until Jemi called out.

"HeadFather Jardien, I didn't lie. I told them that I wanted to speak to you about the crystal. That's true." Jemi didn't care that they could all hear the pleading in her voice. "My ship was the one on which the crystal traveled. The T'Raijek with me is of Clan Hlidskjalff. He escaped the purge in the Highland embassy. HeadFather, I became a criminal and a murderer to come here. Kill us and you lose the last link to the crystal."

Jardien had stopped a few paces down the ramp that led into the main corridors of Salii. The glossy tips of his furs lifted with what might have been a sigh. "I listen," he said, facing away from them. "For a moment."

"Then contact the T'Raijek embassy here on Salii," Ardent said before Jemi could speak. "The ClanMother must be informed—"

"Shut up," Jardien broke in. "I don't listen to *you*. Let the Highlander speak."

Panic made her stutter. Jemi didn't know what to say to the man, didn't know what might make him turn back. Ardent seemed content to simply wait after Jardien's rebuke, silent. She stole a glance down at her companion. Ardent spread his hands wide, tilting his head in a quick shrug. She contemplated lying to Jardien, to tell him that she knew where the crystal was and that they could lead him to it—then she remembered that Gavin Jardien was the man who had destroyed *Starfire,* who had stolen her memories and half of her life with Kenis, all for this crystal. Jardien and those of his family had been responsible—this insolent man in front of her.

He took away half of Ken's life, and he acts as if he's doing you a favor by listening to you.

An anger rose in her. With that rage, went any sense of fear: she didn't care about the guards, about his threats. She took a step toward Jardien, pointing her finger at his back as the guards' weapons tracked her. "You owe me more than a few minutes of your time, HeadFather, so you needn't be so haughty or act as if you don't know why I've come here. You damn near destroyed my ship. You drugged me and stole the last few years of my life for that crystal," she said caustically.

"Holder, shut up," Ardent whispered desperately. She ignored him.

"I believe that my child died because of that crystal as well," she continued. "If you want my life as well, you can have it. What I know you can have, freely. But you owe me answers, Jardien. You owe me for what you stole."

In the midst of her tirade, Jardien had swiveled back. His unblinking stare impaled her. Jemi could see the guards' fingers tightening around their triggers. Ardent tensed beside her. Briefly, she wondered what it would be like to feel the bullets tearing into her body. She wondered if dying hurt.

"Family Jardien stole nothing from you," Jardien said. His eyes narrowed slightly, a twitching of small muscles. "We owe you nothing. That's not a way to bargain with me." He began to walk away again, and Jemi felt her stomach turn. She didn't believe in an afterlife, so she couldn't even comfort herself with the idea that she might soon be with Kenis. She would die here.

Her part in life would be over, the same as those she'd helped to kill. An end with no answers.

But as Jardien reached the hatchway leading into Salii, he paused. "On Salii and the Six Cities we don't waste resources," he said. "Even the poorest rock might have unsuspected value." He nodded, as if reaching a decision.

"Bring them with you," Jardien told the guards.

The seat of Family Jardien was Underneath. Only those directly concerned with intercity governmental affairs lived on Salii: the bureaucracy was there, the embassies of the T'Raijek and the UCN were there—the last currently deserted. Salii was the world of paperwork, the world of law, the buffer between the changing landscape below and the rest of humanity.

The gritty, real work of Mars was done onworld, and it was there that most of the Families lived, in earnest and sometimes dangerous competition. Six cities, six extended families; each charged with the generations-long task of molding this harsh, dry planet into one that would shelter mankind.

Jemi had never been on the surface. Her other trips here had begun and ended at Salii and the docks there. Tourism on Mars was discouraged, if not actively forbidden. She'd never been there long enough to find a shuttle pilot willing to take her downport, nor were there hotels on the Martian surface at which she could stay. Onworld, you had to know someone who was willing to give you shelter.

Mars was gritty. A fine, abrasive dust scrunched underfoot. She and Ardent had both been fitted with nasal plugs and tubes leading to oxy-packs; the plugs itched and made her nostrils sore. In another three or four generations, she'd been told, the air on Mars might be breathable for short periods—at the moment, it was far too thin. Without the packs, a person would be asphyxiated within a few minutes. Collapse would follow after a few steps, the lungs heaving and starved.

And it was cold. Even through the furs she'd been given on the Jardien shuttle, the chill stole their body warmth as they walked from the shuttle landing strip toward the dome of Underneath. Jemi gazed at the landscape around her—the rust-colored, flaking rocks, the pebbly soil, and the impossible few flecks of green from the transplanted earth grasses that were just beginning to change the face of this world. It was much as she had imagined it might be. She didn't think she could ever come to love this place.

Ardent, far too short for any of the coats, grimaced beside Jemi, his jaw clenched. The wind was ferocious, buffeting, a live presence so strong that it staggered Jemi more than once. One of the women guards kept a strong grip on her arm as they walked toward the city.

Inside, even though the temperature rose above 0° centigrade, it was still cold. But at least the air pressure was higher, and Jemi could remove the annoying nasal plugs and breathe normally. Jardien nodded to the workers near the locks and led them to a large lift nearby. He touched the lowest button, and the lift began a quick, whining descent. Rock walls moved past the open sides of the compartment. The stone was marbled with a rusty hue.

When the lift stopped, they stepped out into a short corridor that led into a huge natural cavern. Jemi could hear the drip of open water here: a pool of dark water held the reflection of the room in its mirrorlike surface. People moved under the immense vault of stone, dwarfed by the scale of the cave; buildings of native stone clung to the walls. Jardien led his group toward one of the buildings—as they drew closer, Jemi could see the intricate scrollwork on the stones and the gleam of crystalline windows. This was no casual, rough affair—the city was affectionately made and detailed, created by people who had come here to stay. Jardien led them through a high archway topped by fanciful gargoyles and into an inner courtyard. There, a young man hurried up to them.

"Sorry to disturb you, HeadFather Gavin," the youth said, "but we need you to give judgment. First Brother Aaron was caught pilfering from the stores again—his third offense against the family. You'd asked to be informed."

Jardien nodded. "There's no doubt about his guilt?" he asked.

"He was caught in the act, and has freely admitted it," the young man verified. "He has begged for your pardon."

Jardien gave an audible sigh. He frowned, one small hand stroking his stubbled chin. "Since Aaron has no sense of Family, he should not be Family. I take his kindship from him, Christos.

Tell the boy that he is no longer Aaron Jardien, but Aaron Nameless. He'll work as a menial in the ore factories for five years, for any of the Families that need his body. If he's still alive after that time, we'll see whether he's learned responsibility."

"As you command, HeadFather." Christos nodded, glanced at Jemi and Ardent, and hurried off again, his furs flying behind him.

"A harsh justice, HeadFather," Jemi commented.

"Harsher than you might think, Holder," Jardien answered. He did not look at her but at the doorway through which Christos had disappeared. "Aaron is—*was* my own son. But a HeadFather can't treat his own seed any differently than the rest of his Family. Salii bred realism into her children, Holder. Earth forced it on us, and Mars demands we keep it. There's no other way to survive. We are harsh in our judgments here, I don't deny that. When we believe in something, we tend to be quite violent defending it. You should remember that." He gestured harshly to his companions. They began to move again, across the courtyard to a bank of huge double doors. Jardien swung them back with a abrupt shove—they crashed loudly against their stops.

Jemi thought of Kenis. *I can't imagine being able to do the same with him, no matter how he might disobey*. She wondered if Jardien hadn't somehow arranged this as a demonstration, an object lesson—if he hadn't seemed so visibly upset by his decision, she might have believed it. *No, he's exactly as he paints himself to be. This isn't a man who'd pretend.*

They went into the building and entered a low meeting hall, where Jardien seated himself on a stone stool at the head of a table that was one slab of polished black-and-red rock. *Like everything else here: hard, heavy, and unyielding*. Jardien motioned to the two of them to sit on either side of him at the table, then ordered one of the guards to bring them refreshments. Jemi noticed that the rest of the guards stayed, and that their guns had never left the two of them.

Jardien was staring at Jemi, at the veils that covered her mouth and the nasal tubes. "Take off the k'lyge," he said.

"A Highlander doesn't reveal her face to anyone but intimates," Jemi replied.

"There's no infection to catch here," Jardien told her. "Nor do we let measures taken in one situation become unnecessary habits. I didn't phrase it as a request, Holder."

His stare was intense, the washed-out pupils dilated in the low light of the room.

"You're not going back to Highland as a Holder, Jemi," Ardent reminded her. "Not now. You threw your old life away when you persisted in finding out about Kenis."

Still, she hesitated, knowing that Ardent was right, that the strip of cloth was no longer part of her. Jardien waited. At last Jemi reached behind her neck to unfasten the straps of the k'lyge. She pulled the mask of thin wire and cloth away from her head and, laying it down on the table, ran her fingers through her hair roughly.

She was surprised at how naked she felt. She hadn't known until that moment how irrevocable her decision had been. The air seemed impossibly cold on her cheeks, on her mouth. She lifted her chin to Jardien, defiant. Jardien nodded, as if her action had pleased him, but there was no hint of pleasure in his padded face. His thick lips were set.

The guard returned with a tray of three goblets and a crystalline decanter holding a clear liquid. He set the tray down in front of Jardien and moved back to his position with the others. Jardien picked up the decanter and poured. "Water," he said. "The life of Salii. There is nothing better, and no need to disguise it. This came from the Northern Pole. The great-grandchildren of Jardien will see rivers running on the face of this planet. They'll see Salii become nothing more than a curiosity. They'll visit it as a museum of the past, the place of our origin, rather than a refuge needed when the dust storms make it impossible to live here."

Jardien placed a goblet in front of each of them, filled his own, and sipped at the water as if it were a venerable wine. "The children of Salii will tame this world," Jardien continued. His eyes were half-closed, contemplative. "If we can, we'll leave Mars to tame other worlds in this system or away from it. We have dreams, we of Salii." He tilted his head and drained his goblet, bringing it back down to the table with a crash. "Do you have *dreams*, Holder, T'Raijek?" he roared, and then he leaned back in his chair with a chuckle, one arm draped over the back.

"Other T'Raijek dream." Ardent's bass rumble took Jardien's

gaze away from Jemi. "Not Clan Hlidskjalff. Dreams take away your ability to act. They blind you to the present and what needs to be done at this moment."

"Yes," Jardien scoffed. "Everyone knows the effectiveness of Clan Hlidskjalff."

Ardent scowled. On his stool, he looked like a petulant child before his parent. "Hlidskjalff was giving Salii the ability to leave this sun behind," he pointed out.

"So you say. But the Families who wanted that gift never saw this crystal, though we lost some of our people in making the decision. Hlidskjalff has lost the embassies of Earth and Highland. Salii's embassy was stripped of anything of importance. Your ClanMother has only a title, no authority. A Njialjiad watches every move she makes, and she waits for word to come from your home world that even this embassy must be given to your clan's enemy. I'm very impressed with your ability to judge present situations." His blunt sarcasm tore at Ardent.

"What happened wasn't our fault."

Jardien shrugged. "Put the blame wherever you want. I know only that Salii doesn't have the technology you promised us. That's all I care about. That's the only reason you're here now." He turned to Jemi. "You carried the Crystal, Highlander?"

Jemi looked up—she'd been staring at the k'lyge on the table in front of her, only half listening to the exchange between Ardent and Jardien. She inclined her head toward the T'Raijek. "That's what he told me. I don't remember carrying an alpha male myself. You would know—you were the one who took that memory from me with a drug," she said bitterly.

"You accused me of that earlier," Jardien answered. "From your description, it sounds like Scloramine, and that *is* a drug we make on Salii. But the UCN has it, too, no matter what you've been told. Your story's not true. Your ship wasn't attacked by a Family Jardien vessel."

"It was. I don't need to hear any more of your lies, HeadFather. You were there, and you ran because the *Strolov* showed up."

Jardien's voice held a chill as abiding as that of the room. "You should think before you talk and you'd sound less like a fool," he spat. "Why would I lie to you here? Salii is at *war* with the UCN. They call us pirates, but we take what should by rights be ours. If one of my captains had attacked your ship, I would say so—without any apology. I tell you that such is not the case. You're mistaken, or someone else lied to you."

"Maybe it was *another* of the Families. The ship that attacked me was your Condor class."

"For this orbit of Mars, Holder, only Family Jardien is charged with offworld matters. It could have been no other Family. Salii's ships are ours for the time being. Condor ships have been disabled or lost—one of those could have been used. Strickland either lied or was told wrong."

"I'm supposed to believe the word of a pirate over that of a naval commander?"

Jardien leaned forward in his chair, his hands steepled under his chin, the fingertips lost in his beard. "Pirate," he repeated. "That's only a word the UCN uses to bias their citizens against Salii. We're not pirates, Holder. We're a people doing what we have to in order to survive. We're a colony that Earth left to starve. We survived, instead. It's only their guilt that makes them call us pirates."

"Are you saying that you wouldn't lie if you thought that it would gain you the crystal?"

"I would," Jardien admitted. "What that crystal contains is priceless to humanity. Anyone with any sense of perspective can see that. I also know that Njialjiad hasn't told the UCN exactly what was lost, for that very reason. And I know that Hlidskjalff, despite their protestations of altruism and brotherhood between races, had a price for that crystal. Everything has a price—does it not, Hlidskjalff?"

"You phrase it as a question, HeadFather," Ardent replied, "but somehow I think it's just part of the lecture."

"Tell me you had no price tag attached to that crystal, Hlidskjalff."

"I'm not a ClanMother. I'm not even an omega. All I know is that we asked nothing of you in return for the crystal."

"You asked nothing *yet*," Jardien snorted, slapping the table with an open hand. "You see, Holder? We all lie, we all hold back information. This T'Raijek's probably lied to *you*, as well. I doubt that he told you the T'Raijek had insisted to us that the couriers of the crystal must be killed. You see, we were to disguise the technology and present it as an independent discovery of mankind's own. It was to appear to be an outgrowth of Saliian technology. To guarantee silence, you would have been eliminated, even though you might not have known what you carried. You *and* your son. Did he mention that to you?''

Jemi glared at Ardent. ''Is that true?'' she asked him, but he didn't need to answer—she saw the truth of it in the T'Raijek's angry face, in the look he shot Jardien.

''We had no choice,'' Ardent told Jemi. ''We knew what would happen if the GreatMothers learned what Clan Hlidskjalff had done. We were giving humanity priceless knowledge against the will of our own people, after all. We had to keep the secret for as long as we could. We weren't aware that Clan Njialjiad already knew.''

''You goddamned bastard,'' she hissed. ''You're no better than any of the others, are you?''

''I saved *your* ass, Holder. Do I have to keep reminding you of that?''

''Then you did it because you needed me alive. If you'd found that I had the crystal, you've have killed me then. Or maybe I was never in any danger at all. Maybe you arranged the whole thing to impress me, to convince me to take you along—you wouldn't care that someone had to die to guarantee that, would you? Maybe the two of you planned it out, you and HeadFather Gavin.''

''You won't believe anything I tell you, so why should I bother saying how stupid that sounds?'' Ardent grumbled.

''Don't blame him for his feelings, Holder Charidilis,'' Jardien broke in. ''That's the way of sentience—you do what you must to survive. And I tell you that to survive, we must be able to compete with the rest of the races that the T'Raijek tell us are out there. We have to be able to leave this sun if we need to do so. We're trapped here otherwise, held in bondage by our own sun. There are only two responses to subjugation: you either despair and give up, or you fight until you're dead or have been released. Most of the UCN has given up; Highland has given up. That's why the crystal is so important, no matter what the eventual cost the T'Raijek would have charged. A few of the Families don't agree with Jardien. Family Cole and Family Shiolev want only

Mars as the world of Salii. There was and is a price to pay for *this* world, and we continue to pay for it with our lives. Cole and Shiolev think the Families of Salii have already given enough of themselves, but they're wrong.'' He turned from Jemi to Ardent. ''We'll pay your price, too, Hlidskjalff. Just give me the crystal.''

''The cold must slow down your brain processes, Jardien. I don't have the crystal, Jemi doesn't have the crystal. If I had it, I'd've made you eat your threats back on Salii.''

''Then what good are either of the two of you to me? Perhaps my best move would be to let the two of you work in the ore mines with my son, eh? At least then you wouldn't have been a total waste.''

''You can't do that to me, Jardien,'' Ardent said. ''Even if Hlidskjalff isn't in favor, I'm still T'Raijek. Touch me and you'll lose any chance of help from my people. I'm not afraid of you.''

''If that's true, then you simply demonstrate your stupidity. As you recall, your clan is not in any position to help or hurt me now,'' Jardien replied. The two of them stared at each other for a moment, then Jardien slowly looked back to Jemi. ''There's no more protection for you than for him, Holder. Why shouldn't I make use of *your* body as I will?''

''I don't have an answer for you, HeadFather. I came to Salii to see if I could find out why my son was killed. I wanted to know what you'd done to me and why. I wanted back the two years you took from me.'' She could feel the burning moisture gathering in her eyes as she spoke. Jemi reached to bring the upper veil over her eyes. Belatedly, she realized that there was nothing there, nothing to hide behind.

Jardien had seen the motion as well. He reached out with his thick, callused fingers and snatched up the k'lyge on the table. ''You still don't believe me, do you?'' he said. He rubbed the lacy cloth between his thumb and forefinger. ''I tell you only the truth of things, Holder. Let me ask you another question. What would you do if I let you leave now? Where would you go if there were no answers here?''

Jemi blinked hard, forcing herself into calmness. ''I'd try another way, HeadFather. I'd try another way to find out what happened to me. I'd do whatever I needed to do. I'll *still* do that, no matter what you do.''

One side of Jardien's mouth lifted in a half-smile. "Defiance," he said. "Good. You would have made a better Saliian than Highlander, Holder. You see, you understand exactly what I was saying."

Jardien rose, still holding the k'lyge. "You give me problems that I'd rather not have," he told them. "I have to think about all this. You'll stay here tonight. Tomorrow I'll tell you what I've decided."

He started to leave the room, taking all but two of the guards with him. "HeadFather," Jemi called to him. "My k'lyge—"

He looked down at the cloth and wire apparatus in his hand. With a violent motion, he crumpled it into a ball in his fist. "Whatever I decide, you'll not be needing this again, Holder. Get used to being without it—it only allowed you to hide away from yourself."

The door closed behind him.

Ardent and Jemi were put into separate rooms on another level of the building. The doors were left unlocked, and the woman who'd escorted Jemi to the room began walking away, obviously not caring that no guard was set. When Jemi remarked on that, the woman grinned and shook her head. "Where would you go, Holder? Do you know where the oxy-packs are kept? Can you drive our vehicles? Do you think you'd survive ten minutes outside the dome?" She chuckled, touching the surgically implanted tube in her nose. "Mars herself is quite an effective jailer, Holder. Leave the room and we'll find you or your corpse eventually."

The room was spartan—a gelbed and a stone table the only furnishings. There were no windows, the only light coming from a weak glowtube set in the ceiling. Jemi lay on the bed with her hands behind her head, letting the slow waves rock her. After a time, not realizing how exhausted she was, she drifted from the reverie into a dream-filled, restless sleep.

Kenis was there, as he always seemed to be, an older Kenis than the one she remembered, the pudginess of his toddler stage gone, the lines of his body thinning out to reveal a wiry, athletic child. Ken and Doni were playing some game in the corridors of *Starfire:* chasing each other, giggling and laughing the entire time. Jemi watched from the control seat as they darted in and out of the navigational compartment. "Ken," she called out. "Be careful, please. I don't want you falling."

The blond head turned to her. "We're not on a world, Mom," he said, his voice incongruously that of Gavin Jardien. "I can't fall here."

"The boy's intelligent," said someone with the accent of a T'Raijek, and Jemi turned to see an alpha male floating in the air alongside her, one younger in appearance than Ardent. The T'Raijek lofted what looked to be an smooth chunk of quartz from hand to hand, his long, knobby fingers swaying. "You should be proud of him."

"I am." He handed her the crystal. Jemi took it. It felt warm, smooth; when she peered into one of the facets, there were swirling, tiny lights flickering in its depths. "So much pain for this," she murmured.

"It contains knowledge, and that's life itself." The slurred, lisping voice could only be Doni.

"Your job is to take care of Kenis and help me run the ship," Jemi scolded the vivicate.

"You still don't see what it means," Doni answered. His features seemed to slide from that of the T'Raijek and back—Jemi could not tell which was which. The vivicate/alpha held up the crystal, then slapped it down into his open palm. There was a faint click, as if the crystal had struck a ring on one of his fingers, and the dream faded away into darkness.

She came from the dream feeling troubled and upset. There was an undertone of threat as well, as if adrenaline were being pumped into her. She blinked, but that changed nothing. The room was totally dark, the ceiling light extinguished. Her other senses gave her a sense of place: the sheets rustling softly, the faint gurgle of the gelbed, the sheets cool under her hands. Jemi lay still, wondering what it was that had awakened her. She held her breath, trying to pierce the murk, trying to find what had taken her from the dream.

She thought she heard the softest scrape of a footstep near where the door would be. "Ardent?" she whispered. Her feeling of dread increased. With a sudden move, she rolled from the gelbed to the floor.

The motion saved her.

Blinding violet light cut a swath over the bed, leaving shimmering afterimages and a smell of scorched plastic and acrid steam. Jemi shouted and flung herself to where she thought her attacker might be, knowing that he must be able to see in this darkness, knowing that in another moment he'd find her. She collided with someone who flung her aside despite her clawing hands, slamming her hard into a wall. The impact knocked the breath from her. Jemi struggled to rise and move.

The door was flung open, throwing a wedge of illumination into the room. Shadows moved in that light, someone shouted. The laser fired again—a voice cursed, and the odor of burning flesh filled the room. Jemi felt hands under her arms, and she struggled even as they tried to lift her.

"Holder," a voice said. With the dream's vision still in her head, she thought first of Kenis, then realized that the speaker was Gavin Jardien. "Please. It's over. You're safe."

Jemi leaned against the wall and shaded her eyes against the light. The laser still threw shifting lines across her vision, fading slowly through the colors of the spectrum. The room was crowded with Jardien and two other guards. There was a dark form huddled on the floor which she deliberately avoiding looking at. "The laser—" she began.

"He's dead. He killed himself when we came in," Jardien told her. "He's from one of the other families, probably Shiolev from the look of him."

The overpowering odors in the room nauseated Jemi. With the k'lyge, she could have hidden her disgust; without it, she could only clench her jaw as she glanced at the crumpled form on the floor of the room. The man was young, perhaps in his twenties, with a vaguely Slavic look to his broad face. The muscular arms were sprawled out, the stubby tube of the laser gun lay over his legs. There was a long, irregular burn line through his dark clothing, beginning at the left side of his chest and trailing diagonally down to his right hip. There was no blood, but the scene was no less gruesome for that.

Jardien was looking at her appraisingly. "You should be dead," he said gruffly.

"Are you disappointed?" She didn't bother to hide the sarcasm.

He grunted. "You're more resilient—or luckier—than I thought, Holder. I'll tell you again that you should have been of Salii." He reached down and look the laser from the assassin's body. He held it as if he were used to its heft. The man's colorless, unblinking gaze went from the weapon to Jemi. Small muscles twitched under his eyes. "You saved me from a great shame, Holder. I owe you for that. Family Jardien owes you. If you would ever want to join us, we would welcome you. This should not have happened—I don't know how this man found you."

"Here's how, HeadFather," a voice answered from outside the room. Another of Jardien's guards stood there. Her arms supported a pasty-faced man, bleeding from cuts on his forehead, the oxy-tube torn from his nose, one eye socket a ruin, and the puffy face a mass of bruises. She shoved the man forward, and he stumbled into the room, going down on his knees before Jardien. The man stayed there, his head down. "I found Enrico in the south elevator," the woman said. "The assassin killed two guards at the south entrance to get into the city. Then he found Enrico in one of the computer stations and subdued him. He beat him, trying to learn where he could find the Holder." The woman glanced down at Enrico, and Jemi was surprised to see disgust in her face. The raw hatred in that look startled Jemi: there was no sympathy there for the man who was obviously in great pain, only utter scorn. "Enrico told him," she spat out.

The kneeling man's shoulders shook as the guard said the words. "HeadFather," he said, "he—he took my eye. He seemed to enjoy my pain. He said that he would do worse if—if I didn't tell him. I—" The head started to come up, didn't. "I'm sorry, HeadFather. I was weak."

Jardien suddenly kicked Enrico, who groaned and fell to his side, clutching his stomach and retching.

"No!" Jemi shouted as Jardien's foot came back for another blow. Jardien stopped, looked at her.

"He almost caused you to be killed. He failed to do what he was supposed to do. He knows it, he expects punishment." There was little inflection in his voice, as if he were simply telling her the obvious.

"You don't need to cause him more pain."

"Would you have felt that way if you'd been wounded in the

attack? Would you feel that way toward the persons who caused your son to die?''

"I don't know,'' Jemi answered honestly. ''But I *wasn't* hurt. There's been enough pain and death tonight. I don't want any more.''

Jardien shrugged. ''As you wish, Holder,'' he said. He gestured to his guards. ''Get him up.'' Two of them shouldered their weapons and pulled the man to his feet. He swayed in their grasp, facing Jardien, who grabbed Enrico's chin and pulled his head up.

''You owe your life to the Holder,'' he told the man. ''She owns you now.'' He let the head drop. ''Get him out of here. Clean him up and take care of his wounds. I want him healthy so he can best serve the Holder. Get rid of the body too—put it in the processor; it'll be good fertilizer.''

As people moved to follow Jardien's command, he nodded to Jemi. ''We waste nothing here, Holder. Everything is precious.''

''I don't want your Enrico.''

Jardien shrugged. ''That's your choice. We can make other uses of him—we don't kill here unless we have to.'' He sighed, stretched under his furs. ''You'll be safe now. I'll see to it or take Enrico's place myself. Sleep, Holder. We'll talk in the morning, you and I and the T'Raijek.''

He turned to one of the guards. ''Cara, show the Holder to another apartment.''

With that, he turned and left.

After a glance back into the chaos of the room, Jemi followed Cara out into the corridors.

The only trouble with this future of ours is that it looks iust like the past. It's hung around so long it's gotten all shabby and dirty, and there ain't any money to buy it a new fancy suit. So much for vision. About the only good thing we can say is that we haven't blown ourselves to kingdom come yet. I suppose we'll get to that sooner or later.

—an aside from UCN Head MacWilliams
to U.S. President Hughes at a banquet,
February 27, 2170.

CHAPTER ELEVEN

"Holder, I think we can offer you some of the help you need," HeadFather Jardien told her over breakfast.

Across the table from Jemi, Ardent glowered. "Just be sure that you see all the strings attached to *his* offer, Jemi."

"I'm in the Holder's debt, T'Raijek," Jardien answered smoothly. "There aren't any strings. All I'm offering her is fair payment."

"What do you have in mind?" Jemi interrupted. Since she'd awakened this morning and been ushered into this dining room, she'd heard little but Ardent and Gavin Jardien's sparring. She was tired of it. She had no stomach for the food before her; the violence of the night before had destroyed any hunger.

Gavin Jardien ate with a huge appetite. He put a large forkful of what looked to be eggs into his mouth, stuffed toast in after it. He swallowed, and touched his lips with a napkin, brushing crumbs from the ever-present furs. He reached for his glass of water. "We have no answers for you here, Holder. You'll have to trust me in that, I'm afraid—there's no other way. By your own admission, you can't go back to Highland, and in any case Highland is far too small for you to stay there unnoticed." He shrugged. "You've hardly touched your food, Holder—is there something wrong with it?"

"I'm not hungry," Jemi told him. "It happens every time someone gets killed in my room."

"That sarcasm makes you sound like your T'Raijek companion, Holder. You've spent too much time with him."

"I'll grant you that, HeadFather," Jemi answered. She pretended not to notice Ardent's scowl. "And you don't seem to be leaving me much of an option here."

"You want to discover the truth?" Jardien asked, and Jemi nodded curtly. "Then you have only one path. Highland is closed to you. Salii is innocent." Jardien raised a hand as both Jemi and Ardent began a protest. "I know; that last statement can't be proven, but it's still true. I rule here. None of the other Families had the ships, either at the time of the crystal's loss or when your ship was attacked. Going to Family Shiolev or Cole wouldn't gain you a thing, and the other Families support me entirely. You must go back to Earth."

He tucked a muffin oozing butter into his mouth, looking at them expectantly.

Ardent was the first to react. His laugh was a disconcerting, high cackling. "What's she supposed to do, Jardien? Paint her ship a different color and dye her hair? You think they won't recognize the welds they put in? You *know* they'll get her. She'll be caught thirty seconds after she docks, if they don't simply blow up her ship beforehand." The little alien leaned back on his high stool, roaring.

"You're not saying anything, Holder," Jardien noted.

"I'm waiting to hear the rest," she said.

A slow grin spread over his face at that. "Good. I like you more and more, Jemi Charidilis. What the T'Raijek suggested would, of course, be suicide. I wouldn't be so stupid as to suggest it. You remember our talk of yesterday—to gain, you must pay a price. There is a price for you to pay here, as well."

"I'm still listening."

Jardien pushed a forkful of yolk around his plate but did not eat it. The clatter of steel on pottery accented his words. "You must give up your ship—she's far too easy to spot, no matter how much we did to alter her, and the navy will be watching

Salii for any ships leaving. They know your ship is here—it must stay here.''

''The ship is all I have, HeadFather. It's everything.'' Jemi was amazed at how calm her voice sounded. Inside, that lost part of her railed at the thought of losing *Starfire*, but she knew that what Jardien said was true.

''Your ship will become Family Jardien's, because it has nowhere else it can go. In return, Holder, I'll have you taken to Earth.''

''You're no more welcome there than she is,'' Ardent broke in.

''You know Salii better than to think we'd come openly, T'Raijek,'' Jardien said. ''Beyond that, I won't dignify your objection. We have our own people operating on Earth—we can get her down safely.'' He turned back to Jemi. ''We can alter your appearance here. It needn't be much, mind you. Just enough so that you're not immediately recognizable. We'll have false papers drawn up for you in another name. I will give you contacts on Earth in various cities. You'll be able to use them at need. You'll take my former brother Enrico with you: he knows computer systems well enough to be of use to you in tracking down the information you want and his life is forfeit to you anyway. It's a good offer, I think.''

''I'm supposed to trust you?''

Jardien smiled. His laugh was deep and genuine. ''Holder, do you have a choice?''

''You could just happen to tip off the navy that this ship of yours was coming in. You could sell me to them in exchange for other favors. You could give me a list of what are supposed to be my contacts and I'd find that none of them exists. Enrico could be less than useless to me. Even if I *did* succeed in finding out something, I'd be on Earth, stuck.''

Jardien seemed unflustered. ''I don't betray my own. I wouldn't waste a ship to harm you, and you overestimate your worth to the UCN. I'm putting my own people at risk by giving you their names. And I wouldn't leave you without a way back.''

''All for my ship. In payment of this debt you feel that you owe after last night.'' Disbelief colored her tone.

''Not *just* for the ship,'' Jardien answered. He smiled. ''You'll also be a courier. You'll be carrying back information our people have gathered."

"I'll be a traitor to the UCN, in other words."

Jardien laughed. "Highland's not known as a home of patriots, Holder. You use vivicates despite the UCN's outward dislike for that type of slavery. And I've already noted that your loyalty to the home world isn't so great that you'd give yourself up to its justice."

She wouldn't debate that point. "What else, HeadFather? Certainly you needn't put your undercover agents at risk merely for the sake of bringing some information back—you must have courier systems already in place. What else am I supposed to do?"

Jardien let his fork clatter to the plate. He shoved the dish away from him and leaned his elbows on the table. He stared at Jemi; she wished she had her k'lyge to reduce the intensity of that gaze. "I see a great potential in you, Holder. I see a person who will not let go of her goal. I see someone who *will* have answers no matter what the cost. You will eventually have your answers, Holder. You'll know who destroyed your life and why. When you learn *that*, you may well learn where the crystal is—and *I* want that crystal. It's simple enough. I'm gambling that the crystal's worth the price of a few of our agents within the UCN." He leaned back in his chair, folding his hands on his ample lap.

Jemi knew that she'd made her decision long ago. Still, she sat silent for a moment, glancing first at Jardien, then at Ardent. Finally, she nodded. "Deal."

Jardien smiled broadly, Ardent scowled. The T'Raijek slapped the table with an open palm, causing silverware to jump. "Then I'm going with you."

"Now who's being foolish?" Jardien scoffed. "You think that we can change your appearance enough? Go sit with your ClanMother in the embassy, Hlidskjalff." He laughed and glanced pointedly at the bulge of Ardent's codpiece. "Go screw your omegas while you still have a chance," he said.

Ardent's face flushed at that, the orangish tone going darker and the wrinkled skin of the bald skull smoothing. His body tensed, as if he would spring for Jardien. "Hlidskjalff made a mistake thinking that they could ally with you," he said.

"Alliances are the whores of diplomacy, T'Raijek. One uses them if one must, pays the price, and conveniently forgets them. I know you well enough to suspect that it's the same with you, eh?"

They glared at each other. Slowly, Ardent sat back down. He canted his head toward Jemi, his angry, dark gaze fixed on her face. "Do you agree with him?"

"I don't know."

"I did save your life, in the beginning."

"You keep reminding me of that."

"Then give me the chance to do it again. I'm chasing the same past."

Jemi sighed. "All right," she said. Ardent's sidelong glance at Jardien was triumphant.

"Holder," Jardien said, "what good can the T'Raijek do you? He's a liability."

"I won't stay with her," Ardent answered for Jemi. "I have my own resources. She has to go into the cities to find what she's looking for. In the cities, even I can stay hidden."

"They'll catch you and take her down with you," Jardien insisted.

"They won't," Ardent retorted.

"It's my decision," Jemi broke in angrily. "*Mine*. Do you understand that, both of you?" Jemi pushed her chair back from the table and stood up, pacing the room. "I'm tired of it. I'm tired of being caught up in these damn games. All I want is to know what happened to me and to Kenis. The rest—" She swung her hands in resignation, swiveling to face them again. "Maybe I can care about all the rest later."

She shook her head at Ardent. "If you want to go with me, you can. Or stay. I don't care which. How soon can your ship be ready, HeadFather?"

"A few days," Jardien replied. "No more than that."

"Fine. Find me at that point. Until then, I'd rather not hear anything about it." Jemi swung open the doors to the dining room, startling the ever-present guards, and slammed them shut behind her as she stalked off.

"She has a wonderful power in her," Jardien commented to Ardent as the reverberations died. "She's like the winds of this planet—they rage and sweep away anything that tries to stop them."

"You'd better hope that you've told her the truth then, Jardien," Ardent replied. "Because if you haven't, she'll be back and you'll have to pay *her* price."

Within a few days, Jemi's hair had been drastically shortened and straightened in a close-cropped style fashionable on earth. Her hair color was lightened, the shape of her face accentuated and exaggerated with makeup. Contacts altered the shade of her eyes; her eyebrows were trimmed to slim, high arcs. Jemi found that the change, oddly enough, didn't have a great deal of effect on her. The Jemi she was used to seeing in mirrors was always hidden behind a k'lyge. Her true face, naked and reflected back to her, would have been no less startling than this one. It was quite easy to come to think of this altered Jemi as the only one.

She only wondered what Kenis might have thought of the alteration, whether he might have cared. Beyond that, it made no difference to her; in some ways, it symbolized her break with her old life. By the time they were ready to depart, she was quite used to the new image that stared back at her in the morning. It was harder, more sharp-edged than her former self, but somehow it seemed to suit.

They left Mars and Salii in a licensed trader ship taking ore to the processors of Highland. Two days out from Salii, the freighter dumped some of its garbage—in that mass was a small lifepod, which began transmitting a pulsed signal after several hours. Within another day, a small and fast Saliian cruiser had picked up the pod and its occupants. The cruiser immediately set course for Earth, refueling once at a secret rendezvous several days out from Earth. Within two weeks, the cruiser was nearing lunar orbit, slowing and probing with sophisticated sensors at the area before it. Evading the routine naval patrols was simple enough—the cruiser was packed with electronics to scramble incoming signals and render her transparent to radar and other detectors.

But she could not land in Earth's gravity well and leave again.

For that, Jemi, her two companions, and a pilot were placed in a tiny airfoiled scout and dropped from the cruiser. The scoutcraft, painted satin black and difficult to see against the backdrop of space, blinked its running lights on and then off again in a quick salute to the cruiser. Then the ferocious kick of its engines pinned the occupants to their seats as the tiny ship darted toward Earth.

It was more difficult to pass the screen of orbital defense screens erected two centuries earlier and added to sporadically in the last century. Originally, the web of defense satellites had been intended to be used against weapons and ships in a global war. With the coming of the UCN and a cessation of national hostilities, that screen had been turned to an outward defense against Salii or any unknown aggressor. Admittedly, the system was antiquated and in bad repair. The T'Raijek openly mocked it—the first T'Raijek vessel to arrive in Earth orbit had, in a completely offhand manner, entirely disabled the network within fifteen minutes before proceeding leisurely on its course.

It was not so easy for the Saliian scout. The pilot put them through a series of high-g turns, twisting and accelerating as he plummeted toward the blue-and-white sphere beneath them. With the nose of the craft pointed directly at Earth, he cut the engines, leaving them in an aching, fearful silence. Then there was nothing, only a straight run at the planet as the craft's electronics kept up a blinking display before them. The Family Jardien pilot watched the readouts carefully, his hands on the controls. "A bit of useless reassurance for me," he told them. " 'Cause if one of the suckers decides we're something that needs to be taken care of, we'll be gone before I even start to light the torches again."

"That's a pleasant thought," Ardent commented.

"Ain't it," the pilot drawled. "Keep it—if they *do* see us, it'll be the last thought you'll ever have."

As the first touch of the atmosphere began to transform the forward shields into a glowing orange inferno, the pilot heaved a sigh of relief, the relief in tension visible as he rubbed knotted shoulder muscles. "That's over," he said, looking back at his trio of passengers. "None of the satellites bothered to turn us into scrap metal, so I don't expect company on the ground. I'm letting her come in like any piece of junk: a dead drop until we're under the defense umbrella, then I'll shift her away. We're coming down nightside—if anything, they'll see us as a meteor.''

''You do this often?'' Jemi asked the man.

''Two times—this'n's the third.''

''Do the other pilots say it gets easier the more often you try it?''

''Don't know,'' he answered dryly. ''Nobody's done it more'n me. Eventually, there comes a time when you don't make your rendezvous with the cruiser.'' He shrugged.

There seemed to be nothing else to say to that.

LEDs went from red to orange to green on the console before the pilot. The pilot kicked in the engines once more, making a slow looping bank. They could feel the tug of the world's gravity as he flattened the craft's glide. ''I'll be dropping you near the coast. Make sure you have all your papers. After I get rid of you folks, I'm going to go to ground with this hunk of metal, and I won't be back until I get your call or you go beyond the last day for pickup. I ain't gonna wait for you beyond that, either. If you call, make sure you're somewhere remote—I won't come near the cities with this crate. You get to me, call, or make up your minds that you like it here on this mudball. Okay? You've got about five minutes. Make sure your chutes are ready.'' He grinned at them. ''And thank you for flying Salii Airways.''

''Yeah. Great,'' muttered Ardent.

The scoutcraft slowed, ever closer to the night-shrouded ground below, until the engines cut once again as it swooped below the level of clouds. Jemi, Ardent, and Enrico gathered at the hatch, their possessions in backpacks, the chute packs bulky around them. The pilot touched a switch on his console and the hatch opened in a rush of cold wind.

A spray of stinging droplets lashed their faces.

''Wonderful,'' Ardent muttered. ''It's raining. I'd forgotten why I liked worlds so much.''

The address given to her by Jardien turned out to be a modest home in Mamaroneck, not too far from the harbor and with easy access to the old north–south direct monorail to New York that the older residents still referred to as 95, though there had been no ground traffic on the route in a century.

"I'm Alicia Colter," Jemi told the pleasant-looking young woman who answered their knock. "And this is William Rutherford," she added, using the names on the false papers given to them by Gavin Jardien. "I think you're expecting us."

"Yes, we are." The nonchalance of the woman's voice surprised Jemi. She sounded as if she were greeting her neighbors, and the smile she gave them seemed natural and easy, though it wavered at seeing the patch over Enrico's eye. She was a little overweight, wearing a shabby pantsuit. She looked as if there were no guile or violence in her at all. "Please come in."

The woman stepped back from the door, giving Jemi and Enrico a view of a small living room with well-worn but comfortable furniture. "I'm Helen Martelli," the woman said, brushing strands of wispy, dry brown hair from her eyes and smiling at them with obvious nervousness. "My husband George and I . . . we've been waiting to hear from you."

A older man appeared in the archway leading into the next room, holding a faxsheet in one hand and attired in an old plaid dressing gown. Below the hem were bare legs and felt slippers. He was tall, a little stooped, almost professorial. He went over to Helen and put his arm around her shoulders, hugging her once. They smiled at each other, kissed with the familiarity of old lovers. The affection gave Jemi a twinge of regret. She may have had lovers in the last two years. If she had, they were gone, lost with the rest of her life. After she had kicked Harris out, she'd retreated into herself, letting only Kenis inside the armor around her emotions. She had many times thought that she might have missed something, cutting herself off from love in that way.

George sat next to Helen on the couch and put his arm around her. His fingers idly rubbed her shoulder. As agents of Salii, they seemed uncommonly meek. Jemi wondered if there'd not been some mistake.

Following the identification procedure that HeadFather Jardien had given them, she went to a bookcase and examined the titles there—real books, the spines crinkled from reading, the paper smelling of dust and time. "I see you read Burroughs," Jemi said.

The woman flashed that nervous smile again. "We especially like the Tarzan series," she answered, following the pattern. "We don't get the chance to read much anymore, though," the man commented.

"It's that way for all of us," Enrico said, completing the exchange. George hugged Helen again and tossed his faxsheet on one of the chairs. Some hidden tension seemed to have dropped from the air. Helen nodded to Jemi. "You've come a long way," she said. "Can I get you coffee or something? Then we'll see what we can do for you."

The smile she gave Jemi was genuine and unplanned. Slowly, Jemi felt the tension of the last several days easing. She was here; she would find what answers she could. For Kenis, for herself.

She sighed, running her fingers down the spines of the paper-jacketed books.

"That would be nice," she answered.

They discovered that George and Helen had been on Earth for twenty years, in New York for fifteen. George taught at New York University; Helen worked as an office manager in one of the myriad departments within the UCN administration building in Manhattan. Throughout the chatter that accompanied the coffee and snacks that George brought out from the kitchen, Jemi had the increasing feeling that this was hopeless. These two were small couriers, but little else. They seemed comfortable with their lives here. Jardien had given her no help at all. The Martellis were nice, they were almost normal; that was the problem.

"We actually like it well enough," George said. "We've occasionally done a few things for The Cause"—his voice added the capitals—"but mostly we've been left alone. It surprised us when the message came that said you'd be arriving, that we were your primary contacts."

You've been given the aid of amateurs. You've been abandoned again. "You've been here all that time?" Jemi asked.

"Yes," George answered. "We have our friends here; we do what everyone else does."

"Children?"

A shadow passed over both of their faces at that, freezing the polite smiles they wore. "No children," George answered at last. "Not now, not here." Jemi could see that she'd touched a raw nerve with that, and empathy made her want to ask more. *I can see your grief, I can understand it. Tell me so we can cry together. Let me understand.* But she couldn't say it. She could only nod when Helen quickly changed the subject.

"I'll take William and you in with me to work tomorrow night," the woman said. "I have papers identifying both of you as consulting programmers—that'll be enough for the night guard, along with my authorization. You can do what you need to there, but it'll have to be done quickly. When we get home, we'll get ready to leave—we'll be going with you to the pickup." Jemi could see the unasked question beneath the words. *They're blowing our cover for this one. We were deep-buried, we were safe. HeadFather Jardien must feel he's getting value for our loss. What is it? Why are we being sacrificed for you?*

She wanted to answer them. They seemed to be genuinely caring. There was sympathy in the way Helen looked at Jemi, at the sisterly way in which she touched her arm as they talked over coffee. *Maybe it's for nothing,* she wanted to tell them. *Most likely you're being sacrificed to placate the T'Raijek, so that Jardien can stay in good with them. We're all pawns here, overpowered and weak in comparison to the other pieces on the board.*

But she said nothing. She made her excuses and stood up to go to George's study, given to Jemi as a bedroom for the night. She felt a gnawing sense of loss, of frustration. Before, she might have called Kenis when she felt that need, might have hugged him until he pushed her away with an exasperated "Mommy!" But there was no Kenis, was no Harris, no Doni. Only herself.

As Jemi left the room, Helen called out to her: "Alicia." Jemi didn't immediately turn, as she would have at the sound of her own name. She hesitated, then smiled back to Helen. "Yes?"

"You're a Highlander, aren't you." It was phrased more as a statement than a question.

For a moment, Jemi was dumbfounded. She could feel the false nonchalance of her shrug. "How did you know?"

"You did this as we were talking." Helen moved her fingertips across her face as if sliding a veil across the k'lyge. "You have faint calluses in either side of your temple from where the k'lyge sat all the time, and you have their way of averting your eyes at any hint of emotion. Small things, Alicia, but you should be aware of them. Remember that we're all in the business of being more than we seem. HeadFather usually knows what he's doing."

Jemi knew there was a second message being given. She could only nod. "I'll remember," she said. "Good night."

She was still awake, lying in the darkness, when she heard the soft knock. She pulled the covers over her and whispered, "Come."

The door opened, spilling light from the hall into the room. She saw Enrico silhouetted against the glare, then the door closed again, leaving the image moving across the back of her eyes. She felt the bed move as he sat down near her feet.

"They're taking quite a risk for us," he said without preamble.

"I know."

"They lost parents to the navy, both of them, in childhood. They were on a freighter that the navy mistook for a cruiser. HeadFather Jardien had them sent here not long after. They were raised by agents we'd had here for years, and they were never allowed to forget what the UCN did."

"And you Saliians never kill any parents when you blow up a ship, is that right? You have missiles that only hit single people."

Jemi could sense Enrico's shrug.

"It'd be easier to hate an enemy who was utterly evil, or to choose sides when the choices are black and white, but that's never the case, is it? All you can do is choose for yourself, as best you can. Saliians are brought up to be loyal. We're a small community with a shared ideology. We're taught it from birth; it's not something we question. Overall, I think we're probably more in the right than the UCN. I think the Clan Hlidskjalff made the right choice deciding to trust us, even if that hasn't worked out."

Jemi felt something land on the bed. She reached out to touch a small plastic cube. "That's something I stole from the Jardien computers," Enrico explained. "I thought you'd like to see it, but I can tell you what's there. There wasn't a Saliian ship anywhere near you when you were attacked. There wasn't even a Saliian cruiser out at that time. The craft that attacked you wasn't one of ours. Look at the data—there's a terminal on the desk in here."

"You tell me that after your little speech about loyalty and expect me to believe it?"

"I was given to *you,* remember? My loyalty's yours now. Believe it or not, Jemi, it's true. And I'll find out what I can tomorrow as well."

The bed jiggled as Enrico rose. She heard him pad across the floor and turn the door handle. The patch was a darker shadow on his face. Warm yellow light moved over the bed. "Look at the data," he said. "I stole it just as it is—HeadFather Jardien doesn't lie. If you were his enemy, he'd do what he had to do, but he wouldn't hesitate to tell you that." He waited a moment. Jemi said nothing, her fingers still clutching the cube. "One other thing," Enrico added. "The man who attacked you last time you were in New York—he *was* one of our agents. But I couldn't find anything to indicate that he'd been ordered to kill you or even to contact you."

"HeadFather Jardien didn't bother to mention that to me."

"You didn't ask. I said he'd tell you the truth. I didn't say he wouldn't hide what he could, and I didn't say he was perfect."

Jemi nodded. "I'll look at it, Enrico."

"Uh-huh." The door started to swing shut. The night moved across the wall, and Jemi felt a hopeless emptiness.

"Enrico," Jemi said with a sudden impulse.

"Yes?"

"Thank you. I appreciate it."

"I owe you, Holder. I almost caused your death. This is only interest on the principal, huh?"

"You don't owe me anything. Not really."

"You got a raw deal in the last year or so, Holder. If I can make up for some of that, I will."

Jemi didn't know how to respond to that. She sat on the bed, cradling the cube to her and staring at the blank darkness in front of her. "Enrico," she said before he could close the door. "Would you . . . would you want to stay with me tonight? I think I could use the company, someone to hold. I'm not asking for anything more than that. Just companionship."

He didn't reply. The door closed; she could see nothing. For a second, Jemi thought that perhaps he'd already gone. Then she heard his soft breath. "Sometimes I think I can't feel anything anymore," she whispered. "I'm so damn out of practice."

She felt the bed move as he came in beside her. There was a warmth at her side, though he didn't touch her. His voice was rough and pleasant. "I could use the company, too," he said. "We're both a little lost, huh?"

There isn't a nasty, horrible inhumanity we can think of that we haven't already done to one another. Maybe that's one of the reasons we have such a hard time conceiving of a truly different and better world. None of our images of Utopia match those of our neighbors. Hell, look at the T'Raijek—for all their technological superiority, do they seem any happier than us?

We're much better at constructing hell rather than heaven.

—comment by amateur sociological
analyst on "Open Forum Holo."

CHAPTER TWELVE

Commander Nys glared at the report in front of him as if his scowl could erase the words printed there. He looked up to find an amused expression on the face of the Office of Internal Affairs lieutenant who'd brought the report; that expression vanished when Nys's stare fixed on him.

"You're certain that Charidilis is back in the UCN, Lieutenant Perez?" Nys snapped.

"Her ship was tracked heading toward Salii, Commander." Perez cursed the impulse that had made him smile as he'd watched Nys skim the report. *You'll catch it now, as if the fact that I wrote the damn thing makes me personally responsible for the content.* "She was monitored talking with Salii Port, requesting to be met by Gavin Jardien—OIA sent you a transcript of that conversation, as I recall." *There. Maybe that'll placate the cold bastard and make him realize that we're doing what we can.* "Our agents within Family Cole confirmed her arrival there. Charidilis was escorted to Jardien's city on the surface. We know that she hasn't been seen in the two months since then. *Starfire* has remained empty and unvisited, guarded by Family Jardien members. That's unlike the woman."

"That doesn't mean she's *here*."

"Commander, we have reports that a Jardien pirate ship was lurking in near lunar orbit a few days ago. They don't come in that close unless there's good reason, and two months is about how long it would take Charidilis to come from Mars under high acceleration. We both know the fallibility of the satellite defenses—the orbital fence can be penetrated."

Nys snorted. He punched a contact on the side of his desk and part of the wall slid back to reveal a viewscreen, with the half-globe of a shadowed earth hanging there. The North American continent was beyond the umbra now. Dawn raced eastward across the Urals. " 'The orbital fence can be penetrated.' " Nys snorted, throwing the lieutenant's words back at him, laced with sarcasm. "That's the understatement of the day, Lieutenant Perez. The defensive screen's a huge, expensive, and outmoded joke. We're trying to hold back tanks with muskets and spears, and we don't have the budget to fix it. A halfway smart *ape* could figure out ways around it. And none of this speculation by your department has any proof to go with it, does it?"

Perez allowed himself an inward sigh, keeping his features locked in neutrality. *Exaggerating as usual, aren't we, Commander?* "That's not all, sir. We had a report of a large meteor from several radar tracking stations in the southern hemisphere. By all indications, portions of it should have reached ground, but we can't find any fragments at all. We've looked. There should have some grounding of a rock that big."

"You're saying it was a Jardien shuttle?"

"Possibly, Commander. Add it together, and it all makes sense. Charidilis can't go back to Highland, and while it's conceivable that she's been kept on Mars by Jardien, I think that it's more likely she's continued on after she's learned what she could from the HeadFather. Which leaves her only one option."

"To come back here."

Isn't it nice to know that your superiors can state the obvious, too. My two-year-old daughter could have done the same. "Yes, Commander."

"And what are your orders regarding this report?"

"The Office of Internal Affairs has alerted all civil authorities onworld. The description of the woman's been circulated, and all governmental agencies are on a stage-one alert. We've told the T'Raijek embassy here, and they've furnished us with a list of the names and locations of all their alpha males onworld who are not within the embassy itself. If she's found, she's to be apprehended. She's listed as armed and dangerous since the incidents on Highland."

Nys nodded. Perez wished he could read the man. He'd known the Commander since his assignment to Uphill Port. In that time, he'd rarely seen the man show much outward emotion—that was most of the reason he'd been pleased to see the obvious chagrin on the Commander's face when he'd first read the report on his desk. Now the Commander had bottled himself up again, sitting stiffly at his desk with his hands laid primly before him, as proper and formal as the flower arrangement that sat on the file behind him, as stylized as the Japanese prints on the wall. "Tell me, Lieutenant, do you have any theories on why the Charidilis woman has been so, ahh, elusive?"

"I suspect that she's a trained agent, probably Saliian all along, Commander. We know that they have some deep-cover operatives within the UCN."

There was nothing readable on Nys's face. He might as well have been wearing a mask. "I wonder, Lieutenant," he said softly. "I think you might overestimate the situation. She may be nothing more than she's claimed to be—a woman trying to find out what happened to her son. It could simply be that she's tired of being manipulated."

"An innocent, Commander?" Perez nearly gave vent to an incredulous laugh, catching himself at the last moment. "You can't believe that, Commander, not after all this."

"There's a power in innocence, Lieutenant. Those who have never had such a quality tend to forget that axiom."

Which means what, Commander Inscrutable?

Despite his thoughts, Perez nodded dutifully. The Commander's gaze was directed at the wall behind Perez, and it did not move. The fixed meditation on nothing seemed almost eerie to Perez, making him very uncomfortable. "With your permission, sir?"

"You may leave, Lieutenant." Softly; a whisper.

As Perez was about to leave the office, Nys stopped him. "Lieutenant, one more thing, if you please. Has Admiral Strickland asked for this same report, by chance?"

Perez didn't bother to keep his puzzlement from showing. *Now why in the world would he want to know that?* "Why, yes, sir, he did. He's asked OIA to keep him appraised of anything pertaining to the Charidilis woman."

Nothing showed on Nys's face. He merely nodded, his hands folded neatly in the exact center of his desk top, his wide Asian features composed and neutral. "Thank you, Lieutenant. That will be all I require at the moment."

Jemi was surprised at the ease with which they entered the UCN building. Only a few lights were on in the offices of the tower set in the center of downtown Manhattan—mandatory budgeting measures precluded night hours for the staff unless absolutely necessary. There were two guards in the lobby: a balding, rotund man lolling in front of an array of flatscreens showing various hallways within the building; a much younger woman leaning back on a battered wooden chair. Between the two of them stood a small table littered with disposable cups of coffee and the crumbling remains of pastry. Seeing their approach, the female guard let the chair drop forward, the metal-tipped legs scraping against tile. "Evening, Ms. Martelli. Late night again for you?"

" 'Fraid so, Kathy." Helen smiled at the woman. Jemi tried to smile as well, nodding. "Mark should have given you the authorization chit."

"He did. Who'd you bring with you?"

"Alicia Colter and William Rutherford. Programming consultants from ICC. They're supposed to get rid of the bugs that have kept me here at these awful hours."

"Miracle workers, huh?" the guard said, looking at them. Her gaze was more intense than Jemi had expected, and she had to resist the compulsion to bring her hand up to the k'lyge that wasn't there. *Think, woman—you're not allowed to have those old reflexes anymore.*

"We hope so," Jemi said. She handed the guard the leather case Helen had given her that evening. "Here's my ID."

The guard flipped it open, glanced at the holographic image there and then quickly at Jemi. She did the same with the one Enrico gave her, then gave his eye-patched face a long, second look. She tapped the two cases together for a moment. For a heart-sickening instant, Jemi thought that something had gone wrong. She could feel her heart hammering against her ribs. Then Enrico touched a forefinger to the patch. "Infection," he said. "The doctor said I have to keep this on for another week or so."

The guard nodded at that and handed the cases back. The woman gave each of the three of them a plastic clip. "Here's your building passes—there're only good for your particular floor, so don't let yourself out of Ms. Martelli's sight, eh? And I'll need you to sign yourselves in."

Alicia Colter—Jemi scribbled that strange name in the passbook and followed Helen to the elevator in the center of the lobby. A minute later, having shown their clips to the guard at the floor desk, they were in the offices. Enrico quickly put on the temple contacts of the computer and accessed the main program with the pass-code Helen supplied. "Archaic stuff," he commented, tapping the keyboard and terminal in front of him. He looked up at Helen with his disconcerting, one-eyed stare. "You're not using mind-interfaced imagery yet? We've had it on Salii for years. Saves all the damn keyboard work."

"Not in the budget," Helen answered. "Not for the last twenty years. Or the *next* twenty. You don't realize how bad it's been here."

"Just as well," Enrico commented. "This'll be easier, then. Except that I haven't typed in years." He pulled the keyboard toward him, and flipped up the screenfoil. "Just so the two of you can watch, too," he said. The screen filled with code-strings, and as Enrico tapped the keys, they began to shift and move. "Hexadecimal," he commented. "I hate it. This stuff belongs in a museum, not an office. Helen, tell me if you see something I should know about."

Over the next half hour, they watched as Enrico made his initial incursion into the system. Bored with watching the endless display of meaningless figures, Jemi wandered around the office. The large room, full of desks and chairs, seemed lonely and too quiet in the night. The ghosts of the people who worked here still seemed to lurk—she expected to see someone in one of the chairs as she passed. The tension burned in Jemi's stomach; she felt entirely helpless. She wanted to do something, to have some task to perform, if only to take her mind off the possibilities.

Brushing against the back of one of the chairs, Jemi felt an unaccustomed bulge at her hip, and she touched the flat, hard shape under her waistband. Helen had given her a compact, plastic-cased gun; now that Jemi had noticed it once more, the gun's weight dragged at her waist like an accusation. To take her mind from the possibilities the gun represented, Jemi stared down at the lights of Manhattan, wondering how the city must have looked in its glory before the endless economic struggle had dimmed her lights and made her filthy.

"Okay, that's got us into the part of the net we're after." Enrico pulled a small flat case from a briefcase he'd brought along and attached it to one of the ports in back of the terminal. "Virus program," he said as he connected it. He talked without looking at them, his gaze on the screen. "Just a bundle of information. It'll move into residence in the mainframe memory and start taking out the password cues to the restricted menus and files, reproducing itself in the files as it goes. At the same time, it'll be keeping a running tabulation on the content in those files so that I can make the choice of whether to go in or not. Our job's mostly to sit and wait—and to hope that our little intruder doesn't set off alarms buried in the system. Alicia, you have that list of questions you wanted to ask that weren't on HeadFather Gavin's list?"

Jemi still gazed out at the panorama of the city. "Alicia?" Enrico repeated, and Jemi started. *You can't even have your own name now.* She slid her hand into a pants pocket, pulled out a rumpled sheet of paper. "Here," she said sourly, walking over to him.

"Don't look so pleased that I managed to break in for you, huh?" Enrico's soft smile took away the sting the words might have had. Jemi shook her head self-deprecatingly and tried to smile in return.

"Sorry."

"It's okay, lady. Let's see what we can do for you."

Enrico typed as data scrolled across the screen. Helen and Jemi leaned over Enrico to watch, Jemi putting her hand on his shoulder. As she did so, she thought she heard a muffled noise and jerked away.

"What's the matter?" Helen asked.

"Did you hear that?"

"I didn't hear anything."

Jemi listened for a moment. It was quiet, with only the clatter of Enrico's fingers on the keyboard. Jemi shook her head. "Nothing. Just jumpy, I guess."

Helen smiled nervously at her. "I can understand that. I feel the same way. I'll be glad when this is over and we can pick up George and leave." She shrugged at Jemi. "We don't really remember Salii; it'll be good to be back there again after—"

"Here's some of what we're after," Enrico interrupted. "This is the log of communications from the T'Raijek embassies to the UCN naval headquarters on Uphill Port. There's rarely anything coming in from Highland. Yet there's a record of three messages on April fourth of this year—that's the date you left Highland before the attack, right?"

"Yes," Jemi confirmed. She leaned closer. "Who did those go to?"

"Let's see." Enrico touched a key and lines scrolled across the foil. "There." He pointed. "Admiral Strickland, Eyes Only." His dark brown eyes glanced back at Jemi. "That say the same thing to you it says to me?"

Jemi remembered Strickland, recalled how kindly and gentle the man had been and how softly he'd broken the news of the attack to her. She remembered the pain in his eyes, the sound of his voice. Jemi shook her head. "Not him," she insisted, "not Strickland. It can't be. Maybe someone in his office intercepted it. Isn't Commander Nys assigned to Uphill? I'd believe it of him. He tried to keep me away from the T'Raijek. Can you check to see whether or not the Admiral ever received the reports?"

Enrico shook his head. "Not from this."

"Then did the messages go to Uphill, or some other way?"

"Uphill, definitely," Enrico said. "That's the normal route, I'd think."

"Then Nys or someone else could have intercepted or copied the communications. Maybe they were never intended for Strickland at all." That explained it, she was sure. Nys was there, always there between Strickland and the messages from Highland. Uphill Port was the hub of the UCN wheel: everything passed through there. He could see it all.

"There's no way of telling. All I have here is a log—we can't get to the message itself without accessing Uphill, and I don't dare try that. That's going to be too well protected for my virus." Enrico's fingers stroked keys; the foil flashed and the log disappeared to be replaced by another menu. "Any other ideas?"

"Let's try another tack," Jemi said. "We know the T'Raijek don't have the crystal or Clan Njialjiad wouldn't have bothered telling the UCN anything. We also assume that the UCN doesn't know exactly what they're looking for, that all Njialjiad told them was that it was something of importance to them—they'll have given the UCN a description of the crystal and they'll have some minor reward for the UCN if they turn it up, but the crystal itself is going to have to be returned."

"Fine—and where do we go from there?"

"I know someone's trying to cover up Kenis's death—they don't want me to look too closely at it. So that's somehow connected with all this as well. Kenis died in December '69, just after Njialjiad took over the Highland embassy. Are there any records of messages between Strickland and the embassy then?"

Again letters danced across the screenfoil. Enrico shook his head. "No."

Jemi scowled. "Damn. I thought . . . " She sighed.

"It would have been a civil matter," Helen commented. "Something between the Highland authorities and the navy. What about checking that?"

"You're right," Jemi said. "Njialjiad wouldn't have necessarily known. Enrico?"

"Already checking." The wait seemed interminable, but after a few minutes, he leaned back in the chair and gestured at the screen. "There it is," he said softly. The words glowed softly on the screenfoil.

To: Commander Nys, Uphill Port—Eyes only

From: Adjunct Michaels, Highland Security

Re: Arrest of Strolov Shipman Louise Martel, suspicion homicide

For a moment, Jemi was literally dizzy. Homicide. Without knowing, she was certain that the murder referred to was Kenis's. The screen seemed to waver, and she clutched Enrico's shoulder tightly. Then she took a deep breath. "Nys again," she said, despite the certainty in her mind.

"You're thinking that it's about your son," Enrico said. His hand touched hers. "You don't know that."

"It could have been on some other matter," Helen commented.

"Easy enough to find out," Enrico said. "We can access navy files—if this Martel was accused of killing a Highlander under normal circumstances, it should be on public record. All we have to do is check naval court-martial proceedings—it shouldn't even be classified if it's a routine matter. I might even be able to find out from here."

He leaned forward, but as he did so, the door to the office was suddenly flung wide. The three of them whirled around to see a quartet of men. The gleaming muzzles of automatic weapons were aimed directly at them.

"Don't move," one of them said tersely. "You're all under arrest."

But Helen was already reaching under her jacket. In a motion that surprised Jemi with its suddenness, she brought out her gun and fired. Jemi cried out.

Then the racket of the guns deafened her.

Ardent had found it easy enough to move within the city. In any large population center, there were shadows enough and cover enough to move at night. An alpha male was humanoid enough and might be taken for a short, fat child in darkness—from a distance. Yet caution was needed as well. If reports reached the T'Raijek embassy here that an alpha had been seen, they would know who it was. There couldn't be more than one or two Njialjiad alphas on Earth at any one time. Ardent himself had killed one of the Njialjiad alphas the night before he'd met Jemi—a private quarrel. Since then, alphas would be stringently accounted for, especially since Ardent's escape from Highland.

Have to stay undercover until Jemi and the rest of the apes makes their move. If the ClanMother here knows for certain that I've come back, the purge of Hlidskjalff will begin again. More of the clan will die. Damn ClanMother Hlidskjalff for deciding to trust the apes. This crystal's been too expensive for all of us.

Ardent moved through the twilight of New York toward the bulk of the UCN tower. There, he found a convenient alley and waited. It was two nights later before he finally saw them: two days of hiding, of cold and hunger, always staying out of sight of the drunks and derelicts who used the alley as a refuge, passageway, and latrine. Two days of dealing with the stench of urine and decaying garbage. Two days in which he came to hate the dirt and filth of humanity and yearn for the clean, open dwellings of his home world.

Giving the apes the crystal was supposed to save them, to give us an ally in the war that will inevitably come. No wonder Njialjiad thinks that the apes are useless—they see this and wonder if every world the apes touch will become like this one.

Ardent pulled the knit cap he wore tighter over his head, staring dourly toward the UCN offices. Two more days. Two more days and then he'd have to try to make his way alone to where the Jardien scoutship waited for them. He wondered if he could really hope to make it there before he was discovered. Njialjiad wouldn't let him live, not this time. He'd never know if there were children of his alive within the Clans.

He'd die here on this stinking, polluted, crowded planet. The humans deserved their death—it was only just. They'd already proven that they couldn't cope with their own evolutionary success. Left alone, evolution would weed them out as it had a million other species throughout the vast universe. But the T'Raijek . . . *We deserve to live. We haven't made the stupid mistakes. We haven't been the aggressors in that war out there. We knew enough to run.*

A familiar walk, a shape he recognized brought Ardent out of his reverie. Jemi, with Enrico and a woman who must have been their contact. They went into the UCN building. Ardent brought a pair of gel lenses from his coat pocket, bringing them before his eyes and adjusting them to full magnification, peering through the wide glass windows of the lobby. He watched the trio move past the guard. As Jemi and her companions nodded and left, Ardent continued to watch. He frowned as he saw the guard reach down and speak into a phone. At the same time, the woman nudged the other guard, who immediately began scanning his array of camera views. But nothing further happened. The guards remained in the lobby; from his limited view, Ardent could see no further action.

By the ClanMother's eggs, what did all that mean? Coincidence, or are they waiting for something to happen? There was little he could do but wait. He watched the flank of the towering building, but no new lights flicked on—the Saliian contact's offices must be on the other side of the building. Ardent settled down beside an overflowing trash container, ignoring the smell of rotting fruit. He waited, tapping his feet impatiently.

Half an hour later, he watched as a black groundcar pulled up in front of the building and parked. Four men got out of the car and moved quickly into the lobby, where they spoke for a moment to the guards, flashing their identification. The guards pointed; the men nodded and moved quickly toward the ranks of elevators. Ardent pocketed the lenses, exhaling sharply.

They knew, then. Somehow they knew. They waited long enough to let Enrico get into the system so they could find out what Jardien was after, and then they made their move. At least it's UCN Intelligence and not a thousand local cops.

Another car pulled up to the front of the building—one man went inside the building, four others moved quickly toward the rear of the building. Ardent grimaced—the odds were suddenly looking worse. Once Jemi was taken away, there'd be little chance to get her back, and he didn't care to think of the consequences. At best, the crystal would simply stay lost, with whatever unknown consequences that might have. At worst, the apes could find the crystal and use the knowledge there without the guidance of the T'Raijek. Perhaps nothing more would happen; or perhaps the apes would stumble across the Traal and tell them where to find the T'Raijek. *Njialjiad's fault. If they'd let*

Hlidskjalff do as we wished, we'd have had an ally against the Traal in time. We might have been able to stop worrying about them.

Ardent waited until the men had gone around the side of the building. Then he ran quickly across the street. He had no time for preparations, for stealth. The apes wouldn't be expecting a frontal assault—they'd think that stupid, and they were probably right. Instead, they were concentrating on keeping Jemi and her friends in. Fine. He'd hit them while they were looking the other way.

The two building guards and one of the UCN people were watching the elevator—he could see them through the lobby windows. He crouched low and reached out to touch one of the street doors, pushing softly with his fingertips: it moved slightly, unlocked. Still, as soon as he opened the doors, they'd turn—he'd only have an instant before they reacted. Their tension was evident in their stances, in the fact that their guns were already out; he'd be surprised if they didn't simply fire on him. Ardent took his own weapon in hand—the neural disruptor that had killed Jemi's attacker the last time he'd been in this city—and checked that its charge was full and the trigger-contact on the most sensitive setting.

So you kill a few more of the apes without giving them the courtesy of aljceri. So what? You're playing it by their rules. Let that bother you and you'll be the one dying on the floor. They're beasts, most of them.

Ardent exhaled as deeply as he could, calming himself. When he was ready to take the next breath, he leaped to his feet. At full running speed, he pushed through the doors and into the lobby.

He fired even as he dove and rolled across the tiles. Glass-tipped darts from the disruptor shattered against the wall alongside the guards. One of them screamed thinly and collapsed as the other two whirled around. Shots were fired wildly, but Ardent had rolled clear and come up on his knees, steadying his aim. He pressed the contact twice, quickly. The disruptor coughed in response. The guards slumped to the floor.

Ardent knew he had to keep moving—the guards' noisy weapons would have alerted the others. He scanned the list of names by the guard post, found Jemi's alias and a floor number. One of the elevator doors was open—he slid past the bodies and into it, punching the button savagely. The doors hissed shut and acceleration pushed against him. As the elevator began to slow, Ardent dropped flat on the floor, his hands wrapped around the disruptor and pointing the muzzle at the doors.

Yes, the floor guard was waiting. Ardent could see the man as the doors began to open—a glimpse of a uniform, a pallid face, and the gun aimed toward the elevator at what would have been chest level for a human. The guard looked as if he were about to shout, his face half-turned toward the right.

Ardent dropped the guard before the man could readjust his aim, and was out of the elevator before the man hit the floor. Ardent could feel a tense, silly grin widening on his face—it was almost too easy. The apes were so damn stupid. They'd underestimated the possibilities from the start.

A long corridor ran from the floor lobby toward the back of the building where the Martelli woman's office was located. Ardent bent low as he looked around the corner. He could see the four Intelligence people gathered in the hallway just outside the office door. They had automatic weapons out. As Ardent watched, one of them kicked the door open and they went in. Ardent surged to his feet, racing down the corridor even as he heard them shout to Jemi and the other two, as he heard the chatter of weapon fire.

Another gun—a small one, by the tiny sound—barked from inside as Ardent reached the door: he saw one of the UCN quartet go down. Ardent bellowed as he came up behind them, trying to distract them. Two of them turned, their weapons swinging around. Then there was nothing but confusion.

Ardent fired, but then something impossibly strong threw him back against a wall. He saw his own blood spattering the front of his jacket as everything shifted into aching slow motion. There was Jemi, her mouth open in a soundless scream, and one of the UCN people bringing his weapon to bear on Ardent. The T'Raijek tried to lift the disruptor, but his right arm would not move. He could only watch, helpless, as that blackened death centered on him. He could see the eyes of the man that held the weapon: there was only blind fury and hatred in them.

There was no time for surprise. Everything was lost in confusion. Jemi could not think—only stand there numbly. The bullets tore Helen Martelli apart before Jemi's eyes. The woman exploded in blood and bits of cloth and flesh, dead in an instant, though her body still moved with her last defiance. The eyes were open as she fell, and then Jemi felt the concussion as Enrico, beside her, returned fire. Jemi screamed with the shot.

She saw Ardent in that moment. Impossibly, the T'Raijek plowed his way into the confusion as Enrico grunted in pain beside her. Jemi stood frozen in panic.

Only one of the intruders was still up, and that one had turned to Ardent. She saw him fire at the alien, saw Ardent flung back against the wall by the impact of a bullet even as he tried to leap away. Jemi knew that the man would fire again, knew that Ardent would then die as Helen had died and that Jemi's turn would be next. She fumbled for the small pistol Helen had forced her to take, somehow got it out and pointed it toward the man. Incongruously, she found herself wondering whether the man might have a family, if he'd kissed his child good-night that evening.

The gun seemed impossibly small and light—a toy. All she had to do was pull the trigger.

She did. There was a percussive roar and the plastic grip grew warm under her fingers. The man yelped like a wounded dog, one shoulder dropping as a circle of red spread over his shirt sleeve. He began to turn toward her and she pulled the trigger again, deafened by the sound of the thing, but surprised that there was so little recoil. The man went to his knees as a spot of red appeared on his chest and he sprayed a wild path of destruction across the wall nearest Jemi.

She pressed the trigger again, and yet again, not realizing that she was screaming wordlessly at the same time, watching the man crumple and die before her even as she kept firing. The horrible thing of death in her hand clicked softly several times before she realized that it was empty, that this was over.

She looked at the carnage in the room. A stomach-wrenching nausea took her and she doubled over, vomiting again and again until there was nothing left in her stomach.

We always have to have something to worry about. Back in the end of the twentieth century, we worried about the rapid changes of society. Now, a little more than a century on, we're worried because we're not changing enough. We think we might have become stagnant. I feel, instead, that we're just at a long, necessary pause. I think we stand on the brink of a new age.

—from a speech by UCN Head
MacWilliams, July 6, 2170.

Shit, we've been pushed off the edge. We're waiting to hit bottom.

—response of a heckler to the above.

CHAPTER THIRTEEN

"Jemi?" The voice was a rough growl, comforting in its familiarity. "Jemi, come on. We have to leave here."

She spat dryly, on her hands and knees. The room smelled of blood and hate and her sickness. She turned her head, her hair drooping over her eyes. Through the tangled strands she saw Ardent. One of the T'Raijek's arms hung limp and useless, cradled in his other hand. Thick brown-red fluid turned the tattered sleeve there dark and ugly, but the blood flow seemed to have somehow stopped. "Helen, Enrico . . ." Jemi said.

"Dead," Ardent answered tersely. "We'll be, too, if we don't get out of here now. From here on in, they won't wait to see if you'll stop first."

"Helen pulled her gun," Jemi said slowly. Her mind was numb, ice-locked. She kept seeing images of the last few minutes before her, Helen's body arcing back, broken. She struggled to sit up and fell back again heavily.

"Helen was a fool, then, and deserved what she got. Look, I'd love to sit here and chat but there's this little group of people who aren't going to be excessively happy about what just happened here. Get up."

"I'm not sure I can yet."

"You'll have to, and I can't help you. Look at me, damn it." Ardent took Jemi's head by the chin and forced her to regard him. "I just got shot for you. You also saved my life and I'm very grateful, but you can't sit here and mope about your decision. It's *over*. The people that are dead are going to stay that way no matter what you do, so you might as well save your own damn skin." The T'Raijek's sarcasm tore at her shock, and she slapped his hand away, struggling to her feet.

"Get away from me," she raged at him suddenly.

"With a hell of a lot of pleasure. Just as soon as we get out of here."

"Wait a minute." Jemi went to Enrico. She touched his neck, feeling for a pulse. "He's still alive," she told Ardent.

"Fine. I'm ecstatic. Let's go."

"We can't leave him."

"We don't have any damn choice. You think we can take him to a hospital? You think that moving him's going to do him any good? You think your staying here will help him at all?" Ardent grimaced suddenly, clenching his teeth, the wrinkled span of his wide face tightening in pain. "Make up your mind, Jemi. I'm leaving while I can."

Jemi watched Ardent pick his way over to the door. When the T'Raijek reached the door, he turned back. "I'm sorry for you, Jemi," he told her gruffly. "I wish things could be more the way we'd both like them to be. Sometimes we don't get that choice." He looked as if he were about to say more, the bald dome of his head smoothing, but then he shrugged. He stepped out of the room.

Jemi glanced down at Enrico. She smoothed his hair, touched his cheek. "Any debt you had to me is paid, Enrico. I wish . . ." She shook her head. "Thank you. I'm sorry."

Jemi stood up. Trying not to look at the gore that littered the room, she followed after Ardent.

Ardent limped badly as they moved down the corridor toward the floor lobby. The elevator was still open, the sprawled body of the guard lying there. Jemi's breath hissed as she saw the body. "Don't look at it," Ardent grumbled. "Come on; we'll take the stairs."

"No," Jemi said. "They'll bring the elevator down to the lobby first, so that we'll *have* to take the stairs. We'll take it down before it's too late to use it."

"And you think there's no one in the lobby waiting for the damn thing to come down? You're worse than a blind youngling, woman, and an omega at that. They'd have us cornered in that."

"Not if we're not there. Get in." Jemi had already stepped over the body of the guard and into the elevator.

"No," Ardent said sharply.

"You can hardly walk now, Ardent. You'll collapse on the stairs."

"Better than getting shot in that contraption."

"Trust me," Jemi said urgently. "Hurry."

Ardent spat; she could see blood in the spittle. "You were heaving up your guts back there, and all the sudden you're a tactician?"

"I want to live, too, T'Raijek. Are you coming?"

Ardent muttered, but he came. Jemi pointed to the access hatch above them. "I'll hoist you up to that—you open it and get on the roof," she said quickly. "I'll send the elevator down and follow you up."

"They'll check there."

"They'll be in a hurry. What would you think if the elevator came down and when the doors opened, it was empty?"

Ardent's mouth lifted in a half-smile. "That it was a diversion. That we'd done it to make them wait while we took the stairs." He shook his head. "They still might look."

"You got a better idea?"

"No," he admitted. "Lift me up."

The alpha was heavier than Jemi had thought. She could barely lift him, and he groaned in pain as she did so. Still, they managed it. Ardent lifted up the hatch and clambered through as Jemi pushed him from below. Then she punched the button for the ground floor. As the doors began to close, Jemi leaped for the roof of the elevator. With Ardent hauling her up with his one good arm, she reached the roof of the elevator. Standing in the noisy darkness of the shaft, she closed the hatch door. The place smelled of grease and steel, and the walls moved by disconcertingly fast. She remained on her hands and knees as the elevator lurched to a halt.

They heard the doors open, then the compartment shook beneath their feet as gunfire rattled deafeningly, tearing holes in the rear wall. "Not taking chances, are they?" Ardent whispered.

They waited. Nothing happened—the compartment remained steady underneath them and no one seemed to enter it. There was a faint shouting that might have come from the lobby, then silence again. The shaft was utter blackness. Jemi reached out and touched Ardent's hand, giving it a questioning squeeze—it was the first time they'd touched. She was surprised at the softness of his skin, like touching one of Kenis's toy bears. "Yes," Ardent whispered back. Jemi began to lift the access door. Light flooded the shaft, but then Ardent forced the hatch back down. In the darkness, he pressed the strange shape of his weapon into her hand.

"You'll have to go first," he told her, "and you'll have to make sure that you take care of anyone who might be there. I can't do it. When I drop down, it's going to be all I can do to stay on my feet. I'll be one easy target. You can't hesitate as you did upstairs."

"I hate what you're forcing me to become," Jemi answered harshly.

"Hate it all you like," he spat. "I'm telling you what your choices are. You can give up anytime you like. Just walk out there with your hands up—maybe they won't shoot first."

"Is there a way this can be set just to stun a person?"

She knew that Ardent looked at her as if she were a madwoman. She heard his mocking, quick laugh. "Not a chance," he said.

Jemi took the alien weapon. She juggled its strange lightness in her hand for a moment, then wrapped her fingers around it. "I hate it," she repeated. "You've made me into a murderer."

"Yeah. And incest and rape are next on the list," he hissed. "You're trying to survive, that's all. Don't you see that?"

Jemi lifted the hatch again. She could see Ardent's eyes glistening in the light, like an old gnome hidden in a cavern. Taking a deep breath, telling herself that she would not let herself think, she crouched above the access and dropped through. Somewhere in the time it took to reach the floor, the last part of her that was still the cold, reserved Highlander died. She could feel the emotions tearing through her gut like a sword.

She was crying when she hit the floor—deep, gasping sobs full of her own pain.

The shock buckled her legs. Through the shimmer of tears, Jemi could see one guard nearby, already turning at the unexpected sound: the woman Helen had called Kathy. Weeping, Jemi brought up the spiraled tube of Ardent's disruptor and pressed the tiny contact on the base of the cylinder. There was no sound, no feeling of anything happening, but the guard's eyes rolled back into her head and she fell. Jemi gave a moan of pain for her death.

The T'Raijek fell into the compartment, striking the floor with a muffled cry and falling to his side. He tried to lever himself up with one hand. Jemi reached down and helped him to his feet. He stared at her tearstained face and said nothing.

They half ran, half stumbled to the doors of the building. Impossibly, there were no guards there. Jemi flung the doors wide. The wind outside was cold on the wetness of her cheeks. They fled like apparitions from some nightmare. They ran across the sidewalk and into the stream of light traffic as people stared at the sight: the weeping, gasping woman; the stumbling, wounded T'Raijek, their clothing disheveled and stained with blood. They goggled, they pointed, they shouted, but no one stopped them.

They darted between the cars and into an alleyway between buildings across the street.

"I've had enough death. I don't want your ghost howling at my soul when it's my time. There are already too many of them."

"When did you get religion, woman?"

"It's not religion. I can already hear them, Ardent."

The doctor's office, in a Greensboro, North Carolina, clinic, was dingy and oppressive. The walls, once white enamel, were now a nondescript shade of mottled gray. The cabinets that held the assortment of medicines were the same shade of age, with flimsy sheet-metal doors that, bowed, would not close entirely. The doctor looked as if he had grown old with his clinic; a balding, paunchy man with stooped shoulders, his stained gown open over a frayed sweater. A nervous fear wobbled his jowls as he worked on Ardent's wounds. A frozen, meaningless smile curved his chapped lips and he muttered idle reassurances as he swabbed the cuts with antibiotics.

The doctor owned a vivicate, a thin, plain-faced man who stood in one corner, gibbering soft words. Jemi couldn't tell if the shivering of the vivicate's body was the legacy of the rekindling or simple fear. She ignored the vivicate and turned to the doctor.

"How soon can the T'Raijek move?" Jemi snapped.

The doctor glanced over his shoulder at him. "I don't know. He's—he's not like you or me. I'm doing what I can, but—" The man's voice had the twang of the South.

"You'd better be. If something happens to him, you'll pay for the mistake." Jemi brandished Ardent's weapon at the old man, who shivered and turned back to his work. Ardent's eyes narrowed as he looked at Jemi, trying to ignore the doctor's prodding.

There had been a change in her, deep inside. She'd cut off part of herself, locked it away to leave only this hard, brutal woman behind. Ardent had seen it ever since they'd left the UCN building. She'd hauled him stumbling alongside her when the blood loss had threatened to take his consciousness; she'd badgered him, refusing to let him give in to the beckoning oblivion. Two blocks away from the UCN building, Jemi had come upon a woman and a man fondling each other in a parked car. She'd yanked open the door, hauling the man out with pure adrenaline strength. When the man tried to resist, she'd used the disruptor on him and ordered the frightened, hysterical woman to drive them north. They'd left New York that way, leaving the woman behind after crossing the bridge. She'd continued north for several miles, then abandoned the car as well, parking it on a public street in Stamford. There, she'd commandeered the hoverflit of a teenager returning from a late date.

It had not been so easy with the kid, who was obviously a little drugged and full of foolish heroics. He grabbed for her; she flung him back with a warning. The kid didn't listen. Jemi used the disruptor on him when he'd tried to take it from her. She'd left the body slumped in the backseat and flown them south for hours. By that time, Ardent had been only semiconscious from his wounds, and Jemi had left him in the 'flit in deep woods south of Greensboro. She'd come back hours later with this doctor in his own 'flit. With the help of the doctor's vivicate, they'd hauled Ardent in and gone back to the clinic. Ardent had regained consciousness to find the old man working on him at gunpoint.

Jemi looked ravaged, like some demonic thing, her hair filthy and matted, her clothing soiled with dirt and blood. Deep circles of exhaustion ringed her bloodshot eyes. And those eyes themselves: they blazed with a ferocious intensity. Looking at Jemi made Ardent uncomfortable. He did not like the being that stared back at him. *I hate what you're forcing me to become.* Ardent remembered her words from the elevator, and he knew the truth of them. She had indeed become something else.

For the first time, he began to wonder if GreatMother Hlidskjalff had known what she was doing—if the apes were all like this, if they all had these monsters inside, they were more dangerous than anyone suspected.

"Oow! Damn you!" Ardent howled as the doctor probed at the shoulder wound.

"I'm sorry. My hand slipped. It's your friend. She makes me nervous."

"She should. She does the same to me."

"I don't know what I can do to help you," the old man muttered. "I'd give you an anesthetic or a sprayskin solution, but I don't know how your metabolism would react. I don't even know if the antibiotics will do any good."

"Just do it and worry about it later," Jemi told the man. She fiddled with a dusty foilscreen in the corner, flicking across the channels. Colored light from the screen threw changing hues over her face. "Treat him like he's human—he's enough of a son of a bitch for it to work."

The doctor sighed. He looked at Ardent's wizened, bald face. "I'll do what I can."

"That's very comforting." Ardent's voice was full of overdone sarcasm. He closed his eyes and lay back on the table, trying to ignore the pain.

". . . two of the dead were Saliian terrorists. That was confirmed by UCN Intelligence only a few minutes ago." The newscaster's voice made Ardent open his eyes again. He pushed the doctor aside and sat up. Jemi was watching the screen intently.

"It's not known how many more were involved in the action, but at least two others were seen leaving the building and are being sought by the authorities," the newscaster continued. "One of them is a woman who signed the register of the building as Alicia Colter. The other, according to witnesses, may have been a T'Raijek alpha male. The last, we repeat, is still only a rumor. The T'Raijek embassy has made no comment on this, though contacts within that embassy have hinted that there is a possible link between this sighting and a murder on Highland two months ago in which a Highland woman and a renegade Clan Hlidskjalff alpha male are being sought. Commander Nys of the UCN navy confirmed today that Jemi Charidilis, the Highland woman, and Ardent Hlidskjalff fled Highland and were known to have sought asylum on Salii—"

Jemi reached out with a curse and flicked off the foilscreen. The doctor stared at the two of them; the vivicate huddled deeper into his corner. She ignored both of them, speaking to Ardent. "Nys again," she said to the T'Raijek. Then, to the doctor: "How soon?"

"I've done what I can. He needs to rest. So do you."

Jemi's haunted eyes closed for a moment, opened again. "I can't rest yet. Not here. Doctor, what do you have that'll put someone out for several hours?"

He shrugged. "Ten cc of Isonir would do it, I suppose."

"Then get the injection ready." As the doctor began to rummage in the disarray of his shelves, Jemi turned to Ardent. "We can get to the west coast, lie low there for a few days, then fly from there to the rendezvous," she told him. Ardent saw the plea in her pain-filled eyes, and understood: *I don't want to kill again. Let the lie go through and I won't have to kill this one. No more ghosts.* Ardent simply nodded.

The old man filled the syringe. "Fine," Jemi told him. "Lie down on the floor. Then give yourself the injection." They both saw the hope that flared in the man.

"You're not going to kill me," he breathed.

Jemi gestured with the gun. "Lie down," she ordered. "Do as I said." She watched as the doctor plunged the needle into his arm, as his eyes slowly closed and his breathing relaxed.

"Good," Ardent rumbled as the doctor's breathing deepened. But in that moment, the vivicate gave a thin scream. He lunged for Jemi, and Jemi cuffed the vivicate down with the handle of the disruptor. She aimed the weapon at him; Ardent thought that she would kill him, as she'd killed the others.

But she stopped. Muscles moved across her face in indecision.

"It's just a vivicate," he told her. "It's already dead. Do it."

Jemi glared at him. "It shouldn't be that easy," she said. "No matter what, it should never be that easy. They shouldn't have killed Doni, either." The vivicate moaned, staring up at her silently. "Get the Isonir," she told Ardent.

He groaned and hopped down from the table, stretching his arm tentatively and grimacing as the newly stitched wound pulled. He did as she asked, holding the filled syringe out to her. "Inject him," she said.

Ardent did so. When the vivicate's eyes had closed, Ardent threw the syringe across the room. "Now we tell our hotshot pilot to come get us tomorrow night while they're all looking for us across the continent. Is that what you're thinking?"

"Most if it," Jemi said. "We call the Saliian, right? Only you're the only one going with him. I'm staying here. I'm going to Uphill."

"Don't be stupid. You can't do anything there."

"It's where I have to go to get the rest of the answers. With what Enrico found, I know that the navy was involved with Ken's death. I'm sure that Nys, especially, knows more than he's saying. I'm going."

"You couldn't possibly do anything alone," Ardent growled.

"I'm supposed to take you along? I might as well wear a sign saying 'Come get me.' There's no way we can disguise you. Shut up and think, T'Raijek. You can't do me any good now, and I need you to tell HeadFather Jardien what we learned—tell him what happened."

"I'm not going to let you do this."

Jemi sighed. She sat in a chair, leaning back and closing her eyes while she continued the argument tiredly. "Ardent, listen. Once the UCN realizes that a Saliian ship left from this area, they'll think we're both gone. Security'll relax. I still have the names of Saliian contacts here—I can get new ID. At least this way I have a chance. There's no way to get you to Uphill, and no way to learn anything from here. You go back to Salii; I'll meet you there afterward."

Ardent rubbed his shoulder and grimaced. "Not likely," he told her. "You go on to Uphill and the only place I'm going to see you again is during the footage of your trial."

"Don't be so pessimistic," Jemi told him, her eyes still closed. Ardent could hardly hear her.

"Where do you get the idea that I'm being pessimistic? I *actually* think it's far more likely that they'll kill you outright, especially after the bloodbath yesterday. All I'm going to see are the pictures of your shrouded body on some port floor."

Jemi was too tired to even shrug. "If that's the way it has to be, fine."

Ardent glared at her, resisting the temptation to shake her awake, to cause some reaction in that haggard face. "I'll never understand the things that turn you apes into fanatics," he said. "Somebody sure pushed all the right buttons for you. Listen, we'll give the pilot the signal tomorrow night—the delay won't matter much. That's reasonable, Jemi."

She didn't answer. "Jemi?" Ardent said again.

Ardent looked over at her. Her head back against the chipped paint of the wall, she was asleep. Ardent sighed, groaning as he hobbled over to her. He took one of the lab coats from a hook on the wall and covered her with it.

Commander Nys stared unsmilingly at the woman facing him

across the tatami mat. Both of them were dressed in a white, judo-style *gi;* each of them wore black *hakama,* the skirted trousers of the samurai, and their feet were bare. Nys was empty-handed, the woman gripped a *boken*—a wooden sword—in her left hand, holding it at her side as if it were in a scabbard.

Except for the mat and changing screens to one side, the room was empty. On one wall, there was a black-and-white photograph of an elderly Japanese man—O'Sensei, the Great Teacher. Around the picture were arranged a few banners and a shelf with a simple arrangement of flowers.

Nys took a deep, slow breath, and then the two bowed to each other. The woman gave Nys no chance for another breath. There was no pause. Even as they straightened from the bow, the woman quickly drew the boken in a fluid motion, raising it for a strike as she shouted, rushed toward Nys, and struck for his head with full force.

But Nys was no longer there. As the woman's blow came down, he'd moved aside, his hand coming up as he'd pivoted. His right hand snaked between her arms, grasping the long handle of the boken between the woman's own hands. Nys moved with the motion of the strike, continuing it, and then the woman was flying through the air. She flipped easily, rolling across the mat like a wheel down the length of her arm and across her back. Her free hand slapped the mat with a resounding noise, and she bounded back to her feet. Nys had laid the boken on the mat and backed away a few paces. The woman took the boken on the run and attacked Nys once more, this time with a side cut.

Nys moved as if in a dance, circling and moving inside the circle of the blade. He grasped the boken's handle, pivoted—his partner was flung head over heels and crashed into the mat. Nys laid down the boken; the woman sprang to her feet immediately to attack again. Again and again the pattern was repeated: the woman would attack; Nys would evade the blow and throw her, taking the boken in his own hands only to give it back to her once again. They continued until they were both running with sweat, Nys's short, dark hair plastered to his head.

After another of the throws, Nys dropped to his knees, nodding to the woman. She stopped in midcharge, relaxed, and sank into the same *seiza* position. They bowed to each other, then turned to the picture on the wall and bowed to the photograph. For several seconds, Nys merely sat there, his eyes closed, droplets of sweat rolling down his face as he breathed in deep, long breaths through his nose. Then he opened his eyes once more.

"You were very focused today, Akira," the woman said to Nys.

"Thank you, Carol," Nys replied. He still had not smiled, but his voice was warm. "Can you stay for a while longer? It's your turn to throw me around."

"Fine—I don't have to be back on duty for another two hours. I want you to show me that Shihonage throw." Carol lay back on the mat, brushing away her short bangs and wiping her forehead with a cloth taken from under her gi top. She closed her eyes. "God, that felt good. How were my attacks?"

Nys didn't allow himself to relax as Carol did. He sat stiffly in seiza. "They were exactly what they should have been," he said. "You gave me all your energy."

"What kind of attack are you going to make with all the information OIA's feeding you, Akira?"

The only visible sign that the question had registered with Nys was a slow blinking of his eyes. "Perez mentioned that you asked him about the Charidilis woman again yesterday," Carol persisted.

"Your lieutenant can't control his mouth, Carol."

"That's why he's a clerk and a lieutenant and will stay that way for the rest of his career. Still, he's useful—I always know where my sensei's interests lie." Carol sat up, the hakama draped around her. "You don't think that she's gone back to Salii, then."

"I didn't say that."

"But you suspect it, despite the fact that the alert's dropped two stages since the shield detected the Saliian cruiser leaving Earth a month ago."

"Carol, when we bow, we always place our left hand on the mat first. Then the right follows. The right will come off the mat first as well, after the bow. That custom dates back centuries to when the samurai carried swords. That way, even if you were attacked during a bow, you could quickly draw your weapon. It's unlikely such a treacherous thing would happen, but unlikely does not mean impossible."

"I think it's even less a possibility than 'unlikely,' Akira," Carol insisted.

"Put yourself in her place. Think like your opponent. We interrupted them in the process of retrieving information. The program they used to invade the system hadn't dug down into the highly classified areas yet, though it managed to wreck the hierarchy of files rather thoroughly. They were looking for information pertaining to naval communications. They didn't get all they were after, mostly because they would need to access the mainframe here in Uphill. So—where would you go next?"

"That doesn't mean they have to come here. They could go anywhere where there's a computer tied into this network—" Carol stopped. Her lips curled in thought. "Their computer wrecker's dead," she said. "And Charidilis . . ."

". . . doesn't have the expertise." A faint smile ghosted across Nys's face. It looked alien there. "Good. Part of responding to an attack is knowing from what direction it is likely to come. Understand your opponent and you begin to understand yourself. In some ways, I think I might like this Charidilis." Carol gave him a shocked look that he ignored. "Now—let's work on that Shihonage," he said.

"I'm in charge of Uphill security, Aki. Tell me if I should be watching for Charidilis."

"I've been training you to always be aware, Carol."

"And that's all you're going to say?"

Nys bowed to the picture of O'Sensei. "You should talk less on the mat," he told Carol as she swung to seiza and bowed with him. "Learn by watching and by doing."

Nys took up the boken and rose to his feet as Carol did the same. Again, they bowed to each other. "Now," he told her, "I'll attack—you do the Shihonage to me, and then we'll start taking it apart."

"And Charidilis?"

"Worry about the attack that is coming at you now. The rest can wait an hour."

If the T'Raijek demonstrate anything, it is that no matter how different the bodies, there is likely to be an evolutionary similarity between all intelligent species. Despite the physical differences, despite the varying instincts, despite the (to our minds) bizarre social habits of the aliens, they still obey the one prime code of us all: you do what you have to do to survive.

—from *The T'Raijek: An Analysis* by R.M. Jordan; Darwin Press, 2169.

CHAPTER FOURTEEN

By the time Jemi reached Miami, she was a skinhead—the latest new/old renegade fashion of the young. If Jemi was perhaps too old to truly be one of them, at least her age was hidden behind the look. She'd gained the anonymity of the bizarre. The ridge of her skull was lined with small twinkling lights in the shape of a star. She'd lost weight, twenty pounds or more, and her face was stark and hollow-cheeked. Her cheek was rounded with a plug of jimsa, the mild narcotic of the skinheads, and she kept her gaze averted from the more normal-looking people around her, as the skinheads also did. The skinhead rebellion was one of passive defiance. They did nothing to anyone; they avoided confrontation except by the way they looked. The jimsa helped that: Jemi had tried the actual narcotic only once, and found herself in a semi-stupor for hours. After that, she simply chewed licorice, and spat out the black fluid as if it were the bitter jimsa.

In Miami, she contacted one of Jardien's people and arranged for a flight to Paris. Within the UCN itself, there were no longer tedious border checks. Her identification had been in her purse, but no one asked for it. In Paris she'd stayed two weeks with money lent her by the Miami agents, then contacted one of the locals who owned a cosmetics/hairstyling shop. There the severe skinhead "died," to be replaced by a more fashionable version—still hairless but far more elegant. She'd moved on to Rome at the advice of the Parisian.

In Rome another of the contacts had been made, and she'd booked passage with them to Uphill as their niece. The papers were made by a London contact and shipped to her in Rome.

In truth, Jemi didn't expect to pass through the gates from Rome Port to the Uphill shuttle. The Parisian contact had assured her that the detection devices in Rome dated from the terrorist-dominated times of the early twenty-first century. The Susan D'Etrang documents held up as she purchased the tickets. The clerk there glanced idly at her ID, looked up for a moment to be certain that the face was similar enough to that in the ID's holo, and stamped the gate pass. She went back to her "family" with the tickets. Moving through the gate security was just as simple, though once again she separated from her companions in case there was trouble. No one noticed the presence of Ardent's disruptor, strapped to her thigh underneath her full peasant skirt. The gates were built to detect metal and explosives—the plastic, electrically charged disruptor did nothing to the sensors.

When the shuttle finally taxied down the runway and climbed into the air, Jemi began to relax. Her "aunt" patted her hand. As the sky outside the window turned from blue to deep blue-black, the knot inside Jemi's stomach began to slowly relax.

At Uphill, the passengers were herded through the microgravity central port into the spun sections, where their documents were once again checked. That was expected—Uphill was partially a military installation, and the procedure was routine.

Uphill was as grimy and bustling as ever—like Highland, an installation well past its prime, built during the brief outward push of humanity a century before. New coats of paint did little to hide the worn look of Uphill—the same look that all of the UCN's holdings shared. There were perhaps more uniformed guards about than Jemi remembered, but that in itself wasn't unusual—during the times of crisis between Salii and the UCN, that was normal enough as well. She handed her documents to the clerk at the check-in line, watched him examine it, stamp the ticket, and hand it back to her. Jemi smiled back to her companions and walked through the gate into the lobby.

Lulled by the ease with which she'd made it to Uphill, Jemi was too surprised to react when a woman stepped in front of her. At the same moment, two guards materialized on either side of her. The woman stared at Jemi and nodded as if to herself. "Jemi Charidilis," she said, "I'm Carol McGinnis, head of Security for Uphill. You're under arrest."

Entirely naked, Bearer Njialjiad stood on the sands of the Deep Pit with the population of Embassy Salii arrayed in seats around her. Her feet were planted in the middle of a discolored oval of red-brown, the sands there stained by the blood of a Njialjiad female youngling, whose spirit would now be watching above to judge the match. Across the wide pit, ClanMother Hlidskjalff stood in her own bloodcircle. Bearer Njialjiad smirked at the ClanMother's appearance: Hlidskjalff's fur had grown dark over the cuts inflicted during the fight with Njialjiad's predecessor, and the ClanMother was lean. Her fur lacked the healthy sheen of Njialjiad's, and the twinned mounds of flesh that covered her vaginal opening were a weak pink, not the gleaming, brilliant red of Njialjiad's own. Hlidskjalff looked old and tired. Her elongated face drooped; she did not even bother to look up as the omegas filed into the chamber to take the seat in the upper tiers. In the heat of the lamps, Njialjiad could sense a quick victory.

She would win this *aljceri*. ClanMother Hlidskjalff might have recovered physically from her last battle, but the ClanMother's spirit had fled. Even her youngling's spirit could not support her. Hlidskjalff knew that she was the last, Njialjiad was certain. The ClanMother must know that after this night, Clan Njialjiad would hold all the apish embassies.

Already the Bearer was planning her first decrees. First she would have Hlidskjalff's younglings killed, along with any of the omegas that asked to share in that death. She would send the ClanMother's two alphas to her own omegas' chambers. The alpha Hlidskjalff with Charidilis would be told to come here for his death. She would make certain that the crystal was found and destroyed, no matter what that cost.

With unanimity assured, Njialjiad could end this foolish rebellion of Clan Hlidskjalff. Together with the ClanMothers of Highland and Earth, the ClanMothers Njialjiad would petition the GreatMothers for the embassies to be removed. Then the GreatMothers would meet and declare all the works of the hated Clan Hlidskjalff forfeit. The new GreatMother Hlidskjalff would be forced to recant all the deeds of the renegade GreatMother before her, and the embassies would be closed.

Then . . . then all the mounting fears would begin to ease. The T'Raijek could deal with the apes as they should have been dealt with from the beginning. There would be no worry about their becoming like the Traal. The GreatMothers and all the clans would be safe again.

It would all be over. She had trained since birth for this moment. She'd nurtured on the hatreds of the old Bearer Njialjiad, she'd suckled on the bitter taste of her fears.

The brass horns sounded from the last tier—the eldest omegas had been seated. Njialjiad took a deep breath. The lights around the sloping sides of the pit dimmed, leaving only the two combatants in light. Njialjiad held up her hands, palms toward herself. She let her curved talons slide out from the padded fur to tip the wide, fat fingers with deadly natural knives. Across from her, Hlidskjalff had done the same. As challenger, the ritual demanded that Njialjiad make the first move. She did so now, attacking with no feint all, charging across the pit toward Hlidskjalff as blooded sand kicked up under her.

Hlidskjalff, unexpectedly, did not move. In the brief instant before contact, Njialjiad thought that perhaps the ClanMother would simply bare her throat as if already conquered and let Njialjiad rip the life from her.

But in that last instant, Hlidskjalff turned aside. The ClanMother moved with a quickness and determination that unnerved Njialjiad. Hlidskjalff's strength surprised the Bearer. Njialjiad's twisting blow caught only air, but Hlidskjalff's claws tore fur, ripping away one of Njialjiad's nipples on the left side. Warm blood began streaming down Njialjiad's body as she danced away from another slicing blow from Hlidskjalff. The ClanMother let the Bearer retreat: Hlidskjalff still had not moved from her bloodcircle.

Njialjiad knew that if it weren't for the draught of bloodbane that both combatants had taken before the ritual battle, she would be screaming in agony. She refused to look down at the wound, knowing that if she did so she might be sick. The females might be the ones to die in *aljceri*, but none of them were BeastCaptains like the alphas, accustomed to fighting. Hlidskjalff, two meters away, flicked her claws at Njialjiad, spattering the Bearer's face with her own blood in mockery.

For the first time, Njialjiad saw the deception of Hlidskjalff, and she was furious. She should have known—the T'Raijek were all caught in the web of Hlidskjalff's machinations, and she'd been duped as well, thinking that the ClanMother was tired and already defeated. Njialjiad scowled at her own stupidity; the expression evoked a short bark of laughter from the ClanMother. Hlidskjalff hissed at Njialjiad in a whisper that the lower ranks of the gallery could plainly hear. "Did you think I'd give you my throat that easily, Bearer? If you did, then Njialjiad is still going to be Second Clan in Salii, and it will be one of your daughters that will have to revenge you."

Njialjiad knew better than to respond to the taunt. She began to circle, the ClanMother turning to keep her in front. *Because of your stupidity, you're going to have to end this quickly,* she thought. *By the eggs, I'm already stiffening up. She knew exactly where to cut me.* Hlidskjalff cuffed at Njialjiad once, but otherwise let her circle without reaction. "Didn't you learn the lesson of your mother, Bearer?" Hlidskjalff scoffed. "Didn't you know that she was as overconfident as you?"

Njialjiad paced around Hlidskjalff, a full circle. She could see the stain of her blood where it dribbled, staining the sands of the pit. Her mind was racing. Any thoughts she'd had before the combat were useless now. She had never visualized that Hlidskjalff would strike so quickly, so deeply. *You can't rush her again; it didn't work last time and you're even slower now.* Njialjiad burned at the deception of the ClanMother, and with that thought, the glimmering of an idea came to her.

Deliberately, the Bearer staggered, then caught herself; she saw the ClanMother begin to move with that motion, then hold back. Njialjiad knew then that the ClanMother's slowness was only part deception. *She saved herself for one blow, hoping it would weaken me. She'll wait until she sees her opening.* Njialjiad let her breath become audible. A rustling had gone around the gallery as Njialjiad staggered, so she knew that the raking of Hlidskjalff's claws had done terrible damage to her front. Njialjiad staggered again as if unable to keep her feet any longer, letting one clawed hand fall in the sand. As Hlidskjalff leaped from her circle to attack, Njialjiad flung a handful of sand toward the ClanMother, blinding her for a second. With the same motion, the Bearer slashed at the ClanMother. Hlidskjalff howled as the talons opened up new furrows in her flesh. With fury, Hlidskjalff struck back, and then the two closed. They tore at each other in rage—as the gallery rose to their feet in a strange, tense silence; as new blood darkened the ground beneath them.

It was difficult to tell which of them fell first. Both were torn and battered, their fur matted by a gritty mixture of blood and sand. Only slowly did the watching T'Raijek realize that it was Hlidskjalff who lay panting and glaze-eyed on the floor of the pit, that it was the ClanMother who keened the cry of sorrow to her kin and laid her head back so that Njialjiad could, with one brutal slash, rip her throat open.

A torrent of scarlet gushed out to form a new bloodcircle.

Njialjiad raised her hand in triumph and let the claws slowly retract. In the glaring quiet, the gallery bowed to her. Those of Clan Njialjiad gave a shout in unison. Clan Hlidskjalff merely stared.

Commander Nys had not been certain how he'd felt about Charidilis after his first meeting with her. Then, he'd come away with an impression of a person under great mental strain, after the loss of her son and the attack on her ship. The reports in the tabloids painted her as some kind of rabid, hard-edged fanatic. They did all they could to make the woman seem bloodthirsty, short of saying that she filed her teeth and ate her victims. Nys, though, could understand how a person might be driven to do things that she wouldn't otherwise have considered possible. He'd certainly done things himself that a younger Nys would have considered totally out of character.

He suspected that he was about to do another.

The woman Carol shepherded into Nys's office was hardly recognizable as the same Jemi Charidilis that Nys recalled. That one had been a definite Highlander, k'lyged and coldly distant even when angry. She'd borne little resemblance to this Jemi—emaciated, shaven-headed, and still defiant despite her capture. There was a molten quality in this one's eyes, an inferno fueled by some depths in her spirit that Nys had not suspected. He'd thought the old Highlander simply pitiable. Strangely, he found that he felt more kinship with this one. He had more sympathy for her now.

And more caution.

Carol sat the prisoner on the chair before Nys's desk. Her hands were bound in static-charged cuffs and she was clothed in ugly, ill-fitting green clothing. She stared, her eyes sunken into her hollow face but still extraordinarily vital, not at all beaten. He could see the tension in the muscles of her arms and knew that the woman fought against her bonds, that if at any moment they were suddenly released, Charidilis would be moving at the same time. The hatred in her gaze told Nys that she would not flee, but hurl herself at him, as if he were an enemy.

She's been turned into a strange dual-faced monster. She is rage and yet she is softness. She would kill and yet weep at the same time. It is not fair that this was done to her.

Nys kept his face stiff and neutral, his hands folded precisely on the desk in front of him, the right hand under the left. He turned to Carol. "Captain, you may leave us."

The security chief's face revealed her surprise at that. "Commander, my orders—"

"Your orders have just been countermanded," Nys told her. "I'll take any responsibility for that. You may leave the key for her bonds."

He could see the curiosity in his student's face, and he could also see that she knew him well enough—as commander and as instructor—to know that protest was futile. She gave a shrug and then a more proper salute. "As you wish, sir." She hesitated. "It will have to go in my report, Commander."

"I'm aware of that, Captain. I expect you to follow procedure."

"Yes, sir. I'll be outside, then, to take the prisoner back to her cell." Carol laid a small plastic case on Nys's desk, which Nys slid to one side. The Commander glanced back to Jemi as Carol left the room. He was still composing his opening statement when Charidilis spoke in a surprisingly strong voice.

"I know what you've done, Nys. I know you've intercepted messages intended for Strickland from the T'Raijek embassies. I know that it must have been you who ordered *Starfire* attacked. I know about shipman Louise Martel. 'Suspicion Homicide,' wasn't it, Commander? That wouldn't concern my son, would it?"

Nys felt the jolt deep inside, as if the woman had punched him in the kidneys. None of it showed on his face, but the pain was there. *She knows more than anyone thought she ever would. And she doesn't realize how explosive all that information is, or she would have already used it.* He took a deep, calming breath. *Blend with the attack.*

"You've found the outlines of truth, Holder Charidilis," he told her. "I'd caution you to realize that truth is a very deceptive concept."

"You would," Jemi spat out. She wriggled in her seat. Muscles tugged against her restraints. Nys took his gaze away from her, looking instead at one of the drawings on the wall: "Crane and Pond." He'd done the ink drawing himself, back when he'd first embarked on this course he was following, when he'd accidentally seen the first communiqué between Strickland and the Clan Njialjiad. The crane was caught in the first moment of flight, as if startled by something hidden in the shallow waters of the pond. Nys had often watched the cranes in his native Japan; he knew that when frightened they would take flight. A frightened crane would circle in watchful silence for a time; sometimes, as if certain that the threat was real, it would sound an eerie call over the waters, and the others of its kind would take to the air, filling the sky with their splendor, a magnificent array of wide, white wings and long bodies.

Looking at the picture forced Nys to recall the night he'd done the drawing and the emotions that had driven the bamboo brush. "I'll tell you what is true, Holder Charidilis," he said without looking at her. "I've seen messages for Commander Strickland. I do know that shipman Martel was implicated in your son's death, and that the entire incident was"—Nys paused—"hidden." He heard the sudden intake of breath and knew that his words had stunned Charidilis. "I had nothing to do with the attack on your ship, however. Holder Charidilis, you have several parts of the puzzle. But you draw the wrong conclusions about the entire picture."

Now he looked at her. The pain inside the woman was very near the surface now. The wound in her soul had never healed after the death of her son. It had only just begun to scab over when the rape of her memory had torn it open again, gouging it even deeper. Nys could feel her agony as if it were his own. He wished that he could show her that he felt her inner pain, but knew that she would reject any such admission.

"The picture I see tells me that you were responsible for my son's death, Nys," she told him. "The picture I see tells me that you'd kill an innocent child to get what the T'Raijek I ferried had. That picture tells me that you're a goddamn bastard that deserves to die the way Kenis did."

Jemi spoke with such quiet force that Nys trembled. Her softness enhanced the power of the words far more than any shout might have. "I would feel the way you feel in your place," he told her. "Despite that, you are mistaken."

Jemi spat. The globule landed on his desk just before his hands. Nys stared at the thick puddle. "A Highlander would not have done that," he said.

"I've changed a lot since then, Nys. You've taught me a lot of nasty things."

"Tell me what else you've learned."

"It isn't obvious enough for you?" Jemi shook her head; shiplight gleamed on the bare skin over her skull. "You tell *me* something, Nys. What did Njialjiad offer you for my son's life? What would they give you in exchange for the crystal?"

"Technology," Nys answered calmly. "Safe, cheap power and new materials. Energy to rekindle our society. That's what the T'Raijek offered—a chance for mankind to get back on the path we lost a century ago. But they didn't offer that to me, Holder Charidilis. They offered that to those with more power than the commanding officer of Uphill Port. The offer was made to the UCN and the naval heads. To Admiral Strickland."

"Admiral Strickland is one of the few people who have shown me any kindness at all, Commander Nys, and he warned me that there were people under him that he couldn't trust. I hope you're not trying to turn me against him."

"Louise Martel was a shipman on *Strolov,* Holder."

"I saw the log of a communiqué to you from the Highland Security chief concerning Martel, Commander. Are you telling me that I shouldn't draw the obvious conclusion about why the whole affair was hushed up?"

"You didn't see the communiqué itself, Holder," Nys reminded her. "Let me ask you a few other rhetorical questions. Doesn't it seem strange that an Admiral of the navy would spend as much time aboard a cruiser instead of at his desk? Since you confirm to me that the ship that attacked you wasn't a Jardien pirate, doesn't that cast immediate suspicion on the ship that was so readily within range of your distress call? Doesn't that make you wonder if perhaps Strickland didn't have advance knowledge of the attack—that the entire episode was designed to make you trust him so that if you found this missing crystal you'd contact him immediately? Doesn't it strike you as strange that there have been so many messages between Strickland and the Clan Njialjiad?" Nys hammered home the points with quiet force. The woman's eyes narrowed as he spoke, and he knew that she had the same doubts, despite her words.

"I've followed this matter for two years, Holder," he continued. "I've checked on many things concerning Admiral Strickland. When I learned of the incident on Highland with Martel and your son, I simply asked for the details from Highland."

"It *was* Kenis," she whispered, and he knew then that she hadn't actually known, only guessed. Her eyes filmed over, and he looked away from her pain, giving her some privacy. With her hands cuffed, she couldn't hide the grief; still, she made no attempt to disguise it, sitting stiffly in the chair as tears gathered in her eyes.

"I'm sorry for you, Holder," he said. He let some of his empathy show in his voice, and she looked up, her eyes more angry than sad.

"What happened? Tell me how it happened," she insisted.

"I wish I knew. I tried to find out. All I learned was that the crèche-mother said that your son disappeared from the crèche not long after a naval shipman had come by asking for him. Beyond that, everything is surmise. Martel was indicted briefly, but the charges were dropped."

"Then let me talk to Martel," Jemi said.

"Martel's dead. An accident aboard *Strolov* two months later."

Jemi's eyes were dry when Nys glanced back at her. The hardness had returned to her. She stared at him flatly. "Why doesn't that surprise me?" she said. "Do you know why Martel wanted Kenis and not me?"

"I don't," Nys admitted. "The T'Raijek alpha you'd ferried was killed the day before—perhaps that was also Martel. Then Kenis suffered his accident the next day. Perhaps you would have been next if Martel hadn't been arrested the next morning. After that, Strickland couldn't afford to have anything happen." Nys's eyes went back to "Crane and Pond": *What was in the waters that startled you so much?* he wondered. *What's hidden there?* "Strickland had your movements traced. He even went so far as to try to retrace the steps of your vivicate. He pulled the Customs reports for all of you."

"You say all this so well that it sounds rehearsed, Commander. I haven't seen one bit of proof for it, though."

"I have it all locked away."

"Convenient."

"I hope to use it against Strickland and his supporters in the UCN. They violated our laws; they destroyed people to gain power. I wonder, if they were given this gift of the T'Raijek, how they would use it."

"When do you apply for sainthood, before or after the trial?"

Nys grimaced. "I'm not at all a saint, Holder. I've too many faults of my own, and I admit that I wouldn't mind my chance to wield some power. I like to feel that I might use it better than those who have it now, but I don't deny that I'd be willing to fight for my position. But I'm not a casual murderer. I'm not one who would kill your son—not for this crystal or anything that the T'Raijek offered. I wouldn't sell my soul for power."

"You make pretty speeches, Commander." Jemi shook her head. "It's a pity I can't believe them."

Nys stared at the woman, measuring her. At last he nodded. He swiveled his chair around, rose in a lithe motion, and went to the back wall. Under the photograph of himself on the mat, he opened a small, long drawer that Jemi had not noticed before. From the compartment, he took a long bundle wrapped in velvet.

He laid it on the desk. Pulling the wrapping back, he revealed a scabbarded katana, a long, curved sword. He drew the blade from the scabbard. The wicked, thin edge gleamed in the overhead lights. He put the sword on the desk before Jemi, the handle to her right, the edge facing the Commander. Then he sat again. He reached over to the case Carol had left behind and pressed a contact on its surface. The steel bracelets encircling Jemi's wrists parted, leaving her hands free. Nys folded his own hands on the desk.

"The katana is nearly five hundred years old," he told her. "I bought it from a dealer in Japan who gave me a long, detailed history of the blade. Most of it was almost certainly fanciful, however entertaining. Still, every time I hold this, I can feel the many hands that have used it in the past, and I delude myself with the thought that perhaps they were also people like me—frail, imperfect, but wanting to obey what we feel is right. Please, pick it up."

Jemi took the sword, gingerly, holding the unfamiliar weight of water-hardened, layered steel.

"It's an archaic weapon," Nys continued, "but one that I still revere. I wish that all fighting had to be done with swords, so that when we killed, we would have to be close to the person whose life we take. Then we would deliberately have to make our choice. Fighting with ships, fighting with guns—it's all too easy, too impersonal. We've both killed, Holder Charidilis. I fought in the last open battle with the Family Jardien pirates, and the ship I commanded destroyed one of their cruisers, so I know that people died at my hand. It might have been that if I could have seen their faces, if I could have listened to the tales of their lives, could have talked with them about our grievances, I could have done nothing to harm them. But I wasn't given the choice. I give it to you instead. You've heard what I said. I tell you there *is* evidence, and that I will show it to you. I ask you to believe me. I can see that you desire revenge. I can understand that. I think I'd want it myself. If you think that I'm the one who hurt you so badly, then take your revenge now. You hold the blade in your hands and I won't resist. The edge is honed. Swing it at my neck and it will be done."

Nys closed his eyes. He waited, wondering if he had taken too much of a gamble, if he had misjudged the woman. He could hear her labored breathing, heard her rise from the chair. He waited, but the stroke never came. He opened his eyes again after a minute. Jemi stood in front of the desk, the sword grasped awkwardly in trembling hands. She was crying. Great, silent sobs shook her body. Slowly, she lowered the katana, laying it back on the desk. The steel rang against the scabbard as she put it down.

Nys nodded. "The Admiral is already on his way here," he told her. "I'll show you the documents that I have, and we will go to meet him."

Nys took Jemi aboard a naval cruiser, ostensibly after an alleged threat against her. As they stepped aboard the vehicle in free-fall, Jemi looked out at the curved desks and tables of the interior, at the seats arrayed around the ship's sides and control consoles which would be "down" once the ship was under way and given spin. Despite the free-fall, all of the naval personnel in sight were aligned to the up-and-down positions the ship would have when it was given spin. The sight made her squint her eyes in thought, as if there were some import to the scene that she was missing. She stopped, and the guards on either side of her nudged her along.

Locked in a cabin, Nys himself brought the files against Strickland to her. She spent the day reading them, going over the logs and intercepted messages, the memorandums that Nys had ordered sent to him concerning Strickland's actions. Reading them made Jemi physically ill. If what she read was true, Strickland had gone to much trouble to hide himself, and Nys's accusations were well founded in circumstantial evidence. Strickland had gotten everything. Jemi reached to the pile of papers, pulled one out and scanned down it: *Customs Declaration, Vivicate Doni Kyle*. Poor Doni. He'd had so little, only the scant extra money Jemi usually gave him because his employment checks went directly to Vivicate Corporation. He'd had only a few credits and a cheap gift for Mari. Yet Strickland had bothered to dig all that up later, when Njialjiad had asked for help in finding the lost crystal.

Jemi was drained, emotionally and physically: the killings in

New York, the flight away from the city, coming to Uphill to confront Nys, the arrest, the strange meeting with Nys this afternoon. "God, Kenis, if I could just have you back and start all over again . . ." She lay back on her bed. *Fantasy? Is that what it has to be? It's done, it's over; you can't have him back. All you can have is the weregild—the payment for his death. Strickland, if that's who it is, or even Nys, if all his talk this afternoon was a lie. That's all you can ever have of Kenis again. Too damn little. Too damn little.* Her musings floated her into sleep.

There, Kenis played in the wardroom of *Starfire* with Doni and a T'Raijek alpha. They were playing hide-and-seek. The ship was in free-fall, in dock: Jemi lost sight of Kenis and the T'Raijek as they slid behind a table. The alpha was nearly the same height as Kenis, and both were hidden to Jemi and Doni, who called out from his post in the pilot's chair, oriented in the same way as the table. "Okay, Kenis, come on out, we can't see you."

"I know. I'm under the table," Kenis called.

Jemi grinned at Doni and floated out herself. Hanging over the table, she grasped the edges and pulled herself toward it, her feet sticking straight up. Jemi experienced the brief moment of vertigo she always did when she violated the spinward arrangement of the ship's furniture. "Mommy, you're upside down," Kenis said. Huddled beside Kenis in the shelter of the table, his thick arms wrapped around the boy, the T'Raijek alpha also grinned at Jemi. Jemi reached out for the two of them, but Kenis darted away, streaking over to Doni. "Look what I found, Doni," he said in his little-boy lisp. He held out a blue and yellow stuffed toy to the vivicate. "I found it under the table. You're my friend. I'll give it to you."

. . . give it to you. The words still echoed in Jemi's mind. She sat upright in the bed, the dream shattered. She was sweating, as if waking from a nightmare. Her hands shook as she steepled them before her face.

You should have realized it sooner. It was all there. An alpha the same size as Ken, wanting to hide the crystal from the inevitable Customs search, Kenis always prowling all over the ship . . . Strickland realized it was a possibility, too, and that's why Kenis died.

Jemi knew. She knew where the crystal was.

The only thing she didn't know was what to do about it.

A good lie is like a good politician's speech: just convincing enough that for lack of a decent alternative people believe the promises it makes, but with enough slack in it that you can always say that you were completely misunderstood.

—written on a bathroom stall.

Hell, a lie *is* a politician's speech.

—written below.

CHAPTER FIFTEEN

Gavin Jardien grinned. Ardent didn't like that expression at all. It was the wide, meaningless grin of a barracuda circling a floundering swimmer.

"Welcome back, Hlidskjalff," the HeadFather said to Ardent as the alpha swung down the alleyway into a corridor of the Salii colony. Ardent glanced at the ubiquitous guards flanking HeadFather Jardien. He grunted a wordless reply.

"You seem upset. Is it because you couldn't convince the Holder to let you tag along with her to Highland to be arrested?"

"Jemi's been caught?" Ardent's surprise pitched his usual growl higher. "How'd you find out?"

"We received a high-gee capsule to that effect a week ago." Jardien gave Ardent another amused glance. "Now, you want to try to convince me that I received value for expense in this little jaunt? It seems to me that I've lost one programmer, two agents, and the person who might have been able to dig up the crystal. For that I've learned nothing that I didn't already know. Charidilis might have to be convinced that the UCN caused the death of her son—I didn't. And now I'm left with the decision of what to do with *you*, Hlidskjalff."

"You may give the alpha to me, HeadFather Jardien," said an accented voice behind them. Jardien turned, and Ardent peered past him with a puzzled scowl on his face. Between two other attentive Jardien guards, a T'Raijek omega male came toward them. In robes the color of jade, a head taller than the guards, the omega seemed lordly. He inclined his head politely to Jardien, one of his thin, long hands fluttering at his low waist. "I beg your indulgence, HeadFather, but this is in many ways only a T'Raijek matter." His words were tinged with a guttural heaviness, telling Ardent that the omega was newly imprinted with this language. He began to feel a slow dread building within himself. He knew this one was Njialjiad: only Njialjiad would have to imprint one of its omegas—the ClanMother had long ago done that with her own.

The Njialjiad looked at Ardent. He sniffed audibly, as if in contempt. "The ClanMother Njialjiad Salii demands your presence," he said ponderously. The dread exploded within Ardent, leaving only a sagging resignation. *It's over, then. She couldn't keep them off and Njialjiad has won.* Ardent summoned the last shreds of bravado and folded his massive hands over his barrel chest. *At least make it good for Jardien. Let him see how Clan Hlidskjalff acts in defeat.*

"Did ClanMother Hlidskjalff leave any final instructions for me?" Ardent demanded, knowing that the omega would be bound by T'Raijek custom to tell him the truth.

"Her death-oaths were read to all," the omega answered. "To you she gave the command to follow the path given you by the death-oaths of ClanMother Hlidskjalff Highland."

Ardent laughed scoffingly, feeling no amusement inside, only an empty bitterness. "Then you're spending your seed in an empty hole, Njialjiad. The death-oath of ClanMother Hlidskjalff Highland refused me the privilege of joining my people until all hope was gone—I get to keep on playing this useless charade."

"You refuse the order of the new ClanMother?"

"I follow a death-oath, Njialjiad."

"Even when the reasons for the oath are now gone? Surely you see no hope at this point?"

"I follow a death-oath," Ardent repeated. That was all he needed to say. The omega drew himself up to full height. Ardent could see the offended dignity of the Njialjiad—at another time it might have made him want to laugh. All omegas were haughty and self-important; it had always pleased Ardent to deflate their egos. Not now.

The omega turned to Jardien, his face serious. "You see why it is said that alphas should not be given death-oaths to fulfill. They are too stupid to understand when an oath has been adequately followed. The self-centered youngling that he once was never leaves any alpha, the older they get, the more sour and pitiful that childish spirit becomes." Now his voice became honeyed, and he leaned toward Jardien as if in confidence. "Will *you* give him to me, HeadFather Jardien? He will have kept his oath if you hand him over to us as a captive."

Ardent could see the barracuda gleam of Jardien's eyes. "And if I don't?" the HeadFather inquired.

"Clan Njialjiad rules the embassy now," the omega answered. "The mistakes of the Clan Hlidskjalff are being unmade. Our ClanMother has declared the alpha Hlidskjalff renegade. She has decreed that his death-oaths are now void. We will take him as we must, HeadFather, no matter where he would hide himself or who would protect him."

"Indeed?" Jardien purred. "Am I to interpret that as a threat?"

A brief puzzlement washed across the omega's face at the HeadFather's words: no T'Raijek would have asked that—they would have *known*. They would have known and either submitted or given formal challenge. "I simply tell you what will happen, HeadFather Jardien," the Njialjiad said at last.

Jardien turned to Ardent. "What do you think, Hlidskjalff? Do you think it'd serve me to keep you alive?"

For an instant, Ardent felt a resurgence of hope. *This is why the GreatMother wanted the apes—they don't follow the rules of the group, but look only to their own survival. Like the Traal, very like the Traal.* "You no longer have Charidilis. Njialjiad won't give you the crystal. I still would, and I know Jemi's mind better than anyone else."

"But you don't know where the crystal is."

"No," Ardent admitted. "But I've other things I can tell you. Things you should probably know—things Clan Njialjiad won't tell you. Things Clan Hlidskjalff never mentioned either."

The omega was glaring at Ardent in fury. "You betray all of us, alpha—your own clan as well as the others. Your new GreatMother will die like the last for this."

Ardent shrugged. "I follow my death-oath."

Jardien glanced from one to another. He scratched at his chin thoughtfully. "I'll tell you what," he told the Njialjiad omega. One pudgy forefinger rubbed his neck, his lips pursed. "I'll hold on to the Hlidskjalff for the moment. I'll let you know what I decide . . . later."

The omega's nostrils flared. "That's not acceptable."

"I'd be curious as to how you intend to stop me." The dead, flat grin was back again: a mask. Jardien fluttered a thick hand. As the omega watched, the guns of the Jardien's guards came to bear on the T'Raijek.

The omega's eyes narrowed, his lips stretched thin. "I protest this treatment, HeadFather."

"I've done nothing to you. I've simply told you what I'm going to do—take this alpha back to Underneath."

"You make a decision that could affect all of your people on this world, HeadFather, not simply your own Family. ClanMother Njialjiad might well consider this affront severe enough to call for *kinjtha*." The omega lapsed in his own tongue. Jardien glanced at Ardent. "Satisfaction," Ardent said. "War. By our rules."

Jardien nodded. "Tell your ClanMother that I send her my regards. You might also mention that you didn't see too many people here on Salii. That's because they're all downworld. You may also mention to her that war doesn't have many rules for Salii. We've fought too hard to get where we are. Tell her that at the first sign of any attack, I will blow up Salii—and her. I had the explosives placed beneath your embassy when you first came. They'll rip the whole damn place apart and every last Saliian will walk out on the sands to see the meteor shower as the pieces hit the atmosphere."

The omega's skin had gone dark. He seemed in shock, unable to say anything. He gaped at Jardien for a moment, then turned stiffly and walked away without another word. Jardien's guards chuckled at the sudden retreat. "Let's go," Jardien said to his people as the alien left. "Tell the staff here to go to Family homes except for the minimum. And you''—he turned to Ardent—''had better have something interesting to say.''

''I do,'' Ardent told him, ''I do. But tell me, would you really blow up Salii just to get the embassy?''

Jardien snorted laughter. ''What do you think?'' he asked.

''What are you going to do with Strickland?''

Commander Nys had asked Jemi the question over a week ago now, before the ship on which she found herself had left Uphill to go meet Strickland aboard the *Strolov*. ''You had better decide whether you want revenge or something else. To a point, I can help you, but your interests aren't mine. We have a common enemy, but perhaps not a common goal, eh?''

Jemi was still held under ship arrest, locked in a room of the small vessel that Nys had somehow commandeered from the naval docks at Uphill: a packet cruiser named *Inverness*. ''I thought that I was a prisoner of the UCN, not the navy,'' she'd said. He'd replied with an amused smile.

''And you are. But your Admiral Strickland was entirely right. There are those within the UCN and the navy who have wondered at his abuses. Captain Burgess, who commands this vessel, is one who has seen the files you've seen. She's willing to take the risk.''

''Then I suppose I can trust you a little further yet.''

Nys had given her a strange smile then. He'd touched her shoulder with an odd affection, holding the contact a moment too long. ''I admire you, Jemi Charidilis,'' he'd told her. ''You've bent under the pressure, but you haven't allowed it to break you. You force it to compromise.'' Then he let his hand drop. She didn't see him again for two days.

For two days, Jemi stayed aboard *Inverness*. Nys boarded then, and they left Uphill for the rendezvous with Strickland. ''I'm sorry, Admiral,'' Nys had told Strickland, ''but my security chief tells me that Uphill is not safe, and that Saliian threats have been made. It would be better if you simply ordered her to be brought to you.''

Surprisingly to Jemi, Strickland had agreed.

Jemi waited for him now in Nys's quarters. The room seemed more like the quiet, formal office on Uphill than a cramped ship's room. A low table of polished wood had been bolted to the floor; a ceramic vase holding two silk flowers was attached to it. An ink-and-brush sketch hung from a wall, a row of Japanese *kanji* streaming below it. Jemi sat in one of the three chairs in the room. Nys knelt *seiza* before the table, his eyes closed, looking oddly wrong in his naval whites. Captain Burgess was there as well, a young woman looking worried in her dress uniform, seated across from Jemi. Jemi noticed that when Burgess caught Jemi staring at Nys, the woman frowned but said nothing. She wondered if perhaps Nys and Burgess weren't more than fellow officers. Then Burgess looked away from Jemi with a sudden intake of breath.

"What is the matter, Captain?" Nys asked without opening his eyes.

"He's here. I felt the shuttle dock."

Nys opened his eyes and nodded. He rose smoothly to his feet.

"What are we going to do, Commander?" Burgess asked.

"We are doing our duty, Captain. We've brought a prisoner to the Admiral at his own request. Beyond that"—Nys shrugged—"we'll simply have to see. This isn't our confrontation at all, but the Holder's."

"Mine?" Jemi asked, surprised. "What can I do, Commander?"

"I don't know," Nys answered. "But it would surprise me if you have no resources left. You have surprised me a number of times already, Holder Charidilis. I fully expect you to do so again."

They all heard the ring of steel-clad boots in the corridor outside, and there was a quick knock. "Come," Commander Nys called. An ensign stuck his head into the room. "Admiral Strickland to see Commander Nys," he said.

"Tell the Admiral to come in," Nys told him.

Jemi didn't know what she expected to see. In one scenario, she had thought that Strickland would enter with his head bowed, looking guilty. In another, he would be angry and furious, denying everything. Somehow, she'd never conceived that he would look exactly as she remembered, like someone's kindly old grandfather. The Admiral limped into the room, the stiff leg dragging a bit. His white hair was softly combed, the dress uniform perfect. His sad eyes belied the soft smile he gave them as he entered. He nodded to Nys and Burgess. "Commander, Captain," he said, then glanced at Jemi. As a Highlander, she had years of practice reading the subtleties of faces. She would have thought that his guilt would have shown, in his eyes at least. Yet she couldn't see it. He gave a small nod. "Holder Charidilis," he said, and his voice was gentle, understanding. "I wish we could have met again under pleasanter circumstances."

"Ensign," Burgess called out to the officer still in the doorway. "Please bring some coffee for the Admiral—I believe you prefer Colombian, do you not, Admiral?" Strickland nodded. "The Commander will have tea. I would like coffee myself. Holder?"

"Nothing," Jemi said. Her voice husked from a dry throat.

Burgess nodded; the ensign fled. The four of them sat in uncomfortable silence until he returned a few minutes later with a tray. As Strickland measured and stirred sugar into his coffee with the same precision that Jemi remembered from the *Strolov*, the Admiral turned to Nys. "I would have thought your security better than to require moving the Holder to a ship, Commander," he said. "Holder Charidilis is simply an unfortunate woman caught up in a trap, not some beast that must be caged. I assume there's a reason." Said any other way, Strickland's comment might have been scathing, but there seemed to be genuine sympathy. Again, Jemi began to wonder. She knew that it was possible for Nys, figuring that she would come to Uphill, to have faked the documents she'd seen. *All he wants is an indictment of Strickland, and he thinks I could help with that. One of them killed Kenis. One of them wants the crystal so badly that he would do whatever he needs to do to get it.*

And I know where it is . . .

That's the only weapon I have left. What does Nys expect me to do, attack Strickland with my bare hands?

With the Admiral's words, Captain Burgess rose and took her mug from the tray. She saluted the Admiral and Nys. "If you gentlemen will excuse me, I have business on the bridge."

"Certainly, Captain," Strickland answered. Jemi saw a quick, odd glance pass between Burgess and Nys, then the woman left the room. "Commander?" Strickland queried.

"I thought it best that you meet with her in private. She was told, by you, not to pass information to any other naval personnel.'' Nys's lack of inflection made him sound insolent. Strickland sighed as if very tired and turned to Jemi.

''You've been very active since we last met, Holder Charidilis,'' he told her. ''I told the Naval Secretary that there were extenuating circumstances relating to the charges against you, that much of what was attributed to you can instead be laid at the feet of Salii. I hope that's true, Holder.'' Always gentle, like her father had been when he'd scolded her. *Jemi, why are you being such an imp? I know you aren't usually that way. Something must be bothering you. Tell me what it is.* ''You seem to have changed a lot in that time, and not for the better. You've lost weight, you look malnourished and frightened. I'm very sorry for that. I feel responsible.''

Jemi shrugged. She glanced at Nys, but the small man was watching Strickland.

''I want you to know that I've not let the matter of your ship simply drop,'' Strickland continued. ''I've continued the investigation into it.'' He groaned under his breath as he shifted his weight on the chair. ''I have my reports aboard *Strolov*. You're welcome to examine them.''

With a feigned irritation, Jemi shook her head. ''You're being awfully kind to a prisoner.''

''*I* would not have treated you as a prisoner had you come to me, Holder. I don't blame Commander Nys, however. He was simply doing as he thought he must. You've been through quite a stressful time, Holder. You were plunged into matters that had little to do with you directly, and it's not surprising that they overwhelmed you. I doubt that anyone within the UCN is looking to punish you for that.''

''Are you offering me amnesty?''

Strickland smiled wearily. He chuckled, sipped his coffee, and set it down. ''I'm saying that I'll do what I can to see that the charges against you are dropped or minimized. I won't lie to you, Holder—some of the charges are serious, and I can make no promises. But I'll try. A person in my position isn't without power, after all.''

''And what do you want in return?''

''Is this where I'm supposed to turn into an ogre, Holder?''

Strickland smiled, and his glance toward Nys completed the sentence for Jemi: *as the Commander told you to expect.* "I'm not one," he said quietly. "I doubt that you know anything I don't know at this point, so I've nothing to bargain for here. I'm simply trying to do the right thing."

Jemi shook her head, now more confused than before. She wanted to tell Strickland yes, see what you can do. *Let me go. Just let me return to Highland and forget this thing. I'll even give you the crystal. Just let me out of this. All I ever wanted was Kenis, and I can't ever have him again.* She wanted to turn and rage at Nys, to scream that she knew that it was all lies, that she knew the Commander had been the one to hide Kenis's death, perhaps even to order it. A year ago, she would have hidden herself behind her k'lyge. Now she could not. But before she could say anything, Nys spoke.

"Do you think, Admiral, that she could still lead you to the crystal?"

Strickland's face went quickly red, and his hands fisted at his thighs. Jemi watched the hot flush climb the older man's neck and glow like a live coal in his cheeks. "Commander, you're discussing sensitive information for which you're not cleared. You are ordered to cease—"

"This room is verified secure, Admiral," Nys interrupted. "And I know about the crystal because the prisoner talked quite freely with me after her capture. She—and I—know what her attackers were looking for aboard her ship."

"Commander, I don't much like you or your ways. This will be noted in your report, and if you've made any statements to the Holder, you'll be held accountable for those as well. I trust you understand that."

"Perfectly, Admiral."

"Good," Strickland grunted. He turned away from Nys and his voice softened. "Holder, you know about the crystal?"

"Yes."

"Are you aware of what it contains?"

"The alpha Hlidskjalff told me that . . ." Almost, Jemi told him. Yet a certain caution held her back. She hoped her hesitation would be attributed to nervousness. *Another lie, another deception.* ". . . that they were T'Raijek diplomatic documents, something about the feud between Clan Hlidskjalff and Clan Njialjiad.''

Nys stared, but Strickland nodded. ''We thought that might be the case. It was on our list of possibilities.''

''But it doesn't explain why Family Jardien and the Saliians would want the crystal so badly they'd attack her ship, does it, Admiral?'' Again, Nys spoke with his curious flatness, so that no meaning could be implied beyond the words themselves. Still, they hit Jemi like a blow. She immediately saw the implication behind Nys's comment: a double-edged sword. First, Nys wanted to remind Jemi that she had claimed no Saliian ship had attacked her before Strickland's rescue. And second, it begged a question: wouldn't Strickland be puzzled about why a Saliian pirate would be trying to rescue T'Raijek diplomatic documents? Yet it was obvious that Strickland was satisfied with the explanation. He had reached down to pick up his cup again, and the flush was beginning to fade from his cheeks. Jemi glanced at Nys, but he was still paying her no apparent attention. *So that's to be the game—like the one in your office. Give me the sword and see what I do with it.*

All right. This time I'll use it. For Kenis and for me.

''Admiral, that doesn't make sense,'' she said. ''Why would Jardien attack my ship to recover documents? No one would do that unless they thought that they had a lot to gain from finding that crystal.''

Strickland seemed to puzzle over that, and the flush began to creep back upward. ''Perhaps they had allied themselves with Clan Hlidskjalff for some reason, Holder. I don't know—HeadFather Jardien would have to be the one to answer that question for you. I have no idea why they might be driven to that.''

Liar. Watching for it, she could see the evasion in his face. Jemi knew that he could have told her what she already knew—that the Clan Njialjiad had offered a reward for the return of the crystal. If Strickland thought that the document contained diplomatic information, then Njialjiad could have made the same offer to Salii that they had made to the UCN. That might have explained the attack. But no—Strickland instead chose to lie and keep Jemi in the dark. That said nothing about his guilt, but it told her that she could not trust the man's sweet words.

And you're no better than he. The thought pained her. Her eyes were suddenly very bright, stinging with salt. Deliberately, she lied again—a lie laced with truth to use the edge that Nys had freely given her. Jemi remembered what Highland had taught her: The liar tries to trap you with the lies so that you can see nothing else. The eyes don't care about truth, but the mouth hates the taste of a lie. Watch the mouth and don't get snared by the eyes. "I've learned something during all this. I found that Kenis had found the crystal. He had it." Talking about Kenis made the tears gather and spill over the rim of her eyes, but that only made the lie more effective. "He had it when he was killed—I'm certain a Saliian agent killed my son, but didn't find the crystal."

The Admiral's eyes were full of moist sympathy, but Jemi didn't look at them. She watched the other muscles of his face, his mouth, his hands. She saw him shaping the words before he spoke, and she saw their falseness. "That's my conclusion as well, Holder. We think Ruth Diesen, the crèche-mother, might well have been that agent. Tell me, do you suspect where your son might have hidden the crystal?"

Strickland was smooth—there was no eagerness in his voice at all, only a slow concern. Yet he leaned forward slightly in the chair, and the fingers clenched. Jemi could feel Nys's gaze on her and she turned to look at the Commander. He stared at her, and she knew that he was asking her a question. She also knew that she had reached a decision. Still looking at Nys, she nodded. "I think I might have an idea," she said, knowing that Nys would not realize that she spoke the truth. "Take me to Highland and I might be able to find it."

There was no mistaking the joy in Strickland's voice. "I'm afraid that's not possible, Holder," he said to her with that gentle, friendly sympathy. "After all, you are under arrest, and in any case, it would be dangerous for you. All you need to do is tell me—I'll take care of the rest."

"Take me to Highland," Jemi insisted, and Strickland's mouth turned down as if in irritation, though the eyes regarded her with pity.

"I can't do that, Holder. It's not necessary, for one. Give me a general idea of where to look and I can have my people go there. They'll find it—with the crystal's recovery, I can easily plead your case to the UCN."

"And if I refuse to tell you?"

"Please, Holder," Strickland said, his voice pained, pleading with her to be reasonable. "There are other ways—drugs, primarily—to get the information from you. I'd rather not have to use them. Please don't force me to do that."

"It's happened to me before." Jemi paused, took a breath. "And you were responsible for that time as well, Admiral."

He shook his head as if to a hopelessly errant child. "Holder Charidilis, as I told you then, a drug such as the one used on you isn't available in the UCN, and in any case, I was on *Strolov* at the time."

Jemi was not listening. She had turned back to Nys. "You were right," she told the man. "And I do know where the crystal is. Exactly."

"You're certain?" Nys asked.

"I am. It's on Highland."

She didn't say that she also knew what it contained. She reserved that, waiting to see how Nys reacted. *You've given the sword back. Now Nys faces the same test.* Nys rose to his feet with a sigh and went over to the wall, standing near the Admiral. Strickland followed his movements with a puzzled glance.

"Commander Nys, I will be taking Charidilis back to *Strolov*," the Admiral said. "Please tell Captain Burgess to prepare my launch."

Jemi thought for a moment that Nys would simply nod and follow orders. But instead the Commander came up to stand beside Strickland in his seat. He stared gravely at the older man. "I'm afraid that's not possible, Admiral," he said.

"Not—" Strickland began, blustering, the flush returning to his face. He turned, half rising. "Commander, I won't tolerate your insubordination."

"You've no choice, Admiral," Nys said. "At the moment, Captain Burgess has the guns of *Inverness* trained on the drive of *Strolov*. She did so when she left here, not knowing if this was an option we would need to take. I would have preferred to let you go and bring charges against you later, but the Holder has forced my hand, as I think she intended." Nys glanced at her and nodded. "When I tell Captain Burgess to do so, she will inform the captain of that ship that you have been taken hostage and will be killed at the first sign of hostility from *Strolov*. At that point we will disable *Strolov* and make our way to Highland."

"You're a fool, Commander. You've nowhere to go but Salii, and if they take you in, that action will precipitate a full-scale war."

"I don't think so, Admiral. Please, I'll take your service revolver." Strickland's hand had gone to the pistol grip. But now the fingers opened and dropped limply to his lap. Shaking his head, Strickland unfastened the holster belt and handed it to Nys.

Strickland remained silent. Jemi rose from her seat and went over to the Admiral. She stood directly in front of the man, confronting him. "You killed Kenis," she told him, her teeth clenched. A slow rage filled her. "You can't believe how much I hate you for that."

Strickland blinked. "It wasn't me," he said quietly. "I have children and grandchildren of my own. I wouldn't have wanted anything like that to happen. I don't know why your son died, Holder. I don't know anything about it." His chin jutted out stubbornly. Muscles bunched in his jaw.

He was lying. She knew he had to be lying.

Her rage was a giant's hand clutching her throat, choking her in a red haze. Jemi wanted to scream. Through the mist of the fury, she could see Strickland's revolver, held in Nys's hand, the grip toward her. She knew she could reach for it, might be able to grab it and fire before Nys could react. The Commander might not even try to stop her. She could pass judgment on her son's killer, could exact the punishment she'd wanted for the last several months, could strike back against the nightmare that she was caught in.

Her breath was ragged, gasping. Her hands were claws. She looked at Strickland and hated. The bile was a deep poison within her. If she had been sure, if she had been utterly sure, she might have moved then and ended it.

She screamed. She slapped at Strickland with her open hand, dragging nails across his cheek.

"Get him out of here!" she shouted. She swatted air with her palm, backing away. "Get him out!"

She wept, covering her face with her hands, crying for Kenis, crying because she felt no satisfaction. Nys's hand clenched her arm and pressed gently. When she looked at him, he nodded to her sympathetically. Then he ushered Strickland out of the room.

When the T'Raijek came, it was as if some cosmic magician had suddenly conjured an entirely new reality from the empty box of space. Some of the effects on humanity were immediate and public; we all know those. Others were subtle and hidden. You have to search through the statistics of that time to see them. For one, our own scientific research died a quick and painful death. What reason was there to continue developing our own spacecraft when the T'Raijek ships were so obviously far better? Why explore the tiny limits of even our own solar system when the T'Raijek already knew it?

It would be like doing calculus on our fingers when everyone else has calculators.

And surely a race that is our technological superior is also our moral superior.

—from "The New Magi" by Ellis Wilson.
New Lifestyle magazine, July 2170.

CHAPTER SIXTEEN

In his mind, Ardent saw the destruction of Clan Hlidskjalff. The memory of his act of defiance to the omega Njialjiad before HeadFather Jardien was a mockery of his feelings. He did not feel defiant. He felt sick.

It would be *aljceri*, the fight of authority, or it would be *kinjtha*, the fight of equals. Ardent could smell them coming, like the spoor of some sick beast.

And if they did come, if the T'Raijek warships arrived here, the humans would feel compelled to fight. They would not follow the rules of *aljceri* or *kinjtha*. They would fight as Ardent had seen Jemi fight—like a base animal cornered and trapped. And once they did that, once they revealed that nature, that was how the GreatMothers would judge them. They would hunt them down as beasts, not as equals. They would let the alpha BeastCaptains deal with them in any way they wished. If he lived long enough, Ardent would see Highland twisting like a broken toy in the sky. He would see the cities of Earth as burning pits in the ruined soil. He would see Mars left empty and barren again.

Njialjiad was no different from any of the rest of the T'Raijek. They would follow the rules of conflict—inexorably, no matter what the situation. No matter that the more Ardent saw of the apes, the more he thought that maybe the old GreatMother Hlidskjalff had been right. The apes would not have reacted to the Traal as the T'Raijek had. If the apes had the T'Raijek technologies, the Traal might not be a threat always to be feared, a reason to look constantly over their shoulders. They might have fallen, yes, but not so meekly, not so quickly. And perhaps, *perhaps*, not at all.

The winds of Mars buffeted the little Jardien shuttle heading downworld from Salii. Sparks of light in the upper atmosphere, other shuttles followed, leaving Salii almost deserted. Over the shrill scream of the jets, Ardent shouted to Gavin Jardien, seated near him in the shuttle's cockpit. "You put on a good show, HeadFather. Would you really blow up Salii?" He again asked the question that had nagged at him since the confrontation.

Jardien grinned back. "Absolutely. Without hesitation. *If* I really could, and if I thought it would do any good. Neither of which is the case."

Ardent's eyes widened. The apes, the damn apes—despite what the Njialjiad had said, they were far worse than any alpha. They lied and they deceived, and they laughed about it. T'Raijek could lie—the lie of omission. Ardent himself might lie; he had found that he had picked up too many of the apish ways. But not the Mothers, not the omegas. The only falsehood they knew was that of simply not saying all. "You were bluffing?"

"All the way. The same way as you, eh?"

"I wasn't bluffing," Ardent said stiffly. "I *do* follow a death-oath. T'Raijek wouldn't bluff, HeadFather. They would simply go ahead and do it."

"Then I want to get in a poker game with you sometime," Jardien replied. "The higher the stakes, the better. Now you can answer one of my questions. Tell me, Hlidskjalff, what would your clan have gotten in return for the crystal? You give us a stardrive—what's your fee?''

Ardent hesitated. He looked at the sandy oxide soil that was looming up at them. Here and there were specks of green where nothing had once been, the legacy of Saliian determination: the apes' determination to survive. Their linked economies in shambles, the initial resources of their solar system failing, still some of them continued to fight. Ardent would have bet, when the first reports concerning the apes had reached the T'Raijek, that the GreatMothers of the time had been convinced that the apes were ready to destroy themselves. They'd watched. For two of the apish centuries they'd watched. And they hadn't died. They hadn't lashed out at themselves in frustration. They'd come close several times, but each time had lurched aside from the death waiting for them.

HeadFather Jardien should have never been born. He should have been a skeleton bleaching on the cold sands of Mars. But he was alive. He was here.

The death-oath nagged at Ardent. *Do not obey the commands of any ClanMother who is not Hlidskjalff until all hope is gone. Follow the path the GreatMother set for us.* Fine, he would do that, despite the fact that he could feel the utter uselessness of it. It would be *kinjtha*, probably, and the apes were not the Traal. When the apes met the T'Raijek retaliation, they would die.

Finally.

Ardent sighed. He looked at the surface of Mars, at the meager holdings the apes had carved in the world's surface, and he began to tell HeadFather Jardien the tale of the T'Raijek and the Traal.

''You mean that you've never actually talked with the Traal? You met them only once? *Once?*'' Gavin Jardien nearly laughed with the unbelievability of it. He had never been so struck by the true alienness of the T'Raijek until this moment. He had somehow always had them in his mind simply as odd humans. But this . . .

They were still in the shuttle, which had grounded near Underneath. A minor sandstorm was in progress outside, so Jardien had given the order for the crew and passengers to wait until the storm passed in a few hours. It had given the Ardent time for his tale. Jardien shook his head and tapped at the windshield, where orange sand collected in the corners. "It was a settlement expedition, HeadFather," Ardent said. "All our ships were escorted by fully armed warships. The command ship carried two GreatMothers. They were fired on without warning. When the GreatMothers offered *aljceri*—leader to leader combat—there was no reply. The Traal continued to attack. *Kinjtha*—full war between equal forces—was proposed, but still there was no answer. So the GreatMother declared them beasts, and gave control of the fight to the alphas. Our ships swung to attack. But the Traal . . . the Traal destroyed all the warships. Then they began to fire on the undefended expedition freighters. It must have been utter chaos. The ships tried to flee—two made it back."

"And you decided to hide from that point on."

Ardent shrugged, his ancient face puzzled. The ship rocked in the winds. "Don't you understand? The Traal force was far smaller than ours. Yet they beat us. Their ships were faster than ours, their weapons were devastating. We hardly hurt them at all. Can you imagine what that means?"

Jardien scoffed. "Evidently not. You lose one battle and concede the war?"

"The ships that did return brought back a few of the Traal dead, retrieved from the carnage. From what we can tell, their evolutionary ancestors were predators. Ours were more like your herd beasts. And your own . . . a little of both. The Traal are truly warlike, more like you than like the T'Raijek. In *aljceri* or *kinjtha*, we would have become subject to them. But there are millions upon millions of stars in this arm of the galaxy—there was only an infinitesimal chance that we would come across them again, and almost none at all should we expand outward in the arm instead of inward to where we had found them. Their worlds are toward the galactic core, on the other side of the T'Raijek worlds from your sun, and are a well-developed society. Still, it was an awesome coincidence, considering the odds and the number of suns, that we would hit a world that was theirs. Yet we knew that there was still that possibility.

"We're not at all like you or like the Traal, HeadFather. We don't understand individual initiative very well. We tend to follow the rules of our society; when others fail to do that, we often don't know how to react. You'd probably say that we lack imagination."

"It still doesn't make sense." The gale howled, sand scoured the thick glass of the windshield. Jardien pulled his furs tighter around him.

"To you. Nor do you make sense to us," Ardent sniffed. "We're different."

"And you thought you could use us."

"That was the thought of my GreatMother Hlidskjalff. It was a new thought for us, and new thoughts aren't easily accepted. We thought that perhaps if the Traal find us, or should we meet them again, that it would be good to have your people between us and them."

"You could have asked."

Ardent laughed. "Asked? HeadFather, we stumbled across you apes not long after the Traal—another cosmic coincidence. The GreatMother Hlidskjalff who proposed our course did so two hundred and fifty of your years ago. We simply watched you for two hundred years, judging and arguing." He shook his head. "Asked? The other GreatMothers would never have allowed it. We were surprised when GreatMother Ktainias AllMother permitted contact. Clan Hlidskjalff had been petitioning for it for fifty years. Now the Ktainias and the other clans may well try to rectify that mistake."

The ClanMother Njialjiad Salıı lolled in her nutrient pool. The younglings were all sleeping in a far corner of the pool except for the lone alpha, whom she kept near her. The alpha wasn't of her body, but of the late ClanMother Hlidskjalff's, the only youngling left of that brood. But alphas were too rare to kill for the sake of *aljceri*. She stroked the wrinkled face, the pudgy body; the alpha stirred in his sleep and snuggled closer to her warmth.

"I should have you feed the pool," she said to the omega who stood near the entrance, waiting for her to notice his presence.

"I will do it if you order it, ClanMother," the omega said, bowing to her. "As I would do anything you asked me to do. I'm sorry I've failed you."

"I wasted the imprint on you, omega Sabist. You were supposed to bring the alpha Hlidskjalff here. That was simple enough."

"He claimed a death-oath."

ClanMother Njialjiad sighed. "I know that. That's the only reason you're still alive. You've checked out the HeadFather's threats?"

"For the last two turnings of this world, ClanMother. I checked the records of the growing of this building, and we have examined the foundations. I myself personally supervised a crew to dig under the subfloor. I found nothing."

"And the station itself?"

"As far as we can tell, there's nothing there, either, though of course the Saliians could destroy the station from a ship—we are watching for that possibility. Salii itself still has only a minimum crew of the apes aboard, though."

"And what's your conclusion?"

"That HeadFather Jardien *lied,*" Sabist said, using the apish word. "That there is no threat to you or the younglings or this embassy. That the HeadFather simply wanted to keep the alpha despite your wishes." The omega's face was strained. It didn't help his discomfiture that the ClanMother stared at him, stroking the youngling alpha. "The apes are too like the Traal," he said. "There have no sense of the order of things. That's why Hlidskjalff's folly was so tragic."

The ClanMother nodded. The omega confirmed what she had suspected. "They insult us. They beg to have authority shown to them." The ClanMother began to rise from the pool, the gelatinous broth of the nutrients clinging to her fur. The wounds inflicted by the old ClanMother were scabs across her chest, the fur just beginning to cover them. The alpha opened his eyes, found the ClanMother missing, and began to howl. "Get one of my daughters to care for the younglings, Sabist," she told the omega. She came very close to him and let one of her claws slip out from the pads of her hands. She tucked the sharp tip under Sabist's chin and lifted it so that he looked into her eyes.

"Send one of the fastships," she said. "Tell GreatMother Ktainias AllMother to come for *kinjtha,*"

The two pieces of news reached HeadFather within a day of each other. The first to come was a paper stuffed inside a high-gee capsule and recovered by a Jardien cruiser. The headlines screamed at the HeadFather when he unrolled the faxpaper: STRICKLAND TAKEN HOSTAGE, SALIIAN/HIGHLAND REBEL INVOLVED. That in itself made him draw his breath in. The story itself was a collection of rumors and speculation—it was obvious that the UCN would not release precise information. But it said that the commandeered ship—the UCN small cruiser *Inverness*—was on a heading for Highland. Jardien pursed his lips and decided to wait.

He was glad the next day that he had done so, for that was the day that a small, unmanned fastship left the T'Raijek embassy on Salii. Saliian instruments tracked it for three hours, after which the thing suddenly left all screens. Ardent confirmed what Jardien already knew—a message was being sent.

HeadFather Jardien nodded. With his authority, he ordered all Saliian cruisers into orbit and planetary defenses put on alert. He took command of one of the cruisers himself: the *Lowell*.

Ardent had only one question. "Where are you going?"

"Highland," Jardien answered. "Why?"

"Take me," Ardent said simply.

Jardien shrugged. "Let's go," he said. "They'll almost be there."

Her world was locked in night. Boiling, angry clouds threw lightnings across a swollen sky. In the fitful, aching glare, Jemi could see Kenis across a wide expanse of water, his back to her. He seemed to be playing in the sand of the small island on which he sat. The wind began to rise, lashing Jemi's cheeks with his hair; rain came pelting down—huge, warm droplets that made Jemi squint and protect her face with her hand. "Ken!" she called. "Kenis, I'm here, honey!"

Slowly, he turned to look at her. He smiled, but the smile made her want to gasp, to cry out. There was nothing there, nothing behind his eyes and that smile. It was the empty grin of a death's-head. "Hello, Mommy," he called back. His soft voice carried impossibly in the wind, and it was as dark and low as the clouds—an adult's voice, ominous.

"Ken?" she whispered hesitantly, and he laughed, a sound as vacant as the smile.

"You can't ever have me back, Mommy," the mocking,

grown-up thing told her. "Not ever. You lost me except in your head, and all you've done is cover me with your hate." He smiled again, incongruously, and reached over the sands to dip his hand in the water. Lightning flared like magnesium. He palmed a handful of the strange, still lake. The water ran thick and dark from his pudgy, little-boy fingers, and in the next blue flash, Jemi saw that it was not water at all. It was blood—black instead of red in the night, but *blood,* thick and pasty and clinging to his hands.

He held his hand over his head. He let it drip down over him. "See, Mommy, see?" the apparition said under the drooling flow. The flow was impossibly huge, as if his cupped palm held an endless pool of the stuff. "It didn't do any good, did it?"

"God," Jemi muttered, horrified. "Kenis—"

And then the thing let his hand drop, and suddenly it *was* Kenis again, lost and frightened. "Mommy!" he screamed. The sound of his voice dragged her to her feet as if shocked. She began to step into that viscous, obscene water.

"No!" Kenis shouted. "No, Mommy!"

"Kenis, I'm not going to leave you, love. I'm coming, don't worry."

"Holder?"

A hand pulled her back, and Jemi turned to see that it was Doni. The vivicate shook his wan, sad head at her. "No, Holder. I'll go get him," he said in his slurred, pathetic voice.

"Why should you?" Jemi demanded. "He's my son. And what good did I ever do you?"

"Holder Charidilis, please . . ."

"It wasn't your fault, really," Doni said. "You were better than most Holders, usually. I liked you. In some ways, you reminded me of Mari. It wasn't your fault that you responded to me in the way you were taught to respond. It wasn't your fault that Kenis died, either. No fault, no need to go looking for forgiveness." He stepped into the water. His pants went dark, but it seemed to be only water that he waded in. "I'll go get Kenis," he said.

"Jemi, wake up."

The voice dragged her from the dream. Jemi opened her eyes, feeling a sense of loss and disorientation. *Kenis* . . . But there was no Kenis, no pool of dark, strange water. There was only the cabin around her and the face of one of the officers of the ship. The woman's face was grim, her manner hurried. "Holder," she said, "Major Nys sent for you."

With a start, Jemi noticed that the woman was floating in midair. The ship was no longer spinning. A dull growl reverberated through the deck plating; the ship shuddered a few times and seemed to shiver.

"Sorry, ensign. I was—" Jemi grimaced, remembering. "Never mind," she said. "What's happening?"

"We're near Highland—you can see the colony from the ports. The naval patrol ships there have ordered us to surrender." The officer pressed her lips tightly together. "Please come with me."

"All right," Jemi said. "Let me get dressed."

The ship's bridge was in the middle of *Inverness*. Flatscreens gave a view from the ship's hull cameras and instruments. Most of the personnel sat in front of their stations. Major Nys hovered near the middle of the room, tethered to a stanchion beside an empty acceleration seat. He wore a throat mike; Captain Burgess dominated the room's center in a small booth crammed with panels. The ensign led Jemi over to Nys and then left.

"Holder," Nys said.

"What's going on?" Jemi asked again.

"Patrol ships," he answered tersely. "There weren't any cruisers in Highland dock, but the naval base, under orders, sent over what protection they had. I'd hoped that the patrol vessels would be farther out from Highland, or that they would have been ordered to avoid confrontation. I misjudged my superiors in that."

"The ensign said that they'd ordered us to surrender," Jemi said.

The little man nodded; his dark eyes glittered, mirroring the pinpoint flecks of light from the panels around them.

"Can they force it?"

"Perhaps," he answered. He gave a half-shrug that moved his body up. He adjusted his position quickly—Nys moved gracefully in free-fall, seemingly comfortable. Jemi slid toward the stanchion, hugged it to herself. "Please," he told her. "Strap yourself into the chair if you're to stay here." Jemi did as he requested, Nys speaking as she moved the restraints over her shoulders. "We've told them that if they fire on us, we will return fire," he said. "That's not a decision I like to make, Holder. It bothers everyone on this ship. There are probably those who will not do it in any case."

The dream came back to her momentarily, making her close her eyes. She clutched the armrests of the chair; she knew Nys saw the strain it revealed. "God," she sighed. "Do we have to fight?"

"No," Nys answered flatly. "More to the point, we won't. I've played my bluff, Holder. I will order the crew to defend this ship, but I won't make an offensive move first. I don't believe in that. The crew of this ship has taken enough of a chance already. They've done so only because they've seen the abuses of Admiral Strickland and others in the UCN, because they've all seen the documents I've compiled against the Admiral, and because of Captain Burgess's leadership." Nys indicated the dark-haired woman, speaking urgently into her throat mike, her eyes worried as she scanned her instruments. "I won't ask them to kill people who are, after all, only obeying orders. We're at an impasse at the moment, each of us circling the other."

Jemi relaxed. "Good," she said. She rubbed weary eyes. "I'm tired of it, Commander. I don't need to be responsible for more. I'd rather take my chances with UCN justice."

"It may come to that," Nys told her. "But it also may be more important that we recover the crystal. That's why I asked you to come up here." His dark, intense stare riveted her. "You're not bluffing me as I am doing to these patrol ships, are you, Holder Charidilis? You do know where the crystal is?"

"I'm fairly certain that I do," she answered wearily. "No, I can't be sure, but I'll be surprised if it's not."

"You're still holding something back," Nys said, his brows lowering. "Are you certain that all the crystal holds is diplomatic messages? Is there something else?"

Jemi shrugged. *I still don't know that I trust you, Commander. I'm sorry*. Jemi could tell that Nys would not let the subject drop. She could see his frustration with this encounter. He had taken an immense chance—not directly for Jemi, but because of her. Jemi had tipped the scales for Nys, moved him into action. *I would tell you, but I may need something of my own to bargain with, nor am I certain that I want to give the UCN the gift of this crystal.* "I'm sorry, Commander," she said. "I've nothing else to say."

She thought he would continue the argument, but then Captain Burgess called to him. "Major—screen five."

Nys spun to see a wallscreen behind him, stopping his momentum with a chopping motion of his hand. On the screen, three dots moved across a grid, a phalanx of numbers moving with them. "Condors?" Nys asked.

The captain nodded. "Saliian ships," she said. "HeadFather Jardien is aboard the command vessel and has given a warning to the ships blocking us. The patrol ships are peeling off. Jardien is hailing us."

Nys nodded. "Open the link," he said. "Put the cameras on me, but let him see the Holder as well."

"Aye, sir," Burgess said. "Communications, you heard the Commander." Another screen flared into life to one side, and Nys turned to face it. HeadFather Gavin was there, and he grinned like a cat.

"Hello, Commander, Holder," he said. "I've just come for a visit. I've always wanted to see Highland, and this seemed like a good time. It even looks as if we've saved you from a little trouble. What do you say, Commander? I tell you that it's time enemies became friends. I've no quarrel with you, and we both want what's best for our people. I say we should follow the Holder's example—she's shown me that there's power in following her path. Let's say we have a momentary truce?"

"Can I trust you, HeadFather?" Nys queried.

"The Holder's my reference. Ask her."

Nys glanced back at Jemi.

She nodded.

Nys stared at her for long seconds. In older times, she would have drawn her k'lyge across her eyes at such an intense scrutiny. But she only looked back at him. She let him see whatever it was he wanted to see in her. His lips curled in the slightest indication of a smile. Then he turned back to Jardien. "Truce, HeadFather," he said. "For the moment."

We do everything for our children, either the children of our flesh or the children of our minds. Without some part of us to travel into the future, there is no reason for existence. The prime directive is to perpetuate yourself in one way or another. If there's no chance of leaving your autograph on the walls of eternity, we might as well go ourselves, for we face an empty void.

—preface to *My Father's Fault* by
Meg Stevens. Lee Books, 2171.

CHAPTER SEVENTEEN

Highland had only minimal defenses other than the navy. She had originally been, after all, only a colony for mining the ore of the Belt. Faced with the massed firepower of Nys's cruiser and the three Saliian ships, the council of Provosts had capitulated within hours, without much debate at all. The UCN would send cruisers to save them, but that might be a week, a month, or more—in the meantime, they would do what they needed to do to survive.

As Adjunct Michaels told the assembled provosts: "We're not fools. Why die for useless pride?"

The vote was carried by acclamation.

And aboard the cruisers—the three Saliian ships and the larger *Inverness*—an uneasy watch was kept, each on the other, as they made the final approach to Highland.

The night before they finally docked at Highland Port, Jemi came to Nys with a request. "I want to talk with Strickland," she said. "Alone."

Nys was wearing his *gi*. He and Burgess had been practicing in the cruiser's gymnasium. Both were sweaty; Burgess, seeing

Jemi approach, had gone off to another corner, where she practiced a solo *kata*—series of movements—with the boken. Nys pulled a cloth from underneath his top and wiped his face. Seated in seiza, he looked up at her.

"I hope you've not changed your mind about revenge, Jemi," he said.

"No," she said. She started to say more, then closed her mouth. She rubbed a hand over her scalp. Her hair was beginning to come back, a prickly fuzz that reminded her of that on Ardent's face.

"We need Strickland," he told her. "All of us on this ship face charges at home. He's our only chance to escape those."

"I know that. He also killed my son. I want to know more about that, and he might be more likely to talk if I'm there alone."

Nys closed his eyes. She thought for a moment that he had slipped into some meditation. Then they opened again, a dark, nearly pupiless stare. "All right," he said. "I trust your judgment. Go now."

"Thank you," Jemi said.

"We *all* need to trust each other," he said with an odd inflection. "Neither of us has had that kind of faith in anyone else for too long. I'll write you a pass for the guard."

Strickland's cabin was no different from any of the others. Small, cramped, a tiny desk and chair bolted to the floor and a bedshelf the only furnishing. A lamp was set in the ceiling, giving off a sharp-edged light that put the deep hollows of his eyes and cheeks in shadow. He was stretched out on the bed when she entered. She nodded to the guard to leave, standing silently until the door closed behind him.

She thought Strickland might be asleep, but his tired voice came as the lock clicked behind her. "I hope you don't think that I'm more likely to talk without the guard," he said wearily. "I'm not that much of a fool."

"You won't tell me anything about Kenis?"

"There's nothing to tell, Holder. I don't know what happened. I wasn't there."

"You thought his life was worth what the T'Raijek offered to give you. You thought that my memories of him were just as expendable, and that Doni's life was nothing.'' Jemi blinked. She could feel the cold hatred in her voice, the gall that spilled out of her with each word. Her arms were folded tightly under her breasts; her hands were claws digging into the skin. The Admiral stared at her dully, either not seeing the venom in her or not caring. Jemi came near him. With a sudden movement, she pulled a hypodermic from her blouse pocket and with a cry, jabbed it into his bicep. The Admiral cursed and started to slap her away. ''Don't!'' Jemi cried harshly. ''Move and I'll inject the stuff. It's Scloramine, Admiral. Do you know what it is, what it does?'' She felt him fall back, and she knew that he *did* know. With that motion, she knew that he had lied to her again.

''I'm telling you that we couldn't have done it,'' he had told her back then. He had told her that by UCN technology it was impossible. He had lied. He had known all along.

''So you're familiar with Scloramine, Admiral. You know exactly what it is. You know that I could put this in you and peel back the layers of your memory, let you relive it all for me one more time. You know that I could take you back in time and see exactly what the truth is. The only trouble, Admiral, is that after it was over, *you* wouldn't remember it at all. It would be as if it had never happened for you. Wouldn't it?'' She nearly shouted the last words. Jemi's thumb trembled on the plunger of the hypo, and the Admiral moaned. ''Tell me the truth, Admiral,'' she whispered. ''Tell me the goddamn truth this time or I'll use the drug to do it. Did you send Martel for Kenis?''

For a second, he resisted. She thought he would defy her. But as she watched, she saw his resolve shatter. He slumped in the bed, all the muscles limp, and his shadowed eyes half closed. The word husked out from between dry lips.

''Yes,'' he said. A quiet sibilance.

Jemi shivered with the admission. A moan escaped her, and she pressed her lips together. ''And me and Doni?'' she said through the beginning of tears. ''Did you send someone after my ship?''

He simply nodded. ''I thought . . . There were others . . . We could have used the T'Raijek technology for everyone.''

''After you were installed as UCN Head.''

Strickland didn't answer. The grief struck Jemi fully then.

With a wail, she yanked the syringe from Strickland's arm. She threw it blindly at the wall, sobbing—glass shattered, a clear liquid darkened the gray paint.

"Holder," Strickland said from the bed, "I'm sorry. But no one in power can make a decision that doesn't hurt someone. Quite often, it ends up killing too. That's the way of things."

Jemi fled the room. She could not stand to be near him.

She ran into Nys. His arms came around her as they collided. When she struggled, crying, he let her go. They stared at each other for a moment, then Jemi fled down the corridor. Nys shook his head at the guard who began to pursue her. He went into Strickland's room. After a glance at the Admiral, he went to the wall. His shoes crunched against broken glass. He sniffed the wetness, touched a fingertip to it, and put it to his tongue.

"Sterile water," he told Strickland, and left the room.

This time there was no old vivicate tending the garden. The Rekindled House seemed deserted and almost ominous, though that was perhaps more in Jemi's mind than anything about the way the place looked. With her entourage of Nys, HeadFather Jardien, Strickland, Ardent, and an assortment of guards, Jemi's group was far more threatening.

She felt strange walking Highland's streets without a k'lyge, her hair shorn. She felt odd seeing Harris among the Provosts who greeted them deferentially at the port; he didn't seem to recognize her at all. Walking up to the house in company with the others was just another strangeness among several.

Mari answered the door. She looked the same, leaning on a cane, her dark hair flecked with gray, wild hairs, the once handsome face twitching as she stared at the group on the doorstep. Surprise twisted one side of her mouth, though the other remained slack. A film of saliva sheened her chin. "What do you want?" she said, with a bravado that Jemi remembered all too well—the memory of their last meeting stung her, and Jemi replied as gently as we could.

"We'd like to talk with you, Mari. Please."

Mari grimaced. She let the door open wider and hobbled back from it a halting step. "Doesn't look like I can much stop you if the provosts couldn't. Wipe your feet, though."

The vivicate waited until they were settled, the guards along the walls, all the rest except for Jemi seated. Mari glanced from one to another, standing on a braided rug in the center of the room. From the archway leading back into the house, they could hear voices, but no other vivicates could be seen. "What do you want?" Mari asked again. She tapped the floor with her cane for emphasis. Gnarled, disfigured fingers clutched the knob of the cane tightly. She looked at Jemi with a curious sympathy. "I remember you now," she said. "You're Charidilis. You've changed."

"More than you'd think," Jemi answered.

"Did you bring this zoo here?"

Jemi nodded. "It has to do with Doni."

Mari's face went slack. She blinked slowly. "Doni again. What's the matter, Holder? Did you have a thing for vivicates that Doni never told me about? Did you like dead meat?" She tottered on the cane, caught herself. "I had enough trouble after you left the last time," she said. "People asking about you, about what we'd talked about. I don't know what trouble you're in, Holder, but I don't want any of it, and I'm glad Doni's gone—I don't want to see him hurt anymore. Why don't you leave me alone? I've enough problems all by myself. Every vivicate does."

"I might be able to help with that," Jemi told her.

Suspicion lifted one corner of Mari's mouth. Her fingers moved on the cane. "I'm listening."

"Doni gave you something just before we left Highland last time. Remember it?"

"A paperweight," Mari said. "A crummy, cheap paperweight he bought on earth. What about it?"

"Would you get it?"

Mari stared at them. Then, with a shrug, she limped from the room. Jemi didn't look at anyone while the woman was gone, though she could hear them fidgeting behind her. "He *did* buy the paperweight on earth, Holder," Strickland spoke to her back. "I saw the receipt on the customs manifest. I talked with the customs official who saw it, and I know there were a hundred more just like it in the ship where he bought it."

"Kenis would have been about a meter tall," Jemi told him

without turning around. "About the same height as a T'Raijek alpha male. I kept spin on *Starfire* as much as possible. Kenis always prowled the ship, looking into odd corners—he could have gone anywhere the T'Raijek did. He would have had the same viewpoint. And he and Doni always played together. Kenis showed Doni all his toys, all his little discoveries."

Mari came back into the room. She held Doni's gift in her right hand, clutched against her thin chest. It was a round globe about four centimeters in diameter, a poor representation of Earth dappled blue and green and set on a small piece of driftwood. Jemi had seen them in the stores of Uphill Station—this one was perhaps worse than most. But she heard Ardent's intake of breath behind her.

"I won't give it to you," Mari said. "It's all I got of him."

Nys had given her the sword. He had given her the gift of her own choice. "I wish that all fighting had to be done with swords, so that when we killed, we would have to be close to the person whose life we take, so that we would have to deliberately make that choice." You can do no less for her, for Doni and for Kenis.

"I'm not asking you to give it to me," Jemi said. "Just scratch it. Scratch the paint with your fingernail."

Glancing oddly at Jemi, Mari did so.

Underneath, there was a lambent glimmer.

Jemi sighed. "That caused Doni's death, Mari. It killed Kenis too, and more others than I care to remember."

"What is it?" Mari whispered.

"Knowledge," Jemi said. She laughed bitterly. "Just that. Not everybody here knows exactly what it is. But I'll tell you, Mari. I'll tell you because it was Doni's. The crystal holds a stardrive. With that knowledge, humanity can have entire other worlds. New beginnings, perhaps." Jemi heard the collected intakes of breath behind her, and knew the words had shocked both Nys and Strickland. "It's yours, Mari," she continued. "You can do whatever you want with it. Strike any bargain you desire. The Admiral thinks it could buy back his freedom and power. Commander Nys believes he might be able to use it to change the UCN. HeadFather Jardien would send his people to find new suns. The T'Raijek might be able to save his clan. I don't have any use for it at all—it won't give me Kenis back.

Doni might have suspected that it was worth something. I think he probably intended to use it, but he never had a chance. It's Doni's gift to you." Jemi's shoulders slumped; she sighed. She wanted to sit down—she simply felt weary. She had thought that she would feel exhilaration at seeing the crystal. Instead, it made her sick to see it.

Mari's thumbnail scratched over paint, flecks of blue and green drifted to the rug. Below, a milk white gem gleamed. Iridescent colors swirled in the surface, moving. *Kenis would have loved it. He held that, he played with it, and he gave it to Doni. His friend.* The thought made her eyes burn with tears, and she blinked hard. "You can even destroy it. The Hlidskjalff tells me that it's relatively fragile. Throw it against a wall—it'll be gone, the way it took Doni and Kenis."

Mari seemed startled, unsure. The others began to speak now, adding to her confusion. "Salii has never used vivicates," Jardien shouted over the others. "Give it to me, and I'll make certain that the research is done that should have been done before. Vivicates won't be slaves to the Saliian economy."

"I can promise the same," Strickland said.

"Any of us would," Nys interjected. "All of us will."

Only Ardent remained silent.

Mari gaped. She looked at them all, clutching the crystal to her breast. Her gaze rested longest on Jemi, searing. "I hated you," she said.

"I know. I can understand it."

"Doni hated you, too."

"I can understand that, as well. I didn't hate him, but I wish I'd been kinder to him, Mari. You were right; I didn't know him. I didn't think of him as a person. Only Kenis did that."

Mari nodded. She stared at the crystal in her hand. "I want what every vivicate has always wanted," she told them. "I want Vivicate Corporation dissolved. I want the contracts of all vivicates destroyed. I want money channeled into death research. I want—I want a second chance, not this mockery of life you gave me." She pressed her lips tightly together. "Would that be what Doni would have said, too, Holder Charidilis?"

"I think so, Mari."

"He loved your son, Holder. He thought of Kenis as his own,

in a way. He told me that he wished he and I could have a child like yours.''

Mari held out the crystal to Jemi. ''Take it,'' she said.

Jemi shook her head. ''Mari—''

''You'd promise to give me what I asked for?'' Mari's rheumy, bloodshot eyes peered at Jemi, her head tilted to one side.

''Yes, but—''

''Then take the damn thing. If it killed Doni, I don't want it. And no matter what you do for the vivicates, it's too late for me. I'll always be an ugly thing, a drooling monster. Doni loved me; no one else but a vivicate could.'' Muscles worked in her thin face. ''Take the damn thing.''

Jemi held out her hand. Mari twisted the crystal; it came off easily from the driftwood base. She let the wood fall to the floor and placed the crystal in Jemi's palm. ''There,'' she said. ''Now get the hell out of here.''

Celebrate the common person. Celebrate those who rise from obscurity to make their mark on history. If you look to someone to change the world, don't cast your gaze to those already in power. Those who have made their niche are too busy trying to secure it. They don't want change; it's in their best interests to retain the status quo. In a crisis, the changes will come from a Cincinnatus, a Joan of Arc, or even a Hitler. Those are the ones who will smash the current order.

Forget the already titled ones. Look instead to the person next to you on the street.

It was probably no coincidence that Jesus was a carpenter or Muhammad a merchant.

—from *Another Fanfare* by Aaron Bernard. NY University Press, 2171.

CHAPTER EIGHTEEN

GreatMother Katainias had intended to go first to Earth and the UCN, and there issue the necessary first step of *aljceri* challenge. She did not expect the challenge to be accepted. The apes could have wasteful *kinjtha* then, if they desired, but the moment that they ignored the rules of the ritual warfare, she would declare them beasts and give the alpha BeastCaptains free rein.

The T'Raijek warship blinked into existence near the orbit of Mars, and the GreatMother used the ansible to contact Salii and ClanMother Njialjiad Salii. The plans changed on learning that HeadFather Jardien was on Highland, that the alpha Hlidskjalff was there as well with the renegade ape Charidilis, that UCN naval ships were even now nearing that colony. GreatMother Ktainias could feel the disturbances focusing there like the ripples spreading outward from her hands as she stirred the Waters of Life.

She hoped that this would all soon be over. The apes were a threat, she was certain of that. Hlidskjalff had made an enormous error in judgment. Yes, as AllMother, Ktainias had given them the formal permission to open contact with the apes, but Hlidskjalff had gone too far. Too far.

GreatMother Ktainias, as AllMother, would rectify that error.

The GreatMother stirred in the nutrient pool that she rarely left during spaceflight. Her scarred, massive body moved slowly, wading the thick waters. The other two GreatMothers, Hlidskjalff and Njialjiad, watched apprehensively. This had not been a good or pleasant trip for them. GreatMother Ktainias—old, sour, and undefeated in her time as AllMother—had been petulant and savage during this trip. Hlidskjalff's favorite two omegas had gone to feed the pool after an unintentional slight to GreatMother Ktainias. The fading memory matrix of the last GreatMother Hlidskjalff stirred in GreatMother Hlidskjalff's mind as she recalled the way her two omegas had looked at her as Ktainias ordered their deaths. Hlidskjalff forced the matrix personality down and pretended calmness.

Next to her, GreatMother Njialjiad had her own apprehensions. Njialjiad's younglings had been confined to the lower pools after cavorting too clumsily near Ktainias's huge flanks. Njialjiad was careful to see that the younglings stayed well away from Ktainias.

It didn't seem to be a good time to antagonize her.

"It's your fault, Hlidskjalff," GreatMother Ktainias grumbled. Ktainias had lost an eye to *aljceri* spans ago. She'd never bothered to have it replaced. The empty socket was more intimidation than an eye could be. Five times in the thirty spans since then, the GreatMother Ktainias's position as AllMother had been challenged. Each time, she had been the one to walk from the Deep Pits. For the last ten spans, no one had had the temerity to dispute her rule.

The GreatMother Hlidskjalff wished that her predecessor had possessed the honor and desire to challenge Ktainias instead of flatly disobeying her and hiding the treachery she had committed with the apes. Maybe then all this would never have happened. With that thought, she felt the stirring of the matrix again—that layering of the experience of all the past GreatMothers of her clan; the ghost of the last GreatMother strongest among them. *Not my fault,* it seemed to say. *I couldn't have beaten her. Yet this had to be done. All the alphas advised it. The apes might have saved us.*

The ruined gaze of Ktainias turned on the young GreatMother Hlidskjalff.

"It was the GreatMother before me that started this," Hlidskjalff reminded Ktainias carefully. She pushed down the protesting matrix, pretending to relax against the pool's stony sides. The red light of the pools seemed suddenly too cold. "The GreatMother Ktainias AllMother knows that I have followed all her commands."

Ktainias sniffed. Turgid water peaked in slow swells from her body. "Then advise me, GreatMother. Should we go on to the ape home world, or should we deal with those on that flimsy toy they call Highland?"

Hlidskjalff snuck a glance at Njialjiad; all she could see there was smug satisfaction. She knew that Njialjiad was enjoying this. "ClanMother Njialjiad Salii thinks the crystal is there," Hlidskjalff answered slowly. "My alpha *is* there."

Ktainias nodded. "We can at least pick up the crystal—*if* Njialjiad knows what she's talking about," Ktainias added irritably. From the corner of her eye, Hlidskjalff saw Njialjiad suddenly frown and sink lower in the pool. "We can also retrieve the alpha, though I feel that he's worthless at this point, too tainted from contact with the apes. Any value he has as seed is marginal. I will order him destroyed."

At the words, the matrix howled in Hlidskjalff's mind: *No!* it wailed. *No!*

Ktainias reared up in the pool as if she'd heard the mindsob. She smoothed the fur between the rows of nipples as the splashing echoed in the chamber. Her chest and abdomen showed the ridged scars of old *aljceri* wounds; the gleaming tips of her claws shone through the pads at the ends of her fingers. Hlidskjalff had no doubt that the display was quite deliberate. *I don't care that the alpha is valuable*, Ktainias was saying. *I don't care that he carries all that's left of your apish embassies' lines. Challenge me now if you must,* Ktainias insisted. *Challenge me now or submit.*

Hlidskjalff hesitated. The fact that Ktainias insisted on an alpha's death spoke of her deep displeasure with Clan Hlidskjalff. GreatMother Hlidskjalff had thought that Ktainias might claim the alpha as her own in punishment for Hlidskjalff's meddling with the apes. But she'd not thought that Ktainias would destroy him outright and lose the genetic bloodline he represented. This told her that Ktainias knew all too well that the matrix of a strong GreatMother could sometimes force an unwanted decision on her successor. Ktainias knew what Hlidskjalff must be thinking: her empty, horrid eye socket impaled her. The clawtips combed fur laced with gray.

No! the matrix pleaded. Hlidskjalff shuddered with the feel of it.

"Whatever the GreatMother wishes," Hlidskjalff said at last. "I release the alpha to you. I will follow your decision for the apes."

"Then you don't share the delusion of your predecessor?"

"No, GreatMother Ktainias."

"Good," Ktainias said. She allowed her body to sink back into the pool's dark, moving waters. She swam to one of the deeper ledges, until only her head remained out of the water. The long, graying muzzle was lapped by wavelets.

"Then we will go to Highland and settle this," she said.

The alarms had begun to shriek over Highland before Jemi and the rest reached the port. After a hurried consultation with Captain Burgess, the others, along with Strickland and a guard, went to the war room off the main navigational compartment of *Inverness*. The ClanMother Njialjiad Highland was already waiting for them there.

"GreatMother Ktainias AllMother has asked for *aljceri,*" the ClanMother said without preamble as they entered. Her gaze lingered for a moment on Ardent. "The alpha Hlidskjalff is to be given to me."

"I still claim a death-oath," Ardent said.

"GreatMother Hlidskjalff has released you from it."

Jemi saw Ardent's shoulder slump with that. This was the first time she'd seen one of the female T'Raijek's in person. The ClanMother, sleek, in appearance almost like an upright, muscular otter, stood a head taller than any of them. She wore a loose tunic woven with glittering, metallic threads; a faint odor of musk exuded from her, a pleasant spice. But the ClanMother was tense and expecting a confrontation: there was enough similarity between the races for Jemi to see that. It showed in her tight stance, the uneasy, darting stare as she faced them.

Jemi clenched the crystal tighter in her palm, and the motion drew the ClanMother's eyes. "GreatMother Ktainias AllMother has said that the crystal is to be returned to us as well," the T'Raijek told Jemi. The ClanMother held out her hand to Jemi, palm up. Jemi could see the tips of long claws nestled in the sleek umber fur, and she knew that the ClanMother could rip her open with one cuffing blow.

The old Jemi, the one whose ship had been destroyed by Strickland's puppets, would have given over the crystal without hesitation. She would have shrugged and thought nothing of it—what happened afterward would happen. But Jemi looked at the tiny sphere in her hand, its surface still flecked with the awkwardly painted continents and seas, and her fingers closed around it again. The crystal was Kenis. The crystal was the deaths she had caused. The crystal was blood and violence and her own shattered life; it was a promise made to Mari. Jemi hated the crystal. She longed to be rid of it because of how much it had cost her. But not this way.

"No," she said quietly.

The ClanMother's intake of breath was audible to all of them. The clawtips emerged slightly from the fur. Then the T'Raijek's hand dropped to her side and she glared at Jemi. "As you wish," she said. "We'll have it anyway—it won't do you any good to keep it. But I will take the alpha."

"Only if he wants to go," Jemi said. The statement was half-question, her inflection rising as she looked from Nys to Jardien for confirmation. Jardien shrugged. Nys nodded. The ClanMother seemed furious, but Ardent ended it. He walked over to the ClanMother and bowed. "I submit to GreatMother Hlidskjalff's command," he told all of them. "I'll go."

"Ardent?" Jemi questioned. He seemed entirely unlike the alpha she had known. All the fire had gone out of him, all the passion. He was empty, like a scolded little boy. She'd seen

Kenis act the same way after defiance had gotten him spanked. The alpha shrugged.

"I've no reason to stay," he said. "It's all done now."

"You forced me to keep going," Jemi told him. "You wouldn't let me quit."

"I did that because I had to. I keep my oaths," he said.

"What will you do to him?" Jemi asked the ClanMother.

"GreatMother Ktianias AllMother has called for him," Njialjiad replied. "She may kill him. I haven't asked, but I know she's angry. That's all I know, and none of our concern. If you stop me from taking him, you lose all your options. GreatMother Ktainias will declare you all to be beasts. That will be the end of it. Your two worlds will be laid waste, the pieces of Highland will circle the sun like the rocks around it. You can have *aljceri*, the fight of leaders; you can have *kinjtha*, the fight of clans; or you can have the BeastCaptains leave your cities in ashes. No one else must be hurt but the leaders or a picked group of warriors who know they risk death. If you're more than animals, you'll submit."

"Ritual combat," Jardien muttered. "That's barbaric."

"More barbaric than *your* warfare, which kills anyone who gets in the way? That's true barbarism, HeadFather, allowing the innocents to be killed because of a question of dominance."

"The Traal are the same kind of barbarians, then, but you ran from them," Jardien shot back.

The ClanMother glared at him. "The Hlidskjalff talks too much," she commented. "We offered the Traal the same alternatives. Even the stupidest beast can be dangerous, HeadFather. It's sane to fear and avoid something that can hurt you. It's also sane to make sure that a potential threat never has the chance. Even an ape would know that. An ape would run from a tiger, but you'd crush a wasp that got in the same room with you, wouldn't you? It's all a matter of relative danger. And when we have a gun for the tiger, we'll go after it as well."

"And *aljceri? Kinjtha?*" Commander Nys pronounced the alien terms slowly.

"If the wasp could talk and agree to accept your terms for life, would you give it that chance? *We* would, Commander Nys."

"We have no GreatMothers," Jemi told the T'Raijek. "We don't have one leader."

"We will deal with your clans separately or at once, it doesn't matter. Or if you wish *kinjtha,* the AllMother's ship will fight one of your own. As the challenged, it is your choice."

Ardent laughed at that, jarringly. "You haven't seen a true T'Raijek warship—the *jthacalin,*" he said to the three humans. "The ships that brought the embassy was only a transport, yet it wrecked the UCN's orbital defenses. You think one of your cruisers will fare better against a full *jthacalin?* That would be your wasp against an eagle. It would swallow you whole."

The ClanMother gestured, and Ardent fell silent at the command. "GreatMother Ktainias AllMother has said that she would accept Holder Jemi Charidilis as your representative for *aljceri,*" she told them.

"What?" Jardien scoffed. "The Holder—"

"First, she is female," the ClanMother interrupted. "That in itself is more pleasing to the GreatMother—it is not soldiers who fight *aljceri,* but the representatives of the clans involved. Second, the Holder has been the one most affected by the manipulations of the Clan Hlidskjalff; if there was any truth in that Clan's speculations, she will show it. Third, she was able to find the crystal against all the plotting of all of you, even the efforts of Clan Njialjiad." The ClanMother made a sour face with that admission.

"She doesn't represent any of us," Nys interjected. "And even if HeadFather Jardien and I were to agree to this, that's still only Salii and a rebellious UCN officer. Not the UCN itself, which is still the majority."

"GreatMother Ktainias will accept your acknowledgment of Holder Charidilis as your representative in *aljceri*. She will do the same with Admiral Strickland for the UCN. If you fail to keep your word afterward, then she will declare you beasts."

"And what does this gain us?" Jemi asked quietly. The ClanMother turned to her.

"Acceptance will tell GreatMother Ktainias that the apes are sentient and not beasts. You will tell her that there is a chance you can be trusted. You will return the crystal to us. Your people will be watched, you will be confined to these worlds around this sun, but you will live so long as you do as GreatMother Ktainias AllMother asks."

"And if I would win?"

The quick smile the ClanMother gave told Jemi that she thought the possibility unlikely. "You would then have proven that Clan Hlidskjalff was correct. GreatMother Hlidskjalff might well use that advantage to become AllMother herself. As for your own people, GreatMother Ktainias has said that her death-oaths will tell the Clans to leave you as we left the Traal. You may keep the crystal—we will show you the way to unlock its matrices. In time, you'll be able to build your own drives. If you should find us again, we will see what will happen then. Or perhaps it will be you who find the Traal. You will be left to your own destinies."

"We can't trust you to stick to any of that," Jardien said.

"No GreatMother would tell you that and fail to abide by the death-oath," Njialjiad answered. "That is truth. If you don't wish to believe it, that's your choice. But if you feel that way, then you had best prepare to be treated as the beasts I think you are."

Jemi had listened with a growing sense of despair and resignation. *The old Jemi,* she found herself thinking once more. *The old Jemi would have sat here and said nothing. She would have let the others handle this.*

"I'll do it," she said. She spoke the words without consciously thinking them, without mulling it over. They came from a compulsion in her. It was not that she felt she had nothing to live for. In one sense, the decision was more an affirmation of life. Yes, she fully expected to die, having heard Ardent's description of *aljceri,* having seen the ClanMother Njialjiad and knowing that only one person would walk from the combat. But it would also be some small payment for the debt of life given her by Mari, by those that had died along the path she'd been forced to walk. "I'll do it," she repeated forcefully before she could think about it, before she could convince herself of the stupidity of saying the words.

HeadFather Jardien roared his disapproval, but Nys only shook his head. "That's the way the branch is being bent," he said softly. "I will give you my acknowledgment of the Holder,

ClanMother Njialjiad. I want to find another way, but if it happens, I accept her."

"You're crazy!" Jardien bellowed. In the heat of the UCN cruiser, Jardien was sweating under his furs. The fringe of his hair was plastered darkly to his forehead. "What's your word worth, Commander? You can give the T'Raijek nothing but a cruiser."

"A cruiser *and* its people," Nys answered calmly. "At least it's something, HeadFather Jardien. I've seen films of the day the T'Raijek arrived. I am—was—an officer of the UCN navy. I know that no ship of ours will be likely to stand against them. Yes, I'll trade one life for several."

"Easy to say when it's not your life, isn't it?" Jardien retorted.

"If the GreatMother Ktainias would take me, I'd gladly be the one to go. I can't prove that. You'll have to accept it for what it's worth. The ClanMother Njialjiad has said that there are no soldiers allowed in *aljceri*."

The ClanMother nodded, and Jardien gave a scoffing bark of a laugh. "I'll tell you what," he said. "This *beast*"—he spat out the word—"will let the Holder represent Salii also, as far as my authority lets me. And for as much as my word is worth," he added, and laughed again.

The ClanMother gave the HeadFather a look that could only be disgust. "Your word is all the GreatMother has asked for," she said. "I'm sure she knows how well you will keep it. Clan Hlidskjalff has already given her a lesson in apish ways. All she cares is that the proper form is kept. What of Admiral Strickland?"

They turned to him. The Admiral had been silently observing the meeting from his chair. He shook his head; Jemi could see the sense of defeat in the man. His shoulders sagged, the face was sunken and pale. It was as if the finding of the crystal had heralded an ending for him. He no longer seemed to care. "The T'Raijek have lied from the beginning," he said. "Clan Hlidskjalff never told us what they wanted in return for the crystal; Clan Njialjiad never said what it was, nor did they tell us what finding it might mean."

"Clan Njialjiad would have kept its word, if you had found the crystal," the ClanMother told him. "You failed."

"You never told us all it would entail."

"How can one predict all the possible futures?" the ClanMother responded. "All we can know is what each of us will do."

"Which gives you an excuse to say nothing?" Strickland asked with a trace of his former animation. Then he sagged back into the chair once more. He waved a hand to the Jemi. "You're just another useless sacrifice," he told her. "You're doing this from guilt."

Jemi shrugged.

Strickland sighed. "Do as you want, then. Fine. It's on your head. I'll do what I can with the UCN once it's over. Is that satisfactory, ClanMother?"

"It will do," she said. "GreatMother Ktainias AllMother expects that you will be called beasts no matter what may happen. She only wants to be sure." She bowed to them and opened the door to the room. "The alpha and I will leave now," she said. She gestured to Ardent to precede her.

Ardent looked back at Jemi. She waited for him to say something, but he only gave her a half-grin, the faintest touch of a shrug.

As a farewell, it seemed pale.

Who says we're not like the T'Raijek? We're ruled by old compelling instincts that have their roots in our homo ancestors. That's no different from the T'Raijek, in whose blood runs the passions of a herd beast. Why do you think that we watch the apes in the zoo with such curious intensity?

It's because we see ourselves peering back through the bars.

—from "Apology for the Alien"
by Akira Nys, published in
The T'Raijek Anthology.

CHAPTER NINETEEN

The Deep Pits of the *Jthacalin Ktainias* were as ornate as any in the ClanHomes. One did not stint on ritual, after all. The walls were smoothed; the building coral that had built the walls had been chosen for their varied, gleaming colors; and so the Deep Pits nearly glowed in the long wavelength light. Purple streaks marbled the basic pink, tinged here and there with glowing, electric blues. The tiers swept back from the sands of the pit itself in steep ranks. *Jthacalin Ktainias* had been built (or more precisely, grown) some fifty years before. In that time, the Deep Pits had seen *aljceri* several times, mostly because of disputes between the ClanMothers underneath the GreatMother Ktainias. The sands had been taken from the Old Pit of Wjthir, where centuries of the ritual combat had taken place. The sands had licked the blood of nearly all the T'Raijek clans, including those whose lineage was no longer counted. There were times, to most of the T'Raijek who came to the Deep Pit to meditate, when the sands seemed to be alive with the memories of the Mothers who had died there. "Each grain of Wjthir holds a life" was what all younglings were told.

All of which meant little to Jemi. To her, it was a warm, dark hole in which she would soon lose her life.

The Deep Pits smelled of the T'Raijek. The few humans there were lost in the swarm of aliens, mostly omega males with a scattering of females and the occasional alpha male. The GreatMothers Hlidskjalff and Njialjiad sat apart from the rest in the lowest tier of the Deep Pits. Ardent sat between the two GreatMothers, his face reflecting a dour resignation. Directly across the sands from the GreatMothers was the human entourage: Jardien, Strickland, Nys, Burgess, and two representatives each from the Saliian crewmen, Highland, and the UCN naval complement nearest Highland. It would be days yet before any of the cruisers dispatched from Earth after the kidnapping of Strickland entered Highland space.

The T'Raijek had made concessions to this *aljceri*. The human Charidilis had no younglings to feed the sands of the cleansing ritual; she had been horrified at the suggestion, in any case. Since Clan Hlidskjalff had been most responsible for the Holder, one of the Hlidskjalff younglings had been used instead. The human had no natural weapons with which to fight: GreatMother Ktainias AllMother had insisted that the Holder be given a knife for each hand, the blades carefully sharpened and curved, tapered to look very much like the claws of the T'Raijek. They were ripping and tearing weapons, without edges.

Brass horns sounded, an atonal dissonance with no Earthly harmonies. The lights dimmed around the Deep Pits and the whispering of the watchers fell away to a hush. GreatMother Ktainias AllMother stepped out into the sands. As she stepped into the bloodcircle of the Ktainias youngling, Jemi was ushered onto the sands to stand in the other discolored area. She was naked, as was Ktainias. Against the bulk of the GreatMother, Jemi looked pale and fragile. The claws laced to her fists seemed insignificant against the six paired rows of Ktainias's natural weapons, against the huge muscles that rippled under her fur.

Jemi felt that she looked ridiculous. The scene was ludicrous, a mockery—it proved nothing, nothing at all. She wanted to run away from here, but it was too late.

The Pit was cleared. A gong sounded

Jemi stood in the heat, feeling the sweat dripping down the

length of her body. her nakedness made her even more vulnerable, knowing that there were hidden watchers in the shadows around the Pit. She shifted her weight, feeling the harsh grains of the sand rasp under her soles. Sand clung to her feet, sticky with the blood of the youngling. Jemi tried to remember what Nys had whispered to her before the T'Raijek had taken her to prepare for the *aljceri*.

"Don't try to directly oppose her force with your own," he had said. "If you do that, the strongest will always win, and she's far stronger than you, physically. You know this is laughably overbalanced in the T'Raijek's favor. Keep turning, keep moving. If she strikes with her right hand, pivot to your right. Follow the energy of her strike. Turn your hips. Try to use some of her own force against herself. Get behind her. Push her. Trip her. If you see an opening, use the claws. If you want to live, Jemi, you won't stand toe to toe with her. Be the monkey that they call us—badger her, worry her, and don't fight her the way she wants to be fought."

"I'm going to die, Commander," she'd replied. She knew the words should have bothered her, but she felt nothing, as if in accepting the challenge, she had become numbed to emotion. They were just words, empty of anything but facts. She held up the claw knives one of the Ktainias omegas had given her. "These are nothing," she said. "They're a joke. Can't you hear fate sniggering?"

She'd expected him to deny it, to give her meaningless encouragement, but he only put his hands on her shoulders. His eyes would not let her gaze drop. "You're right," he said. "Do you want to back out of this? No one would blame you, certainly not me."

Jemi shook her head. "Too late," she muttered.

Nys took a deep breath, let it out. "I know you. I've watched you. You didn't give up after Kenis died, after you were attacked. You won't do it now. You'll fight her as well as you can."

She'd only shrugged. After a moment, he let his hands drop, though she could feel that he wanted to say more. "Good luck, Jemi," he'd said.

"I'll need more than that," she'd replied flatly.

A few minutes later, GreatMother Ktainias AllMother herself had come to the small room under the tiers of the Deep Pit. Her fur was slicked with some pungent oil; she exuded a floral scent that mixed with the natural musk of her body. Against the glossy brown fur, the brilliant scarlet of her vaginal mounds was prominent. Ktainias eased into a chair near Jemi and waved away the omega who had followed her into the room. She uttered a string of guttural syllables toward him, and as he bowed as he retreated. GreatMother Ktainias stared at Jemi, at the lightness of her skin. The GreatMother's fingers unconsciously touched the long row of nipples down either side of her own chest; Jemi knew that the T'Raijek was looking at Jemi's own small breasts. "I wanted to meet you," Ktainias said. Her voice was slow and hard to understand, laboring with the human words, yet the tone seemed far less haughty than Jemi had expected. "I wanted to see what you were like before we met on the sands."

"I'm as you see me," Jemi replied, shrugging.

Ktainias nodded. "You lost your youngling because of us," she said. "I'm sorry for that. I know that you have fewer younglings than we. I feel for your loss. I cannot imagine what it would feel like to have only one youngling and then to lose him." The sympathy in the T'Raijek's voice warmed Jemi.

She turned more fully to the alien. "I lost him due to our own greed, GreatMother," she said. "The T'Raijek were only part of it."

"Do you hate us?"

The question made Jemi lean back in her chair. She could not answer right away—there were no words in her head. She thought, pondering. "No," she said at last. "I don't hate you. If I hated the T'Raijek, I wouldn't be here."

"Odd," the GreatMother mused. "I thought perhaps you would. I was certain that was why you agreed to meet me on the sands."

"I don't really know why myself," Jemi told her. She started to say more, then stopped. "Why me?" she asked the GreatMother.

"Didn't the Njialjiad tell you?"

"Some. But not all, I suspect."

"I wanted to know whether Hlidskjalff may have been right. They said that the apes were a strange melding of aggression and passivity." She spoke a few phrases in her own language, then shook her head—quickly, like a mare. "Fire and ice," she said. "Honorable and devious. They said that you were something like us, that our races could exist together as the Traal and T'Raijek could not. They felt that if we gave you help, you would give us help. Njialjiad said that instead you could not be trusted, that we would only turn you into another Traal, an enemy who would know where we were. On the whole, I would agree with Njialjiad. But I offer *aljceri* because I'm not entirely certain."

"It's a farce, GreatMother." Jemi held up her hands, with the claws strapped to them. "Look at me. This is stupid."

"I know it," Ktainias said, surprisingly. "Yet it's the way. I find that I've no enthusiasm for this *aljceri*. But I must know if you're beasts or not."

"There are other ways."

"This way I must risk my own life to find out. *Aljceri* means that no one will challenge someone else lightly. I might have been wrong about you apes."

"You'd take a chance on death because you might be wrong? Isn't that a little backward from the usual reasoning?"

The GreatMother's snout lifted in what might have been amusement. Jemi caught a glimpse of long canines among molars. "Looking at you, I doubt that I'll die, Holder. And the GreatMother Ktainias that follows me would have my experiences to guide her. Holder," she asked, "haven't you also had to pay for your decisions? Aren't you doing that now? Neither one of us wants this. Neither one of us thinks that it will prove things one way or another. But we each have things we can't change. If I don't fight you, one of the other GreatMothers will challenge me for failing to follow the laws of my people. You see, I have little choice."

GreatMother didn't wait for Jemi to respond. She rose to her feet. Nodding to Jemi, the T'Raijek went to the door. "Among the T'Raijek, we say that there aren't any final answers," she told Jemi. "We simply change the shape of the questions."

Now, on the sands, Jemi waited for the second gong to signal the beginning.

Ktainias, as the one who issued the challenge, was compelled to be the first to leave her bloodcircle. Looking at the huge T'Raijek female, Jemi knew that Ktainias would not hesitate; she would bull her way across the few meters of sand that separated them and try to end it quickly. Meeting the GreatMother had not helped Jemi at all—it had only made the T'Raijek more sympathetic. She'd hoped that here, at risk and with the adrenaline of the moment, she might find hatred for the T'Raijek and use that energy for herself. She had intended to think of Kenis—his name would have been the mantra of passion.

There was nothing there. She was empty. Alone.

Caught in a folly.

The air shivered with the note of the gong.

Before the sound had died, the feet of GreatMother Ktainias kicked sand. She moved much faster than Jemi had thought she could. The T'Raijek was on her in the space of a second; Jemi barely had time to lift her arm, all of Nys's advice forgotten in the panic of the moment. Claws raked across her arm as she instinctively ducked, falling to the sand as she let Ktainias's charge go past. Jemi screamed with pain. Flesh peeled away in meaty ribbons; sticky, warm blood flooded her arm from elbow to wrist. She looked down and nearly fainted, seeing the stark whiteness of bone at the bottom of the deepest cut. On her knees, her mouth open as she gulped for breath, cradling her arm to her, she gaped at Ktainias. The T'Raijek only stared at her. She seemed to be waiting. "Do you submit?" Ktainias asked. Her wide, liquid eyes were soft in appearance, as if she could feel some of Jemi's agony. "Give me your throat. It will be quick."

"No," Jemi gasped. She staggered to her feet, let the hand fall to her side. She clutched the hilts of the claw knives in her good fist; the muscles shorn from bone, her other fist would not close. Sand clung grittily to her sweating body; she could taste it in her mouth. She blinked heavily, forcing her eyes to focus as she crouched, waiting for the next charge.

Ktainias came at her again, brutal and simple—a straight charge. This time Jemi moved, sidestepping as Ktainias swung. She half shoved, half cut at the GreatMother as she passed. Jemi felt her claw knife dig into Ktainias's side; the weapon was nearly torn from her grasp as the force of the charge, her shove added to it, propelled Ktainias toward the sides of the pit.

Ktainias tried to turn, planting one foot and going down to one knee as sand sprayed underneath her. Jemi could see blood dappling the sand underneath her, and the tightness of the GreatMother's lips told Jemi that she had hurt the T'Raijek. Then Ktainias thrust herself up again, charging before Jemi could move or react.

Again Jemi simply tried to get out of the way. She pivoted on her left foot as Ktainias cuffed at her. Claws ran ugly furrows along her left side, but shallower this time. Jemi slashed/shoved Ktainias again, grunting.

The GreatMother stumbled in the loose, treacherous sand.

The T'Raijek tried to right herself, but her leg collapsed underneath, the ankle turning. Her clawed hands flailing, Ktainias slammed into the side of the pit. Her head hit rock with an audible thud. She fell sidewise to the ground. Her hands slashed sand.

Jemi could barely hear the sudden roaring of the crowd through the pounding of blood in her temples. She limped over to the GreatMother. She brought her hand back to tear at the unprotected throat.

It might have been the shock, the blood loss she'd already suffered. But, her hand raised, the GreatMother's alien face seemed to dissolve before Jemi. Ktainias was layered by ghosts. Jemi could see Helen Martelli, her guts slithering onto the floor of the UCN office in obscene coils. She could see the guard she herself had shot, slumping down to die before her. She could see the purple, strained face of the Highland security man whose windpipe Ardent had crushed. She could see New York and the warehouses and the dead Saliian agent. She could smell the vile odor of their decay. She could taste the vomit in their mouths as they died, the choking gout of thick blood. There was nothing pretty or noble or beautiful about their deaths.

They all had Kenis's face as well. They all looked up at her—and she could not strike.

The GreatMother's eyes blinked. She roared. Her clawed hand raked up; Jemi moved too late. The talons tore her right side open, exposing the curve of ribs, and Jemi fell helplessly to the sand. Ktainias stood over her. The GreatMother stared, her eyes like that of a huge, savage doe. "You should have killed me," she said. "You should have struck when you had the chance. It's too late now."

"I couldn't," Jemi whispered. She found that she was crying helplessly: pain, loss, frustration; all of it melting together into a wail. She huddled into a fetal position, waiting for the last blow. "I couldn't," she sobbed.

Ktainias gave a sound somewhere between growl and curse. She said something in her own tongue, then spoke to Jemi in her thick accent. "Hlidskjalff was utterly wrong," she grated. "Njialjiad was just as wrong. But we learn. We learn."

Impossibly, she retracted her claws. She glanced up at the shadowed tiers. "There is no *aljceri* here," she shouted. "Get a doctor for the human. Send my omega to me."

Then she hunkered down on the sands beside Jemi to wait. Her fingertips felt curiously gentle on Jemi's face.

She awoke once to the face of an omega.

When she opened her eyes again and lifted her head, she saw only one person in the room: Nys. He was sleeping in a chair beside her bed. Jemi tried to move and could not. Her body was swathed in bandages; a monitor unit lay over her chest, and she could feel the prickling of IVs.

Nys had awakened with the rustling of her sheets. His dark eyes regarded her. He smiled fleetingly.

Jemi licked dry lips. "Commander."

"It's Akira," he said. "Would you like some water?"

"Very much."

He brought her a glass, held the straw out to her mouth. She sipped, closing her eyes at the velvet feel of the cool liquid. "Thank you," she told him. "Where—?"

Nys set the glass on the nightstand beside her bed and returned to his chair. "You're on *Inverness* now. It's all over."

"GreatMother Ktainias . . ."

"Gone. Along with the rest of the T'Raijek. Four days ago. She kept her bargain well," he told her. "The GreatMother made certain that she extracted public promises from all the leaders that they would abide by the oaths she made them take. She made them promise that there would be no reprisals against you or anyone involved in the search for the crystal. Strickland was court-martialed and jailed for what he did to you, but beyond that, the rest is to be forgotten. She did it by threatening to name as beasts any of the governments that failed to abide by the terms of her treaty. There wasn't much opposition. She even made certain that the promises you gave to Mari Coyle were incorporated in the agreements. She signed the treaties, gave us the information that was in the crystal.'' He stopped, canted his head. ''And left,'' he finished.

''Gone? Like that?'' Jemi felt a sense of emptiness. She had wanted to talk to the GreatMother. It was as if the ending had been left off a song, so that one hung forever waiting for the last notes. There was a jarring disorientation.

''She said to tell you that it didn't matter. She said that you had changed the question on her. Do you know what that means?''

''I think so.'' She knew that Nys waited for her to elaborate, but she only shook her head. After a moment, Nys spoke again.

''She said that we were to give you whatever you wanted. I think she expects you to be the GreatMother Sapiens.'' There was a gentle teasing in his voice that made her smile despite herself, and she rolled her head over to look at him. His eyes were bright with silent laughter. ''You could run the UCN tomorrow, and Salii the next day. What do you want, Holder Charidilis?'' he asked.

The question dissolved her smile. ''I want my memories of Kenis back. I want the two years that were stolen. That's all I ever wanted.''

''You can't have those.''

''I know,'' she said. She heard the choking emotion in her voice and she cleared her throat. She sniffed. ''Then I want *Starfire*,'' she said.

''That's all?''

''It's all I need.''

''You're easy to please, Holder. For the moment, that will do, then. I'll tell HeadFather Jardien that you'll be coming for your ship.'' Nys rose. For the first time, she noticed that he no longer wore his naval uniform. He stood by her bed, touched her arm as he glanced at the readouts on the monitor. ''You'll need a second pilot,'' he told her. ''There won't be any vivicates to buy. Not anymore.''

"I'll find someone," she told him.

Nys nodded slowly. He took a breath. "I thought I might apply. All I ever wanted was to see the UCN work as best as it can. I'm tired of the intrigue, and what I set out to accomplish seems to have been done. If not, it needs other hands than mine. I could use a quieter life." He paused and seemed to consider his words. "None of us got what we looked for," he said at last.

"I can't afford union wages," Jemi told the man.

"The Hlidskjalff alpha told me to say that I charge half-union scale."

That brought the smile back to her face. Jemi shook her head softly. "I'll think about it," Jemi told Nys. "I'll let you know."